A page torn from
The Bachelor Chronicles . . .

Thomas Dashwell

Captain of the *Circe* (a privateer, he is called. Harrumph! A pirate is more like it.)

b. in America (which renders him completely unfit to grace these pages, but my cousin Pippin insists I include him.)

Current residence: At the bottom of the sea if I had my druthers.

Notes: Captain Dashwell is the worst sort of bounder and quite rightly should be in jail, as I have told my cousin often enough. I fear Pippin is more taken with Captain Dashwell than ever before; I must find her a proper husband before she throws caution to the wind and does something foolish.

Addendum 4 June 1814: This wretched bounder has escaped from prison. Worse yet, I suspect Pippin has had a hand in this impossibility and it will be her ruin if she has. If only she would marry someone respectable . . .

Addendum 7 June 1814: Thank heavens. Pippin has married Lord Gossett and Dashwell has fled England. For good. At least I can only hope it is for good . . .

The Duchess of Hollindrake

By Elizabeth Boyle

MEMOIRS OF A SCANDALOUS RED DRESS
CONFESSIONS OF A LITTLE BLACK GOWN
TEMPTED BY THE NIGHT
LOVE LETTERS FROM A DUKE
HIS MISTRESS BY MORNING
THIS RAKE OF MINE
SOMETHING ABOUT EMMALINE
IT TAKES A HERO
STEALING THE BRIDE
ONE NIGHT OF PASSION
ONCE TEMPTED
NO MARRIAGE OF CONVENIENCE

ELIZABETH BOYLE

Memoirs of A Scandalous
Red Dress

AVON
An Imprint of HarperCollinsPublishers

This is a work of fiction. Names, characters, places, and incidents are products of the author's imagination or are used fictitiously and are not to be construed as real. Any resemblance to actual events, locales, organizations, or persons, living or dead, is entirely coincidental.

AVON BOOKS
An Imprint of HarperCollins*Publishers*
10 East 53rd Street
New York, New York 10022-5299

Copyright © 2009 by Elizabeth Boyle
Excerpts from *Memoirs of a Scandalous Red Dress* copyright © 2009 by Elizabeth Boyle; *Lord of the Night* copyright © 1993 by Susan Wiggs; *Don't Tempt Me* copyright © 2009 by Loretta Chekani; *Destined for an Early Grave* copyright © 2009 by Jeaniene Frost
ISBN 978-0-06-137324-4
www.avonromance.com

First Avon Books paperback printing: May 2009

Avon Trademark Reg. U.S. Pat. Off. and in Other Countries, Marca Registrada, Hecho en U.S.A.
HarperCollins® is a registered trademark of HarperCollins Publishers.

Printed in the U.S.A.

10 9 8 7 6 5 4 3 2 1

To my Aunt Susie.
You never stop amazing me
with your resiliency and wry humor.
Our family's other storyteller,
please continue to make us all laugh,
for there isn't a day when that isn't needed.
All my love,
Lizzie

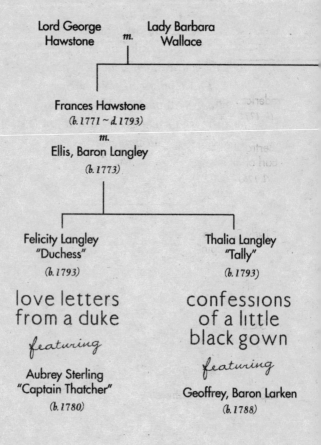

Lord George Hawstone **m.** Lady Barbara Wallace

Frances Hawstone
(b. 1771 ~ d. 1793)

m.

Ellis, Baron Langley
(b. 1773)

Felicity Langley
"Duchess"
(b. 1793)

love letters from a duke

featuring

Aubrey Sterling
"Captain Thatcher"
(b. 1780)

Thalia Langley
"Tally"
(b. 1793)

confessions of a little black gown

featuring

Geoffrey, Baron Larken
(b. 1788)

For the complete Bachelor Chronicles Family
Tree, please visit www.elizabethboyle.com

the BACHELOR CHRONICLES

family tree

Frederica Hawstone
(b. 1771 ~ d. 1800)

m.

**Bertram Knolles,
Earl of Stanbrook**
(b. 1765 ~ d. 1812)

**Lady Philippa Knolles
"Pippin"**
(b. 1793)

**Carlton Knolles,
Earl of Stanbrook**
(b. 1796)

memoirs of a scandalous red dress

featuring

**Captain Thomas Dashwell
"Dash"**
(b. 1788)

Memoirs of A Scandalous
Red Dress

Chapter 1

The London Pool, 1837

Philippa, Viscountess Gossett, followed her escort through the crowded docks of London toward the HMS *Regina*, where the most recently christened ship in the fleet was about to gain a new captain.

Her son.

Lady Gossett shivered, with a sort of uncontainable pride that she shouldn't admit to. He wouldn't like it. Serious and stalwart, noble and utterly British through and through, John, the current Viscount Gossett, and about to be named Captain Lord Gossett, would never approve of his mother's bubbling enthusiasm for this remarkable promotion.

So she'd leave it to the headlines in the newspapers to shout his accomplishments.

Youngest commander to be raised to captain in nearly twenty years. Bravest officer in the Royal Navy.

The hero of the *Cadmus*. Saved all one hundred and fifty souls with his daring.

Lady Gossett shivered. How like his father he'd been that day. Reckless. Rash. Courageous. Diving into a storm-tossed sea to swim a line over to a floundering ship. Nearly drowned doing it, and by all accounts had come out of the icy Atlantic grinning like a mad fool.

Too much like his father, she mused.

Yet that was the last time she'd seen that side of her son, for shortly thereafter her husband had died so very suddenly, and John's once devil-may-care existence had been buried that same day.

The responsibilities of a title, inheritance, and the people who relied upon the family for his governance and benevolence had been at war with his one true love: the sea. The heavy obligations of his new duties had clipped his spirit, leaving him somber and far too proper.

As she approached the ship, the lieutenant who'd been awaiting her carriage turned to her. "There she is, my lady. Isn't the *Regina* a grand beauty? Give those new Yankee clippers a run for their money, I'd say."

"Yes, very much so," she told him, smiling graciously as he offered her his hand and she made her way up the gangplank to the deck where her son awaited her, along with Admiral Fairham and several other high-ranking officers from the navy.

At first John smiled at her, until he noticed her gown. Then his jaw set into a stubborn, nay, disapproving line.

"Madam," he said, taking her hand. "Why have you put off your mourning?"

Oh, yes, John would notice. So suddenly proper to the point of creaking, he would notice her choice of gown. Which was mauve, and still well within the proper confines of respectful grief.

But still, a far cry from the raven's black she'd worn since her husband died.

"Gracious heavens, John," her daughter, Virginia, the Countess of Claremont, said, winding her arm into her mother's and shaking her head at her brother. She and her husband, the Earl of Claremont, had come a little earlier and were already manning their places of honor. "Father has been gone for two years, and Mother's dress is hardly, well, it's not the least bit—" she started to say, but there wasn't time to continue the discussion.

Thankfully, thought Lady Gossett.

For just then, Admiral Fairham stepped up, disengaging the viscountess from her daughter and bringing her fingers to his lips. "Lady Gossett, you look enchanting today."

A gallant from another time, the admiral still considered himself the rake he'd been in his younger days, and Lady Gossett could feel her son's spine stiffen at the man's familiar tone.

Oh, what was it with these young people today that they so disapproved of their parents' rakish and devil-may-care manners? You'd think the British with their youthful new queen would quite embrace life as they had done in generations past, instead of standing so upright that one expected them to snap in the first good wind.

"My Lord Admiral," Lady Gossett demurred as she politely tried to pluck her fingers free with little success. "I am quite honored to see you again, and on such a capital occasion."

"Ah, yes, my lady, most excellent," he said winking at her in a way that suggested he had other ideas for the day.

She paused for a wicked moment, then replied, "And how is Lady Fairham? Still in London, or has she gone down to Bristol for the rest of the summer? I do say, I haven't seen her in an age, and must make sure to write to her this very afternoon a full accounting of the day."

At the mention of his terror of a wife, the admiral released her hand, and Lady Gossett folded her fingers demurely in front of her as an impeccable matron should, but not before she shot a glance at her son as if to say, *There. Is that dignified enough?*

John looked as if he wanted to keelhaul her, but then again, she doubted her proper son would ever entertain such a disreputable thought.

"A most excellent sailor you've raised, my lady," the admiral said, slapping John on the back and changing the subject, obviously more than happy to avoid a discussion about his wife. "Takes after his father, doesn't he?"

"Yes," she replied. "He does." Or rather he did . . .

"Like father, like son," the admiral bustled, his muttonchop whiskers working up and down. "Gossett was quite the yachtsman, wasn't he?"

"Yes, my lord. He loved sailing," she said, glancing away at the mention of her husband, images of him flashing through her memories. Idyllic days at the seaside, the children playing on the beach, laughter ringing over the waves. And Brent, always Brent, smiling over the children's heads at her, love shining in his eyes.

They'd had a good life together, until . . . until . . .

"Shall we begin, Lord Gossett?" the admiral asked, and John nodded and led the way to the raised deck at the stern of the ship.

As the ceremony began, with the crew standing at attention on the lower deck, reporters milling about, and spectators crowding the docks below, Commander Lord Gossett, England's beloved hero, became Captain Lord Gossett. And as the admiral droned on and on—Fairham did love the sound of his own voice—Lady Gossett found her attention wandering.

Her gaze drifted across the deck of the ship and out toward the docks.

She tried to pay attention, but, botheration, Fairham was a dull old bag of wind, and the salty scent of the sea was in the river today. While others might pinch their noses shut in dismay, Lady Gossett loved the sea. Her toes curled in her half boots, and she wished for a wild, crazy second she was sailing away with John, on a ship, toward the edge of the horizon and all the mysteries that the world beyond held.

Beyond London. Beyond the green, tame meadows of England.

A bit of a breeze curled at her hair, all done up properly beneath her bonnet, but teasing her nonetheless, like a lover's secretive, tempting kiss.

Like a whisper from her past.

It was like having a life, long lost, dangled before

her, where she was Lady Gossett no more. Not even Lady Philippa Knolles, as she'd been known before her marriage. No, when the sea whispered to her, she was Pippin, the nickname of her youth, the girl who'd risked too much . . .

Risked everything . . .

Fixing her gaze on her gloves, she told herself she needed to appear the admiring, proper mother, but something inside her, something long-forgotten, clamored to be let loose.

Remember, Pippin, a voice whispered in her ear. *Remember me?*

She blinked for a moment, and she was no longer on the deck of John's new ship, but on a beach at night. The stars overhead twinkled seductively to the chorus of waves crashing near her feet.

Come with me, Circe . . .

She took a steadying breath and shook off the errant vision, focusing instead on John's solemn expression. But all too soon her gaze wandered again, this time over the railing and into the crowd gathered on the docks, pressed together to witness this historic promotion.

Seeking refuge from her memories, she focused on the mass of people, common and noble alike, until her sweeping gaze halted at the sight of a solitary sailor, atop a vast wall of crates. It was impossible to miss him, at least for her, what with the bright red scarf tied around his head. Or maybe it was how he had his dark hair tied in a queue at the nape of his neck, or the tan of his face against his stark white shirt, or those high boots and breeches that made him look more like a pirate of old than an ordinary, common sailor.

And he saw her as well, his gaze fixed on her and her alone. As their eyes met across the distance, it seemed as if an ocean opened between them, his haphazard smile calling her to cross it.

Pippin, remember me?

Oh, yes, she wanted to cry out. *I do.*

Then he made a jaunty salute and, she swore, winked at her, before jumping from his perch and disappearing into the crowd.

"No," she whispered. Then her protest came out louder. "No!" Loud enough to stop the admiral's lofty speech and have everyone on the deck turn toward her, staring in horror at Lady Gossett's untimely and unseemly interruption.

She staggered back just a little as that trembling, dangerous desire, the one she'd tamped down tighter than a keg of powder all those years ago, ignited.

How could this be? How could he be here?

Then Lady Gossett made the day all that much more memorable by dropping like an anchor onto the deck.

It might have been "the hot sun overhead that caused Lady Gossett's distress," as one reporter wrote the next day in his newspaper, or her "overwhelming maternal pride," as another put it.

But neither of them had the right of it.

Lady Gossett had fainted dead away for only one reason. She'd looked across the deck of the HMS *Regina* and seen her past.

She'd seen a ghost.

Twenty-seven years earlier
Smuggler's Cove
Hastings, 1810

Captain Thomas Dashwell waded through the black churning surf and darkness, pulling the rope tied to the longboat behind him, dragging it and its occupants ashore. Wet to his chest, chilled to his very bones, the breeze only adding to his discomfort, he couldn't have cared less.

He'd collect his gold, unload his passengers, and get the hell away from England.

Not that he had any illusions that he'd get all the gold he was owed, but one could hope. After all, he hadn't expected this delivery to take two nights. An extra day that would have been better spent speeding home with a hold full of French brandy and silks.

And toward a tidy profit.

His boots, now full of seawater, sloshed and pulled at his legs, slowing his pace, but he was nearly to the rocky shore.

Dash took a deep breath and heaved the rope a bit harder. He didn't need to make these illicit trips, as his first mate, Mr. Hardy, liked to remind him, but he couldn't resist the hefty purse the English paid him to help bring their agents home from the Continent, smuggled out of France right under Boney's very nose.

Dash grinned. He liked that part. Thumbing his nose at the snooty Frenchies and taking English gold for the privilege. Lots of gold.

Ah, yes, gold. It was an odd thing, he mused as he pulled again on the rope but made no progress. This time one of his crew jumped into the surf beside him and lent a hand. He scowled at the man, for he'd ordered them to keep in the boat with their heads down, lest there be trouble.

As there had been last night.

He glanced up at the cliffs towering overhead where on the previous evening the king's militia had peppered the beach with bullets as they'd tried to deliver their passengers. Pompous fools. Shooting up a bunch of sand and probably spending tonight down at the local inn, bragging how they sent that "demmed smuggler" running.

Only out of range, he would have told them. Dash had no desire to die, no matter the risks he liked to take, but he never left a job unfinished.

Or wages uncollected.

Dash laughed to himself and tugged one last time on the rope until the bow of the longboat crunched against the rocks.

So far, so good.

That was, until he looked up and found himself faced not by his usual contact, Lord John Tremont (Mad Jack to the likes of Dash) but nose to nose with the man's harridan of an aunt, Lady Josephine.

Christ. This didn't bode well. Not at all.

"Well, if it isn't the old girl herself," he said, plucking his hat off as he offered her a regal bow. At least he hoped it was good enough to charm her a bit. After all, she was supposed to be dead. "I see the reports of your demise were premature." He leaned closer to her. "That or the devil tossed you out of hell."

As he planned, the bit of Irish charm he'd inherited from his mother worked in his favor.

Lady Josephine grinned and reached and took him

into a hug. "Dash, you are the most incorrigible, impertinent, young man."

"And you wouldn't have me any other way," he said, slipping quickly from her wily grasp before she had a chance to clean out his pockets. She might have been born the daughter of a duke, but Lady Josephine would put the finest Seven Dials foyst to shame with her skill.

Again he searched for any sign of Jack, but to his shock, Lady Josephine stood flanked by two girls, a pair of coltish chits whose wide eyes and stiff stances said they hadn't their companion's experience in these matters.

"And who do we have here?" He winked at the tall, lithe creature to the lady's right, and damnation if the chit didn't blush like an innocent.

As if she'd never been kissed.

Well, he could take care of that problem. Moving toward her, to get a better look he would aver, his real problem cut him off.

"You leave her alone, Dashwell," Lady Josephine blustered. "She isn't your type. And I'll warn you, I taught them both to shoot a rat when they see one."

"My lady, you wound me," he said, bringing his hand to his heart while his gaze wandered back to the tall, fair miss beside her. Sure enough, there was a pistol in her trembling hand.

Misses with pistols and Aunt Josephine back from the dead? He rather preferred the militia . . . Though they didn't have pretty blond hair, or sweet lips that looked in need of kissing.

As if Lady Josephine could read his thoughts, she started nattering at him again, giving his theory that the devil had indeed tossed her out of the afterlife some credence.

"Enough of this nonsense," she was saying, waving her own pistol about like it was merely a lady's fan. "Unload your passengers right this minute."

Ah, yes. The devil probably hadn't liked being ordered about any more than he did.

"—furthermore, Thomas Dashwell, why in God's name didn't you put them ashore last night? It isn't like you wouldn't be paid."

Wouldn't be paid! He snorted. If there was one thing he did know, an Englishman and his coins were difficult to part. And Lady Josephine, like her pinchpenny husband, was even worse. "You'll get your cargo when I get my gold."

Lady Josephine nodded toward a pile of driftwood behind them, where a mule stood tied to a weathered branch.

He grinned and strode up the beach, flipping open the first pack. Even before he dipped his hands in, he knew the contents.

Gold. And plenty of it.

Mr. Hardy was wont to say, "The captain can smell it, he can." There was some truth to that. And right now Dashwell's nostrils were filled with the scent of newly minted guineas. Enough Yellow Georges to make even the dour Mr. Hardy happy. Nodding in satisfaction, he whistled low and soft like a seabird to the men in the longboat.

They pulled up one man, then another, and cut the bindings that had their arms tied around their backs and tossed the two over the side and into the surf.

That ought to cool their heels a bit, Dashwell

mused, as he watched the Englishmen splash their way to shore. His passengers had been none too pleased with him last night when he'd abandoned their delivery in favor of saving his neck and the lives of his crew.

Untying the mule, he led the beast down the shore toward the longboat. It came along well enough until it got down to the waterline, where the waves were coming in and the longboat tossed and crunched against the rocks. Then the animal showed its true nature and began to balk.

The miss who'd caught his eye earlier came over and took hold of the reins, her other hand stroking the beast's muzzle and talking softly to it until it settled down.

"You have a way about you," he said over his shoulder, as he walked back and forth, working alongside his men, who were as anxious as he was to gain their gold and be gone from this precarious rendezvous.

"Do you have a name?" he asked, when he returned for the last sack. This close he could see all too well the modest cut of her gown, her shy glances, and the way she bit her lip as if she didn't know whether to speak to him.

Suddenly it occurred to him who, or rather what she was, and he had only one thought.

What the devil was Josephine doing bringing a lady, one barely out of the schoolroom, into this shady business?

"What? No name?" he pressed, coming closer still, for he'd never met a proper lady—he certainly didn't count Josephine as one, not by the way she swore and gambled and schemed.

As he took another step closer he caught the veriest hint of roses on her. Soft and subtle, but to a man like him it sent a shock of desire through him like he'd never known.

Careful there, Dashwell, he cautioned himself. If the militia didn't shoot him, he had to imagine Josephine would. "Come sweetling, what is your name?"

There was no harm in just asking, now was there?

The wee bit of muslin pursed her lips shut, then glanced over at her companions, as if seeking their help. And when she looked back at him, he smiled at her. The grin that usually got him into trouble.

"Pippin," she whispered, again glancing back over toward where Josephine was haranguing his soaking wet passengers, Temple and Clifton, for news from the Continent.

"Pippin, eh?" he replied softly, not wanting to frighten her, even as he found himself mesmerized by the soft, uncertain light in her eyes. "I would call you something else. Something befitting such a pretty lady." He tapped his fingers to his lips. "Circe. Yes, that's it. From now on I'll call you my Circe. For you're truly a siren to lure me ashore."

Even in the dark he could see her cheeks brighten with a blush, hear the nervous rattle to her words. "I don't think that is proper."

Proper? He'd fallen into truly deep waters now, for something devilish inside him wanted to make sure this miss never worried about such a ridiculous notion again.

But something else, something entirely foreign to him, urged him to see that she never knew anything else but a safe and proper existence. A thought he extinguished as quickly as he could. For it was rank with strings and chains and noble notions that had no place in his world.

"Not proper?" He laughed, more to himself than at her. "Not proper is the fact that this bag feels a bit lighter than the rest." He hoisted it up and jangled it as he turned toward the rest of the party on the beach. "My lady, don't tell me you've cheated me yet again."

For indeed, the bag did feel light.

Lady Josephine winced, but then had the nerve to deny her transgression. "Dash, I'll not pay another guinea into your dishonest hands."

No wonder she'd brought her pair of lovely doves down to the beach. A bit of distraction so he'd not realize he wasn't getting his full price.

"Then I shall take my payment otherwise," he said, and before anyone could imagine what he was about, he caught hold of this tempting little Pippin and pulled her into his arms.

She gasped as he caught hold of her, and for a moment he felt a twinge of conscience.

Thankfully he wasn't a man to stand on such notions for long.

"I've always wanted to kiss a lady," he told her, just before his lips met hers.

At first he'd been about to kiss her as he would any other girl, but there was a moment, just as he looked down at her, with only one thought—to plunder those lips—that he found himself lost.

Her eyes were blue, as azure as the sea off the West Indies, and they caught him with their wide innocence, their trust.

Trust? In him?

Foolish girl, he thought as he drew closer and then kissed her, letting his lips brush over hers. Yet instead of his usual blustering ways, he found himself reining back his desire. This was the girl's first kiss, he knew that with the same surety that he knew how many casks of brandy were in his hold, and ever-so-gently, he ventured past her lips, slowly letting his tongue sweep over hers.

She gasped again, but this time from the very intimacy of it, and Dash suddenly found himself inside a maelstrom.

He tried to stop himself from falling, for that would mean setting her aside. But he couldn't let her go.

This Pippin, this innocent lass, this very proper lady, brought him alive as no other woman ever had.

Mine, he thought, with possessiveness, with passion, with the knowledge that she was his, and always would be.

He wanted to know everything about her, her real name, her secrets, her desires . . . His hands traced her lines, the slight curve of her hips, the soft swell of her breasts.

She shivered beneath his touch, but she didn't stop him, didn't try to shy away. Instead, she kissed him back, innocently, tentatively at first, then eagerly.

Good God, he was holding an angel!

And as if the heavens themselves rang out in protest over his violation of one of their own, a rocket screeched across the sky, and when it exploded, wrenching the night into day with a shower of sparks, Dashwell pulled back from her and looked up.

As another rocket shot upward, he realized two things.

Yes, by God, her eyes were as blue as the sea.

And secondly, the militia wasn't at the local pub bragging about their recent exploits.

"Christ!" he swore. And as eagerly as he had held her just moments before, he shoved her down face-first into the sand and threw himself over her as the first of the bullets started to kick up the sand around them.

Where before she'd been so alive in his arms, now she felt small and fragile beneath him.

From his ship, Mr. Hardy was swift to return fire, opening up the cannon ports and laying a ball just over the top of the cliff, while the men in the longboat had pulled out their pistols and were firing as well.

With all that cover, all he had to do was get up and run for his longboat. They'd push off and be out of the line of fire before the militia could reload.

"Come with me, Circe," he whispered in her ear. "Don't stay here, come with me. I'll keep you safe, I promise."

But beneath him, she didn't respond. In fact, she wasn't moving in the least.

"Give me your hand, lass. Give me your hand and we'll make a run for it. There's no use staying here to die."

But she didn't move, not even a wiggle of protest, as once again bullets pierced the beach all around them.

Well, the boys in the village could reload quicker than he gave them credit, but their aim was wide of the mark.

Thankfully.

"Now's our chance, my little Circe," he said, pulling his hand out from beneath her. It came out warm and hot.

And covered in blood. Her blood.

Dashwell turned her over and saw to his horror the truth of her silence, her eyes staring at the heavens as vacant as the emptiness above.

Oh, God, no. No.

"Cap'n, we need to get going," one of his men called out.

"Hold there," he shouted back, looking up and down the beach for someone to help him.

Help her.

Temple, quick and wily, scurried across the sand toward him. "Demmit, Dashwell, what have you done?"

"I tried to save her," he whispered, his gaze fixed on Pippin's blank gaze that moments before had been filled with life, with innocence.

"You've killed her is what you've done," Temple shot back, pushing him aside, shoving him toward the surf. "She's dead because of you."

Aboard the Ellis Anne
The English Channel, 1837

Captain Thomas Dashwell jolted awake in his bed, his body slick with sweat and his mouth dry.

It took a moment for him to find his way off that distant beach, shake off the dream that haunted him night after night, and remember where he was.

On his ship. At sea. Far from that night. Far from her.

He rolled over and reached for the bottle that was always close at hand. Tugging the cork free with his teeth, he spit it into the far corner of his quarters and drank.

You've killed her is what you've done . . . She's dead because of you.

The haunting words left him shuddering in his damp sheets, so he took another pull to quell the shakes, to ward of the chill of his nightmare, banish the lies the images held. The lies he was telling himself as the hot, fiery liquid flowed easily down his throat, the lie that the brandy would stop the hurt.

If there was one thing that was true, it was that he hadn't killed her that night. She'd never even been shot. And more to the point, she'd escaped the beach that night and grown up to be the enchanting vision her youthful bloom had promised.

As far as he knew, she lived still. In her lofty world not so far away in London.

If anyone had died that night, it had been he. She'd killed him, torn his heart out and left him adrift all these years, with only a brandy bottle to dull the pain.

And so he took another drink and rolled over, nursing the wound that had festered for more than twenty years, trying to forget her.

Trying to forget what she'd done to him . . .

Chapter 2

London, 1837

*T*he argument in the parlor below carried quite
easily to the room above. It wasn't that Lady Gossett
was eavesdropping on her children, rather, it was hard
to ignore them as they loudly debated her future.

As if she were suddenly a child to be cared for.

She heaved a sigh and rose from the bed where the
doctor had recommended she rest for the remainder
of the day, perhaps a few days, he said, patting her
hand as if she needed such bland reassurances.

What she needed was to get back to the docks.
What had it been? Two, maybe three hours since she
fainted. Perhaps he could still be found . . .

When she wandered toward the window, the voices
became clearer, more distinct, but she was only half
listening, parting the lace curtain with her fingers and

staring out at the park that made up the middle of Grosvenor Square.

"Something must be done," the newly christened Captain Gossett said, as if he were issuing an order. "Obviously she isn't well."

Lady Gossett could almost see his spine going stiff, his shoulders drawing into a taut line as he instructed his sister on what must be done.

Oh, John. Tread carefully. You of all people should know how well Ginger takes your ordering her about.

"She fainted, John," Lady Claremont said. "It is hardly cause for alarm."

"It isn't just the fainting, madam," he said, the click of his boots punctuating his words as he paced in front of the sofa where Ginger was most likely playing hostess. "Didn't you have a care what she was wearing?"

Oh, botheration, not the gown again, Lady Gossett thought, looking down at the elegant mauve creation. It was the height of fashion and perfectly respectable, even if she personally found the modes of the day rather overdone.

Fluffing the lace and taking a mincing glance at the puffed sleeves, Lady Gossett longed for the cool and comfortable muslins of her youth. Elegant gowns, simple and pretty in their long, slim lines—without the need for all these corsets and cages and hoops and excessive froufrou.

Ginger's voice rose a bit, marking her irritation with her brother. "John, there is nothing wrong with a woman of Mother's age wearing such a dull color. I have to admit, I was surprised when she asked me to go shopping with her, but then again I suppose she saw today as a celebration of your success and didn't want to appear like some old crow."

Lady Gossett sniffed. *A woman of Mother's age.* While she knew her daughter was defending her, she needn't have added the "old crow" part. She glanced over her shoulder at her dressing room where row after row of black gowns hung in a mournful line.

Dull and boring. And terribly depressing. Like a flock of ravens on a clothesline.

"I would rather she show our father his due respect. At least when she is wearing mourning, we needn't worry about the likes of Fairham taking it into his head that she's . . . she's . . ." He stammered over the last of it, for she had to guess he didn't want to even think of his mother being . . .

Alive. Available. Still capable of passion.

"Shocking notion, isn't it, John," she said softly, taking another glance at the park. The summer blossoms and roses made for cheery respite from the dreary conversation below. The rest of the square was empty, as it usually was this time of day, save for a governess pushing a baby carriage across the path.

Claremont waded into the fray. "Must say, I'm with Gossett on this. Thought it shocking, myself. And Fairham isn't the sort of man I'd want around my mother."

You aren't the sort of man I'd have picked for my daughter, you dreadfully dull coxcomb, Lady Gossett thought uncharitably.

"Oh, you are both making much too much of this. Fairham slavers over every woman's hand. She need only be drawing a breath," Ginger shot back. "Not that it wasn't a tad disconcerting to see him looking at her like that, but really, I think the admiral was being more gallant than solicitous. Men his age are like that."

There was a decided harrumph from Lady Gossett's chamber.

"Well, I don't like it," John said, back to his formal, proper tones. The sort that issued dictums and rules that weren't mere suggestions, but orders. "She's a widow and she should behave as one. If Father could have seen such a display—"

Ginger groaned at her brother's pomposity. "He would have said she looked quite pretty. And the mauve doesn't make her look so pale, so frail."

Pale? Frail? This was her daughter rising to her defense?

Lady Gossett leaned over and looked at herself in the mirror. The woman staring back at her was hardly the decrepit crone they described. To her eyes, her face was still unlined, her fair hair still pale and blond without a streak of gray, and despite having two children and living to what they thought was such an advanced age at forty-three, she'd kept the figure of her youth.

Well, for the most part, she thought, glancing at the way this horrible gown disguised every bit of her curves, what with the hoops and the wretched corset.

Downstairs, Ginger was adding, "You are making much too much of this, John. All she needs is rest and some gentle attention. It isn't as if she's gone and put on some red silk monstrosity and paraded about the park."

Lady Gossett sighed. Did they really think her as addled as that?

Quite a pair, John and Ginger. She should be so very proud of them, but right now she wanted to knock their heads together.

"Red silk!" John was sputtering, his voice filled with horror. "I don't even want to consider such a vision."

Upstairs, his mother was of half a mind to go into the back of her closet where there was indeed a red gown to wear, a notorious silk from her youthful folly, and put it on. So attired, she'd proceed downstairs to toss them all out of her house.

At least it was hers until John married . . .

"Perhaps we should consider . . . well, this is sort of presumptuous of me, but I do say—" Claremont began.

"Consider what?" Ginger prodded gently.

"Well, moving her to Claremont House," the earl announced. "At least for the rest of the summer, just until she's back to her old self. Could move her into the dower house with my mother."

"An excellent notion," John said, snapping up the idea like a fish at a lure. "You could keep an eye on her, Ginger, and see that she doesn't . . . well, you know what I mean. Come to any further problems."

Lady Gossett clenched her teeth together. Now she was a problem?

Standing in front of the window, with the square before her, she began to gather together a set-down that would send them off for at least a fortnight.

Enough of this nonsense! I won't be moved any-

*where. I intend to live in London. And I have no
intention of—*

I have no intention of . . .

Every word, every rebuke, every bit of anger that
had been inside her fled in an instant.

Catching hold of the window frame, she could
only stare at the sight before her.

For there in the park, on the bench that faced her
house, sat a young man. A sailor, to be exact. His red
bandana, jaunty hat, and striped duck cloth trousers
as sharp a relief from the grays of London as the roses
blooming around him.

Lady Gossett closed her eyes and considered for
half a second that perhaps her children were right
and she had gone round the bend.

Then she opened her eyes and found him still sitting exactly as she'd seen.

The very same man she'd seen down at the docks
earlier.

Her first thought was to race after him, without
the least bit of propriety, without a care of what her
children would say . . .

Her children . . .

Oh, demmit, Ginger and John! How could she
have forgotten? She glanced at the floor and took a
deep breath, smoothing her trembling hands over her
skirt and forming a quick plan.

Silently treading her way to the door, she only
glanced at her bonnet and gloves, ignored the matching shoulder cape, even though stepping outside without them would be scandal enough.

There isn't time, she told herself, as she made her

way down the side of the hallway with every bit of stealth her cousins had taught her years ago.

Tally and Duchess. Lady Gossett smiled. Her dearest friends. She had to imagine they would laugh uproariously at the sight of her sneaking through her own house, trying to slip past her children, much as they'd done in their youth to escape their schoolmistress, Miss Emery.

The Duchess would probably suggest, and rightly so, that Lady Gossett had completely lost her wits to go chasing after this phantom sailor, but what else could she do?

It was him. And there was nothing else she could do but follow.

Rounding the landing on the stairwell, she put a finger to her lips to silence the maid dusting in the front hall. The footman who usually waited by the door, as well as the ever-present Lockley, were nowhere in sight. Taking their tea, she surmised.

She crossed the hall, while even inside the parlor she could hear Ginger saying, "I've asked her half a dozen times to come to the country with us, but she refuses. What do you suggest we do, John, carry her off against her will? Kidnap her? She'd be scandalized by such rough treatment."

Not as much as you think, Ginger, dear. For it wouldn't be the first time, Lady Gossett mused. *If only they knew . . .*

But there was no time to enlighten them about their mother's past. Her youthful sins.

Instead, she fled out the front door, quietly as a mouse, and the moment she closed it behind her, something inside her broke free. As if she'd clipped the ties that bound her to this house, this life, to the proper existence John and Ginger expected her to maintain.

Lady Gossett was gone, and for the first time in years, she was Pippin again.

With one eye fixed on the bench in the park, and the other on the traffic, she dashed across the street, dodging the carriages and wagons like a madwoman, until she came to a tumbling halt before the bench. This close, right here, toe-to-toe with him, words failed her.

It isn't him, Pippin. It isn't.

For it wasn't him.

A searing disappointment ran through her, a sense of grief she hadn't expected. Hadn't felt in years. Then again, if she were being sensible, she'd have known that already.

How could it be him?

But surely it was like looking at her past, seeing Dash again, as he had been that night on the beach in Hastings. All youthful arrogance, and ruggedly handsome. The hair, the cut of his jaw were the same, but the nose and eyes were wrong, and she suspected he hadn't quite Dash's height.

In fact, he held a rather uncanny resemblance to . . . She glanced over her shoulder and looked at the parlor window, now realizing the real scandal of what she was doing.

If they saw her here and came out, she'd have to explain . . . something there was no easy way to account for.

"Lady Gossett?" the young man asked, his words

crisp and sharp, full of brash American confidence. He rose to his feet, doffing his hat, the red scarf still tied around his head. Without the cap, he looked even more like a pirate, and her heart beat a little quicker.

She nodded, rubbing at the gooseflesh rising on her arms. The voice. It was so similar.

Again she glanced at the house, and this time caught up his arm and steered him across the square.

"My name is Nathaniel. Nathaniel Dashwell."

She stumbled a bit, but of course he was a Dashwell. His introduction shouldn't have surprised her. She took a quick glance at his tanned, handsome face.

"Dashwell?" she repeated.

He stopped, and thankfully they were well enough away from the house that if John and Ginger happened to glance out a window, they wouldn't notice her. "Captain Dashwell is my father. You knew him, didn't you? You remember him?"

Remember him? Was the man mad? As if she ever could have forgotten Captain Thomas Dashwell.

Still, all she could do was nod in shock.

He worried his hat in his hands for a few seconds and then said the words that changed her life.

Offered her the sort of scandal she'd avoided for years. If her children were convinced that just wearing half mourning was beyond the pale, what this Nathaniel had to say would have put John in an early grave. Turned all of London Society on its ear.

"Lady Gossett, I beg you to come with me. You see, he needs you. I think you're the only one who can save him."

A fortnight later
Aboard the Ellis Anne

Captain Dashwell woke with a start and automatically reached for his ever-present bottle. But the space was empty.

"Christ!" he muttered, raking his hand through his hair and casting a bleary gaze toward the window. Outside, night still claimed the sky, and from the way the ship rocked, the fresh, crisp wind that had filled their sails at sunset was still blowing, for the ship was cutting a true, steady line through the waves.

He got up and tottered over to the cabinet on unsteady legs, pausing before it to steady himself, then opening it and searching around inside. Instead of bumping his hand into the heft of a full bottle, his fingers came up wanting.

He peered inside the shelf that held his private reserve and found the entire thing had been emptied. Pilfered. Stolen.

This time the curse he muttered wasn't fit to repeat.

Where the hell had all his brandy gone?

He glanced at the decking over his head. More of Nate's meddling, he suspected. Demmed cheek was what it was. He, Thomas Dashwell, was still the captain of this ship, still in charge, and it was about time his son understood that.

No *matter that it's him the crew looks to more than naught*, a nagging voice whispered traitorously in his ear. *The men follow Nate without hesitation, 'cause he keeps the ship on a true and profitable course.*

Dash shook his head, tossing aside any thought

that he wasn't still in charge. This was his ship, demmit. His.

He reached farther inside and clicked the panel at the back of the cupboard, and when the false back opened, he reached in and brought out both pistols.

Been a while since he'd shot anyone, but he could still aim. And he was in a foul enough mood to prove his ruthless reputation of old had been well-earned.

He took a few wavering steps toward the door and then realized he had another pressing problem to attend to. He needed to take a piss. Fine, he'd do that first, then he'd see about murdering the bastard who took his brandy.

Shrugging on his coat, he pulled his hat low over his brow and made his way onto the deck, his boots hitting the planks with a stormy thud.

Catching up a lantern, he made his way to the stern, set the lantern down, and was about to drop his drawers and relieve himself over the back railing, when a soft voice from the shadows stopped him cold.

"Dash, is that you?" a woman whispered.

He stood there, frozen in place. His hands on his waistband, the sea at his feet below.

Jesus! How long had he gone without a drink? Too long, if the waves were talking to him. For there was no other explanation.

"Dash?"

Then he remembered Nate saying something about bringing on a passenger, not that he'd paid much attention to these things. Now he wished he had.

What the hell had Nate said? A widow who'd booked passage to Baltimore. Paid in gold.

The gold part had been the only thing he'd cared about. Now he knew he should have asked one more question.

What woman?

"It's me," she told him. "I've come to find you."

The ship rose and fell, heaving in the thick seas, and Dash thought he was going to be sick. Forty years at sea and he'd never cast up his accounts. Until tonight.

"Dash, I've come back," she said, coming closer. " 'Tis me."

Oh, that voice. He knew it only too well. Like a siren it called to him in his dreams, haunted him.

Not her. No, for Christ sakes, not her.

It can't be her, he told himself. 'Twas some demmed joke. Probably the same rotter who had stolen his cache of liquor. Well, there was one way to end this prank.

Slowly, he reached for the lantern, while his other hand reached inside his coat to pull one of the pistols free. He turned around, lantern raised, pistol aimed.

Oh, Christ, no. For there before him, staring back in shock, was a pair of blue eyes he knew only too well.

Blue as the West Indies seas and filled with grief.

He'd been shocked once before like this, to turn around and find himself facing her, and the memories of that day rushed over him.

London, 1814
The Thames Frost Fair

Bloody frozen. The entire demmed river. Dash shook his head and frowned. While the rest of London frolicked atop the frozen Thames in this spontaneous Frost Fair of theirs, Dash was of another opinion as to this wretched state of weather. One not shared by the multitude of citizens and gawkers who'd come down to enjoy the novelty of walking atop the river and partake in the carnival it afforded.

And me stuck here as likely to be arrested as I am to find me balls drop off from cold, he thought as he rubbed his hands together over the makeshift brazier he stood before and called out to passersby, "Chestnuts, roasted chestnuts."

"A bag of those," a toff said, tossing his coin down on the table and holding a handkerchief to his nose. He passed a dismissive glance over Dash, then looked over his shoulder at the young lady waiting for him and waggled his brows at her. "Be quick about it, my good man, demmed cold for a lady to be standing about." The fellow winked at the girl, and she giggled.

Both of them were dressed in heavy coats, trimmed in fur with thick gloves and boots to ward off the frigid temperature and the bite of the wind.

"Yes, m'lord," Dash said, remembering to put the bit of English to his words. He was after all an American. On English soil. Well, ice, but with their countries at war, one slip, one man who recognized him, and he'd be hanging from the nearest yardarm as a spy.

He handed over the bag of chestnuts and collected his payment, calling out for more customers, "Chestnuts. Hot chestnuts."

This certainly hadn't been what he'd planned when he'd snuck into London on a Dutch trader a fortnight earlier. Before the river had frozen solid, trapping the ship and all its passengers and cargo in a river of ice.

Arrogantly he'd thought to come into the London Pool, gather enough information about the ships about to set sail, their cargoes and their destinations, and then return to the *Circe* and pick them off one by one as they sailed out of the mouth of the Thames and past Shoebury Ness.

Instead, he'd found himself marooned. And the captain he thought he could trust, well . . . Dash's gold had run out, and with it the Dutchman's loyalties and silence.

So, resourceful as ever, Dash had stolen a brazier from the galley, pawned his watch for some extra coins to buy a bag of chestnuts, and then set up this makeshift booth on the ice to parlay enough money to find his way back to sea.

If anything, he was gathering enough intelligence to make him a very rich man . . . when he got back to his ship, that was.

A watchman strolled by, casting a long glance at him, and Dash bobbed his head respectfully at the man. "Warm your hands, sir?" he offered, and the man smiled his thanks, thrusting his hands over the small nestle of coals.

"Terrible chill today, eh?" the watchman asked, wiggling his fingers over the bit of heat. "But it hasn't stopped the gentry and nobs from coming out, eh?" He tipped his head at the crowds filling the frozen river—skating, strolling through the booths, shopping at the impromptu market stalls that had sprung up almost the moment the river froze. "My thanks, sir."

Dash bowed slightly, smiling like an idiot and hoping the man thought him nothing more than a simpleton.

Better that than the truth.

That he'd just shared a few moments with the notorious privateer, Captain Thomas Dashwell. The most hated man in England, one newspaper had declared.

Dash rather liked that headline. He had it in his cabin, and his crew liked to tease him about it. The scourge of the merchant ships, he and his *Circe* were. How many English prizes had he taken? Twenty-two at last count. Single-handedly had made insurance rates for shipping soar to astronomical levels and raised the price of sugar to make it too dear for most.

That didn't even include the three naval packets he and his feisty crew had captured over the past year. One of them carrying a small fortune in wages for the fleet in the West Indies. And there was the small matter of the Scottish town he'd robbed recently.

Sailed right into their harbor, leveled his guns on the village, and ordered his holds filled.

No, he'd find no friends anywhere within English or Scottish shores.

Save one . . .

That gamine bit of muslin from the beach at Hastings. He didn't know why she haunted him, but she had all these years. What had it been? Three, nay, four years since he'd stolen that kiss from her.

Absently he rubbed his chin, and let out a low, long breath.

Pippin. That was her name. At least the name she'd

given him. Shyly. Not quite honestly. For it had only been her nickname.

Lady Philippa Knolles, he knew now. Mad Jack had told him sometime later who his mysterious little minx had been. A daughter of an earl. Far too lofty and above the likes of some American smuggler and pirate, his English friend had told him. Destined for a good match and life.

But her eyes, those blue eyes, he'd never forgotten them. The light shining there held a sadness that said the life she wanted and the one destined for her would never be the same.

Late at night, while he was standing watch, he could swear he heard her soft voice whispering across the waves, calling to him. That he could smell that soft hint of her rose perfume mingled on the breeze. And those eyes, wouldn't he love to see them alight with something other than sadness.

Pippin. His own Circe. She'd cast a spell over him with just a glance. He looked over at the snowy banks lining the ice, beyond the buildings rising behind them, toward the vast maze that was London and wondered where she was.

In Town? Or long married and far from the trappings of the city? He shrugged and looked away. Most likely. Not that he had any business wondering about her. Not her or any other lady.

He was naught but a curse to the likes of her, and well he remembered that. But still . . .

A soft sigh interrupted his reverie, and he glanced up to find a young woman fumbling with her reticule, a few coins jangling in the bottom of the silk bag. She glanced back over her shoulder, as if looking for someone, but the moment she'd raised her head, Dash's heart slammed against the wall of his chest at the sight of her eyes.

Blue and sad, soft and pure. The same light. The same tip of the chin. The very same lass. As if he'd conjured her here by his own musings.

Pippin. His Circe. And all grown up. A lady, with all the curves and temptations that left him speechless. Gone was the gamine bit on the beach. The woman, yes, woman, before him was now a tempting, irresistible minx.

"One bag, if you please," she said, still distractedly digging through her reticule. She was a million miles away from this place, and he wondered if she even remembered him.

Remembered him? Holy Christ! What was he thinking? The last thing he needed was her remembering him. He'd stolen a kiss from her and then tossed her down onto the beach, leaving her in a hail of bullets.

Hopefully she'd forgotten that part and remembered only his kiss.

That she'd liked being kissed, he had no doubt. And not by some pompous, flowery gentleman, he mused, the sort Jack had averred she was destined to marry.

Dash drew a slow, unsteady breath. Here she was. The one woman in London who had every reason to hate him . . . every reason to turn him over to the Watch in an instant. Yet what could he do? Turn tail and run? He'd never done that in his life. So carefully he filled the bag, and then handed it over to her, and for the merest second, their fingers brushed together and Dash wondered why he hadn't kidnapped her that long ago night and kept her always.

Lost in the spell she continued to cast over him, he said the words that would forever change his life.

"Is that all you want, little Circe?"

Chapter 3

Aboard the Ellis Anne, *1837*

*L*ady Gossett stared in horror at the man holding the lamp. This was Dash? This disheveled, stinking shipwreck of a man was Captain Thomas Dashwell?

She shook her head. *No. It can't be.*

He came closer, the lamp raised, and not only could she see the bleary set of his eyes, but she could smell him. Well, she could smell the brandy. And not even good brandy. The rank, sweet odor hung about him with the same disarray as his ragged jacket and tousled hair.

"No," she whispered.

Nathaniel had told her that Dash needed her help, that he was ailing. That he'd never stopped loving her.

What Dash's son had neglected to tell her was that his father was a ruined man. A drunk.

She backed up until she bumped into a large coil of rope.

Lady Gossett's hand went to her heart, for it felt as if it was about to break yet again.

What had happened to the pirate who had stolen her heart?

London, 1814

Coming to the Frost Fair had been her cousin Tally's idea, one that Pippin had thought might be a fun diversion from their wretchedly empty house on Brook Street.

Tally's twin sister, Felicity, had come up with an outlandish scheme to come to London for the Season. One Pippin had agreed to if only to get out of the dull boredom of their cottage in Sussex. Felicity had convinced them that by pooling their meager funds and taking the risk of stealing a proper house, they could quite easily launch themselves into Society. Then, with the help of Felicity's *Bachelor Chronicles*, they would be able to make good, albeit hasty, matches to lift them out of their poverty.

Oh, Pippin didn't mind all that much that she was as poor as a church mouse, it was just that as the daughter of an earl, Lady Philippa Knolles knew all too keenly how Society viewed those with pockets to let, and if Felicity's plan was discovered, if one hint of scandal touched them . . . well, they'd be back in Sussex for the remainder of their days.

Sussex. She shuddered, even though the place offered her only saving grace—a small country house

Pippin had inherited from her mother, that thankfully her father had never been able to get his hands on. If he had, it would have been lost as well in some gaming hell or at one of his favorite horse races, like everything else her family had possessed that wasn't either nailed down or entailed.

Not that her house was anything to brag about, a small cottage at the end of a lane, where the surrounding country society were only too aware of the poverty and lack of connections of its occupants to bother including them.

At least in London there was a chance, Felicity had argued, of finding good marriages.

Something that would have eluded them in Sussex for the rest of their lives. Would elude them here in Town if Felicity's scheme failed.

Oh, heavens. A good marriage. Pippin sighed. Whatever did that mean?

For Felicity, nothing short of a duke would do. Pippin smiled at her cousin's grand aspirations, for she really didn't want that sort of life, and would be quite content with someone a little less lofty.

Tally, on the other hand, wanted some scandalous sort of rogue, a rake of the first order, some Byronic, despondent sort that she would lift out of his desperation and loneliness—a nobleman, certainly, but she wasn't quite in the hurry that Felicity seemed to think necessary to find a suitable *parti*.

Then again, Tally never paid much heed to the trivial aspects of life, such as how to pay the greengrocer, or that the Watch could descend upon them at any time and evict them from their less-than-legal habitation of the town house on Brook Street.

No, in truth, Pippin's affections had been steered off course a long time ago. By a pirate of a man who'd stolen a kiss from her, and in that moment, made off with her heart as well.

It was hard to find Felicity's litany of eligible men interesting when none of them had ever smuggled silks or sailed across the oceans. When none of them smelled like anything other than bay rum or some flowery perfume, rather than the crisp salt of the sea, a hint of tar, and that whisper of danger that had enveloped him.

Captain Dashwell.

She glanced over at the ships, locked in the ice of the river, and wondered where he was.

At sea, she knew. Bedeviling the English fleet and merchants, if the reports in the papers were to be believed. She shouldn't smile, shouldn't be amused by his daring and exploits, for he was an American. A privateer. England's enemy.

She shivered and rubbed her mittens together, wondering if he remembered that night. Remembered that kiss . . .

As she had every night since. Recalling what it had been like to be held by him, how his lips had felt on hers, the liberties he'd taken, the ones she'd let him take because she'd been lost in her first taste of passion.

It was a wonderful memory, but one that didn't serve her well as she walked across the ice and nearly slipped in her distracted state.

Oh, Pippin, what a foolish nit you are, she scolded. *He is far away and probably has never once thought of you.*

Then her stomach growled and reminded her of her errand to find something to eat. She shook her head and continued on to the chestnut vendor she'd spotted before, and ordered up a bag, digging in her reticule for some coins. She shouldn't be squandering her few pence on chestnuts, but she was hungry.

Though really, she was hungry for something that had no price, that no coins could buy.

"One bag, please," she said as she dug into her reticule. For such a small purse, it always seemed to manage to swallow up her coins.

"Is that all you want, little Circe?"

Pippin's world stopped. Only one man had ever called her that.

And he was far from here, she told herself. Off at sea, fighting a war that would keep him well away from London.

"Come, my sweet Circe," the deep, rich voice teased, as he came around his stand. "Don't tell me you've forgotten me?"

Then she glanced up and found herself looking at the very same bright, mischievous light in his green eyes, that same rough-hewn chin, the same pair of stone-cut lips.

Forgotten him? How could she have?

"Captain Dashwell, whatever are you doing here?" she asked, taking a step back from the man who had haunted her dreams for far too long. She still couldn't quite believe it, but there he was.

Oh, gracious heavens, it was one thing to dream about a man for four years but quite another to find him standing right before you.

"So you do remember me, Circe," he said, coming

up to take her hand and kiss the tips of her mitten. He didn't seem to mind or notice her homespun. "I must say, you have grown up since last we met, though you still blush quite prettily."

She pulled her hand free and put it to her cheek, which she knew was ablaze. "Captain Dashwell—" she managed, but was unable to say much more.

Whatever did one say to the man of one's dreams? *Oh, heavens, Pippin*, she scolded herself. *Steady. You aren't sixteen still and he's no danger to you . . .*

Danger. Oh, good God! She was standing here talking to Captain Thomas Dashwell—the most hated man in England. England's most notorious enemy, shy of Bonaparte.

Her enemy.

Well, nearly enemy, she told herself. But that didn't mean he wasn't in danger. "Captain Dashwell, you shouldn't—"

"Shhh, Circe. Thomas, plain and simple, if you don't mind." He caught her hand again and pulled her close, whispering into her ear, "The name Dashwell isn't much loved in these parts. Most of England and a good part of Scotland, for that matter. There's a rich price on my head . . ." He paused and looked at her.

Pippin shivered beneath his scrutiny. "Yes, I know."

He leaned back and grinned at her. "So you've been following my adventures, have you?"

"Your exploits are hard to avoid, sir," she told him, glancing over her shoulder and looking for her cousins. For whatever reason, here he was in London, which couldn't bode well. Not for him. Or her, either, if she was found with him. "You've caused a good many merchants to lose their goods."

"Better they lose their tea and silks than I have my neck stretched." He leaned forward. "For however would I steal another kiss from your sweet lips if I were to find my head stuck up on a pike?"

A kiss? He meant to kiss her? Again?

If only he would, she thought almost immediately, then realized exactly what it was she was about.

Why, she'd be ruined, not to mention that Felicity would have *her* head on a pike for bringing scandal down on them when they had so much at stake, had risked so much to come to London for the Season.

No, kissing was definitely out of the question.

At least not here and now in the plain view of all of London, a wicked little voice whispered in her ear. *But later perhaps . . .*

What was it he'd offered her all those years ago?

"Come with me, Circe," he'd whispered in her ear. "Don't stay here, come with me. I'll keep you safe, I promise. I'll teach you to be a pirate."

She should have gone with him that night instead of running from him like a frightened child. If she had followed her heart that night, she had to imagine she'd know more about kissing than just those wisps of memories she clung to . . .

Pippin stumbled back, looking left and right to see if anyone else had noticed them, was looking at her, for she felt the heat of blush rising up on her cheeks once again. "Whatever are you doing here?" she asked, changing the subject.

"Stranded, I fear. At least until this ice melts,"

he told her. "I came in, to do some business you might say, and found myself landlocked. Merely an inconvenience." He waved at the ships held fast in the ice. "And without a friend to be had. At least until now." He tried again to take her hand, but this time she was quicker and tucked it safely under her cloak.

Not that such a thing would stop Captain Dashwell, she realized as he slanted an assessing glance at her elbow, which still poked out.

Pippin took another step back. "I daresay you haven't done yourself any favors on that score. There is no doubt why you are friendless. Lady Josephine says you're a scurvy, dishonorable, wretched—"

She stopped her description, for it seemed the man held each word of censure like praise from on high.

"But sweet Pippin, I think that is why you like me."

"I don't," she lied. "I don't even know you."

He tipped his head back to gaze at her, and she could see the shadow of a tawny beard on his face. For a moment as he studied her, she swore she could smell the sea on him—the tar and the pitch and the salt that had been his calling card that long ago night they'd first met.

Yet he'd changed as surely as she had. His shoulders had grown in breadth, and now he loomed even larger over her—not like the popinjays and pampered Corinthians of London that Felicity constantly pointed out, but as a man used to living by his wits and fighting for (or stealing, most would say) what he wanted.

And from the light in his eyes, she realized he might even want her. Her! Penniless Lady Philippa Knolles.

"So you've been reading about me in the paper? Seen the accounts of me and the *Circe*?" He rocked on his heels and studied her. "But lass, I don't think it is my exploits that have you remembering me, but something else that has held your fancy all this time."

"I wouldn't know what you mean," she said, drawing herself up into a proper, standoffish stance. Even when she knew exactly what he meant.

He shrugged, then leaned dangerously close. "I wouldn't suppose you've given any thought to that kiss of ours? When was that, two, nay, three—"

"Four years, sir," she corrected him without even thinking. Oh bother! She'd fallen right into his trap. Then again, it was devilishly hard to be proper with him standing so close. That didn't mean she shouldn't at least try. "I was but a child then," she reminded him. "And you a regular villain to be so bold."

He laughed, whether at her censure or her haughty stance, she didn't know. "A child! With a gun in her hand and doing a man's job for her country." Captain Dashwell shook his head. "My lady, you were no more a child than you are now. And might I say you've grown into quite a lovely lady. As pretty as I am dishonorable." He reached over, and with one finger gently tipped her chin up. "I've never forgotten those eyes of yours. As blue as my heart is black." His words came out with a ragged air of longing.

One she understood so very well.

His rough fingers, poking out of the holes in his tattered mitts, held her gently, and there was almost a sad light to his gaze as he looked at her. "Tell me you haven't gone and married someone else."

There was an almost wistful air about his words. A refrain that haunted her, a hint at something she couldn't quite put her finger on.

"No, I'm not married," she told him distractedly, searching his face for an answer, but only finding that grin that sent her heart racing.

He came closer still and whispered, "I'd be sorely disappointed to discover that you hadn't waited for me—"

Waited for him. Why, of all the arrogant—

A very English part of her, the part of her that had spent years in a Bath school being drilled and trained to be a proper lady, rebelled at his presumption.

No matter that it was true.

She steeled her shoulders and lifted her nose as Felicity did when she was practicing to be a duchess. "I haven't been—"

"No, of course not," he said solemnly, but his eyes sparkled with the truth. He knew her secret. "No, I have to suppose you're living in Mayfair in some grand house," he said, in a voice that held not envy, but, well, pity. "With servants aplenty to do your bidding."

She shook her head, unable to speak, once again lost in the intimacy of being with him again. Just as she had dreamed. Imagined. Desired.

"Not in Mayfair?" he teased.

"Oh, the house is in Mayfair, on Brook Street, though it is hardly grand," she confessed, glad to have someone to talk to who held not a care of Society's rules or pretensions. "It's empty and cold. And it isn't even ours. Since we've no money, we had to steal it."

Dashwell gaped at her. "You stole a house?"

"Shhh!" she warned him. "Borrowed is how Felicity likes to explain it."

He let out a low whistle. "You stole a house? And here I thought myself a fine privateer." He crossed his arms over his chest and looked at her long and hard, from the scuffed boots on her feet to her careworn bonnet. "But you're an earl's daughter, what have you to do with this felonious nonsense?"

Apparently stealing, or rather, borrowing a house wasn't such a grievous transgression in his world, but it was something else that struck Pippin.

You're an earl's daughter. "How do you know—"

There it was, that cocky grin again. "I asked, I did. After our, shall we say, last meeting."

Pippin felt her cheeks flush again.

"Tremont told me," he confessed. "Actually it was the last time I saw him. Just before this war broke out. Threatened me with a bullet through my heart if I ever came near you again."

This brought her gaze up. He'd wanted to find her? She almost sighed, that was if she hadn't been more miffed with Lord John Tremont. Oh, of course he'd have warned Dash off. Bothersome fellow! For a former rake, and the sort of fellow that most people referred to as Mad Jack, he was too protective of his "trio of troublemakers" as he liked to call Pippin and her cousins.

Dash, meanwhile, was chuckling at the memory, as if it was fondly held. "I think he thought your lofty state would frighten me away."

She ruffled again, but this time for entirely different reasons.

"Apparently it did," she said, "For it's been four years since last we met, and naught a word from you . . . Not one word, 'cept what one reads in the papers." She paused again, feeling a bit tossed about. "Not that I've looked."

He laughed, loud and clear. "You little minx. You almost had me convinced you didn't care—but you do. Not looked, have you? I'd wager you've scoured the columns for me. And tell me, little Circe, how was I supposed to come calling?" He paused, for the watchman was coming by, and they both lowered their gazes as he passed. Even with the man out of earshot, Dash lowered his voice to add, "What with our countries at war—that, and there's been the Atlantic and a good part of the British navy between the two of us—it hasn't been a simple matter of dropping by your fashionable Brook Street mansion for a pot of tea, now has it?"

"Hasn't stopped you from coming to London," she pointed out. "And selling chestnuts like some beggar."

He grinned again, stepping back to doff his ridiculous hat at her. " 'Tis a fine cover, lass." He waved at his little cart. "Gives me a chance to hear all kinds of talk. The merchants can't get their wares out to sea, so they come down here, and, well, wagging tongues . . ." He shrugged, then drew closer, lowering his voice to barely a whisper. "When this ice breaks up, I'll be sitting off Shoebury Ness waiting for them like flies to honey."

Pippin shivered. Well, of all the dishonorable, ignoble notions. War or not. "You can't do that, 'tis wrong."

He roared with laughter, loud and strong, at her indignation. Then he paused and gazed at her, his eyes sparkling and his lips set in a tempting grin. "Care to come with me, sweet Circe, and see just how wrong I can be?"

Come with him? Pippin's knees knocked together at the very notion. Why, it was scandalous, ruinous, and wrong for a hundred and one other reasons.

So why did she want nothing more than to catch hold of his hand and run away with him? From London, from the proper future bearing down on her like a mail coach.

Go with you? Oh, yes, Captain Dashwell. Please, she wanted to say, but somehow her cousin Felicity's practical voice invaded her thoughts. *How can you trust this bounder, Pippin? He's a pirate. An American.*

Felicity held the same horror of Dashwell as Jack's crusty old Aunt Josephine.

Yet what he was offering tugged at her soul, at a secret longing to be free that she suspected this man could unlock for her.

Oh, it was a heady, impossible notion. Run away with Captain Dashwell, sail away from Society and all its strictures.

And leave in your wake a raft of ruin, a stern, imposing voice rained down on her dreams. *Ruin your cousins' chances, add to your family's already shaky standing in Society.*

No, she couldn't do that. Not to Tally and Felicity who had done so much for her already. Stood firmly beside her when others tucked up their noses at the penniless Lady Philippa Knolles.

Shaking her head, she backed away from him,

away from everything he offered. Everything she desired.

She steeled her shoulders and stood with perfect Bath school posture, every inch the earl's daughter. "Come with you? Why, you aren't even a proper gentleman, and I shouldn't even be—"

Captain Dashwell paid little heed to her imperious manners, saw right through her lofty put-down. He moved much as he had on the beach in Hastings, as he must at sea—recklessly, arrogantly, swiftly, without any thought of the consequences. He caught hold of her and pulled her into his arms, as if it were his right, as if she belonged there and nowhere else.

She glanced up at him, thinking halfheartedly of putting up a struggle, that was until she saw the serious turn on his features. She was his. His to hold, and as he bent his head to hers, she knew another truth.

His to kiss.

She tried to breathe, and what little bit of air she could manage was rich with the sea. How was it that he seemed to be made of salty breezes?

And this wasn't like the last time, when she'd no idea what to expect. This time as his head dipped toward hers with the audacity of a thief, stealing away her senses, a jolt of passion ran through her. She clung to Dash, for that was what he was to her, Dash.

Her Dash. Her greatest temptation.

"Now tell me you haven't thought of that kiss in all this time," he whispered in her ear. "Tell me you haven't wished for me to come ashore and steal you away?"

Pippin shivered and tipped her head upward, praying he'd kiss her again, praying the ice would never melt. That he'd never sail away again. That she'd never have to choose . . .

But eventually she would.

Aboard the Ellis Anne, *1837*

Dash gaped at the woman on his deck. It was truly her. Pippin. Bloody hell!

His heart did a double wallop. Like the heave of a cannon fired with a little too much powder. Then again, he'd never been one to go the safe and sensible route when it came to loading powder.

"Dash, would you put the pistol down?" she asked softly, nodding at the weapon in his hand.

"Oh, so sorry," he mumbled. Christ, he'd forgotten he was holding it, setting the hammer carefully back in place and hastily tucking it in his waistband.

"How the—" he managed to begin.

"I've come back," she said, smiling at him, but it wasn't the smile he remembered. The one that lit up at the sight of him, then one that devoured him.

What do you expect? You aren't the man she left.

She left . . .

And then the rest of their history tumbled into place. The part where she'd married another . . .

Any warmth, any love he'd felt in the last few seconds sank like a stone to the bottom of the ocean, replaced by the icy chill of her betrayal.

And there was still enough brandy in him to give him the courage to tell her exactly where she could put her pity or charity or whatever it was that had brought her here.

To his ship.

"Lady Gossett," he said, letting his lip curl into a sneer and stalking closer to her. "How is your husband, or have you had a change of heart when it comes to that promise?"

She flinched as if he'd struck her, and she backed away from him.

He didn't know what infuriated him more—the twinge of guilt he felt over being cruel to her or that she backed away as if he carried the plague.

"My husband is gone," she told him, her shoulders squaring.

He glanced at the soft green gown. "Put off the mourning, have you, and come around for a toss, is it? Lonely for a bit of company and decided to look up old Dash, is it? Good for a tup and bit of scandal." He came right up to her, and the moment he got close he realized his mistake.

Because to be close to Pippin was to remember.

Remember the way she smelled like roses and everything that was good and proper in the world.

And God, how he longed to catch hold of her and never let go. It was like seeing land after months at sea. Standing on solid ground and knowing one was safely home.

And he hated himself all the more for wanting her still.

"What is it, Lady Gossett? Overcome with longing at the sight of me?"

She shook her head, her mouth opening as if to say something, but then she shut it just as quickly, her nose wrinkling in dismay. "I thought . . . that is to say, Nathaniel told me." She shook her head again.

"Oh, how could I have been so mistaken! Whatever have I done?"

She turned from him and looked about to cry.

Apparently the joy of their reunion wasn't mutual. So he reached out to catch hold of her, but to his shock, she reacted faster.

Her hands planted into his chest and she shoved him. And while he'd had enough brandy in him to be cruel, he'd also had enough to make him unsteady on his feet.

She upended him easily. With a whoosh his feet flew out from beneath him, which was followed too quickly by a sharp thud as his arse hit the oak deck, leaving him dazed and gaping at the canopy of stars overhead.

"Mr. Dashwell!" she called out, marching past him, raising her skirts as she swished by. "Mr. Dashwell, a word please!" She sounded like she was about to ring a peal in the lad's ear. As if she had a list of grievances to lie at Nathaniel's feet.

Well, she could get in line. She wasn't the only one about to keelhaul his son.

"Mr. Dashwell!" she barked again.

Dash tried to right himself with some measure of dignity, but in the end he was a tangle of dull wits and limbs.

But to his feet he finally got, and he stumbled after her.

"Mr. Dashwell, I demand you attend me this very moment!" she was saying.

There was an imperious, all-too-British lilt to her words that sparked a rebellious fire in Dash's very American belly. Besides, he was also still hung over from yesterday's bottle, so her sharp notes pierced his ears with an unholy and painful clamor.

"My lady, is there a problem?" Nate was saying as he came down from the top deck. He descended the stairs with a graceful leap, and stopped before her. "How can I help you?"

There was an innocent air to his question that didn't fool Dash in the least. Nate only used his best manners when he was neck-deep in trouble.

"You lied to me," she exploded, prodding his chest with a finger to punctuate each word. "When you came to me in London, you told me—"

Dash stopped listening. Nate had gone to Pippin? Sought her out? Brought her here? Holy Christ.

That moment, that heart-wrenching notion that she'd come back to him was a lie. Because apparently she hadn't returned to him of her own volition.

For the second time in his life, betrayal burned in his chest. She hadn't come back to him. Not willingly.

For her part, Pippin wasn't tongue-tied over the matter. "You told me he needed me. That he was ill—"

Ill? He wasn't sick. He was as fit as he'd been the first day he'd become a captain.

He swayed in his boots and rallied to steady himself. So he was a bit drunk. He'd gotten drunk the day he'd become a captain. Though for other reasons . . .

Nate was rallying his defenses. "Now, my lady, I hardly think I—"

"You lied," Pippin said, going toe-to-toe with him. "You told me he still loved me, wanted me." She glanced over her shoulder and shuddered at the sight of him. "What he wants is a good bath and his ration of rum tossed overboard."

He wanted to correct her that he never drank rum, vile stuff, but that seemed a lesser point at the moment.

"It wasn't entirely untrue, my lady," Nate began. "You can see what the situation is, so you can hardly blame me for wanting to see him—"

Dash's spine straightened. They were talking about him as if he weren't even there. On his ship. And the last time he checked, he was still the captain of the *Ellis Anne.*

"Mr. Dashwell, I demand—"

He stepped between them, cutting off her aristocratic "demand" with a curt one of his own. "Nathaniel, what have you done?"

"Captain," he said, with a nod of his head. "I see you have met our passenger."

"Yes, Lady Gossett and I are well acquainted, as you already know."

Nate, cheeky bastard that he was, only grinned. "I thought you might—"

Dash didn't let him finish. "You didn't think, is what you did. You shouldn't have brought her here."

"Demmit, Da, you need her."

Need her? Need Lady Gossett back in his life? Like an anchor around his neck he needed her.

"I don't need anything—" There was a snort from the lady at his elbow, but he ignored her disagreement. "I'm the captain of this ship and you have no right—"

Nate rose up and met him. "Are you? Are you

really the captain here?" The mutiny in his voice sent a dangerous shiver down Dash's spine.

"Look around, Da, and tell me how you are the captain of this ship? What watch is it? What's the second mate's name? What's our cargo? You can't answer any of those questions. And you're a . . . a . . ." His words faltered, his hands fisted at his sides, frustration setting his jaw in a furious line. "You're a wreck. You make everyone around you as miserable as you are, and I wasn't going to spend the rest of my life defending you, propping you up, pretending that the great and heroic Captain Dashwell, the hero of '14, isn't anything more than a common dockside . . ."

Drunk.

The word hung there between them, as shaky and damning as the way Dash's hands trembled. Would continue to shake until he found a demmed bottle.

"That's enough, Nathaniel," Pippin said quietly. "He's your father, and due your respect."

Dash rounded on her, not because he couldn't defend himself against his son's accusations—not when every word was true—but because the last thing he wanted was her help. "This is none of your business."

"Harrumph!" she snorted again, her scathing glance saying she was in Nate's camp. That he did indeed need a bath. A shave. A clean set of clothes.

And a lot less brandy.

"This is none of your business," he repeated, but even to his ears his words sounded hollow.

She turned back to Nathaniel, her hands going to her hips. "You will return me to London immediately."

Hell, why hadn't he thought of that?

Because, Dash, you don't want her to leave.

"Oh, don't worry, Lady Gossett, you will be back in your Mayfair mansion before the week is out," Dash told her. He swung around and stomped to the edge of the top deck. He looked up at the man at the wheel, and for the life of him couldn't remember the fellow's name.

Rogers? Williams? Shit. Dash clenched his teeth together and refused to admit defeat. "You at the wheel, turn this ship around. Right now."

The man glanced down at him, his brow furrowing into a line of worry. Then he did the unthinkable.

He looked to Nate. "Sir?"

"Belay that, Mr. Glover," Nate told him.

Glover! Demmit, how could he have forgotten? He'd sailed with the lad's father. Well, the man was about to learn who was in charge. "Mr. Glover, turn this ship around."

The poor fellow took a deep breath, glanced again at Nate, holding the wheel straight and true.

Mutiny was what this was. His own demmed son. Bringing her on his ship. Nate was probably the same traitorous bastard who'd removed all the brandy from his cabin. The captain's cabin, he would like to remind him.

Murder erupted in Dash's heart, and he pulled his pistol out and aimed it at the young man. "Mr. Glover, turn this ship around or you're relieved. Permanently."

There wasn't a man on deck who didn't know that a captain was well within his rights to shoot a sailor who wasn't obeying a direct order.

"Da, don't be a fool," Nate told him, stepping in front of the pistol. "If we turn around we'll lose every bit of profit we are to see."

"I won't be the one losing anything. If we lose anything it will come out of your shares," Dash told him. "Now turn this ship around and then go fetch me a bottle."

"We can't go back," Nate told him, in a deadly calm voice.

"Oh, yes, we can," Dash said. "It's very simple. You turn the ship around and sail right back the way we came."

Nate shook his head. "We can't return to London. Not now."

Dash shivered, and not from the shakes, or even the breeze that seemed to be freshening, pushing them farther and farther from England's green shores. No, there was something to Nate's words that hinted that his son had done more than lure Lady Gossett aboard the ship under false colors.

"Why the hell not?" he asked, afraid to hear the answer.

Nate took a deep breath. "I left a ransom note."

"A what?" both Dash and Lady Gossett asked at once.

When she'd arrived at his elbow, he didn't know, but she was there now and with murder in her eyes. He put the pistol down, for fear she'd take it up and put a bullet in Nate.

"I left a ransom note behind," he repeated.

Beside him, Pippin trembled, as if she could see the coming disaster and knew there was no way to avoid it.

"As far as Lady Gossett's family knows," Nate explained, taking a sturdy stance before them, "she's been kidnapped by Captain Thomas Dashwell, and won't be returned for anything less than twenty thousand pounds."

Chapter 4

London, that very same day

*W*hat makes no sense about this is why this devil would choose our mother to kidnap?" John said to the two ladies seated on the settee in his family's town house.

The Duchess of Hollindrake, the former Felicity Langley, shifted in her chair. One of the foremost matrons in London Society, she let nothing ruffle her demeanor, but ever since she and her sister, Thalia, now the Baroness Larken, had arrived, and brought John and Ginger into this room for a "good heart-to-heart," he'd had the suspicion that none of this dastardly business was all that much of a shock to them.

"Explain to me why it is that this bastard has kidnapped my mother," he demanded pacing before them.

The duchess glanced over at her sister, her lips pressed together as if she feared speaking. Lady Larken, however, exhibited no lack of constraint. "Your mother and Captain Dashwell were once lovers."

John's gaze swung over to meet hers. For a diplomat's wife, she had an appalling lack of discretion.

Seated in the armchair, Ginger sat with her eyes closed, a handkerchief clenched in her grasp, exhibiting the ramrod posture she'd gained at Miss Emery's school. He didn't think she'd recovered a bit of color in her cheeks since she'd received the note that had been forwarded from his London address to hers at Claremont House. She had immediately sent a messenger to him, catching him just before he sailed.

Now, three days later, they were all here, convened in this family conference.

"That is preposterous," John declared. "My mother was the daughter of an earl, a respected lady—"

"Your mother is all those things," the duchess told him, cutting him off. "But she also loved Captain Dashwell, and intended to marry him before . . ."

John wasn't used to being interrupted, but the Duchess of Hollindrake wasn't a woman who was easily naysayed.

Or one who told falsehoods.

No, if there was one thing he knew about his godmother, it was that she was going to be completely honest with him.

And do everything in her power to get his mother back. Even if that task was his responsibility, and his alone. Still, what she was saying was outlandish.

"This is impossible, ridiculous!" he declared. "My mother was never this man's . . . this man's . . ."

"Lover," Lady Larken supplied, her hands folded demurely in her lap, a small black dog at the hem of her gown. But her eyes glittered with a mischievous light.

Well, she needn't look so pleased to add to his discomfort.

"John, this isn't the least bit ridiculous," the duchess began. "They loved each other very deeply. It was a scandalous situation, all agreed, and would have been the ruin of all of us if it had been discovered, but luckily for them . . . well, it was a long time ago . . ." Felicity glanced away, her lips pressed together.

"Did Father know?" Ginger asked, so softly and quietly that for a second her words didn't sink in.

Their father? John's horror sunk deeper. "Impossible, why, he would never have—"

"Of course he knew." Again, Lady Larken offered him a slight smile that dared him to find a way to contradict her.

"And still he married her," Ginger marveled aloud.

John felt none of his sister's wonder. He was nothing but incredulous. He marched in front of his mother's cousins, her trusted confidantes, the women who probably knew her better than anyone else, and sputtered with conviction, "I find this entire conversation impossible—"

But he stopped when the Duchess of Hollindrake bounded to her feet and stepped into his path, her finger prodding into his chest as if he were still in short pants.

"John, you may have inherited your father's title, hold a seat in the House of Lords, and command your own ship, but you are a pompous, ridiculous nit without the least bit of understanding of what it means to love someone." She looked him up and down and made a loud *harrumph*.

"Stop being such a shortsighted prig," she continued, clearly having lost her patience. "This is no time for your self-righteous objections to your mother's past. It is what it is, and there is no getting around it."

His temper began to get the better of him. "I will remind you—"

"Silence, John," Ginger said, coming to stand at the duchess's elbow. "You know Papa loved Mama. Worshipped her. And if he could look past her . . . her . . . indiscretions, then we should as well." She paused. "Besides, none of these arguments are getting us any closer to finding her."

He paced before the empty grate, tugging at his suddenly too tight cravat. "Ginger, you wouldn't be so willing to overlook all this if you knew who this man is." He shot a glance over at the duchess, who had retaken her seat. "He's nothing more than a pirate, a bounder—a criminal to boot. Why, he'd be bones and dust right now if someone hadn't helped him escape from Marshalsea Prison—"

Those words, so quickly uttered, brought John to a faltering halt. For even as he'd said them, he'd caught out of the corner of his eye Lady Larken sending a guilty glance over at her sister.

Marshalsea Prison. Long ago, someone had helped Dashwell escape its walls.

"No," he said, his collar now threatening to stop his breathing altogether; that, or somehow the room had suddenly lost all its air.

Oh, it couldn't be . . .

"It was her," Lady Larken said.

Again, John went back to shaking his head. "My mother? You expect me to believe my mother masterminded the most infamous escape in naval history?"

"She had some help," the duchess said, casting a baleful glance at her sister.

"This is unbelievable! What you're saying is treason. That my mother committed treason for this man?"

Lady Larken nodded. "She wasn't the only one, if that helps."

He snorted and stomped around in front of the fireplace.

"How do we get her back?" Ginger asked, steering the conversation back to the problem at hand, not unlike how her mother would have done it.

"The money is of no matter," the duchess said. "Hollindrake has pledged the amount and has sent a note to his banker and solicitor to see to having it turned into gold immediately." She sighed. "Dashwell has always had a fondness for gold."

John spun around. "Madam, the money is not your husband's concern. Besides, there will be no ransom paid."

Ginger gasped. "But John, how else do you propose to get her back?"

He stalked toward the door, paused with his hand on the latch. Then he turned and faced them one last time. "I'm going to sail after them, fetch her aboard the *Regina*, and then burn that bastard's ship down to the waterline."

Aboard the Ellis Anne

Not even a bucket of cold seawater over his head could have sobered Dash up quicker.

A ransom note? He shuddered to think of the stink this was raising in London this very moment.

Having caused more than his fair share of those during his illustrious and nefarious career, he knew what was happening right now. And what would happen to all of them if they were caught with Lady Gossett aboard.

"You told them you kidnapped me?" Lady Gossett shook her head. "It won't work. They will know the demand is a fraud, for I posted a letter to—"

Out of his coat, Nate pulled out a missive addressed to the Countess of Claremont. "Your letter was never sent."

She snatched it out of his hands. "How dare you take such liberties!"

Dash glanced over at her. One hand fisted at her side, her jaw set just so . . . oh, he remembered that look. All too well.

For a moment he nearly smiled. So she hadn't mastered her temper in all these years. He'd always liked that about her—that sudden pique of temper, so at odds with her soft smiles and fair, sad eyes.

But then again, if she still had that bit of spirit to her, he'd need to intervene quickly, or Nate was about to find himself swimming in the briny deep.

"What the hell were you thinking?" he demanded, coming right up to his son.

They were a well-matched pair, but Nate had the

advantage of youth and not having consumed the better part of a brandy bottle. A point Dash knew too well.

And so did his son.

"I was trying to save you," Nate said. The hint of anguish in his words should have hurt, should have made him see the light, but Dash was too far gone to care. "To see you returned to your rightful place."

His rightful place? Bah! They could all take his once heroic reputation and shove it up their—

"Have you gone mad?" he asked instead. "Do you have any idea what you've gone and done?"

"Aye," he said. "Got your arse out of your cabin and your eyes open to the world around you for the first time in years."

Dash gritted his teeth together. "Hell, Nate, you could have done that by taking on a crew of doxies, which quite frankly would have been a fine sight better."

An indignant *harrumph* sputtered from their unwanted guest.

Obviously she didn't like the comparison.

The young man stood his ground. "Da, you've been in the bottom of a brandy barrel for too long. It was time you came out, came out and lived a bit. Were the man you once were. The man people expect."

Dash blew out an exasperated breath. *The man people expect.* Oh, he knew what that meant. The great Captain Thomas Dashwell. Hero of '14.

That man was long gone, and good riddance, he wanted to say.

He'd been a cheeky, arrogant, foolish bastard most of his youth. No, make that all his youth and a good part of his adulthood. How many times had Hardy held him in check, saved him from nearly killing himself and taking the entire crew down with him?

And now his son was following in his footsteps. A path rife with holes and traps. All sorts of ways for a man to lose his way and end up . . . end up just as Dash had.

Leaning in close to his son, he asked in a tight, dark whisper, "Where the hell would you get the notion to bring her aboard, to do all this?"

" 'Twas Mr. Hardy's idea," Nate told him, rocking on his heels.

"Hardy's idea? Mr. Hardy would never have suggested such a thing," Dash told him with every bit of conviction he possessed.

Besides, Hardy knew everything. Hated Lady Gossett as much as Dash did. Hardy's idea, indeed! Not Hardy. He'd never have betrayed Dash like this. Brought his past up into his face to haunt him. To hurt him.

To save him. Dash staggered back as the truth burned through all the denials he'd thrown up.

Demmed old man. Of course he would.

Die lonely and beached like me, if you don't do something, lad. The old man's voice, cragged and rough, drifted across the waves, sending a shiver down Dash's spine. He wasn't a superstitious man, but if ever he'd felt the hand of the beyond send a chill through him, it was right now.

Hardy, you bastard. If you weren't dead . . . well, you would be in short order.

In his mind's eye he could see that Irish devil standing at the stern, watching the sails with the eye of a sea hawk, and sniffing at the wind as if he could discern its moods.

You're killing yourself, lad, he'd said the last time Dash had seen him, a few days before Hardy had breathed his last. Just before they'd sailed on this trip.

Dash had scoffed at his warning then, but apparently Nate hadn't.

"Exactly what did he tell you to do?" Dash asked his son.

Nate crossed his arms over his chest. "Mr. Hardy told me the lady in red was the one person you'd be willing to listen to."

At his elbow, Lady Gossett blanched. The lady in red. It was probably a long time since anyone had called her that. Remembered her treasonous past. Including her.

But Dash had never forgotten. No matter how hard he'd tried. And, apparently, neither had Hardy.

Nate jerked his head. "Her. Lady Gossett. She's the one, isn't she? The one who broke you out of Marshalsea Prison?"

For a moment, there was that recoil of doubt in his son's eyes. That perhaps he'd snatched the wrong woman off the streets of London.

While for Dash it was no stretch to imagine the still slight and stunning matron before him in a scarlet gown and wielding a pistol, for someone of Nate's years, the notion was probably akin to imagining Mr. Glover in such a dress.

Meanwhile, she'd turned to Dash, her blue eyes wide with horror, as if she was shocked to be reminded of her past.

But it wasn't shock that had her shaking, but anger, and it was now starting to blaze forth.

"Hardy? Who is this Mr. Hardy?" she demanded, coming into the fray with that aristocratic, overbearing English tone at her command.

"My former first mate."

"This Mr. Hardy told you to tell this horrendous lie?" she asked Nate.

Nate paused and glanced at her and then at his father. While his son was usually good at holding his cards close, Dash knew the truth.

"You came up with the kidnapping notion, didn't you?" he asked. Not that he needed to. He hadn't seen Nate looking so guilty since he'd stolen ten guineas from Dash's cabin to buy his first whore.

Expensive, overpriced piece that she'd been.

Dash shook his head. So was the one before them. Likely to cost them their necks.

"Why would you do this?" she asked. "I agreed to come quite willingly, you didn't need to—"

"You did what?" Dash asked, before he could stop himself, stop his heart from making that tumbled thud as it always did over her.

She'd come with Nate willingly. Because she wanted to . . . Which meant . . .

It meant nothing.

"I came because your son told me you were ill and needed my help." She glanced away, her lips drawn in a tight line. Whom she was more furious with, him or Nate, was a debatable subject.

"I risked everything to come to you," she began, her heart in her words. Not that he cared a whit over her problems. "I left my family, my home, my reputation to come here to help you because I thought you were dying."

So that was it. She'd come because she thought this was her last chance to make up for all those years ago.

When she'd traded his love for a title and a string of grand estates. A house in London and all the money a lady could ever need, instead of a pirate's heart.

"Well, I'm very much alive, so you can go home," he said, waving his hands at her, dismissing her from whatever obligation she felt, ridding her from his life for good.

He turned to Nate. "Now that this is all settled, turn the ship around."

Nate shook his head, stubbornly so. "Not and risk the entire crew, the ship, and a hold that is filled with a fortune in silks and wine."

Dash glanced up at the mate at the wheel, as well as the collection of crew on this last watch before dawn, as each of them took a determined stance—legs set wide, arms crossed over their chests, and faces set with the same dogged expression. Not one of them looked willing to face English justice.

So there it was. Nothing or no one was turning this ship around, short of a hurricane.

He muttered a dark, frustrated curse, and turned to the rails. Christ, he needed to drink, and he had yet to take his piss.

In addition to the fact that he had a mutiny on his hands.

And that wasn't even the worst of it. She was on his ship.

His fingers wound around the rails and dug into

the oak. How he longed for the good old days when a mutiny meant the crew shot the captain and threw him overboard to feed the sharks.

"Oh, dear God," Lady Gossett was sputtering behind him. "This is a disaster." He heard the swish of her skirts as she turned on Nate. "You have no idea what you've done. They are going to think the worst."

Out of the corner of his eye, Dash spied Nate shaking his head.

"I explained to your family," Nate was saying, "that you would be safely returned to London when the money was paid. I made it very clear that no harm would befall you."

She made that *harrumph* noise again, the one that said the damage was already done.

Well, hell, she wouldn't be here if she hadn't . . . if she hadn't . . .

Traded her life for yours all those years ago, he could almost hear Hardy say.

Some trade. Now here they were. He was a drunk and she . . . Well, what was she now?

Dash turned to her and looked and knew the truth of it.

The same beautiful woman he'd loved all those years ago. Her pale hair glistened in the lamplight. He doubted there was a trace of gray to it. Her skin still shone; even her cheeks held that same soft, rosy pink that whispered of a blush, and her lips, God, her lips were still as ripe and full and lush, the same pair of kissable temptations that had captivated him the first moment he'd spied her on the beach in Hastings.

And anyone who thought her fair face and hair made her look frail, thought her like a china figurine meant to be gazed upon and not enjoyed, missed the lady entirely.

Beneath her fragile exterior was a woman with a spine of oak and nerves of steel. And a passionate heart to match those demmed and delightful lips. A kiss that could drive a man to risk everything . . .

"You must return me to London, Mr. Dashwell," she was telling Nate.

"I'm sorry to say, Lady Gossett, I cannot put you off this ship until we reach Baltimore." Then he crossed his arms over his chest, and his face set with the same Yankee stubbornness that the rest of his Maryland crew wore.

Lady Gossett muttered something under her breath that sounded suspiciously like Russian, and while he might not know the words, her tone held nothing but contempt for both of them. Then she swept past them, nose raised in an aristocratic tilt, her hemline tugged aside to avoid touching anything associated with either of them, and with a determined click of her boot heels, she headed to her cabin.

Dash didn't know what it was—his own fury at himself for wanting her still or her haughty demeanor—that sent him into a temper, but he was hard on her heels and caught her by the elbow before she got to the ladder down to the cabins.

Twenty-three years. Twenty-three demmed years he'd waited to ask her one thing, and if she thought she could just walk out of his life a second time without a "by-your-leave," she was sadly mistaken.

He was going to have his answer.

Catching hold of her, he stopped her cold, and she whirled around on him, her face a mix of emotions, none of which was promising.

"Why did you do it?" he asked. "Why did you marry him?"

After all these years, the heat of her skin beneath his fingers brought back a flood of memories. Her dress had short sleeves, so her forearms were bare. That same silken skin he'd worshipped now lay in his grasp.

He let go of her immediately and let her catch her own footing as the ship swayed in the rising waves.

"Why?" he repeated.

She stared at him. No, more like gaped. "I had no choice. It was you or . . . or . . ."

"Or what? Death?" He shook his head. "Madam, you risked your neck to save my life. Whyever would you stop then and just give up?"

She pressed her lips together, unwilling to give him even that. "I am going to my cabin," she told him, turning toward the gangway.

Well then, if she didn't want to talk about her choice, then he had another question. "What happened to Gossett?"

Pausing at the opening to the stairwell, her hand on the wood frame surrounding the opening, she glanced over her shoulder at him. "He's gone."

"How?"

She closed her eyes and let out a long, slow breath. "Does it matter?"

"To me."

Her lips pressed together stubbornly, and he thought she was going to dismiss him again, but instead she opened her eyes and looked directly at him as she said in an anguished voice, "The surgeon said it was his heart. He was with me one moment, and then the next . . ."

Dash moved closer. He saw the grief in her eyes, wanted to fold her in his arms and tell her how sorry he was, but then again, Gossett had stolen everything he'd ever wanted, so he could hardly grieve for the man.

Pity the man's widow.

And besides, he still had a score to settle with her.

"Tore his heart out, did you?" he said, letting years of anger chill his words. Mask the pain beneath them. "I know how the poor bastard felt in his final moments."

Chapter 5

$\mathscr{P}$ippin closed the door to her cabin and sank against it, her fist against her mouth to stop the sob that threatened to escape. *Oh, dear God, why have I come here?*

Because you never stopped loving him. Never stopped wondering what had become of him . . . Never . . .

What she should have done was to never come flying back after him like some foolish, headstrong schoolgirl. Yet after she'd heard all of Nate's plea . . . the hasty words that had followed his first request . . .

Lady Gossett, he's ill. I fear for the worst . . .

Oh, how the images Nate's speech had brought forth had tugged at her heart, and she'd been fool enough to believe him. She glanced up at the ceiling, where atop the deck she could hear Dash's son casting orders about and wished she could cast him overboard, the lying wretch.

All her dreams of seeing Dash were now tossed

over the railing. Gone were her visions of finding an older, wiser Dash, albeit frail with illness, yet stalwart and stubborn enough to still be on the deck of his ship.

He'd have turned at the sound of her voice, and suddenly he'd have been filled with hope and strength, and the years of separation between them would have melted away, and she would have rushed to his arms and everything would have been . . .

Pippin blew out a loud, disgruntled breath. What a cartload of manure she'd dreamed up. Why, one would think she was still sixteen and full of girlish dreams. She should have known better, considering she was a matron of . . . well, enough years to know better.

But that was one of the problems, she realized, of living inside a dream for so long. The dream never changed, but unfortunately, the world around one kept turning.

And changing. Especially in Dash's case. No longer the man of her dreams, the pirate of her heart.

"Oh, whatever am I going to do?" she whispered.

Here she'd stayed in her cabin the last week at Nate's urging, his telling her he had to prepare his father for her arrival, that the shock of seeing her might be too much in his frail state.

Harrumph. What Nate meant was she had to stay hidden until they were far enough out to sea that turning back would only lead to their arrest. That, and he needed time to sober Dash up enough, clean him up as much as possible so she wouldn't immediately see through his lies.

She shook her head and pushed off from the door, pacing the three steps it took to cross her cabin (Nate's cabin, she knew), and turned and paced back, until she faced the door.

The one that led to Dash. One she had no intention of opening again until they reached Baltimore.

She shuddered. How long would it take to reach the American port? Twenty-five to thirty days, Nate had said when they left England. And then she'd have to find a ship to book passage on to return, and by the time she got back, the scandal of her "kidnapping" would have . . .

Pippin closed her eyes and shuddered. Oh, what Ginger and John must be going through! She could see her son pacing about the library making plans for action and ordering his sister not to tell a soul about their disgrace.

With good reason! What would it do to his reputation, let alone his career, to have his mother kidnapped by someone as infamous as Captain Dashwell?

And there were still enough ladies around who had lived through her first scandal with Dash—who would love nothing more than to dust off their old gossip and give it a good airing all over London.

Which would leave Ginger and John in a terrible position—not that Lord Claremont's lofty reputation wouldn't shield his wife from most it, but John . . . Pippin shuddered. Her son was too much like his father, too proud and too set in his ways to be able to ride out this storm, not when all of London would be circulating such wayward tales. He'd rise to her defense, and then . . . he'd do something rash, which would certainly put an end to his plans to marry Admiral Rothton's daughter.

The admiral's wife, the former Lady Oriana Dalderby, was more of a high stickler than her husband, and any hint of immorality on Pippin's part would have the old cat hauling her daughter in the direction of the nearest respectable baronet rather than taint their name by association.

She cringed. John would never forgive her. And her daughter . . . well, Ginger had a good head on her shoulders, but she was like so many of the young ladies of her generation—not so very different from their brand-new queen—sheltered and proud, proper and without a hint of scandal associated with her.

She only hoped Ginger had the good sense to send word to Felicity and Tally. They'd be able to tell her children the truth.

Oh, yes. The truth. That will be a comfort to them.

Pippin groaned. Yes, that would make it all better. She could see Ginger's face and, worse, John's at the notion that their proper mother had taken a lover before she'd married.

She paced again, and this time ran her knee into the corner of the bunk. She cursed roundly, not caring that it wasn't ladylike or proper. Demmit, she'd ruined her life; she had the right to a bit of salt in her vocabulary.

Besides, hadn't she always wanted to curse? And run away to sea with Dash? And feel the deck of a ship beneath her feet and the roar of the cannons as they chased after a fat merchantman?

Now this was the fat merchant ship, and Dash . . . oh, Dash, what had happened to him?

She sank to her bed, rubbing her bruised knee, and wondered at the changes in him.

Surely he had to understand why she'd done what she had.

And it wasn't as if he hadn't gone and married someone else—for there was Nate, and he must be close to John's age, meaning . . .

Meaning Dash had married the first woman he'd encountered after he'd escaped. Married and had a family.

Pippin chewed at her lips, not all that happy with the notion of Dash with another woman, sitting by the fire with her, taking her to his bed.

Oh, yes, and what did you do for twenty-one years? The very same thing with your husband. The man you chose over Dash. A man you grew to love deeply, despite how much you tried not to.

Brent had been easy to love—so kind and generous and funny and faithful.

Perhaps that's what prodded at her guilt the most. She'd loved Brent, when she'd never once considered loving anyone other than Dash.

Well, none of it mattered now. Dash wanted nothing to do with her, and she certainly didn't want anything to do with him. Which was for the best.

She rubbed her knee and sniffed. So why did she feel like crying?

She didn't love Dash. She didn't care.

Oh, but she did. He was just as Nate had said, a man in trouble.

He needed a bath, a shave, his coat patched, and he needed to stop drinking before it killed him. If it wasn't too late already.

Pippin opened her eyes, her gaze falling on a book she'd brought along with her. The one her cousin Felicity had sent over recently.

None of this is your fault, Pippin. None of this, she could imagine her cousin saying. *That man chose his path, as much as you chose yours. You haven't spent your years wallowing in self-pity, and neither should he. You saved his neck and gave him back his life when his own reckless ambitions had seen him captured—not once, but twice.*

And as right as her cousin would be, Felicity's "advice" didn't make her feel any better.

For at the sight of Dash, of his green eyes, the stubborn set of his jaw, she remembered all too well why it was she'd fallen in love with him.

Swiping at the tears welling up in her eyes, she leaned over the bunk and pulled her valise out from beneath it. Opening it up, she dug around inside it and fetched out the box of Turkish delight she'd stashed inside when she'd packed.

She undid the string around the package, and when the box opened and that heavenly scent of rose water and sugar wafted up to her nose, she was transported back to a winter's day when her life was no less complicated, but she hadn't the years of experience to tell her she was courting disaster.

London, 1814

"Lady Philippa," Mary whispered from the door, "Lady Philippa, could you come with me for a moment?"

"What is it, Mary?" Tally asked the maid, looking up from the desk she and Pippin were working at.

Pippin glanced up as well. Was it her or did the girl look nervous? Not that their housekeeper's daughter was very bright, or all that good of a maid, but she'd come with Mrs. Hutchinson nonetheless, and none of them were going to turn down a free maid.

Especially when they hadn't even the money to pay her mother.

"Uh, me mum has a question for Lady Philippa on some cooking," the girl stammered. "Yes, that's it, some cooking."

"I'll be of no help there." Tally laughed. "Best you go, Pippin, or we'll be eating toast for dinner."

Pippin smiled at her cousin's jest and rose from her work to follow Mary as she skittered down the back stairs.

But when they came to the landing before the turn to the cellar where the kitchen was, the often befuddled Mary came to an abrupt halt. "I'm so sorry, m'lady, but I wasn't telling the truth. Me mum doesn't need you, but I didn't know what else to say," she confessed, her hands worried into knots in her apron.

Pippin put a hand on the girl's shoulder to steady her. "What is it, Mary? Is there a problem?"

"There's a gentleman, m'lady."

"A what?"

"A gentleman, in the back garden. He's here to see you." Mary's eyes were wide as saucers as she said in a bare whisper, "But I don't think he's a real gentleman, even though he's got a present with him, and bit of posies as well."

Pippin's gaze bolted up at the door. Dash! He'd found her. Just as he'd promised.

Mary's fingers curled around her apron again. "I didn't know what to do, other than fetch you. Mum is in no state to be answering the door and I feared she might run him off. And I was more afeared that Miss Langley would discover him back there. I don't think, m'lady, pardon me for sayin', that Miss Langley would approve of him. He seems a wicked sort, and not at all proper." Mary looked down at her feet. "But he's here to see you, not Miss Langley, and he gave me a bright shiny penny to come fetch you, so I'll leave you now." Then she nudged past Pippin and left her alone, bolting back up the stairs, obviously as afraid of this caller as she was of Felicity discovering her part in letting an unwanted man breach their proper female sanctuary.

Pippin glanced at the door that led to the garden.

Don't you dare go out there, Philippa Knolles, she could almost hear Felicity saying. *Why, if anyone were to see you associating with . . . with . . .*

Pippin bit her lips together and considered what she should do. Send him away. Not even go outside, rather send Mrs. Hutchinson and her infamous carving knife, with which, if Mary's rambling tale were true, she'd chased the greengrocer off just yesterday, when the cheeky merchant had possessed the nerve to ask for his bill to be paid.

Send him away, she resolved, even as her heart did a double thump.

Dash. He'd come to see her. Since the Frost Fair, she'd vacillated between a fervent hope he would find her and prayers that he wouldn't. She shivered, and not from the cold.

For she'd also scoured Felicity's old editions of the *Times* and knew the danger he was in. If he was caught on English soil, he'd hang for certain.

And so would anyone who helped him.

That wouldn't mean just her life, for Tally and Felicity would be implicated as well. As would their chaperone, Aunt Minty; Thatcher, their footman; and Mrs. Hutchinson and poor Mary to boot.

No, there were too many lives in the balance for her to have Dash coming around. Even if it was only until the ice on the Thames broke free. Which would be any day now, and then he'd be gone.

Gone . . . Oh, that was a terrible notion! Almost as bad as the treason part of this muddle.

No, she must send him away. Even if Mary claimed he'd come bearing gifts.

Pippin couldn't help herself; she smiled. A present? It had been so long since she'd received a gift—not counting the red wool socks Aunt Minty had given her for Christmas, the old dear having knit a pair for each of "me diamonds," as she liked to call them.

But this was a gift of a different sort. From a man. For Pippin couldn't imagine what sort of present Dash would bring her . . . besides his kiss, she thought wickedly as she ventured out into the small, tumble-down garden behind their London town house.

She walked down the narrow path between the snowbanks, shivering in the cold. "Dash?" she whispered. "Are you here?"

He stepped out from behind the ramshackle rose

arbor that should have been torn down years ago and grinned at her. "Didn't think you'd come—or that girl of yours wouldn't be able to remember what I told her."

Pippin laughed, glancing furtively at his empty hands. Oh, bother, Mary had gotten the present part all wrong.

Still, that didn't stop her heart from pattering with an excited tremor. *He found me. He found me*, it thudded.

"She told me," Pippin said, "but you shouldn't—"

Her words failed her, for she couldn't bring herself to say the rest of her admonishment. *You shouldn't be here*. Instead she asked, "How did you find me?"

"It wasn't that hard. I just had to look for the stolen house on Brook Street," he teased, taking a glance up at the cream-colored stone that rose four stories above them.

"Shhh," she warned him. "That is a secret."

"I daresay, my lady, that a stolen house is going to be a hard secret to keep."

"Oh, it shouldn't be all that difficult after—" she began, unwilling to finish it. *After we are all married*.

Dash did it for her, taking a different tack. "After the owner comes back and wants to know how it is an earl's daughter is living in his house like some sort of poacher?" His hands went to his hips. "Does Lady Josephine, or for that matter, Mad Jack or that proper wife of his know what you and those trouble-some romps you call cousins are about?"

Pippin shook her head. "Oh, no. I don't think even Jack would approve."

"That isn't much of endorsement for this scheme

of yours," he said. "Because I have to imagine Jack would steal the coppers off . . ." He paused and looked at her. "Never mind that. Whatever were you thinking, stealing a house?"

"It isn't so much my plan," she said, feeling a bit defensive. "More Felicity's." She paused for a moment. "No, it's mine as well. Believe me, a drafty house in London is a far sight better than a drafty house in Sussex."

"And your family lets you three just gad about like this?"

Pippin ruffled a bit at this. Dear heavens, he was starting to sound like Felicity's long-winded solicitor. "We are all the family we have. My parents are both gone, as are my cousins. My brother is not of age and is at Eton."

"And look at the three of you! Poor as mice with dreams of being the cat, I suppose?"

It was a deeply personal question, but looking into Dash's eyes she knew he wasn't asking so he could tell her how foolish it was, but because he was concerned.

And it had been a long time since anyone had been concerned about her welfare.

"There is no money. I have the little bit my mother left me, and the house in Sussex, though it's naught but a draughty little cottage." She glanced down at her boots. "My father died up to his neck in debt, and his estate has been neglected terribly, with no one but my brother's guardian to oversee it. I suspect whatever income there is from it ends up in his pockets."

"And your cousins?"

"Much the same kettle. Tally and Felicity have a

miserly allowance that their solicitor holds on to as if
it came out of his own pocket," she explained, using
Felicity's favorite lament.

He glanced at the house and shook his head, but
there was a light of admiration in his eyes. As if he
understood why they were taking such a calculated
risk.

"Really, Dash, you shouldn't . . . Oh, you just
shouldn't have come. If Felicity were to see you, or
even worse . . ." Pippin shuddered to think if someone called the Watch.

"Shouldn't have come," he scoffed, reaching inside
his coat, even as he stepped over the small snowbank
separating them and drew closer. "And however
would I have brought you this present if I hadn't?"

"You did bring me something," she said without
thinking. Her gaze flew up to his as she realized what
she'd confessed. "I mean—"

He laughed. "That maid of yours isn't as cork-
brained as she appears if she remembered the present." He reached out and stopped her flutter of words
with a single finger pressed to her lips. Even though
he wasn't wearing gloves or even mitts, his touch
warmed her. "Shhh, little Circe, how could I come to
see such a lofty and pretty lady as yourself without a
wee token of treasure." He put the box in her hands,
and let his hand curl around her fingers, holding her
just longer than was proper.

Perhaps it wasn't just his touch, but him, standing
so close that all she wanted to do was throw herself
into the heat of his embrace and never leave.

But first she had a gift to open. Treasure, he'd said.

"You didn't steal it, did you?" she whispered, sounding shocked, but quite frankly hoping he had.

A gift was one thing. But a pirate's booty, stolen and spirited away, seemed magical to her dull existence.

Dash laughed. "No, I fear it isn't that sort of gift, but one day I will steal you a chest of jewels and a hold filled with gold. And I'll spend my nights pouring pearls and diamonds at your feet."

Her toes curled inside her red wool socks and thin boots at such an offer. Even though it was a wild boast, in her imagination she saw them alone together, in some velvet and brocade harem, and she would be wearing some enticing red gown and Dash would be in the wild pirate costume he'd worn the first time they'd met.

The heat of a blush stopped her wayward thoughts, and she turned her attention to opening her present. Slowly she untied the string, tucking it in her pocket to save always, and then she opened the box and found it was indeed filled with a treasure.

"Oooh," she whispered, glancing up at him, wide-eyed.

"I thought you might like that," he said, grinning again. Then he leaned closer and whispered in her ear, "Your kiss always tastes so sweet to me, I thought only to give you a taste of it when I am gone."

Her fingers dipped into the box and came out covered in white sugar. "Turkish delight," she whispered. "My favorite."

"I hoped as much," he said, his head cocked to one side. "Try it. The man said it is the best in London."

Staring down at the candies, she wanted nothing more than to eat them, enjoy them. As she took a furtive glance back at the house, a pang of guilt tweaked at her. Part of her considered saving it and sharing it, but then however would she explain to Felicity and Tally how she had been able to buy a box of candy when they had barely enough food to eat, not enough coal to get them to the end of the week, and no more than twenty pounds between them to launch themselves into Society?

No, she doubted her duke-mad cousin would be all that understanding about Pippin having such improper callers, even ones bearing gifts, even when she knew Felicity had a fondness for lokum, as she called it, having been spoiled with it by their Nanny Rana in Constantinople.

Sadly there was nothing left for Pippin to do but hide the evidence, and so she did by popping a piece into her mouth. She nearly moaned aloud with delight as the sweet sugar teased across her tongue, then came the soft chewy candy, the crunch of a nut, and finally the hint of rose water.

"Mmmm," was all she could manage.

When she held out the box to Dash, so he could try some, he shook his head. "Those are yours, Circe, as is this." He reached inside his coat again and pulled out a small bunch of flowers. How he'd gotten them in the middle of winter . . . well, they must have cost a fortune, that and he'd gone to great risk to be scouring London where on any corner he could be recognized.

Pippin didn't know whether to be honored or terrified for him. "Oh, Dash, you shouldn't," she whispered. "What if you are caught?"

"Never, not until I finish what I came to do," he told her.

"And what is that?"

"Why, fetch you away from here, of course."

Fetch her? Pippin, reaching nervously inside the box for another piece of candy, didn't know what to say. "M-m-me?" she finally stammered, before she put a second piece in her mouth, chewing quickly.

"Yes, you. If you can steal this house, then I think I shall have to resort to kidnapping English ladies to make my mark in this world. Can't have a novice like yourself bettering me. Stealing houses, indeed! Why, I've a reputation to maintain." He laughed at her, and reached over to wipe the traces of sugar from her lips, but the moment his fingers touched her cheek, something happened.

Something so very magical.

She felt it right down to her toes. For all his jokes and teasing, when he came closer to her, it explained more completely why he was here than any word could.

And when Dash touched her, Pippin knew in her heart that he was hers. This man was her destiny. Just as Felicity and Tally's other nanny, Jamilla, liked to say.

When the right man kisses you, you will know for certain.

Kiss me, Dash. Kiss me, she prayed silently as she looked up into his eyes. *Kiss me again so I can be certain.*

So I can run away with you, be your pirate queen, let you cover me in diamonds and pearls, and your kisses . . .

"Circe," he murmured, as his head dipped down, his lips gently brushing over hers as if seeking permission, and Pippin answered by opening up to him, letting him press closer and kiss her thoroughly.

In that moment, her heart sang as he drew her into the heat of his arms, pulled her against the muscled strength of his body, and held her close, as if he would never let her go.

He is mine. Mine alone. Mine always.

Aboard the Ellis Anne, *1837*

Pippin stared into the box of Turkish delight in her lap. She'd bought it the day before she'd left London. She hadn't had a bite of it in years, for even the smell of it brought back too many memories. Yet there she'd been, walking down the same street she walked every day, past the same confectionary shop, but this time the tray in the window had all but yanked her to a halt.

And sentimentally, she'd bought a box and brought it along. Like a good luck charm. Something to share with Dash. An offering of treasure.

Harrumph. I need more than a box of candy to save me from this mess, she thought as she glanced around her narrow cabin.

Then she took another furtive glance at the box and took out another piece. She ate it, and for a moment let the sweet memories wash over her again. Of Dash's kisses, his touch, the first time he'd come to her when they'd made love in the attics of the house on Brook Street. The simple taste of the candy unleashed a torrent of lost passions and forgotten memories that had been tucked away for far too long.

And when she started to cry, she reached for a third, and then a fourth piece, as she remembered the Dash of her youth. So strong, with his hawklike eyes and his rakish good humor. Remembered how his body had felt covering hers, inside hers, bringing her to a release that had awakened every nerve in her body.

And as she reached for a fifth piece as if she were starving, she stopped and put the lid back on the box. Twenty-three years. Twenty-three years she'd done her best to forget.

How could she? He'd been her heart and now he was lost.

No, she thought, shaking her head, unwilling to let go so easily. *There has to be some part of him left. Some bit of the man I knew still lurking beneath the ruins.*

But, oh, how he'd changed. How bitter he'd become. He carried deep wounds that wouldn't be easily salved over, easily healed.

"Perhaps it's been too long," she told herself as she rose and went to the door.

And Pippin didn't mean it had been too many years between them to ever find their way back.

It had been too long since they'd kissed . . .

Chapter 6

Once she'd disappeared down the ladder, Dash had turned from the opening and stormed over to the railing.

He saw the man at the wheel glance at Nate in alarm, as if the fool thought Dash meant to throw himself into the sea.

No, he didn't deserve such an easy ending, drowned and lost in the arms of the only mistress who'd ever been loyal to him.

He gripped the railing and looked at the rising waves, and that innate part of him, the side that had salt running through his veins, as Nate like to say, took over. Sniffing the air, he let the crisp tang fill his lungs, and with only one thought, he tipped his head to check and see if the sails were trimmed as they should, to catch the freshening wind.

And of course they were. Nate, in all his efficiency, had ordered it. They rose like lofty white clouds above the deck, entrapping the wind, as eager as lovers.

Ships and waves, those were all he'd ever been true to—women; well, with the fairer sex his record wasn't as spotless.

The waves curled and undulated before him, and they made him think of Abigail, with her thoughtful eyes and rich curves. Nate had her eyes, and at times his son's glance reminded him of how Abigail had looked at him . . . with the sad knowledge that she'd gained a poor bargain in marrying Thomas Dashwell.

Just as her son had gained a poor excuse for a father.

She'd had a way of glancing at him across the table, a look that had always left him knock-kneed and hieing his way off to sea as fast as he could get the *Circe* refit to escape the guilt. The truth.

That they both knew. That he didn't love her. He'd married her because her father was the richest, most notable shipbuilder in Baltimore.

And she? He shook his head. He'd never understood what Abigail Jamieson had ever seen in him, what she'd thought to gain in the bargain. A hero, he supposed. The other pride of Baltimore. The daring Captain Dashwell.

He pushed aside those memories and glanced over his shoulder at the darkened doorway that led down below. To her.

The one woman he had loved. Lady Philippa Knolles. The daughter of an earl. Far too lofty for the likes of him. And yet Pippin had loved him in return, without a care of what would become of them.

And what was it he had just said to her?

Tore his heart out, did you . . .

And if that hadn't been cruel enough, the look of shock, the sheer horror on her face should have been enough to tear his own heart out all over again. At least it should have been.

If she'd possessed any thoughts of finding the lover of her youth, he'd ripped those dreams out of her and cast them off like so much flotsam.

He pushed off the rail and crossed the deck, taking another glance at the sails and then nodding to Nate, who stood on the raised deck watching him.

Oh, yes, she'd come out of some misplaced notion of making peace between them. That, and Nate's dire tales of his imminent demise.

Oh, he could well imagine his son putting just the right bit of brown to the entire speech. *My lady, I fear this time . . .*

And there she'd been, always such a soft-hearted, kindly sort. Sweet and pretty, innocent and too trusting.

At least she had been before she'd come into his company.

He yanked open the door to his cabin and went inside, closing it behind him, raking his hand through his hair and staring at the mess around him.

Hardly the room of a hero. The man everyone expected to discover when they learned who he was.

Captain Thomas Dashwell. Hero of '14. The scourge of the British. Baltimore's darling son.

And how disappointed they always were when they discovered the truth.

Even his own son looked at him with wary, sad eyes, as if he, too, hoped to find that man, that legendary hero.

He kicked aside the discarded clothes, the spare pair of boots, and an old logbook. He glanced down at it. That book was filled with exploits, with sailing records he'd never boasted of, with times he thought he and the *Circe* and his crew would never survive.

But they had—and for that, he was hailed as a hero instead of the lucky son-of-a-bitch that he was.

He was an ordinary man, he wanted to tell the world. And not even all that good at being ordinary. As he glanced once around the room, he spied his reflection in the dirty, stained mirror in the corner.

Just a man who wished the world would forget him as he wanted to forget the world, the reflection said.

He shook his head and drew closer to the image, his fingers reaching out to touch the cold, impersonal glass.

It only reflected what it saw, uncaring that the image it held came as a shock to the viewer, told a truth that no one liked to discover.

Dash didn't recognize himself.

Bleary eyes met his wary gaze, while straggly, ill-cut hair hung limply in an old-fashioned queue. But it was his face that told the tale better than Nate's lies.

For his son hadn't been lying to Lady Philippa. He did look like death.

There was barely a hint of the arrogant, headstrong man who'd kissed her good-bye in Hollindrake House and thought to see her again in a fortnight's time.

No wonder she'd recoiled from him in horror. He looked like a Seven Dials beggar. All he lacked was the tin cup and the missing teeth.

"At least I've still got all my teeth," he muttered, rubbing his chin, covered as it was in a week or two's worth of stubble. "Listen to you," he chided. "You make yourself sound like you are an old man."

He glanced up at the ceiling. Well, he wasn't that old. Nor was he on his last leg, or ready to turn over his command to that no-account, arrogant whelp of his.

And he knew one other thing. As long as he looked like he was ready to take his place in Davy Jones's locker, she'd hover about until either he turned up his toes, or he showed her how hale and hearty he actually was beneath this wreckage.

He'd show them both. Make them both look like fools.

She'd see the man she left behind and regret every day she spent closeted away in her Mayfair palace like some bloody princess or viscountess or whatever the hell the title was that she'd traded herself for.

He scoffed at the very notion. He didn't give a fiddler's damn what she thought. Just wanted her off his ship and out of his life. And to do that he needed to let everyone know who was in charge around here.

Without even thinking, Dash reached for the bottle he kept close by, his hand shaking even as his fingers came up empty. It was then he remembered why he'd gone up on deck to begin with.

Because the bottle had been empty and his thirst, the emptiness inside him that he never seemed able to fill, had prodded him in search of more . . .

So what had he found instead? Her. On his ship.

His insides tightened, his legs going weak beneath him.

Clutching his trembling hand to his chest, he gritted his teeth together.

Oh, yes, it was time to end this mutiny.

The one aboard his ship, and the one inside his heart.

Pippin came out of her cabin, determined to do something—just what, she had no idea—but she didn't relish the idea of hiding from her past in that cramped space for possibly the next twenty days until they reached Baltimore.

So lost in her plans, or lack of one, she didn't see the sailor in the hallway and barreled right into him, smacking into his broad chest, even as the ship rose with a rough pitch and the rolling deck sent her scrambling to find her footing.

The man caught hold of her and held her close, his feet planted firmly to the rising and falling ship as if the movements were as familiar as a mother's gentle rocking.

The hands cradling her elbows kept her sure and steady, and Pippin couldn't help herself, she clung to him as she sought to find her footing, her heart suddenly beating wildly.

It was like a scene out of one those interminable plays she and her cousin Tally had written all those years ago. *Imogene's Moral Dilemma, or The Pirate of Her Heart.*

Oh, heavens! Here she was, Imogene all over again, although she was hardly the innocent virgin kidnapped by some pirate, caught in his grasp and trembling from feelings "she didn't understand, but longed to discover."

Oh, she could just hear her children. At her age, she should be immune to such things, be long past finding herself trembling like an unwitting debutante.

But she couldn't help herself.

This man, with his wall of a chest and straight, commanding shoulders, stood before her like a hero out of a dream.

The scent of the sea filled her nostrils, running deep into her lungs as she inhaled, and to her shock it wasn't the bit of spray coming down the open gangway but him.

It was like being held by Neptune himself, for he smelled exactly like the briny deep, with a bit of lye soap and the hint of tar mixed in. It was a masculine air that she hadn't succumbed to in so long, it sent a shiver of desire through her limbs.

Oh, gracious heavens, it sent a tidal wave through her, and to her horror, she found herself leaning closer to him.

"Careful, Circe," he whispered. "Seems a bit rough for a lady like you."

Dash!

Her gaze swung up, and she found herself face-to-face with the very man she'd come seeking.

The ragged, disheveled wreck she'd seen on deck was gone, and in his place stood the pirate she remembered. A bit older, but it was Dash.

Shaved and washed, his jaw still set with a square, solid line. And while his green eyes didn't sparkle with mischief or that impish arrogance she recalled, they held a more sensuous light, the dangerous glimmer of a man who knew exactly what he wanted and had never failed to get it.

Circe, he'd called her. His siren. And he was the pirate she'd longed to bring ashore. And even now, with his dark hair tied back in his old pirate's queue, a red bandana covering his head, she could almost see the buccaneer who'd stolen her heart.

He was just missing his old grand hat and that greatcoat with the burnished buttons he'd been wearing the night she'd met him.

Her heart raced to life, beating wildly as the memories of what it had been like to be held by him, to be kissed by him, assailed her.

She thought he felt the same passion rising between them, had the same reaction, because his lips parted slightly, his head tipped as if he was going to steal a kiss, and then he paused, looking down at her and searching her face as if he, too, was looking for the woman he'd loved.

I'm here, Dash, she wanted to force past her suddenly dry throat. *Remember me? Remember us?*

Oh, this was exactly how she'd imagined their reunion, not that frightful scene from earlier. No, in her dreams, he'd kiss her, and the years would fall away. They'd be as they were when they were young, utterly transfixed by each other, of one mind, reckless and indulgent in their passions. Willing to be together despite the scandal.

If Dash would but kiss her again, Pippin had to imagine it would be worth any amount of scandal, any censure.

Kiss me, Dash. Just once more, she wanted to beg.

That was, until his gaze fell to her hand, which was still clinging to his coat, her fingers twined around the lapel. It wasn't so much her hand that turned his green eyes to the color of a storm-tossed sea, but her ring finger to be exact.

Where Lord Gossett's emerald ring still marked her for what she was. Or what she had been.

Another man's wife.

She heard the deep inhale of his indignant breath, and knew even before he did that he was going to set her aside. And he didn't even take that much care, for in truth, he pushed her out of his arms as if she carried the plague, and she stumbled away until her back hit the other side of the narrow hall.

They stood there in the swaying corridor, staring at each other, his chest rising and falling in anger and hers . . . well, hers was still shaking for other reasons.

Oh, yes, he'd cleaned up, but that didn't mean his fury at her, over what he saw as her desertion, had gone the same way as the stubble and the patched coat he'd been wearing.

Her hand caught hold of the latch to her room and she considered fleeing back inside. It was what she should do. It was certainly the safe and sensible thing.

But when had she ever been safe or sensible when it came to this man?

Pippin stood her ground and faced him. Yes, she'd married another man. And in doing so had saved Dash's wretched neck from being stretched by a good English rope.

Couldn't Dash see how it had been for her? The choice she'd made, when she'd thought there was no other decision to make.

Tell him why you did it, a voice from the past urged

her. *Tell him why you changed course so abruptly. Give him the truth.*

Reflexively, her hand went to cover her stomach, to protect the precious gift of life that had long since left her womb, grown to adulthood, and had lived without ever knowing the truth.

Just as Dash had lived all these years without it.

What was it her cousin Tally always said? Confession was good for the soul.

Oh, yes, Pippin mused. Tell Dash the truth. That will help immensely. By putting him in enough of a temper to toss her overboard, instead of just out of his grasp, out of his reach.

They stood there for a few moments longer, like a pair of wary alley cats, Dash in his anger, Pippin in her guilt.

For all the tales of Dash's ruthless reputation at sea, of his exploits and daring, not once had she ever feared him, but there was always a first time for everything, for he wasn't the same man she'd loved, given her heart and innocence to.

When he finally spoke, he confirmed that only too clearly.

"What are you doing here, Lady Gossett?"

Lady Gossett. Not Circe. Not even Pippin. But that sneered use of her married name, as if he wanted it off his lips before the taste settled in his mouth.

He moved, taking a short, halting stride across the space between them, and leaned over her.

Pippin clung to the latch with one hand, her knuckles probably gleaming white as she held on to it, for it seemed the only solid thing on the ship.

His ship. His world. His realm. He could do any-thing he wanted to her. Exact any revenge.

And all she could think about was his lips. How they would feel on hers. And not gentle like a lov-er's, but covering hers and taking exactly what he wanted.

Oh, botheration! What am I thinking? She hadn't come here to have him take her and then toss her aside like some Southwark doxy.

Pippin tried to breathe, but it was nearly impos-sible with him so dangerously close. A slow, burning heat rose in her cheeks; she shifted slightly, trying to find some stance where her body would stop shiver-ing, stop wanting . . .

"What did you come looking for, Lady Gossett?" he asked in a low, tight voice. "Did you come seeking something in particular?" He reached out and pulled a strand of her hair free from its pins.

Without so much as a by-your-leave, he fingered the blond tendril like he was weighing its worth, and when he was done, his gaze met hers.

Pippin felt the years melt away, and remembered another night when he'd looked at her just like that. When she'd given him her innocence. Trusted him so utterly.

That, she discovered, had been a long time ago. With another man.

Not the one whose head dove down, his lips cov-ering hers, with the same audacity with which he'd plucked her hair free. This was no gentle kiss from an earnest lover—Dash took what he wanted, his hands catching her in his grasp and hauling her body right up against him.

Then, as if that wasn't close enough, he pressed her into the solid door behind her. His lips plundered hers, his tongue tasting her, pulling pleasures from her that had been long held dormant.

One of his hands cupped a breast, his thumb curling over the nipple, bringing it to a tight bud. Desire, raw and aching, coursed through her limbs, and God help her, she arched like a cat against him. She would have purred at the passion he was unleashing, but instead a soft moan escaped her lips.

Oh, Dash, yes. Yes, please . . .

As if he heard her silent plea, he answered it by delving deeper, his fingers plucking at her skirt, pulling it up until his hand found her bare leg. Higher still went her skirt, and then he let his body ride up against hers, pressing her even harder into the door with an unmistakable intent.

For he was hard and hungry, his mouth still devouring hers, his hands claiming whatever they wanted, raking over the curves of her body, his manhood stiff inside his breeches, riding against her. Long and hard; she knew only too well how it felt inside her, how much she'd desired him then.

Still did.

His fingers curled around the front of her gown, opening the prim buttons there, and then pulling a breast free from her corset, taking the hard peak in his mouth and sucking it until she moaned again, this time aloud.

He pulled back a bit and looked at her. Studied her. A look on his face she couldn't discern. Satisfied. Hungry. Angry. All at once.

It should have frightened her. And she suspected

that was why he was mauling her like she was a dockside whore. She should be insulted, incensed at his treatment. But instead, she stood there, one hand clinging to his coat, the other still hanging on to the latch to her room, with every bit of her in between trembling with desire. All she wanted to do was open the door, pull him inside, and make love.

No, not love. Hot, hard, unforgiving sex.

It was hard to think of anything else with this raw, hungry passion flooding her veins, clouding her wits. When all she felt was this reckless need that as a matron of a certain age she shouldn't be feeling.

"Is that what you came for, Lady Gossett? A tumble with your past?" He didn't wait for an answer, rather he covered her again with his lips and his unforgiving body, kissing her hard and savagely.

This was not the Dash she remembered.

Then again, she wasn't the innocent Bath miss he'd known.

She pushed off the wall, hard enough to send them across the narrow hall until his back was against the wall and she had him trapped. Allowed herself to forget who she was supposed to be and rubbed up against him like an unrepentant barn cat, her hands roaming over him.

The strong, steady chest she remembered, the muscled arms and shoulders. Probably not as thick and corded as they'd been in his youth, but still . . .

She drew an unsteady breath. Still . . .

He scrambled to catch up with her, to take command of the situation, but she was one step ahead of him. She hitched her leg up and wound it around him.

"Is this what you want, Captain Dashwell?" She

caught his hand and towed his fingers from her knee to the upper reaches of her thigh. "Do you want to take me, right here? Right now? Is that what you want?" It was a dare issued by a woman, grown and experienced.

The hallway stilled around them; the entire world seemed to pause, even the restless sea beneath them. They stared at each other, lost in the passion that was theirs, always had been.

Always would be.

I didn't come for this, she tried to tell herself as her wits began to find their voice again. *I didn't.*

But she had. It was like being awakened after years of being asleep and finding that, while the entire world had changed, some things—love, she dared to consider—never slipped away.

But on this Pippin was wrong. At least for the moment.

He caught her by both shoulders and pushed her off him, as if he, too, had suddenly awakened, and instead of finding a long-lost dream, had found himself in the arms of a banshee.

His lips curled; his eyes darkened, narrowed. "You needn't have bothered coming if that was all you wanted, Lady Gossett. I am sure London is still filled with men willing enough to overlook your age and respectability to tumble you senseless." He flicked a glance at her disheveled figure and snorted. "But I am not so desperate."

Then he turned on one heel and climbed the ladder to the deck. "Go back where you come from, my lady. There is nothing here for you." And with that, he swung the hatch shut, leaving her in darkness.

And it was good he had.

For the last thing Pippin wanted him to see was the tears of shame . . . no, regret, decades old regret . . . that spilled down her cheeks.

Dash stormed up the stairs, cursing himself for succumbing to the madness that was her kiss.

He should never have kissed her. Kissing her had always gotten him into trouble. Always.

He'd done it to punish her, to use her like some barmaid and toss her aside. Humiliate her as she had done to him.

Then he'd kissed her.

Christ, she'd tasted of Turkish delight. How the hell could it be that her lips still tasted as sweet as candy? And just as demmed tempting.

Back at the rail again, he clung to it and stared at the sea, trying to make sense of what had just happened. He wanted her. Still wanted her.

Dash shuddered from head to toe. He couldn't.

Oh, yes, her. The waves seemed to taunt him. *Just as she wants you. Always has.*

He snorted. Always has? Not always.

"Da, is everything all right?" Nate asked, having come quietly up alongside him.

Dash glared at his son, but then his gaze caught sight of the other sailors on the deck. All nervously watching their captain as if he was about to go mad.

Well, he was. He hadn't had a drink in hours and he'd just been accosted on his own ship. So yes, demmit, he was going mad.

But that didn't mean he wasn't the captain of this ship.

"Da?" Nate asked softly.

"What?" he fired back, loud enough for all to hear. He took a steady stance, his arms crossed over his chest, his feet planted wide.

Nate bowed his head slightly, in deference, giving Dash his due as captain. "Orders, sir?"

Dash took a long glance over the clean deck, the perfectly trimmed sails, the orderly crew. A few of the men had leering grins on their faces that quickly vanished when Dash glared at them.

So the news of his encounter in the hallway was already being whispered around the sails.

"No, it all seems in order. Continue on, Mr. Dashwell."

"Aye, aye, Captain," Nate replied, before turning toward the wheel.

"Mr. Dashwell," Dash called after him. "There is one other thing."

Nate stilled. "Yes, Cap'n?"

"Keep our passenger out of my sight and out of my way. You brought her on board. You deal with her. I don't want anything to do with that woman, do you understand me?"

"Aye, aye sir," he replied, his voice neutral. But it was a good thing Nate had his back to his father.

For if Dash had seen the grin on his son's face, he would have probably keelhauled him.

Chapter 7

"Mr. Dashwell," Pippin whispered from the door-way of the gangway. "Is he about?"

They both knew what she meant. Was Dash close at hand?

Nate shook his head, and then quickly waved her up on deck.

Pippin happily scrambled up the last few steps and sighed as she felt the breeze wash over her.

Three days. Three days she'd spent inside her cabin. Hiding like a mouse. She'd read all the books she'd brought. Mended her socks. Mended two pairs for Nate. And started knitting another.

But she was bored senseless, and the confinement in the cabin with little to do was driving her mad. Pippin was used to running a household, taking a long walk every day, and having someone to converse with.

Anyone. Even Lockley, her taciturn butler back in

London, would be an improvement on her current situation.

Why hadn't she brought more to do?

Because you thought you were here to nurse Dash back to health . . . Or would be whiling away the hours in his bed, making love as you had when you had him hidden away at Hollindrake House.

She shook off that notion. She most certainly hadn't come looking only for pleasure.

Then why did you pack that dress . . .

She closed her eyes, but when she did, his kiss, his touch ran through her thoughts like a herd of dolphins riding ahead of the crest of a ship. His kiss in the hall had reopened a flood of memories, and she couldn't tamp down the passions he'd pulled free from her matronly restraints like the finest cutpurse.

He'd stolen her reason and replaced it with lust, a burning, hungry lust to be beneath him, to have him inside her, to feel as she had when she'd first fallen in love with him, when he'd taught her the finer points of lovemaking and given her a hunger for it that hadn't been sated as thoroughly since.

It wasn't that her husband hadn't been a good lover, he had been.

But he'd never been Dash—and she'd never felt, well, as utterly wicked, as completely sinful with Gossett as she had with Dash.

"Damn him. Damn him to hell," she cursed softly under her breath. Not that he had far to go, she mused. He looked like hell, and if he continued in his current course, he'd be dead before long.

She clung to the rail and was about to send another lament up to the heavens when the sight of the stars stopped her.

Having lived in London so long she'd forgotten what it was to see the sky at night without a cloud of coal smoke blotting out the stars.

Millions of twinkling lights greeted her, and as always she sought out the one constellation she couldn't resist seeking.

Orion.

And there, just overhead the three stars of his belt sparkled.

Reminding her of the night Dash had given it to her, bestowed the heavens upon her starry eyes as if it had been his to give away.

And fool that she'd been, she'd believed such magic was possible.

Dash reeled out of his cabin and climbed the ladder to the deck. After some concentrated searching, he'd managed to find where Nate had hidden his store of brandy, and consumed enough that he was still able to walk and not pass out. A bottle more or so and he'd be able to sleep.

Without dreaming about her.

He stumbled up the stairs and took a deep breath. "Blast her to hell," he cursed under his breath as he made his way to the railing.

And as if only to provoke him further, there she was, her blond hair winding down her back in a thick braid.

Go to her, a voice whispered. *Tell her how sorry you are.*

Sorry? Like hell. He was only sorry he wasn't

drunk enough to toss her overboard without feeling a lick of guilt over it.

Still . . . there she was, and for the life of him, he couldn't help himself, he was drawn to her like a moth to a flame.

But he got no farther than a few steps, when Nate anchored him to a stop.

"Leave her be, Da," his son ordered in a tight whisper, before doing his best to tug him back toward the gangway.

Dash jerked his arm free and faced down the man before him. Traitor of a son, he amended. "What the hell is she doing up here? I ordered you to keep her in her cabin."

"She's not a prisoner," Nate said, standing his ground. "She's a passenger. A paying passenger." Then he looked Dash up and down and sniffed, his nose wrinkling. He eyes said what he would not. *You're drunk*. Moreover, his tone dared to imply that she had more of a right to be aboard the *Ellis Anne* than Dash did.

"Harrumph!" Dash crossed his arms over his chest, willing his feet to stay planted. Not to betray his inebriated wits so he could go after her . . . take her in his arms and see if she was as willing as she had been the other day in the corridor.

"Da, go back to your cabin before she sees you, before the crew notices you about."

"This is my ship, Nate," he told him. How he wished his words sounded as dangerous as he'd once been capable of making such a simple state- ment sound; instead they came out slurred, while he swayed like a mast in a gale.

Nate's right, Cap'n. Go below afore she sees you, he could hear Hardy whispering. From the gates of hell, most likely.

He took another glance at her, a part of his heart, long dormant, tightening. *Pippin* . . .

"I just came up to . . ." Hell, he couldn't remember why he'd come above deck. Whatever his reason had been, it had gone overboard the moment he'd spied her standing there by the rail looking up at the night sky.

"Never mind. I'll leave her be, if that's what you want," he said, more as a vow to himself than to Nate, but still his gaze followed hers, seeing the sky above, a sight usually as comforting as the waves and wind at his back.

What the devil was she looking at up there? he wondered, stepping closer. Then to his shock he spied them, the three stars he always avoided. Orion's belt.

And when he realized what she was doing, the years between them shifted and he was back in London. On a cold winter's night, with the dawn about to pierce the darkness.

Still, he didn't quite believe that she'd be remembering that same moment. Not her.

Especially after the way he'd used her the other day, roughly and arrogantly. She must despise him. She had to despise him. *Please let her despise me*, he wanted to plead. Everything would be so much simpler then.

"I'll see that she goes back to her cabin when she's done looking at the stars," Nate was saying. "Now why don't you go below before—"

. . . before it is too late. But it already was.

Pippin turned around just then, her fair blue eyes filled with tears.

Because there was no doubt in Dash's heart that she remembered that same night all too well.

London, 1814

Pippin stole down the back stairs of the house on Brook Street and shivered as a draft whistled past her. Was there a single spot in this house that wasn't freezing? Having left the warmth of her room, she'd all but forgotten that the rest of London was trapped in the worst winter in memory, with the Thames frozen solid and the city buried in ice and snow.

And though she lived just off Grosvenor Square on fashionable Brook Street, the house Pippin and her cousins had "borrowed" was nearly as cold on the inside as it was on the outside.

Too bad the former owner hadn't laid in a good stock of coal before he'd gone to his reward and left the house in a hotly contested dispute among all the heirs. Then not only would they have the house, but something to put in the grate.

Pippin sighed and then shivered again. If Felicity's engagement to the Duke of Hollindrake didn't come to fruition soon, it would be back to Sussex for all of them.

Sussex. What a dreadful notion! Pippin tugged her wrapper tighter around her, and came to a stop before the garden door. For back in Sussex she'd be far away from . . .

Outside, the gate in the garden creaked, followed by the soft crunch of boots in the fresh snow that had been falling since afternoon.

Dash . . .

Her heart beat wildly, and she pressed her lips together to keep from grinning with joy. After three nights of letting him into the house after everyone else had gone to bed, she would have thought she'd be well past this trembling, wild desire that shot through her just at the sound of his boots.

If that was so, you wouldn't have unbound your hair and put on your best night rail . . .

Pippin blushed at the stray voice that whispered past her ears. Why, it was like having Felicity or their former teacher, Miss Emery, at her shoulder.

Well, certainly it was quite improper for her to be meeting him in her night rail and wrapper. But it was only out of the utmost necessity, she would argue. For it would hardly do for her to be dressed. However would she explain to Felicity or Tally if they found her out of bed at this time of night, wearing her day gown and gloves?

They'd discover what she was doing.

Letting a wanted man into their house in hopes that he might try to seduce her.

Oh, if only he would. Not that her hopes had gotten her much. Why, for the last two nights she'd all but prayed he might take some sort of liberty, but instead he'd been circumspect in his behavior. Much to her chagrin.

And here she'd always heard that pirates were such a rakish lot. She supposed that was why he was merely a privateer, not a real pirate.

But to her, he was the pirate of her heart, of her desires. And they were his for the taking. If he only would . . .

A soft scratching at the door wrenched her back to the matters at hand. She took a deep breath and shook off the last vestiges of her trembling, anxious demeanor and opened the door for him.

Dash swept in, bringing with him the bite of the icy breeze and a flurry of snowflakes. Closing the door quickly, she clung to the latch as she turned around to face him.

It never stopped amazing her how grand he was. So very tall, with his dark hair and broad shoulders. Was there ever a more handsome man? She couldn't think of one. And every time he stood so close to her, she felt as if she were being transported into some heavenly, scandalous French novel.

Then he opened his mouth and looked about to say something to her, so she put a finger to her lips, shaking her head furiously.

No, please. Don't get us caught tonight. Because Pippin was resolved that tonight would be the night.

Grinning, he acknowledged her silent greeting by leaning over and putting his hand on the door, just over her shoulder, and placing a lingering kiss on her cheek.

Even as his lips brushed over her skin, Pippin grew as light-headed as the time she and her cousins had stolen a bottle of wine from their teacher's cabinet and drunk the entire thing in one daring night.

" 'Tis a bitter, cold night, Circe," he whispered. "But you are a warm sight for sore eyes."

Pippin shivered, and not from the cold. He leaned

back and gazed down at her, and it was all she could do not to throw her arms around his neck and beg him to take her innocence.

But that was how he made her feel: tipsy and desired.

For a second they stood there in the empty hallway, until a bit of winter wind stole through from one of the many drafts in the house and ran up her night rail.

The icy shock was enough to wake up her dizzy senses. She was standing in the hallway in naught but her night rail with a man. A wanted man.

"Follow me," she whispered, catching up the candle she'd tucked into the holder on the wall with one hand, and with the other reaching for the basket she'd stolen from the kitchen a few hours earlier. But her fingers never got to the handle, for he brushed her hand aside and took up the burden, carrying it for her.

"We got a bit of coal today," she told him once they were well up from the room Tally and Felicity shared on the first floor. "So the rooms are not quite so cold, and I daresay the chimney will have warmed the attic up a bit for you."

"Anything is better than being out there," he told her, nodding toward a window, where the snow swirled past the panes. "How did you manage the coal?"

Dash knew only too well of their dire financial straits, and didn't find it the least bit mortifying as Pippin and her cousins did.

"Felicity has promised to help Lady Rhoda find matches for her three nieces. Her Ladyship sent over two footmen with buckets of it, and has promised more before the end of the week."

"Now that is a fine trade," he teased as they entered the room where Pippin had been stashing him—the one up in the very attics where the maidservants would sleep.

If they could afford them, that was.

"What is it tonight, Circe?" Dash asked, as he settled down on the bed she'd pushed over next to the chimney flue where it was warmer, and plucked the napkin covering his supper from the top of the basket. "Let me guess, roast beef and a fine pudding?"

"How I wish," she said with a sigh, settling down on the stool nearby. "But I fear it is only brown bread and butter. Oh, with a bit of cheese."

"If the bread has no weevils and the cheese isn't full of mold, then I consider it a feast fit for a king."

"Then you'll eat like a king tonight," she teased back, "for it is what I had for supper and there wasn't a weevil in sight." She tipped her head and glanced up at him. "You don't eat the weevils, do you?"

He paused, about to take a bite of bread. "Well, not if they are wiggling."

Her face must have shone with the horror of it, for he laughed, and then she knew he was teasing her. At least she hoped he was teasing.

Weevils, indeed! But that really wasn't so farfetched, she knew, for in the last two nights he'd regaled her with harrowing tales of his adventures—from chasing Barbary pirates, to robbing a Scottish village, to outrunning an English frigate in a gale.

While she and Tally spent their days writing far-flung and wild tales of romance, here was Dash actually living real adventures.

She shivered with anticipation of what he would tell her about tonight. Being marooned perhaps? Finding treasure?

How much he desired her . . .

Dash sat peering into the basket and then glanced up at her. "You needn't steal so much. What if someone notices?"

Pippin shook her head. "Mrs. Hutchinson . . . well, I fear she . . ." She pantomimed tipping a bottle back.

Dash nodded. "Ah, she drinks, does she. Sad state to see a woman in. Sad for a man as well. Robs them of their wits and their life."

"Well, she won't notice if a bit of food goes missing."

Dash dug into his pockets. "That was my sentiment exactly when I discovered this," he said, holding out a bundle in his handkerchief.

She took it and unfolded the cloth to find several squares of Turkish delight inside. "Oh, Dash! You shouldn't," she said, but her protest hardly stopped her from eating a piece with relish. Then she paused mid-bite. "Did you really steal this?"

"Like I said, I don't think the shop owner will notice a bit gone missing." Then he cocked his head and stared at her. "What's this? A bit of conscience from the lady living in a house she pinched right out from beneath the rightful heirs?"

"I suppose when you put it that way," she said, looking down at the delicious bounty in her hands.

"Eat your treats, Circe. You've few of them in your life, from what you've told me."

For when he hadn't been filling her ears and heart with stories from the sea, she'd been filling him in on her life—so very dull in comparison—her mother's death when she was just a girl, how her worldly cousins Felicity and Tally had joined her at Miss Emery's after their diplomat father had determined they needed an "English" education after years of being educated by his mistresses.

There in the confines of Bath, Felicity and Tally had given Pippin hope for her future, what with their wild continental manners and scandalous notions, that was, until her father's untimely demise had ended her first Season before it had even begun. Then worse yet, the realization that his estate was mortgaged to the hilt and the coffers emptied after years of his ruinous habits.

"Without Tally and Felicity, I don't know what I would have done," she'd confided to him. "I was so lonely before they came back to England. And then it was like we'd always been friends. Despite our lack of funds, our life isn't so terrible. We have Aunt Minty to watch over us, and Tally and I have our writing to keep us occupied."

She certainly hadn't meant to pour out her heart to him, such private matters that weren't shared even with the dearest of friends, but he listened and coaxed her stories from her, listening to her recite her plays and short stories as if her ordinary scribblings were as magical as his extraordinary life at sea.

"The ice is thinning," he announced after a few bites of biscuit.

"Already?" she whispered.

"Aye."

"Then you'll be gone." She shook her head. "But you promised, Dash. You promised me you'd teach me to be a proper pirate before you left."

Dash laughed. "Ah, yes, your pirate lessons. How could I forget?"

"Yes, how could you?" she scolded, smiling at the same time. "Sailing, navigation, scuttling enemy ships, sword fighting, pillaging, and the proper loading and shooting of cannons, I believe was our agreement."

"And where do you propose we find a cannon?" he teased, his eyes alight.

Pippin shivered, for she loved that mischievous fire that illuminated his green eyes. "Hmm, finding a cannon might present a problem, but I'd agree to pillaging Almack's for practice until a suitable twelve-pounder could be found."

He laughed, shaking his head at her proposition, but after a few moments he paused, glancing down at the floor. "I fear we will have to belay our lessons."

"But Dash, you cannot leave," she insisted, not even caring how it sounded.

"Aye. I must." Then he looked up at her and grinned. "But not before I buy you a red silk dress."

"A dress? For me?" Pippin had blushed at the notion. Unmarried ladies didn't let gentlemen buy them clothes, unless . . . "Oh, I couldn't wear it."

"Whyever not?"

She laughed. "Because I don't think red would suit me." Nor would it be proper. No more than it was for her to be up here with him. Alone. Wearing only her night rail.

He eyed her, a flash in his green eyes and a hooded expression that burned with a rare fire. "I disagree. I think you would be enchanting in red. You'd mesmerize every man who saw you." He paused for a moment. "Then again, perhaps that wouldn't be a good idea."

She glanced at him. He'd changed his mind? "Why not?"

"For then," he began slowly, "you would be swamped with offers, and spending your nights with me would be poor fare in comparison."

She waved her hand at him. "Oh, I'm hardly much of a catch." Besides, her nights with him were all she'd ever wanted.

"Men have eyes beyond a lady's purse, my love," he said, his voice low and full of passion. "There are men enough in London, I would wager, who wouldn't think twice of marrying you, penniless and as you are right now." He paused, his hot gaze traveling from the hem of her plain yellow wrapper to the lacy neckline of her virginal white night rail.

Oh, gracious heavens, he did desire her. He did.

"Dash, you are a terrible tease," she said, waving him off, and hoping desperately he was one of those. The sort who could love her as she was. Poor, without a penny to her name.

But to her chagrin, he'd gone back to eating the fare she'd purloined. After a few bites, he asked, "How is it that meddlesome cousin of yours hasn't found you a proper husband?"

Pippin groaned, and not from her lack of husband, but at the wretched word. *Proper.* "Not from lack of trying, let me tell you. She's determined to marry me off to some dull earl, or at the very least, a viscount."

"Poor, poor girl," he said with a solemn tsk, tsk. "Nothing in your future but three square meals—without weevils, I might note—and a solid roof over your head. I can see why you would find such an idea so utterly wretched."

"You wouldn't be so glib if it was your life," she shot back. "I envy you, Captain Dashwell. Your freedom and your adventures. You wouldn't marry just for money and position, as my cousin thinks is so important." She paused for a second. "I'm trapped in this world without any hope of escape, naught but a dull future stretched out before me."

He shook his head. "Don't envy me, sweetheart. I most likely will end my days swinging from a hangman's noose. In comparison, that will make your dull earl look a prince." He held out a piece of bread for her, but she waved him off, pointing at the Turkish delight still remaining.

She gasped at the notion. "They won't hang you, will they, Dash?"

"Of course they will," he told her.

"But after all you've done—for Temple and Mad Jack."

"And I was paid for my services," he reminded her.

Still Pippin persisted. "They would vouchsafe for you."

He smiled at her. "They might have before . . ." His voice trailed off, and he glanced toward the window. "But now?" He shrugged. "Two years of war changes things. We're enemies."

"Never say such a thing," she told him vehemently, edging off her stool and coming to sit beside him on the cot. "I won't let you be caught. You must stay free, you just must."

He reached out and curled his hand beneath her chin. He held her like that for a moment, staring into her eyes as if the sight of them held more sustenance than the brown bread in his lap. "There is always a price for freedom, Circe," he whispered. "Always."

The word washed over her with a strange finality. It was as if it branded her future on her forehead. This man, her feelings for him, and dare she say it, her desire for him, were her ticket to freedom, but the price . . . the price of it could quite possibly destroy them both.

Pippin couldn't breathe, for she feared even a whisper of movement would break the spell, cast them back into a world where she must abide by Society's rules and he . . . well, Captain Dashwell was a wanted man.

"Oh, Circe," he whispered. "You should never have let me in."

And she had to suspect he didn't mean into her house, but into her life, into her heart, for his eyes were full of a stormy passion.

And I'll never let you go, she wanted to say, ready to press forward, to offer him anything to stay with her.

Then suddenly his hand was gone, her face quickly chilled by the loss of his warm fingers.

Dash took one more look at her before he turned to dig back into the basket, searching for the last bit of cheese. When he found it, he continued to eat, but he didn't look at her, and he certainly didn't touch her, or even offer to share as he'd done the other nights.

Pippin bit her lip, and wondered what he was thinking. For he had a faraway look that carried him well beyond Brook Street and even London.

When she looked up at him, she found him staring at her feet.

"Red wool socks," he said, a wry smile on his lips. "I hear those are all the rage this year among well-dressed ladies."

Pippin giggled, tucking her feet beneath her wrapper, a bit embarrassed by her less-than-elegant trappings. Besides, gentlemen weren't supposed to know what a lady wore beneath her gown. "Hardly fashionable. Just plain wool and not silk like, well, like other ladies wear."

"You aren't like other ladies," he said in a tone that warmed her. "I rather like them."

"So do I," she confessed, holding a foot back out. "Aunt Minty knit them. She's teaching me to knit as well. She finds it scandalous that proper ladies only do embroidery and tatting, not useful things like knitting."

"Then you can knit me a pair, for I daresay, they would make an excellent addition to my pirate ensemble." He took another bite of bread. "Strike fear in the hearts of my enemies at the very sight."

They both laughed, and far too loudly. Pippin clapped her hand over her mouth and waited . . . waited for the sound of footsteps coming to investigate, but the house remained silent.

"Do you really want a pair?" she asked.

Dash grinned at her and stood, displaying the ragged pair on his own feet by lifting the hems of his trousers. "Of course. Obviously a better gift than Turkish delight. For what have you left after I bring it to you? Naught but a pretty ring of sugar around your sweet mouth." He reached out and ran his finger across her lips. It was a mesmerizing moment. "And what a waste of sugar," he said softly, his words almost strangled, as if he had forgotten how to speak.

She gazed at him, and without thinking, rose and stepped closer, so he could continue to trace this intoxicating line around her lips, so he could . . .

"So sweet," he whispered. "So very sweet." And then he dipped his head down and kissed her, softly, gently, kissing away the sugar around her mouth, and then with a hunger that had been tempted not by the confection on her skin, but by the taste of her.

Pippin shivered again as his lips sought hers, his hand caught hold of her hip and pulled her up against him. The heat of his body shot through her thin muslin, enveloped her in his desire.

Her hands went to his jacket and she clung to him, as his tongue bid her to open up to him.

And she did. Quite willingly. For she knew only too well what was to come.

At least she thought she did.

His tongue grazed over hers, awakening every memory she'd held of him.

The strength of his arms as they pulled her ever closer, the hard wall of his chest, the tremble of his heart against her breast.

Kissing her deeply, his hand combed through her loose hair.

"Oh, God," he groaned as he threaded his fingers through the strands again. "I never felt such silk."

Her body arched like a cat's as he explored her, for she couldn't get enough of his touch and it seemed he could not stop stroking her. Then the heat of his touch cupped her breast, and she moaned.

Moaned aloud like the veriest courtesan, and Pippin felt the wonder of being shameless—it tasted of a freedom she'd never imagined.

As his fingers curled around her breast, his thumb rolled over her nipple until it was tight and aching, and she knew she was falling happily into ruin.

He kissed her softly and then pulled back, slowly, before tentatively he opened her gown, pulling the ties free of their careful bows, and pausing with each one as if he expected her to protest.

As if she could. Pippin could barely stand, barely breathe. Her lips swollen from his kiss, her skin atingle, her knees trembling . . . and her heart, her heart beat with desire, a rapid, haphazard staccato that left her breathless.

Inside, deep inside her, she quaked. That very private core longed for more.

More . . . she wanted so much more.

Slowly, he slipped her wrapper and night rail from her shoulders, and they fell into a puddle at her stocking-clad feet.

She should be mortified, she should stop him. She should be freezing.

But she wasn't any of those. Pippin was trapped in this moment, watching the desire come to life in his eyes as he gazed at her with a longing she understood.

It didn't matter that she was naked; no, it was that this man, this man she'd loved since the first moment she'd clapped eyes on him, who looked at her with a desire that was only for her.

And hers to give him.

His hand reached out and traced a slow, tantalizing line from her collarbone down to the tip of her breast.

She opened her mouth to breathe, and when she did, he cupped her breast again, and leaned over to take her nipple in his lips. His teeth grazed over her, sending another shock through her, and then he inhaled deeply, sucking her into his mouth, his tongue teasing her nipple until it was round and hard, the twisting passion he left in his wake making her tremble with need.

She teetered on her toes, her fingers twined into the lapels of his jacket. Oh, heavens! How could such a thing be possible?

And yet it was.

"Oh, Dash," she gasped. Her fingers tangling in his dark hair. He caught hold of her bottom with his work-roughened hands and tugged her closer, so she rode right up against his hardened sex.

He pressed his hips against her, and she gasped as she felt him, his hardness rubbing against her.

He pulled himself back, and stared down at her. Oh, finally, she wanted to gasp. He was about to sweep her off her feet, toss her down on the cot, and ravish her.

Like a scene out of one of her and Tally's plays . . .

And now that she had a good idea what it meant,

she was more than happy to be his all-too-willing victim, ripe for plundering.

Yet he paused, his entire body still, and then he closed his eyes, his expression suddenly pained.

"Pippin, I cannot do this."

And then he did the last thing she wanted.

He set her aside.

Chapter 8

$\mathcal{D}$ash tried to catch his breath, dared not open his eyes. The vision of his Circe, naked and willing before him, would be enough to tempt him back . . . back to ruining her.

He stepped around her, catching up her wrapper and handing it to her, not daring to look at her.

What the hell was he doing here? She was a lady. Not only that, an innocent one. Well, nearly innocent.

She wouldn't be for much longer if he continued in this course.

Couldn't she see that she was too fine for the likes of him? No, obviously not. What with those trusting blue eyes gazing up at him with desire and, worse yet . . . love.

No, that was hardly the worst of it. For if he was of a mind to be honest, he would confess that he was in love with her as well.

His Circe. Had been since he'd seen her on that

demmed beach in Hastings, just a wisp of a maiden, on the very cusp of womanhood.

But now, in those four years since, it was so very different.

Their countries were at war. They should be enemies. And she should have stayed that willowy bit of muslin that had tempted him to steal a kiss from her sweet lips—not grown into this tempting, beautiful woman who would haunt him the rest of his days.

Her eyes alone should have warned him away. For one day they would see the truth of him and she would hate him, hate herself for having given him her heart.

Her innocence.

Thomas Dashwell, a man who had stolen, connived, plundered, and pilfered everything he'd ever wanted, couldn't take what she was offering so innocently.

He couldn't.

Then her fingers curled around his shoulder, and with a strength that belied her soft features, the trappings that made her look so very fragile, turned him around.

Fair and sweet she might appear, but he knew the truth about her. She was a woman of passion. She might think herself inconsequential enough never to be able to wear a red silk dress, but Dash knew one day she would don a glorious gown of fire and defy anyone who stood in her way.

And she was on the edge of that awareness even now as she tugged him around and searched his face for answers.

"Dash, what have I done?"

What had she done? "Nothing," he told her. It was him. It was complicated. It wasn't anything he was going to tell her. "But I need to leave."

He might have said the words, but his feet were hardly being compliant, for his boots stayed planted to the floor and his body rebelled. Ached to stay with her. To make love to her.

She slid up against him, as if she saw every bit of the conflict in his eyes and cared naught for his protests. Her hands wound around his neck, and she pulled him down so she could kiss him again. Coax him back into that place from which there would be no turning back.

Her kiss was no longer tentative, her soft tongue curled around his, teasing and stroking.

No! No! No! he tried to protest, tried to pull away, but she held him fast, her bare breasts nestled against his shirt.

He glanced down. How the hell had she gotten his jacket off? But there it was on the floor beside her wrapper.

Dash groaned. This was all his fault. He'd unleashed this scandalous creature with his kiss, with his touch. He'd opened this Pandora's box of desire, and there was no containing her now.

Never would be again.

The innocent and trusting Lady Philippa who'd let him into her house, her heart, let him awaken her to the passions a man and woman could share, was gone.

Replaced by this feminine pirate, this plundering miss. Oh, she knew the power she possessed, and she wasn't about to let him leave.

But leave he would, he vowed. He had to. He must. For he'd destroy them both if he continued this reckless course.

"Pippin, I can't. This is madness," he told her, trying to pull himself away, but still she wouldn't let go, one arm wound around him, the other hand wantonly running down his chest, down to the top of his breeches, and then, God help him, her fingers covered his sex and stroked him through the rough twill, rubbing him and exploring him until he thought he would go mad.

But it wasn't her brazen touch that was his undoing. It wasn't the way his blood pounded in his ears, drowning out nearly every bit of reason he possessed.

It was her eyes. He looked into her eyes and knew he was caught. Trapped well and good. Anchored to this woman. Always had been.

Always would be.

And she knew it as well, damn her.

For whatever reasons, the Fates had bound them together that night in Hastings, and no mortal being would ever be able to cut that cord.

She was his.

And by God, he'd find a way to have her. Always.

As Dash's lips came crashing back down on hers, Pippin knew that whatever doubts he'd been holding were now gone.

His tongue washed over hers, as if begging her to come dance with his. To taste him with the same hunger with which he kissed her.

Catching her up, he pushed her backward toward

the bed, their bodies sinking into the poor mattress, in a tangle of limbs and kisses, to the echo of soft, sweet moans.

He covered her body with his, and his hands touched her everywhere.

And where his hands weren't, his lips were, sucking her nipples into tight points, breathing hot kisses down her belly.

Pippin arched anew, her body trembling with desire as he continued his hot, scorching seduction.

Hardly a seduction; she couldn't think of anything she would want more than this. Having Dash devouring her, pulling such a delicious, heated desire through her limbs.

His hand stroked up the inside of her thigh, his rough fingers padding lightly over her smooth skin. She shivered as her legs opened to his explorations, as he claimed her lips in another searing, searching kiss.

And then his hand brushed over the triangle of curls at the top of her thighs, and she thought she was going to burst, for suddenly her body tightened, anxious and hungry for him.

For more.

"Dash, oh, Dash," she whispered as his hand swept over her again.

He pulled back a bit. "Do you want me to stop?"

She looked up at him in horror. "No!"

Laughing, he kissed her lightly on her nose, his fingers returning to exploring her sex, coaxing her to open up for him. "Is that better?" he whispered, his lips brushing over the curve of her ear, his teeth nipping lightly at a sensitive spot right behind.

It was nearly too much for her, his teasing kisses,

his torturous touch, for just then he parted his way to her very core and found the tight nub beneath, bedeviling it with feather-soft touches, and whispered promises into her ear of more to come.

More?

"Oh, yes," she begged. "More."

And Pippin knew what more meant. She ran her hands over his chest, and pushed his shirt over his head. His broad chest felt heavenly beneath her fingers, the crisp dark hair, the muscled strength, the pounding of his heart.

And then lower her curiosity led her, to his breeches.

When she had touched him there before, she'd known exactly what she was doing, tempting him to come to her, and now she wanted more than to explore him through his rough twill breeches, she wanted to touch him.

She pulled at the buttons, fumbling with them in her nervousness, and then as if he couldn't stand it any longer than she could, he reached down and pulled them off, taking his smallclothes with them and leaving him gloriously naked atop her.

Her hands roamed down his back, and faltered as they came across the evidence of thick scars crisscrossing his back.

Her gaze jolted up to his, and he nudged away her questions, her shock, by kissing her again, and begging her as she had him. "More, Circe."

Pippin pushed aside the vision in her mind of his scarred back and returned to her exploration, running her hands down his sides, to the lean line of his hips, and then to his hard sex, which jutted out in desire, waiting for her, thick and hard for her and her alone.

He groaned as she closed her hand over it and stroked it, touched it, let her hand cup him, ran a finger over the pearly drops forming at the head and using them to lubricate her play, her hand sliding up and down him, even as his fingers continued to explore her, their mouths fused in a hot, ragged kiss.

And then he rolled her completely beneath him, and Pippin felt open and exposed, her legs spread wide to receive him.

"You are the most beautiful creature who ever lived," he said in a low voice. "And you are mine."

His possessive words thrilled her. *His.* She couldn't think of anything that she wanted more. To be Dash's. Tonight and always.

She arched up as he slowly entered her. If she had thought he would ravish her, she was wrong. He moved carefully, filling her slowly, with soft strokes until he came to her barrier, and then he whispered in her ear, "This might hurt."

And before she could make sense of what he was saying, before the words penetrated her desire-clouded mind, he breached her, taking her innocence in a smooth, quick movement.

Pippin gasped, but the shock of it was quickly replaced by his kiss on her lips, whispered words of worship and desire.

He caught her by her hips and pulled her closer to him so he could fill her entirely, and this time when he moved inside her, she felt only pleasure.

Deep, insatiable passion.

As he moved in and out, she fell into a greedy rhythm, arching up and seeking more and more of him. He teased her, stroking her slowly and with steady, increased pressure that left her anxious and pleading, "Oh, Dash!"

He increased the tempo, feeding her hunger, her body tightening around him.

With each stroke, the world around them slipped away, and all Pippin felt was this man, his touch, his desire for her building inside her. She moved with him, arched against him, clung to him as he carried her higher, farther than she thought possible until everything gave way.

"Dash, oh, Dash!" she called out as her body trembled and rocked. A storm of pleasure exploded all at once, as if he'd caught up a tempest and unleashed it inside her. Wave after wave came crashing over her, and he continued to stroke her, continuing the melee until suddenly he stilled for a moment, filled her in a hard, quick stroke, and moaned in thick pleasure as he, too, found his own piece of refuge on this tossing sea of their own making.

She wound her legs around him to hold him close, while he continued to move inside her, continuing the soft, lapping waves that echoed and reverberated through her.

And while outside the night was icy and dark and cold, inside the little attic on Brook Street, Pippin and Dash found a paradise of their own.

And both sent up a silent prayer that it might last forever. Or at the very least, through this dark night.

* * *

Pippin stirred sometime before dawn, the chill of the attic stealing beneath the warmth of the blankets and leaving her shivering. She reached for Dash and found the once warm spot beside her empty.

She sat bolt upright, surrounded only by shadows. "Dash?"

A wisp of icy wind wound past her, and she pulled the blanket back over her as if it could ward off the cold. Blinking in the meager light being put out by the stump of a candle, she searched for him.

The breeze rifled past her again, and then she finally found the source of this wretched draft. The narrow door that led to the balcony overlooking the mews was open.

She rose, catching up her night rail and wrapper, hastily donning them, searching the room for any sign of Dash.

But everything, his clothes, his boots, his coat were all gone.

It was as if he'd never come to her in the night.

Pippin stilled. Impossible. She couldn't possibly have dreamed such a night. Besides, her body offered a different kind of evidence—she moved stiffly, slightly sore from his lovemaking, but not minding in the least, still reveling in the delicious languor left in its wake. No, none of this could have been discovered adrift in a dream.

He'd been here.

And then he left . . . a warning voice whispered.

Her heart trembled in dread. He wouldn't leave her without a word . . . or even a kiss . . .

Dressing hastily and still chilled, she stole a blanket

from the bed and wrapped it around her as she went to close the door and make sure that it was latched securely this time . . . It wouldn't do to have anyone up here investigating her secret little nest under the eaves.

As her fingers closed over the latch, the wind brought a whisper of a voice inside.

"Pippin."

She peered into the darkness, until she spied him there, at the edge of the rail. "Dash," she sighed happily.

He hadn't left her. He wouldn't just leave her . . .

"Were you expecting another?" he teased. "Or do you invite all your lovers up here?"

"All my lovers!" she scoffed swatting his hand aside as he offered to help her out. "What a thing to say."

"You could if you wished," he told her, pulling her into the warmth of his arms. "You could have legions of men waiting for just a mere glance from those glorious blue eyes of yours."

She blushed and tucked her head into his shoulder. He nearly made her believe she was capable of such a feat. It wasn't true, but she loved him for thinking it. "What are you doing out here?"

"The storm has passed." He nodded toward the clearing skies. "The stars have come out." He paused and gazed upward. "I miss them when I'm not at sea. Out on the ocean they sparkle all around you. 'Tis like standing at the gates of heaven."

"Sounds glorious."

He snuggled her up against his chest, let his warmth surround her. "This is my favorite time of day. Just before the sun starts to rise. Before there is any hint of daylight. The stars always seem their brightest now, as if they know they only have another hour or so of life. For in that time they'll all be gone from sight, lost to the sun, and hidden away until night claims the world anew. So they shine their brightest while the world still sleeps."

The poet in her stilled. She'd never heard anything so beautiful in all her life.

"Would you like one?" he asked.

"One what?"

"A star." He snuggled her closer. "Pick one and it will be yours forever."

"Just one?" she teased back.

He kissed her forehead. "I would give you them all if I could."

Silently, they clung together and gazed at the sky, her hands wound around his waist, over his back. There beneath his coat it was only his linen shirt between her fingers and his back.

And even through the thick fabric, she could feel the scars. Ragged ridges crossing over his back. Evidence he'd endured something horrific.

And when she pulled her hand away, he flinched, his entire body tensing.

"How, Dash?" she whispered. "What happened to you?"

He shook his head and glanced away. From the twist of his lips she knew he was trying to find some light quip to toss out, to deflect her, but she persisted. "Dash, I must know. What happened to you?"

He paused and then looked down at her. "It isn't fit—"

"Oh, pish!" she said, nudging him with her elbow. "Tell me."

"If you must know—"

"I must," she insisted.

"Well, then, not long after that night at Jack's beach—you remember that night . . ."

The night they'd met? How could she forget it?

She nodded and urged him to continue.

"Two British frigates came upon the *Circe. Boundless* and the *Princess Caroline*. They had us outgunned and outmaneuvered. I didn't even see it coming or I would have loaded her with sail and outrun them, but once I realized they intended to board us, it was too late."

He glanced down at her, his body tensing. "Why should I suspect them? I helped Temple and his lot and assumed, wrongly on my part, that my assistance to the Foreign Office would have some bearing with the Admiralty." He blew out a hot, angry breath, his body suddenly tense. "They boarded and claimed I was smuggling—" He shrugged. "Which I was, but no more than any other ship out there. But instead of just taking my contraband, they rounded up the crew."

Pippin stilled. Oh, God, no. She knew exactly where this was going.

Impressment.

And while many of her fellow Englishmen saw nothing wrong with the Royal Navy filling out its ranks with English sailors from merchant vessels, the problem arose when the captains didn't always discriminate between those born under British law and those whose citizenship put them well out of British reach.

Personally, she could see why such a high-handed

practice had incensed the Americans to the point of declaring war against the might of England. Why, if it had been the Americans doing such a scurrilous thing to British sailors, the entire island nation would have howled together in fury.

Just as Dash was now shaking with the same righteous anger at the memory of that day.

"And so they rounded up my crew," he repeated, "and began choosing who they were going to take." He shook his head. "My da—he was a captain as well—had it happen once. They took my younger brother, and we never saw him again. I always thought by helping Temple and Jack, they might be able to find him. I know they've promised to look . . ."

"If they gave you their word, they will do what they can," she insisted. Templeton and Jack might be many things, but they were men who could be trusted.

"I know, but not all Englishmen share their code of honor. And, unfortunately, the pair of captains who'd cornered us were not of that ilk. They only saw the profit to be had in stealing my cargo and adding to their crew."

"And you disagreed with them," Pippin said, seeing him all too well standing on the deck of his ship, pistols drawn and furious.

"Hell yes. That's putting it lightly," he told her. "And the captain didn't appreciate either my letter of introduction Temple had given me or the fact that I ordered him off my ship." He reached out and caught hold of the railing, his knuckles glowing white as he held his temper in check, restrained his fury.

"The bastard gave me a choice, let him take who

he wanted or he'd empty the hold and burn us to the waterline. Kill all of us."

Pippin gasped. " 'Tis murder!"

"Yes, it would have been. And before I knew it, half my crew was in irons, and he was about to leave, when he spotted the cabin lad. The mite was only eight, and it was his first voyage. His mother had trusted him to my care, and the hell if I was going to let him go. He was American-born and his citizenship was undisputable."

Pippin closed her eyes. "And he took him anyway."

Dash nodded. "After that, I didn't care. If he thought to destroy my ship, I was going take him with it." He unclenched his hands and nestled her close, clung to her, inhaling the scent of her hair as if trying to stop the flood of horrific memories.

"I nearly killed him," he said a few moments later. "Had my hands around his throat, and just about snapped his neck before one of his marines got to me. Clubbed me with the butt of his rifle—at least that is what I learned later."

"Oh, Dash. And when you awoke?"

"I was in irons in the hold of that demmed frigate and they told me the *Circe* was gone. At the bottom of the sea."

Pippin's gaze flew up to his. "No! But you haven't lost her, have you? They didn't burn her, did they?"

He shook his head. "No. They didn't dare. That would have been an outright act of war, and they hadn't the nerve for anything that open. Just kidnapping and murder." He glanced up at the sky.

"But you didn't know it for certain," Pippin murmured.

"No, I didn't," he told her. "They probably would have been better off telling me my ship and crew were alive and well—for the thought of them dead—Hardy, Glover, Farrar, and Zimmer, those who didn't get 'pressed—drove me nearly to madness . . . especially after . . . after . . ."

"The boy," she whispered, a shiver of dread running down her spine.

"Aye. He made it a week. Then he was caught stealing food for me, and . . ."

"You don't have to say it," she told him, laying her hand on his chest. "I can well imagine."

Dash's jaw worked back and forth, and as he spoke it was in a choked stream of words. "When I heard his body splash into the sea, I swore a vow to avenge him, so his young, brave life would not be forgotten."

"I daresay you've done that," she offered.

He stilled, then looked up at the sky. "Not by any measure," he said in a voice so filled with darkness and hatred, the chill reaching deeper than this bitter January morning.

They stood together for a time, Dash struggling to forget and Pippin struggling for something to say.

"What was his name?" she finally asked.

"Pardon?"

"The boy's name. What was it?"

Again he paused, as if even saying the name cost him. "Ellis."

"Ellis," she repeated, committing the name to memory. Ellis. Someday she would see that name live on, if only to pay back the small share that was her debt. But a boy's life? How could such a debt be repaid? She shivered again, but this time with anger. "I wish I had known what had happened. To you, to Ellis," she said, feeling both furious and impotent.

He glanced down at her and chuckled lightly at her fury. "Ah, Circe, I would almost pity the British navy if you were to take them on."

Pippin shook off his platitude. "But Jack and Temple, couldn't they have helped?" she insisted.

He shook his head. "How were they to know?"

But Pippin couldn't let go. Someone should have done something. Perhaps if someone in the navy had possessed any sense, taken a step back and looked at such practices and seen that bullying American ships was going to eventually cause more harm than good, this entire war could have been avoided.

Pippin wound her arms around him, clinging to him shamelessly. "At least you lived." For it was all that mattered to her—that he'd escaped and come to her. She moved back away from him and faced him. "How did you escape?"

At this, his entire face changed. Dash grinned and opened his mouth to tell her, but just as quickly faltered. "I-I-I . . ."

Was it her imagination or was he blushing? Captain Thomas Dashwell? The most daring man of the Atlantic looked like a boy caught with the jam pot.

"Dash?"

"I fear it probably isn't a story for your innocent ears."

"I believe you've already taken care of the innocent part, so you might as well tell me."

He laughed. "You devilish minx. Give you a bit

of pleasure and you become a lady of the world, do you?"

"Yes, quite," she insisted.

"Well, then, I will have you know I escaped wearing a whore's red gown."

"You wha-a-t?" she stammered. And then she glanced at his wry look and decided he was teasing. "No, really, how did you escape?"

"Wearing a whore's gown," he repeated.

"However would you get a whore's gown on a navy ship?"

He leaned over and kissed her nose. "Not so worldly as you might imagine you are, Lady Philippa?"

Now it was Pippin's turn to blush, and she stole back into the warmth of his arms. "I still want to know."

"Well, I don't want to see this turn up in one of your plays, mind you," he chastened.

She gaped at him and stubbornly refused to agree. Why, the story was rife with dramatic possibilities.

But when he stood firm and refused to tell her a word, she finally stomped a foot and said, "I promise."

He nodded. "When a navy ship comes into a port, some captains will allow whores aboard to . . . to . . ."

"Ply their trade?"

He heaved a sigh. "Yes, that's it. To ply their trade. By letting the doves aboard, the captain doesn't have to let the men go ashore and risk they'll jump ship."

"But you managed—"

"Aye. The captain was feeling overly generous,

having sold the silks and brandy from the *Circe*, and had kegs and ladies brought aboard and it was quite a . . ." Again, he struggled for the right words.

"Celebration?" she suggested.

"Yes, a celebration," he said, grinning at her. "I had managed to gamble with some of the sailors and get a bit of gold set aside. I had it hidden, and I found one of the girls who wasn't very well-favored and offered her a deal."

"Your gold for her dress?"

He shook his head. "No, my gold for her help. Apparently there was another bird who was rather cruel to her, so when the bitty got so drunk that she passed out, my new friend stole her dress. No one noticed us roll her up in a blanket and stuff her in one of the far hammocks. Then when it came time for the ladies to be rounded up, I donned the dress and was rowed ashore with the rest of the lot."

"Didn't anyone notice?"

"Well, most of the crew and officers were rather—"

"Jug-bit?"

He took a double glance at her. "Such a phrase for a lady. But yes, the officers were as bad as the crew. And my accomplice was so delighted to have gotten rid of her rival, she, shall we say, kept the officer in charge of the skiff so well occupied while the longboat was rowed ashore that he never looked much past his own nose."

"And then you were free."

He nodded. "It was only a matter of finding a captain that I knew and working my passage back to Baltimore where Hardy was with the *Circe*, having a devil of a time getting it refit—the war had broken out by then."

"And the rest of your crew?"

"I gained them back a year later when I took the *Boundless* off the coast of Halifax." He smiled. "There was some satisfaction in seeing that particular captain in irons. Ruddy bastard. Cried when I cast him into the hold of the *Circe*." He pulled her close and kissed the top of her head. "You still haven't chosen which one you want," he said, changing the subject.

"Which what?"

"Star. Best hurry, for it will be light soon and I must . . ."

. . . be gone.

Pippin glanced at the sky and wished the sun would never rise, but the hint of pink on the horizon told the truth. So she glanced up and pointed at three stars in a line. "Those. There. I want those three."

"Three? Greedy miss," he teased, glancing up. "Which three would it be?"

"Those." She pointed and watched his face as he followed her direction.

"Orion's belt. You want Orion's belt?"

"Yes, but I prefer to think of them as one star for me, one for you, and the ocean that lies between us."

"No more will there be such a thing," he told her. "There will be nothing to ever separate us again. For tomorrow night we leave London."

We? Had she heard him correctly? "You're taking me with you?"

He nodded, as if the decision was obvious, but there was a strange light in his eyes even as he made the promise, one that suggested he wasn't as confident as he seemed. "Yes, we're leaving." Dash leaned over and kissed her soundly. "You didn't think I would abandon you, did you? Leave you here in London for this Season of yours, only to return at war's end and find you've married some titled fool and that he's been entertaining you with his great big . . ." He grinned, teasing her. "Ah, castle. How would I ever compete with that?"

"I don't want a castle, big or otherwise. Or a fool for a husband. I only want you," she told him.

"You might find the fool a better catch."

Pippin shook her head, stubbornly, furiously. She wanted no other man but this one. "And pirate lessons," she added.

"Yes, your lessons, I promise," he teased, before he turned serious. "But above all, you will always have my heart, Circe. Always. Never forget that." And he sealed his vow with a sweeping kiss.

There wasn't anything else she wanted, she knew as she trembled in his arms, as he carried her back to the bunk and made love to her one last time before the dawn stole entirely across the sky.

How could she want for anything else, she thought as she stood on the balcony and watched him slip through the garden and out into the city.

Pippin glanced at the sky, where the stars were quickly being extinguished by the sun's arrival. For as much as the day would be forever without him, Dash would come to her tonight, at the Setchfield masquerade, and in the crush of the crowd, Lady Philippa Knolles would disappear, and then . . .

She shivered. She would be with Dash for always and there was nothing that would stand in their way.

Two months earlier
Baltimore, Maryland

The cry of a baby, lusty and healthy, pierced the night. The midwife cradled the lad in her arms, and smiled up at the young mother. She was a lithe beauty, too small to bear such a large child, but she'd survived. The midwife had gotten her this far, but as to the days to come, well, that was in God's hands.

" 'Tis a boy," she told her. "A fine, bonny lad."

"A son?" the mother asked, looking up from her pillow, where she lay exhausted and spent from the long, dangerous labor.

"Yes, a son. You've done a fine job for your husband," the midwife replied, shooting a sideways glance at the housekeeper.

The child is well, but the lady . . .

The housekeeper took note, smiling a bit too brightly from her post beside the bed. "Oh, aye, the master will be most pleased with ye, madam. A son, indeed. Better treasure than bringing home the entire British navy if you ask me."

The midwife wiped the newborn clean and wrapped him in a tidy linen cloth before handing him over to his mother.

The lady examined the dark, downy hair covering his head, the housekeeper leaning over to look at him as well. Both women smiled at each other.

"He looks like his father," the mother said softly. "Perhaps . . . Perhaps, he'll be pleased."

"Of course he will be. And I daresay this little wee one will be as brave and true as the captain, God bless 'im wherever he is," the housekeeper declared, beaming down at the new addition to the household. "What do you plan on calling the wee lad?"

Abigail Dashwell glanced first at her son and then up at the housekeeper. "I plan on naming him after my father." Her fingers gently smoothed over the soft hair on her baby's head, before they fell exhausted to the coverlet. "We'll call you Nathaniel," she whispered to her child. "I know it is what your father would want."

"Oh, aye. Captain Dashwell will be pleased as punch when he comes home and finds you've delivered him such a bonny lad." She shot a furious glance at the midwife, who was muttering a "whenever the hell that is," under her breath, for it was well known about town that Captain Dashwell favored his beloved *Circe* more than his wife. "But I daresay he'll insist the next one be called Thomas, after him."

But the look on the midwife's face suggested that the lady would be lucky to live to see her husband return.

Chapter 9

Aboard the Ellis Anne, *1837*

Pippin watched Dash come toward her, swaying unevenly on his feet, and she braced herself. He might be coming closer with each step, but all she felt was the gulf between them widening.

He came to a stop before her, still wavering in his boots, where once his stance had been ready and sure, confident, nay, arrogantly proud.

The man she'd known, the man she'd loved wasn't anywhere in sight.

Yet that wasn't true. For his eyes, despite being bleary and half shuttered, held a bit of that fire that had always engaged her. His jaw still had the rough-hewn set, his lips in a hard line above that deep cleft, determined and so very sensuous.

And he still kisses the same . . . Oh, if only he didn't.

Pippin shivered and drew her shawl tighter around her shoulders.

He flicked a glance at her, and then his gaze rose to the sky, to a point over her shoulder.

To Orion's belt. Their stars. The ones that still shone despite the broken promises and the lies that lay between them. The wreckage before her was all her fault. This was what she'd done. When she'd married another and left him, she'd done this.

Cut out his heart and left him to live this half life.

"Why the hell did you come here, Lady Gossett?"

It wasn't a question, but an accusation.

She turned to him, the odor of brandy on him rising above the clean salt and rich scent of the sea, a sickly air that made her pull back slightly if only to take a breath.

In that moment her head rebelled against her heart and memories.

She hadn't forced him to drink. She'd managed to live without him. He could have done the same.

Oh, aye. But how would you have done if it had been he who'd left you at Hollindrake House without a hope in hell?

Terrible. She'd have been ruined, nay, worse than ruined.

"You know why," she said, biting back the guilt that prodded her. "Nate brought me."

He laughed, a wicked sort of sound that mocked her calm assertion.

And well she deserved so for giving such an answer, half truth that it was.

"No," he said, drawing closer. "Why did you come here, my lady?"

My lady. She cringed as if he'd raised his hand to her. Yet something in his mocking tone snapped her discomfort, and she turned to face him. He wanted the truth? He wanted to know why she'd come? Well, she'd tell him and let him see how it felt to be made to feel so demmed uncomfortable. To be mocked.

"Because I never stopped loving you, Captain Dashwell."

"Pity your husband," he said, glancing up at the sky. "Did he know?"

"Of course he did." Her hands clenched at her sides. "It is quite possible to love twice, Dash. Obviously you did." She tipped her head over to the top deck where Nate stood by the wheel. "You must have loved someone else. Enough to marry her and have a child with her."

But a small part of her, a sliver she wasn't too proud to admit to, felt a bit of jealousy over this other woman. Who was this lady, the one who'd held Dash's heart as Pippin had? Whom had he turned to, loved, even married when Pippin was lost to him?

Oh, that is not the point, Pippin. Whoever she was, she is gone, as is your husband.

"I never stopped carrying you in my heart, Dash." She pressed her lips together and stopped the words that had nearly followed.

Saw your eyes every day staring up at me . . .

She closed her lashes and shook off that truth. There was laying out the truth and then there was the whole truth.

Pippin wasn't about to tell this man, this stranger, the entire truth.

But that didn't stop her faltering speech. "Dash,

I never stopped wondering . . . wondering what had become of you, what would have become of us if only . . ."

"If only you hadn't gotten married to another man?" His bitterness washed over her and brought with it another wave of brandy.

Good God, the man could light a bonfire with his breath.

"Bah!" She sputtered, throwing up her hands and walking around him, if only to stand upwind of him. "Will you forget my marriage to Gossett? I certainly don't regret it, because quite frankly it was what kept you alive."

"Kept me alive?" Now it was his turn to scoff. "You should have left me to hang," he told her. "Let me die a hero."

"Which time?" she asked, elbows jutting out to her sides. "When you were locked in Marshalsea Prison or in the stable at Hollindrake House destined for the noose?"

"Both."

She shook her head. "I could no more do that than I could have stopped loving you." He turned from her and gazed out over the waves, not looking up toward the sky. She caught hold of him and turned him around. "I had no choice but to save you. Both times. And you know why." She paused and fought back the tears that threatened to spill down her cheeks. "It was all my fault you got arrested in the first place. If it hadn't been for me, you would have never been in that ballroom to begin with and we both know that."

The Setchfield Masquerade Ball
London, 1814

Pippin stood in the middle of the crush that packed the Duke of Setchfield's ballroom and tried not to fidget. Her mask itched, the golden rays meant to represent the goddess Circe were too heavy for her head, and her gown a bit too risqué for her taste.

She glanced down at the diaphanous dress, which her cousin Tally had assured her would make her the most sought-after woman at the ball, and wished she didn't stand out quite so much.

For she was garnering too much attention, and her plan with Dash was to slip out of the ball unnoticed and be well gone from London before Tally or Felicity realized she was missing.

But here it was nearly midnight and Dash was nowhere to be found. For the thousandth time this night, Pippin searched the room for any sign of her lover.

Her lover. She shivered at the very notion of it. Such a scandalous, so very ruinous thing, but she cared not. She loved Dash, and after tonight they'd be together forever.

A randy-looking Charles the Second wandered past and winked lasciviously at her, and then, to her horror, he stopped and came back, taking her hand in his and bringing it to his soft, wet lips.

"My dearest goddess! Divine beauty! Glorious ray of delight! I declare I would make you my queen if you would but give me one word of kindness."

She had to imagine it wasn't a word of kindness he

was seeking. "Hasn't Charles a queen already? Catherine of Braganza, I believe," Pippin said, plucking her hand free and wishing she'd brought along the baby pig she'd wanted to have with her costume just so she could hand it off to the rude fellow.

Perhaps with a pig in hand, he'd take a hint.

"Ah, as smart as you are fair!" he said, moving closer, "I shall have to keep a close eye on you."

Then all of a sudden he made a squealing noise, rather like a pig, his hands grabbing his large bottom. When he whirled around, still clutching his ass, there stood behind him a pirate in a large plumed hat, a black domino, and pistols stuck in the leather braces that crossed his chest—more to the point, twirling a dagger in his hand, looking more than willing to use it.

Again.

Dash! Pippin nearly called out, but remembered their need for secrecy and instead greeted him with a glowing smile. He'd come to rescue her.

"Shove off," he told the pretender to the throne, pushing the man aside.

"I do say, how high-handed. I was only—" King Charles began to stammer, even as he rubbed his rump.

"Leaving," Dash finished for him, taking Pippin's fingers in his, the warmth and strength of his touch sending a bolt of desire through her limbs.

Oh, it is him. He's come for me, she wanted to sing.

"Circe, my angel," he said, brushing his lips over her ear. "I'm so sorry I'm late. Do you know how hard it is to find just the perfect costume?"

His touch sent delicious tendrils of desire down her spine.

"I do," she said. "And I must say, Sir Pirate, yours is perfect."

"As is the lady beneath your glorious crown, my delightful Circe," he replied, sweeping off his hat and bowing before her.

The musicians had paused for a few minutes, but were even now returning to their instruments and striking the first notes of a new dance.

Dash didn't even ask, he didn't need to. He led her out onto the floor and they joined the assembly. She wondered where he'd learned the steps or such elegant manners, but nothing would surprise her about Dash. Nothing in the least.

Out of the corner of her eye, she spied her cousin Felicity, leaving with their footman, Thatcher, and she wondered if he was finally going to tell her the truth about his identity. But then again, it wasn't her concern any longer. Her cousin would find her heart's desire with her unlikely beau, just as Pippin had every confidence she would be with hers.

As the music drew to a close, Dash angled her toward a door and they slipped outside into the garden behind the house. Snow lined the walks, which had been brushed clean for the party, showing the outlines of a knot garden.

Overhead, the stars sparkled brightly, as they rarely did in London, but as Dash had said before, the storms of the last few days had cleared away the usual cloud of coal smoke that divided the city from the sky above.

In the cold, crisp air, Pippin shivered in her sheer dress. Now she saw the real problem with this gown. It wasn't such a wise choice for a lady about to make an escape.

Not that she was cold for long. Dash tucked her into his arms and kissed her, his lips covering hers, his tongue tangling with hers, hungrily, anxiously, as if he was as filled with desire as she was.

His large dark coat encircled her, surrounding her with his warmth, and his hands caressed her, warmed her bare arms, pulled her closer until she was right up against him, could feel the thick, hard length of his rod.

And this time when she shivered it was for an entirely different reason.

Oh, why weren't they far from London right now?

In a softly lit room in some country inn, tangled and naked in a cozy bed, where they would have all the hours they needed to explore each other's bodies, each other's needs.

"Come along, Circe," he said, pulling back from her, his eyes smoky with passion. "We'll have all the time we want for this"—his finger drew a slow line along the edge of her jaw to her lips—"when we are well away."

She slipped her hand inside his warm one and started to follow him, when from inside the room, the musicians began another song. A waltz.

Pippin faltered. The sweet, rich notes taunted her already trembling body, and she looked over her shoulder as the couples began to take the floor.

"What is it?" Dash asked.

"A waltz," she said, her gaze still fixed on the

crowded room behind them. "I've never danced one." She paused for a second. "Well, not at a ball." Or even with a man. She and her cousins practiced together, but that was hardly the same.

And since she'd made love with Dash, lost her innocence to him, the strains of the music plucked a different desire from her.

Now she understood how being held so utterly close by a man, the swaying steps and the rich notes were nothing more than a prelude to something far more intimate.

Dash looked up at the crowded ballroom as well and hesitated. "We must be away, Pippin. We dare not wait too long."

He smiled at her and started for the gate again, but her steps remained heavy and she just couldn't shake her desire to dance just one waltz with him.

Never mind that he was right, never mind that he was a wanted man, and that they should have left some time ago, but . . .

He paused and looked at her. "You really want one more dance, don't you?"

Pippin nodded. She was being utterly selfish, but she wanted to waltz with him just once. After years of being penniless, of being whispered about by the other girls at school for her less-than-fashionable gowns and her coltish limbs, she wanted just once to be the most beautiful woman at the party.

Dancing with the most handsome of men. To be the envy of all and then disappear into the night, slipping into obscurity, like a veritable Cinderella.

And to his credit, he could see how much it meant to her; he might not understand it, but he knew it was important. With a resigned sigh and a playful tweak of her nose, they returned to the ballroom and began to waltz.

Pippin beamed with joy and let the music and the attention from the other dancers fill her heart. It was a heady thing, to have all that attention, to be admired and wondered about—for surely no one knew exactly who she was, and that didn't matter.

It was about being someone other than the poor, unwanted orphan of a penniless and dissolute earl.

How could anything ruin this moment?

For it was naught but a prelude to her new and exciting life.

Viscount Gossett deplored soirees and balls. And masquerades even more. His valet had assured him he looked perfectly elegant in this costume—Robin Hood, of all things—but egads, there were about a dozen or more fools gadding about in the same sort of rigging, and all of them looked like veritable idiots.

He could only assume he looked the same.

Now, he wouldn't be here at all if it hadn't been for his aunt prodding him to set up his nursery. Not that she'd really had to remind him about his duty; he knew full well he needed to marry and secure an heir.

Wasn't he here in London for the Season? And if he was honest, it was what he wanted. A lady to share his life and his heart. Not that he'd admit such a sentimental notion to anyone, but there it was.

He did want to find someone. And he held a certainty that when she came across his path, he'd know her. In the meantime, he'd tolerate looking like a

Covent Garden comedy in this unbearable costume.

He did, however, make a note to pay more attention to the costumes Baxby ordered up.

He glanced around the room and spied a man in a plain black domino coming toward him. He set aside the moment of envy when he realized he knew the fellow.

"Larken! I say there, is that you?"

His old school friend Baron Larken pulled to a stop beside him. There were all sorts of rumors floating around Town about Larken, not that Gossett paid any heed to them.

The baron was a good sort at heart, and that was all that mattered. Served his country with the Foreign Office, Gossett knew, and had done some devilish things over there on the Continent.

A man could be excused some odd nighttime rambles and shabby manners for having given so much for King and Country.

Larken glanced at his friend's costume, and, for the first time in months, he grinned.

Gossett didn't take it personally. "Dreadful, isn't it?"

"Could be worse," Larken said. "Could be like Twistleton over there and have three feathers sticking up from your hat and bear a frightening resemblance to the Duchess of Dorney." Both men laughed as they looked over at their hapless friend, and just then Gossett's heart stopped.

For just over Twistleton's shoulder a lady whirled by on the dance floor. Never mind that her eyes seemed destined for only the man who held her, Gossett's heart slammed into his chest.

Her. It was her.

Fair and lithe, she swayed on the arms of the pirate who danced with her.

"Larken," he managed to say past his suddenly dry mouth. "Do you know who she is?"

"Who?" the baron asked, his gaze raking over the crowd as if he was looking for someone as well.

"Her," Gossett said, nodding toward his future wife. Pirate or no, she was going to be his. "The pretty blond chit, dressed like a goddess." And aptly so, for she was a veritable goddess.

"Which one?" Larken muttered, his gaze still sweeping the room.

"The one on the arm of the pirate on the dance floor."

Larken turned, and Gossett swore he'd never seen a man go so deadly still. The only thing that moved was his jaw as it dropped open. Then his eyes glittered dangerously and he reached inside his jacket and pulled out a pistol and aimed it right at her.

Or rather at the fellow who held her.

"Captain Thomas Dashwell," Larken shouted over the noise of the crowd and the musicians. "I arrest you in the name of the king."

And then all hell broke loose.

Aboard the Ellis Anne, *1837*

"Blast and damnation," Dash exclaimed, pushing off the railing and staring at her. "You think my arrest was your fault?"

"Decidedly so," she insisted. "If I hadn't been such

a fool and pleaded with you to return for that waltz, we would have been long gone from London, and your arrest, all of it would be naught but another page in one of those silly plays my cousin and I used to write."

She thought it all her fault? Dash couldn't believe his ears. Then Dash couldn't help himself. He laughed. Actually, he roared. "You think that was your fault? Yours and yours alone?" He waved her off. "More the fool you. I knew exactly the risks I was taking that night."

More than you know of, my dear, sweet Pippin.

"My arrest that night was because I was an arrogant fool." He raked his hand through his hair. "I was Captain Thomas Dashwell, the scourge of the Atlantic, and I was too full of my own myth that I hadn't the wits to run to ground when I found myself marooned in enemy territory. I struck up an affair with you and I flaunted myself in the house of a man who knew me better than any other man in London. Domino or no, I should no more have been in that house or within fifty miles of Mayfair that night." He paused again, moving back to the rail and clutching it with both hands. With the ship to steady him, he was able to tell her what he'd been too cowardly to tell her back then. "And I should never have taken up with you. It was naught but an affair that went awry."

As he expected, she swayed, as if she'd been lashed by a gale.

"You don't mean that," she whispered back.

He took a step closer to her and wished like hell he hadn't had that last bit of brandy. He'd be steadier on his feet. Which was a lie in itself, for he hadn't been steady on his feet in years.

"Lady Gossett, contrary to what you believe, I have never held you responsible for my arrogance or my arrests." Then he reached out and tipped up her chin so she looked him in the eye.

Ignoring the fact that she smelled like a rose garden and her skin was still the softest bit of heaven he'd ever touched, he lied with the most unholy conviction he'd ever possessed.

And that was saying something.

"I never loved you. You were a soft, willing refuge on a cold winter night, but nothing more. I would have left you on some forgotten shore when I tired of you, so you should be thankful that Larken recognized me that night. For it saved you from a life on the docks seeking the favors of men far more deserving of a drowning than the heaven of your willing thighs, even for the coins it would cost them."

She sucked in a deep, indignant breath and slapped his hand away.

At least she hadn't balled it up and hit him like one of her harridan cousins might have done. Just as he deserved.

No, this was better than the truth.

"Dash, you don't mean any of this," she persisted.

He nearly groaned. Damn her to hell, she'd always been a stubborn bit of muslin.

"I know you loved me," she continued. "I've dreamed of nothing else for all these years. You were my hero, the only one I've ever known."

"Then you have wasted your time, madam, because

I am no woman's hero. If you can't see that for yourself, then you are a worse fool than I ever assumed."
He turned on one heel and walked with every ounce
of dignity he possessed to where his son stood. He
looked up at Nate and said in a loud, clear voice,
"Now where the hell did you hide my bottle?"

As Dash descended the gangway for his cabin, bottle
in hand, Pippin crossed the deck. Her boots clicked
over the planks, and each determined, furious step
should have been warning enough for her quarry.

"How dare you bring me here, Mr. Dashwell,"
she said to Nate. "There is nothing I can do for him.
Nothing anyone can do. Whatever possessed you to
believe that I could help that . . . that . . ." Her hand
fluttered in the air as she tried to find the right word
to describe Dash.

Shipwreck . . . flotsam . . . bilge rat.

"Your father," she finally finished, because she
wasn't going to say what was in her heart.

*The man I loved. Loved, being the point that
needed to be emphasized. I loved him.*

But not anymore.

His loud, angry speech taunted everything she'd
ever held dear. Even now his cutting words echoed in
the pitying glances of the sailors who'd witnessed her
humiliation.

*You were a soft, willing refuge on a cold winter
night, but nothing more.*

Nate nodded to one of the other mates to take the
wheel and took her by the elbow and led her to the
back of the ship where they could speak privately.

Pippin caught hold of the rail, as Dash had earlier,

and held on to it. The ship beneath her feet seemed a solid sanctuary as her life tumbled into ruins.

"You helped him once before," he said quietly, not looking at her, but at the churning wake the clipper left behind.

Pippin shook her head. "That was different. I was different." She paused and looked Nate directly in the eye. "He was different."

The young man let out a sigh, a sort of resignation to the truth that tore at Pippin.

Well, it wasn't as if she wanted to see Dash like this, angry, belligerent . . . cruel. But what could Nathaniel expect her to do? What had he thought bringing her here would do other than raise his father's ire to new levels of arrogance?

And if Pippin believed Nate was giving up after his father's latest bout of ill-temper, as she was quite willing to do, she was very wrong.

"He still loves you," he insisted. "He never stopped."

Now it was her turn to push off the rail and cross her arms over her chest. "I don't believe that. Did you hear what he just said to me?"

Nate nodded. "I fear there are few who didn't."

She closed her eyes and shuddered. Wonderful. She didn't care that it was unlikely the ship's crew had any contacts with the gossip columnist at the *Morning Post*, but she still had to face them when she came above deck.

"He doesn't mean what he's saying when he's like that," Nate continued.

"Whyever do you continue to apologize for him?" Pippin said, rounding on the young sailor. "He is a grown man, and knows exactly what he is saying."

Nate shook his head stubbornly. "No, 'tis the drink that has made him like that. My da, the one I know, isn't like that at all. Not the man who loves you."

"No," Pippin told him, shaking her head furiously. "He doesn't love me. Not anymore." She took hold of the rail again. "Never did."

"Then why does he keep an old pair of red wool socks tucked inside his sea chest?"

Pippin froze. The question sent a raft of shivers down her spine. Red wool socks?

He pressed his point. "One of them is unfinished, the knitting pins still holding the stitches. All these years he's held on to them, waiting for the woman who knit them to return to his life and take up what was left unfinished."

Pippin tried to breathe. Tried to blot the image of them out of her mind.

"You knit them for him, didn't you?"

She couldn't speak, only nod.

"Mr. Hardy told me to look for them and if Da still had them, that would tell me what I needed to know." Nate leaned closer. "That he still loves you, and that whatever is left unfinished between the two of you must be completed if you are to save him."

Shaking her head, Pippin was still trying to recover from the notion that Dash had kept the socks she'd started for him. "I can't do what you ask, Mr. Dashwell. I'm not the same woman."

Instead of taking her answer to heart, the younger version of Dash grinned at her with all the audacity that made him a Dashwell through and through. "I think that lady is still inside you, Lady Gossett. If she wasn't, you wouldn't be standing on this deck."

* * *

Pippin returned to her cabin just as the first bit of dawn started to rise behind them.

Nate's words haunted her thoughts. *Then why does he keep an old pair of red wool socks tucked inside his sea chest?*

The revelation had knocked the air out of her. Dash still had the socks she'd knit for him? The ones Aunt Minty had taught her to knit, if only to while away the hours as the two of them had devised a plan to get Dash out of Marshalsea Prison, where he had been locked away after his arrest at the Setchfield ball.

Each stitch had held a little prayer that she would find some way to save him before the king's justice gained the upper hand and Dash's days were ended.

Before the second sock was finished, she'd come up with a daring plot. One that had thwarted the Royal Navy and the king's best agents, and left behind a myth still told to this day in the bowels of Southwark of an angel in a red silk gown who could save a man from the darkest depths of prison.

If he was worthy enough . . .

Dropping down to her knees before her own trunk, she opened it and reached inside. Deeper and deeper she pushed her hand until her fingers came up against the smooth, cold finish of a silk gown.

She needn't have brought it, she realized, for she wouldn't be wearing it. Even if she dared, she doubted the glorious red gown and its legendary powers could save Thomas Dashwell from the hell she'd tossed him into.

Chapter 10

Pippin awoke the next day to a bright ray of sunshine lighting her room.

"Botheration," she muttered, rolling over and pulling the coverlet with her to blot out the light.

But the sunshine persisted, warming the room, and with the gentle sway of the ship continuing to nudge her, she muttered another curse and threw the coverlet off and got up.

After getting dressed, she surveyed her little prison and swore again.

Her knitting sat discarded next to her abandoned book—a romance her cousin Tally said was a delightful romp. Pippin had her suspicions that Tally had written it and published yet another book under a pseudonym. The diplomatic corps rather frowned on wives with a "literary bent," so Tally wrote her books with Larken's blessings, despite the risk to his career, and published them under her nom de plume, Aramintha Follifoot, using their old chaperone's name as a memorial to the good woman.

Pippin grinned. Aunt Minty would have loved the notoriety the books stirred in proper circles, old romantic that she was.

But even the lure of one of Tally's adventures wasn't enough to keep her in her room—well out of Dash's path.

"I paid for my passage," she said, a frisson of determination running down her spine.

She knew what Aunt Minty would have said. *Damn his idiotic hide, dearling. You go have your adventure.*

Her adventure . . .

Pippin had spent most of her life dreaming of such notions. Sailing to faraway places, smelling the spices of the East in their native markets, seeing the wonders of the world by standing at their foundations, not in prints and secondhand accounts in the *Lady's Magazine.* Well, they still had a good twenty days of sailing left, according to Nathaniel, and she certainly wasn't going to spend it down here.

She caught up her bonnet, her one nod to fashion, for it certainly wouldn't do to arrive in Baltimore all freckled; it was going to be hard enough to explain how it was that a respectable English widow, and a viscountess to boot, was traveling without even so much as a lady's maid.

Oh, yes, she mused as she went above deck, she'd found herself an adventure.

The promise of sun hadn't been exaggerated, for the sky bloomed in brilliant blue all the way to the horizon, broken only by a string of white clouds floating along high over the waves and whitecaps.

She smiled and crossed the deck to the railing. Overhead, all the sails seemed to be aloft, the clipper using every bit of sheet it possessed to catch the breeze and fly over the waves.

Brent always said that Britain might dominate the sea, but the Americans would rule the waves, for they weren't afraid to run up every bit of canvas they could rig and run with the waves like a herd of unruly dolphins.

She turned and looked again for Nate, but he was nowhere to be found; in his place at the wheel stood the other mate, Mr. Clemens, she recalled.

All around the *Ellis Anne* and in the lines, the crew worked, checking the rigging, cleaning the decks, keeping the ship in order.

Dash had once told her that the reason he'd been able to take so many ships during the war, larger ones, faster ones, even ones that had him outgunned and outmanned—was that he kept his ship in the best working order, sailed with men who knew their business and minded the ship as they would their mother's immortal soul.

It seemed some things hadn't changed.

While she'd heard John lament time and time again over the sad and sorry state of the Royal Navy's sailors, Dash's crew seemed a decent, hardworking lot, right down to the lad, Finn, who had brought her tray once or twice and was even now having a bite of something over on a coil of rope not far from where she stood.

Not that they weren't casting looks in her direction, some of them openly staring at her, but she had to imagine that having a sole female passenger was a bit of an oddity, even for an American ship.

She glanced again at the sky, and then to her dismay her stomach growled, in a most unladylike manner. Loudly protesting her lack of breakfast, and now, nuncheon.

Finn giggled, as any young boy would at such a noise.

When she glanced in his direction, he covered his mouth and looked away, embarrassed at his indiscretion.

"You heard that?" she asked, smiling at him. She rather liked the lad, for he reminded her of John when he was that age, finding great humor in every bodily noise a person could produce.

"Iffin you don't mind me saying, ma'am," he said, a wee bit of grin turning his lips, "they most likely heard that in China."

Pippin laughed. "I suppose that might be because you forgot to bring me my tray this morning."

He bounded up from where he sat. "Oh, no, ma'am. 'Twas Mr. Dashwell's orders. Said not to disturb you this morning. Said you and the cap'n had a bit of row last night." Finn paused and bit his lips, obviously realizing he'd probably said more than he should.

Pippin rocked on her heels. "Did he now? How kind of him."

Finn reached over to his tin plate, which sat on the other coil of rope. "Biscuit, ma'am? The cook just made 'em and there isn't a weevil one."

She was of half a mind to refuse, but he seemed so earnest and in need of making up for his gaffe that she took the proffered bounty and sat down on a coil opposite and began to eat. Besides, she was hungry, and the biscuit, just as Finn had promised, was freshly baked and quite good.

As they ate, Finn chattered on about the cook's complaints over some matter and a joke someone had played on Mr. Dashwell during the crossing to England, while Pippin listened intently. To her ears, the lad seemed a bit lonely and maybe even homesick, as he spoke in glowing terms about returning to Baltimore and his mother's fine pies.

"The berries will be ripe when I return and me mam will make a berry pie that melts in your mouth," he told her. "Won't she be surprised when I eat an entire one all by myself."

"Yes, quite," Pippin murmured, but her attention had been moved to watching the crew. The men had taken to filing past her, eyeing her and slanting curious glances at her as if they weren't quite sure what was sitting on their deck, a lady or an albatross.

"Finn?"

"Yes, ma'am?"

"Why are the men staring at me?"

He paused, his third biscuit just in front of his mouth. "Oh, they know who you are, but some of them don't think it's really you." With that said, he bit into his lunch and continued eating with youthful exuberance.

She closed her eyes and shook her head at that explanation. "You mean because I'm a viscountess?"

"A what?" he asked.

"A viscountess. Are they staring because they've never seen a lady before?"

"Oh, they've seen ladies afore," he said with a wave and an innocence of the difference between a lady and one of those ladies. "But they never thought they'd see you."

"Me? I assure you, Finn, I am no one special."

Finn snorted. "Oh, aye, you are, ma'am. You're the lady in red."

Pippin paused this time, biscuit halfway to her mouth and her jaw gaping. "The who?"

She needn't have asked, because she knew whom he meant.

"The lady in red," he repeated. "You know. The lady who saved the cap'n from hanging. Mr. Hardy told me all about you afore he died. Most of the crew has heard the story. 'A finer and braver mort never lived,' is what Mr. Hardy used to say." The boy slanted a grin at her. "Never thought I'd meet a legend. Besides the cap'n, iffin you don't mind me saying."

"I don't really know what you are talking about," she said in that practiced way of Society that meant, *I prefer not to recall such an event.*

But Finn hadn't the least notion of polite conversation and continued on. "Oh, sure you do. It goes like this," he said, settling in to tell the story she knew all too well.

Southwark, London
June 1814

"Come along there," the guard said, shoving his prisoner forward. "We 'aven't got all night." The thick chains rattled at the shackles on Dash's arms and legs as he shuffled through the darkness of Marshalsea Prison toward what fate the English had in store for him, he knew not.

But he could guess. And it wouldn't be a warm bath and clean clothes that awaited him at the end of this unexpected rousing from his bed in the middle of the night. No, after five months in prison, he could guess where they were finally taking him.

"Where to this time, gentlemen?" he asked anyway, feeling a bit light-headed. "Hmm . . . let me guess, the king has invited me for a late supper."

"Oh, there's to be a dinner all right." One of the guards laughed.

"Close your trap," the officer in charge ordered.

A naval officer. Dashwell hadn't noticed him before, but then again, going from the pitch-black of his cell to the corridor—even as poorly lit as it was—had left him blinking like an owl.

Not that officers of His Majesty's Royal Navy were unusual at Marshalsea. Though primarily a debtors' prison, the Southwark stronghold also claimed a small, highly secure section where the Admiralty kept their most dangerous offenders, with Dash being their biggest catch.

The reckless, or rather, ruthless Captain Dashwell, as the Admiralty Court had described him. He supposed it hadn't helped his case that he'd grinned unrepentantly at the judges when he'd been bestowed that lofty title.

Instead of turning left toward the common room, the guard shoved him outside. This was the first time he'd taken a clean breath of air or seen the sky in months, and he inhaled deeply. It might be the foul, stagnant air of Southwark, but it was fresher than the bowels of this bloody hole they'd tossed him into.

They moved out through a courtyard at the rear of the prison, and then out the gates into the maze of alleys that ran behind the prison and spread out into the bowels of Southwark like a tangled web.

Escape . . . escape . . . his pirate's heart clamored.

Oh, yes, and how, Dash? His legs, weak from lack of use, wouldn't take him very far, and where he'd been shot in the shoulder at the Setchfield ball still festered a bit. He ached and swayed in his poor boots and was, much to his chagrin, too weak to make it much farther than toppling into the offal and mud that filled the streets.

Making things ever more difficult to discern was the fog swirling around them, but a few steps more revealed what they had in store for him—a black, fortified carriage sat waiting.

Such a dismal vehicle was used for only one thing. Carrying away the condemned.

For all his bravado, for all his heroics, his arrogance, it was one thing to joke about your end, and another to see it sitting before you. A chill ran down his spine, and for the first time in years, Thomas Dashwell knew what it was to be held in the grip of terror. He stumbled to a halt.

So they'd decided his fate without so much as a by-your-leave or bothering to tell him.

Well, he supposed, they were telling him now, and he forced his feet to move before any of them noticed his hesitation. Before he gave them a story to tell to their mates.

Oh, aye, and ye should have seen 'is face when 'e

spied what we 'ad in store for 'im. Weren't so brave then, the bloody coward.

Dashwell straightened, and resigned himself that this was the end. Not the one he'd often envisioned, or the one he would have preferred—standing on the deck of his ship, cannons blazing, his men cheering as they took another ship.

But what man ever had the choice when it came to the end of his days?

Yet if they intended to hang him, why move him in the middle of the night, and with so many guards? Even the driver sat hunched over in his high perch, hat tugged down to his nose and collar up, so as not to call attention to himself.

It was as if they didn't want anyone to know what they were about.

"Why all the secrecy, Lieutenant?" he asked the officer in charge.

"None of your demmed business," the man said, his voice crisp and surly. "Now get in there," he ordered, nodding to the open door in the back.

Dash took one last deep breath of the night's damp air, just as a voice cut through the silence of the night.

"Oh, aye, what 'ave we 'ere?" squawked an ancient old bawd, coming out of the foul, dreary mists, basket in hand and a ratty old shawl arranged across her shoulders as if it were silk. She came into the circle of light the lamp hanging over the end of the carriage afforded. "Now, there, good sirs, why 'ang such a 'andsome fellow?"

"Get away, you old hag," the lieutenant ordered. "This is none of your business." And when she didn't move he went to strike her, but his motion was interrupted by the arrival of another woman.

"No, stop!" she called out, coming out the mist like an angel from on high. While everything around them was dank and dirty and dark, it seemed she was of the mist, ethereal and fair, her red gown clinging to her richly curved body like the marble on a statue. Her long blond hair hung loose all the way down to her waist, and she moved with an undulating sway that promised to make every sensual dream a man had ever imagined come true.

She even wore a red domino, concealing her face, not that one of the guards was looking up there, not when her gown left nothing to the imagination.

One of the men, the one who'd made the joke about his last meal, made a strangled sound at the sight of this vision. Probably the first time he'd seen a real lady, rather than the drabs and whores he was used to.

Dash had a similar reaction. For after he'd gotten over the shock of seeing her, he tried to draw a breath and found his throat was closed, his chest tightened into a knot.

Oh, no! Crazy, impetuous minx! What the hell was she thinking?

"Lieutenant, I believe you are making a mistake," she purred as she drew closer. "This man belongs to me."

She smiled at Dash, the blue eyes behind the mask twinkling with mischief.

"Don't do this," he begged her. "Leave now while you can."

"But I must do this," she told him. "And you knew I would come. How could I not?"

Foolish, wretched chit. She was going to get herself killed. Why, not even two of his best men would take such a risk, not with these odds—six of the king's men against her and her aged friend.

She moved closer still, her breasts pushing up nearly out of the low line of her bodice, gleaming white and shimmering in the light. "Gentlemen, couldn't we come to some sort of an arrangement? A trade, perhaps?"

Another of the guards had the same strangled reaction—but this time Dash glanced over at the fellow to find that he wasn't choking over the sight of this vision, but because a giant of fellow had come up from the shadows and had his hands around the guard's throat.

When the guard slumped forward, his assailant tossed him aside like a rag doll, down onto the pavement next to the other guard who'd also met a similar fate.

Dash's eyes widened. Good God! He knew that fellow.

"Get away from here!" the lieutenant ordered pointing the way to High Street. "Or you'll find yourself hanging beside him. Dobbins, take this woman into irons if she doesn't leave this very instant."

But there was no reply from Dobbins, for he lay on the street with the other two guards. The last two guards on either side of Dash finally looked away from the woman in red to discover their companions lying on the cobbles.

"Christ sakes," one of them murmured, fumbling for his pistol.

Dash froze, for the last thing he wanted to see was his lovely savior die at his feet, but once again, she surprised him.

"Now," she said, with all the authority that the lieutenant had lacked. She moved forward quickly, past Dash and straight for the officer, pulling out her hand, which no one had noticed tucked innocently into the folds of her gown, and shoved the pistol she'd concealed there right up into the man's nose. "Move, twitch, call for help, and it will be the last thing you do."

But the fellow hadn't risen in the ranks of the navy without having a bit of backbone, and he called anyway.

Well, stammered a bit. "D-d-do s-s-something," he ordered his remaining men.

But what could they do? The old hag had moved just as quickly as his Circe, pulling a large pistol out of her basket, and the giant fellow had lurched forward, felling the other guard with one perfectly aimed punch.

And to Dash's amazement, the driver sat up now, pistol in hand, and had it aimed as well at the last guard.

"Get in," Circe told the lieutenant, nodding toward the carriage, while she plucked the keys to Dash's manacles from the belt loop of the last guard. "Get in, both of you," she repeated, as she also took up the fallen fellows' pistols, pointing one of them at the two men. "You can get in there alive or end your days in this gutter."

That was enough for the guard. He scurried into the carriage and took a seat in the darkest corner. The lieutenant still hesitated, until Dash said, "Don't be a fool, man. My life is not worth yours. Besides, do you want him"— he nodded toward the fellow cowering in the carriage—"writing the report of how your life ended?"

The lieutenant cursed, then did as he was told, climbing in with an injured air, his career as tattered as the old hag's shawl and the sails of the garbage scows he'd be left to command after this. To add to his injury, the lady plucked his pistol from his belt.

"You'll all hang for this. All of you will," he said, shaking his fist at the lot of them. "Dashwell, you'll not escape the king's justice."

"I will today," he said, as his manacles were unlocked and he gained the one thing he never thought he'd see—his freedom.

It took but a minute for the unconscious guards to be added to the carriage, tossed inside at the lieutenant's feet by the giant fellow as if they were naught but bales of smuggled silk, and the door closed with a heavy thud, the lock clanking shut with a defiant rattle.

Circe grinned at her conspirators, then strode around the carriage and called up to the driver, "Go on now."

Slapping the reins, the driver took off at a slow, languid pace, making it look like the prisoner was off to his noose exactly as planned.

Meanwhile, the hag reached out and cupped Circe's chin, saying, "Take care. I will not be pleased if I discover you were caught." Then she grinned at

Dashwell and followed her giant companion into the mists from which they'd appeared.

Holy Christ! He knew that woman. No hag, but the wife of . . . No, he didn't even want to think it could be her.

Circe took his hand then, her warm fingers stopping the questions rising to his lips. She led him away in another direction, but he wasn't distracted for long.

"What the devil do you think—"

"Shhh," she warned, grabbing up a cloak she must have stashed earlier in a dank pile of crates and barrels, and throwing it over her shoulders. It fell all the way to her feet and covered her costume. "We must be away unnoticed." And so they continued their mad dash through the byways and alleys of London's infamous district.

Dash was no fool, and as much as he doubted they'd make it any farther than the city's gates—hell, he didn't think he could make London Bridge in his current state—when he looked into her glowing, intelligent eyes, shining with a victorious light, he knew there was a chance, slim as it was, that this half-witted plan might work.

"Whatever were you thinking?" he said, as he took his vision in red into his arms and kissed her as they waited to cross a wide street.

"That I love you more than life itself," she whispered back.

"You'll regret all this, for it will cost you your life," he said, smoothing her hair away from her face and gently untying the domino covering her face. "You'll regret what you've done for me," he said, as they slipped into the shadows and made their escape from the lofty and dark shadow of Marshalsea.

"Not tonight," she whispered back. "For tonight you are mine. Always mine."

Aboard the Ellis Anne, *1837*

"A fine story," Pippin said, getting up and brushing the crumbs from her gown. "But I am not that woman."

Not that he believed her. The boy glanced up at her and winked. A cheeky gesture that said he'd keep her secret.

So much for her decline into respectable obscurity, as her children wanted for her, she thought as she escaped Finn and his excellent storytelling.

Escaped her past.

Then to her shock, he rose and followed her as well. "I asked Mr. Hardy who the old hag was, and the giant, and the driver, but he didn't know. So I suppose I'd best be asking you, ma'am. Who were they?"

She had to admire his cheek and his persistence. Who were they? Looking down into his expectant gaze, she realized he had every hope of gaining an answer.

Not that he was going to get one. Why, such an admission was still treason. Would ruin a notable diplomatic career—for it was bad enough Lord Larken's wife wrote romantic novels, but to discover that she'd driven a prison van kidnapping an officer and marine of His Majesty's Navy? Or how would it taint the dotage of Lady John Tremont, a highly regarded society matron, to discover she'd had a hand in the notorious escape?

And the giant of a fellow? Pippin glanced away, her eyes growing misty at the thought of him.

Bruno Jones had gone to his Maker several years ago, but he'd never been one to turn down the opportunity for "a bit o' fun and the chance to crack a skull or two." That night, his strength and cunning had been their greatest asset.

They'd all helped Pippin in her wild plan to free Dash because she loved him, and they loved her in turn. That, and Lady John—Mad Jack's outwardly proper wife—had averred that hanging such a fine smuggler as Dash made not a lick of sense, not with the war drawing to a close. Then the illicit trade in brandy and silks would be back, and Lady John saw a future partnership with the daring captain.

Being the daughter of a cit, she knew a bit about business matters.

"I think such a question is better left unanswered," Pippin told the hopeful boy before her. "It makes your story more mysterious."

And safer for all those concerned.

Finn pressed his lips together, his little freckled cheeks rosy from the breeze, his gaze narrowed as he studied the waves.

What an imp, she thought, for she could see he was concocting another way to chisel the information out of her.

She reached over and tugged his wool watch cap down over his ears and told him, "Haven't you work to see to? I would hate to see you run afoul of Mr. Dashwell."

The boy nudged the deck with the toe of his shoe and shrugged. "I suppose so." Finn started off, then turned and glanced over his shoulder. "But I want the rest of the story before we get to Baltimore. I want to hear how the cap'n was saved the second time. How he escaped England, 'cause Mr. Hardy said he didn't know that part, and I'm thinking you do."

She waved him off and tried to smile.

But inside her heart clenched tightly in her chest, for what could she tell him?

Oh, Finn, you are too young to understand about such things. To know what it means to betray the one you love to save his life.

Chapter 11

Two days later, Dash found his way above decks and cursed the sunshine that threatened to blind his bleary eyes. He was either not drunk enough or too hung over.

He couldn't tell the difference any longer.

With his hand shielding his eyes, he surveyed the sails and checked the wind. All was in perfect order.

Not that he expected anything less of Nate. The boy was a better sailor than any man on the seven seas, including himself.

But that spoke more of Abigail's solid Yankee blood in his veins than the Dashwell name he carried. She'd always been a stickler for order and precision.

Yet something wasn't quite right, he realized, shaking off a sense of premonition. He nearly called for one of the men to go aloft and check for nearby ships.

To check for any British frigates bearing down on them.

But he shook off such a thought. *We aren't at war*, he reminded himself.

More's the pity, he mused. Perhaps then he could find himself the hero's death he'd sought so long ago and had continually been thwarted in gaining.

Damn his own luck. He couldn't even manage a decent demise. Most likely end his days a doddering old fool, his family sighing in relief when he finally stuck his spoon in the wall and did the decent thing by going toes up.

Still, he shrugged at the niggle that ran down his spine and he looked back toward England, peering at the horizon, searching for what, he knew not.

Then from around the base of the mainmast, he found his answer.

"Mr. Dashwell says I have to learn and so does Mr. Clemens," the lad Nate had insisted they bring along was saying. "But I don't see why."

Dash frowned. He'd been against bringing young Finn Stafford aboard from the moment Nate had shown up at the docks with the lad in tow. It had been another of Hardy's deathbed ideas, taking the boy to sea and teaching him a trade. Finn's widowed mother had four others at home, and the lad was of an age when he was starting to eat the poor woman out of house and home. Hardy had liked the lad and thought him a bright and likely boy who could grow into a fine mate, even, one day, a captain.

But Dash had his own reasons for not wanting a child aboard. Nate had no idea of the responsibility that came with such a bargain.

What if something happened to the little rapscallion? Dash closed his eyes and tried not to think of it, but the images came to him unbidden. The boy being washed overboard in a storm . . . falling from the rigging and breaking his neck . . . being taken in a strange port before anyone would even notice he'd been snatched.

A thousand and one things could befall a lad at sea and if one of them did, God have mercy on them, for Dash would be the one who had to return to Baltimore and tell the Widow Stafford that her eldest son, her pride and joy, was lost forever.

He'd seen a mother's tears and anguished grief before, had offered halting words of comfort when there were none that could help, no excuses to give for such a tragedy, and he had shied away from the responsibility of any other children in his life.

Including his own. But that was another box of troubles entirely.

He took a furtive glance across the deck where Nate stood surveying the sheets and checking the lines. At least his son had had Abigail's parents to see to his upbringing. And Hardy to manage the rest.

It was their steady presence that had made Nate the man he was today. Accomplishments Dash couldn't take any pride in, for he'd had no hand in the matter. His son had come into manhood and stood on his own feet without Dash's guidance or help, and it had left a distance between them that he wasn't proud of.

But then again, a bit of brandy usually dulled that problem as it did most others.

All but one . . .

"Iffin you were to talk to them, ma'am, they might listen," the boy was now pleading.

"Oh, 'tis a very important skill to learn, Finn," a

voice replied. "And if Mr. Dashwell and Mr. Clemens say you need to learn, then learn you must."

Her. Dash straightened, her voice piercing the bottle haze he lived in like a dagger. Since she'd invaded his ship, his life, there was no escaping her. Not up on the deck, not in his dreams.

"But me mam always knits me socks." This was followed by an indignant huff and the soft thud on the deck as a ball of yarn fell and bounced along the smooth planks. Seconds later, Finn followed, gamboling after it like a puppy seeking a stick. "So I don't see why I—"

His voice fell to a stop as he realized his quarry had come to a halt in front of Dash's boot.

"But she isn't here now, so you must try again," she was saying, sitting on a coil of rope with her back to him.

Dash handed the ball of yarn to Finn and nodded for him to return to his lessons.

Knitting.

"Both my children learned how to knit when they were about your age," she was telling Finn, as he settled down beside her again. "And I learned from a wonderful and kind lady, my Aunt Aramintha."

Dash almost laughed. Aunt Minty. He hadn't thought of that cantankerous old harridan in years. Even in her seventies, she'd been able to pinch a purse with some of the best. But Lady Gossett had loved her, loved her as if she were family.

Family . . .

What else had she said? *Both my children learned how to knit . . .*

His gaze shot toward her. She had children. Two

of them. But of course she did. She'd married Gossett and given him the children that they'd planned on having.

He tried not to imagine them, but he couldn't help himself. Perhaps a bonny lass, fair like her mother and with the same keen eyes capable of seeing into a man's soul.

And a son? There he stopped. He had no desire to imagine what Gossett's whelp, the man's heir, was like. Besides, Dash had a son of his own, a young man grown up into a remarkable source of pride. One he'd had without Pippin. Without her love.

But still he couldn't help himself. *They should have been our children*, he wanted to shout. *Ours.*

Oh, aye. Your children. Isn't that a fine one, Hardy whispered across the heavens, over the waves. *She left you, lad . . . Married another . . . 'Cause she knew . . . knew what a poor bargain she'd be making.*

Dash slapped at his ear and shook his head. Damn the man. He'd not only saddled him with Finn Stafford but also persisted in haunting his thoughts, his conscience.

Meanwhile, there was a resigned sigh from Finn, and some quiet moments as the lady settled the knitting pins and yarn into the boy's hands and patiently guided him through a few stitches.

Her boots swung just a few inches above the deck and her hem had edged up, to reveal the hint of red wool socks peeking over the tops of her plain black boots.

Red wool socks. She still wore them. Dash shivered, and not because he was cold, but because he felt as if he'd had his own grave trampled upon.

Red wool socks. A long-lost conversation rose up in his thoughts.

Hardly fashionable, she'd said, holding up the hem of her night rail. *Just plain wool and not silk like, well, like other ladies wear.*

You aren't like other ladies . . .

She still wasn't. Dash glanced back over his shoulder at the gangway that led below, the bottle he had stashed there calling to him.

Forget her . . . forget it all, it beckoned.

"See, it's not so hard," she was saying now that Finn had completed a few successful tries.

"Still, I think me mam does a better job," he said, eyeing the beginnings of a sock, "and it's girl's work, not for a man to be doing."

She laughed. "Girl's work! My heavens, what nonsense. Some say knitting was brought to our shores by sailors from the Arabian Seas," she told him. "And they were men. And in later centuries, knitting socks was a carefully guarded trade—done by men."

Finn looked singularly unimpressed by her history lesson. "I don't see that I have to knit or learn to mend. I bet the cap'n doesn't."

She laughed. "He most certainly does, Finn. And I've seen him do so."

"No!" the boy gasped. "Go on with ya! The cap'n knits?"

"He most certainly does," she assured him.

Only too late did Dash see where the boy's arguments were headed. Straight at him.

The lad turned around and eyed him. His disbelieving gaze filled with questions, sought the story behind this remarkable revelation. The captain knit? Black-hearted scourge of the British, most daring man alive could turn a sock heel?

Dash had the feeling of being washed overboard, being towed down into the depths of the sea. Into the heart of his deepest memories.

Something he'd guarded himself against recalling. But Finn shoved him right into the black, icy depths with his innocent query.

"If you don't mind me asking, Cap'n, is it true? Do you know how to knit?"

Hollindrake House, Kent
June 1814

When Dash awoke he realized the room they'd stashed him in was a far cry from his prison cell at Marshalsea. Ornate cornices decorated the ceiling, pretty flowery curtains hung from the windows, and the bed he slept in felt like heaven.

Then again, anything after the cold stone floor he'd been encamped upon would be an improvement.

But this? Soft sheets, a downy mattress, and fine wool blankets wrapped him in warmth and elegance.

Perhaps he was dead, he thought as he tried to focus beyond these soft comforts, for in addition to being ensconced in luxury, he was also clean—scrubbed and shaved.

For he remembered very little after Pippin had managed to free him. He'd been weak from months of little food and confinement in a cramped cell. All that was only aggravated by the wound he'd suffered when he'd been shot in the shoulder at the Setchfield ball.

Pippin had led him for what had felt like miles, until they'd come to a waiting carriage, and he'd dropped inside like a stone. He vaguely remembered his lice-ridden, filthy clothes being wrestled from his body and tossed out the window and others being pulled onto him.

Then had come Pippin's whispered instructions for the rest of their journey.

"We've told everyone that Aunt Minty is ill, and she needs her rest, so you mustn't speak to anyone." He could barely open his eyes, let alone speak. Not to mention believe his turn of luck. He still wasn't completely convinced that this wasn't just a dream.

After all, what had Aunt Minty to do with all this? That question got answered the next time he'd managed to open his eyes and realized he was dressed in one of the old girl's crowish black gowns, complete with a bonnet and a shawl pulled over his head.

Ah, now it made sense. Not that it was likely to work, but he had to give his Circe her credit. She was ingenious.

Still, that didn't mean her plan had a chance in hell of succeeding.

Pippin, you mustn't do this, he wanted to tell her. *Don't save me, I'm not worth it.*

But save him she had. The journey from London to the country estate of the Duke of Hollindrake was nothing but a blur, jolting along over the country roads, his body worn to the point of exhaustion, his shoulder still agonizing where the bullet had been extracted. Through the haze, whispered conversations between Pippin and her cousin Thalia, her co-conspirator in this entire madness, had reached his ears.

Pippin, whatever will you do next?

I love him, Tally. I'll go with him. Anywhere. To the ends of the earth if I must.

'Tis madness, you know. Duchess will have our hides if she discovers . . .

Madness yes, but somehow it all worked. Hidden in the depths of one of the duke's carriages, the noble family crest on the side had kept their parade of barouches and wagons and carts from being searched. They'd rolled out of London as if nothing were amiss.

They'd arrived just after nightfall at the duke's country seat, and with Pippin and Tally on either elbow, they'd walked him into the grand house, as bold as brass, through the chaos and cacophony of servants and trunks and unpacking that had the house in an uproar.

No one noticed anything amiss about the duchess's sister and cousin helping their aged and beloved chaperone up to her room.

There he'd fallen into the bed and slept, but for how long, he had no idea.

Then from a far corner in the room he heard a soft click, click, click. He rolled toward the noise. Light made its way through the sheer curtains, and he blinked at the brightness. He hadn't seen the sun in so long it was hard on the eyes.

But not on his spirit. Sunshine. It warmed him through and through, as if it were suddenly spring.

Nay, nearly summer, he guessed, opening his eyes and stretching, his body rested and now restless.

There was a pause in the clicking, and a soft sigh. Relief and joy and a bundle of other emotions all in one soft breath.

He struggled up, and then stopped when he saw her.

His Circe. Dressed in a pale green gown, her blond hair done up in a simple knot, she crossed the room quickly, in that graceful manner of hers.

"I liked the red one better," he croaked out.

"The what?" she asked, setting her knitting down on the bed and reaching for a pitcher on the nightstand. She poured him a glass of cool water and then held it for him while he took a few sips.

"The red gown," he managed this time. "I liked the red dress better."

She laughed. "You would." Then she settled down on the bed beside him, gazing at him with wonder in her eyes. "Oh, Dash," she whispered, "you've truly come back to me."

Her hand rose to his brow, the warmth of her fingers like a balm, a reassuring touch that told him this wasn't a dream. It couldn't be, for he'd never smelled roses in a dream.

"Circe," he croaked, his throat still dry and unused to talking. Instead, he drew her fingers to his lips and kissed them, his lips hungry for a taste of her, his body coming alive just by her presence.

No, this was no dream.

He pulled her closer, and this time his lips met hers and he kissed her, tugging her into the bed with him. She came tumbling atop him, rolling with him until he had her pinned beneath them, the red wool tangled all around them.

"Dash!" She laughed, reaching for the yarn and trying to pull it free. "My knitting!"

"To hell with your knitting," he said, kissing her neck, nibbling at the spot behind her ears, his hands cupping her breasts. He'd spent the last five months keeping himself alive on memories of her, her laugh, her kiss, the sound of her soft sighs and feline moans as she found her release. "You can knit later."

And with that said, his lips crashed down on hers and he kissed her, sweeping his tongue past any further protests—not that there were any—and she was his once again.

He had no right to love her as he did, he had no right to take her into his bed, into his heart, but he couldn't stop himself. He loved her, and he ached to discover her again. To give her as much pleasure as he could.

Beneath him, she arched, her hips rubbing up against him. Christ, he was already hard for her, and the demmed little minx knew it. Her tongue taunted his, sliding over him, as hungry for him as he was for her.

Oh, Circe, whatever are we to do? he wondered before he surrendered to the passionate abandon that he found in her arms. Let his heart go, let himself love her once again.

Pippin couldn't quite believe it. Dash. She had him back. After all those months of waiting, of being unable to see him, of being unable to discover any news of his fate.

Not until her former teacher, Miss Porter, now known as Lady John, the wife of Mad Jack Tremont, had come to her a fortnight earlier with the news that Dash was to be hanged in secret. That he was held in Marshalsea Prison and there was little hope.

In those heart-wrenching moments, something inside her had broken free. It was as if the life she'd longed for, the wild stories of adventures and daring rescues she and Tally wrote endlessly came alive inside. All those years of dreaming up crazy tales for fictional heroines had been preparing her for this very moment.

And in her anguish, she'd known what she must do.

Save Dash. There were other reasons, ones that went beyond her heart, her love for this pirate of a man who'd come to live inside her very soul. But those needed no airing now.

Not when she had Dash back. Atop her, rocking against her, his knee nudging her legs apart. And what a regular vixen she'd become, for she parted them quite willing. But oh, how this man made her come alive. How she wanted him. Inside her . . .

She reached up and tugged at the nightshirt she'd put on him when they'd gotten to Hollindrake House, and with one pull he was naked, gloriously so.

"Pippin," he said in a hungry groan. "God, I've missed you, my love."

He'd grown thin during those months, and the red scar on his shoulder showed how he'd nearly died trying to escape capture. She touched him tentatively at first, but it was hard to worry about such things when he kissed her again, his hands pulling her gown, stroking her thighs, slipping down and over her sex, with the same eagerness that burned inside her.

Moaning softly as he started to bring her to that cadence that would give her release, she arched upward again, greedy for every bit of passion he could give her.

Catching hold of his manhood, she ran her fingers up and down his length.

He groaned and looked down at her, his green eyes filled with desire.

They didn't say a word, both knew exactly what they wanted. No matter that she still wore her gown—at least partially—and that they were a tangle of limbs and red wool and sheets. They joined quickly, fed by a hungry, desperate relief that they had found each other again when all hope had been lost.

Pippin wondered, as he entered her, if anything could feel so perfect. His thick staff filled her and she clung to him, her hips matching his hot, eager rhythm. She dug her heels into the mattress, her arms twined around him, all so she could get closer, feel every bit of him as he entered her, drew that sweet passion from her, had her gasping for release.

And then it came, as quickly and surprisingly as it had the first time they'd made love.

Her body rocked, the trembling release leaving her breathless. He'd carried her upward to this place in heaven, and now she fell back to earth in the warmth of his arms and love.

"Dash," she sighed, curling her arms around his neck and nestling closer to him. "I have you again."

"You have me always," he told her, kissing her brow, her nose, her lips.

She shivered at the warmth of his touch, her body stirring anew. "I never thought I'd—"

"Shhh," he soothed. "Never dwell on the past, little Circe. We can do naught about it."

She struggled up out of the tangle of sheets and limbs and yarn. "But I would have lost you."

You still might . . .

She shook off the notion. No. Not now. Never again, she vowed.

"You must have stirred a hornet's nest with your antics," he said, half to himself.

Pippin nodded. "Tally fears they have sent an agent here to the house party to find you."

"House party?"

"Yes, you are at the most coveted house party that Society has witnessed in years—at least if you are to believe my cousin."

"And you brought me along?"

"Yes, in the chaos, we—Tally and I—figured Felicity would never notice that we'd added another guest to the list." She grinned, but then sighed. "That is, until we got here. Tally's become quite anxious of late. She lost her luggage and now I think she is losing her mind. I very much doubt the Foreign Office would send someone here."

Even as she said the words, a shadow fell over her confidence. No, they had made it this far, it was only a few more days and then . . . She glanced up at Dash and sighed. "Felicity's far too busy trying to find us—"

. . . find us . . .

"Husbands?" he finished for her.

Pippin heaved a sigh. "Yes. Oh, how I despise those

Bachelor Chronicles of hers. As if a husband can be found in an encyclopedia of her making."

"Proper ones, I imagine."

She nodded. "That's why we are here."

He glanced around. "Where exactly is here?"

"Hollindrake House," she explained. When he shrugged, she continued. "South of Tunbridge Wells." But she knew what he was really asking. "A day's ride from the coast. To Hastings, actually."

His eyes flew to hers. "Hastings?"

She nodded. "Yes, Lady John has sent word to the *Circe* to pick us up in the cove as soon as we can get there."

"Us?" he asked with a grin.

"Yes, us," she shot back, "I'm a wanted woman now."

"By me," he said, kissing her anew. But when he rolled this time, he reared back and howled. "What the devil!"

He reached behind him and pulled out the bundle of knitting. "I can see you've found a new weapon."

"Aunt Minty taught me," she told him, taking her knitting and setting it aside.

"Red wool socks." He laughed, looking at her work.

"For you." She set them aside. "That pair is nearly done. I've made two others in the last few months."

"Go on with you," he said. "Lady Philippa Knolles knitting wool socks for the likes of me. What is the world coming to?" His hands roamed over her body. "I daresay you've been eating more Turkish delight than knitting, for you've quite filled out since my arrest. Beautifully so," he whispered. "Having your cousin married to the duke has obviously improved the larder." He laughed and continued stroking her arms, her breasts, her rounded stomach.

Pippin's insides fluttered, for she wasn't quite ready to tell him everything that had happened since his arrest. "Oh, you're a dreadful tease, Thomas Dashwell," she said instead. "I've been worried sick over you and I knit those so that when you got free I would have a gift for you. Because I've never given you anything."

Besides the child inside me . . .

"I thought you would like them," she said instead. It was a coquettish thing to say, but she wasn't quite ready to tell him the truth.

Dash, I'm pregnant. I broke you out of prison because my baby needs a father. I need a husband.

"Like them?" he was saying, grinning at her. "I love them. I'll keep them always, for I don't think I could knit a better pair."

"You? Knit socks?" Now it was Pippin's turn to laugh. "I can't see you knitting."

His brows drew together. "I most certainly can. Learned as a lad the first year I went to sea. Had to learn. My mother was across the ocean and my feet were growing. My father showed me how, and Mr. Hardy lent a hand. Most sailors know how. Gives them something to do other than gamble or fight. And there is no one else to do it. I can turn out a very decent pair. Not as fine as these, but I can knit." He leaned back on the pillows, hands behind his head as if there was nothing he couldn't do.

Still, Pippin had the suspicion he was teasing her,

so she caught up the nearly finished sock and handed it to him. "Show me."

He stared down at the jumble of yarn and stitches now sitting on his bare chest. "Show you?"

Pippin leaned back in the crook of his arms, crossing hers over her chest. "Yes. Show me. I don't believe it."

He sat up, hauling her with him. "Doubt me, do you?"

She shrugged.

Then to her surprise, he picked up the tangle and carefully set it to rights and then knit across the first pin, then the second, and went all the way around, until he'd finished the round.

Pippin gaped at the completed row, for she truly hadn't believed his boast. "Is there anything else I need to know about you?"

A funny look crossed his face, but he shuttered it quickly. "Nothing that matters," he said softly, setting the sock aside and moving restlessly, anxiously to get her out of her gown. "Besides, right now I have a lady to capture and pillage."

"Pillage away," she said, letting him kiss her back into that dangerous oblivion she loved so much.

"I wonder what I'll discover down here," he teased as he began to kiss her neck, her breasts, and laid a hot trail down her belly.

Pippin laughed.

There would be time for revealing everything that needed to be said later.

"I do believe I have found treasure," he murmured from beneath the sheets.

Oh, yes, much later . . .

Aboard the Ellis Anne, *1837*

Dash stilled, the memories of that day catching him from a different angle, even as Finn and Lady Gossett's innocent conversation continued. "You're doing very well there, Finn. You are catching on much faster than my son did, and he learned when he was about your age."

"Why did he want to learn?"

"He didn't, but he longed to go to sea, and I wanted his feet to always be warm . . ."

Finn laughed. "I don't think that is possible, ma'am."

"I daresay I know that now," she told him, holding up the hem of her skirt. "Don't tell anyone, but I have two pairs of socks on."

The boy laughed again, and his wiggling antics sent the ball rolling out of his lap yet again. As he chased after it, he asked, "How old is he now?"

There was a pause before she answered, and when she did, her answer seemed guarded. "He's about Mr. Dashwell's age."

Nate's age? Dash swallowed. Or rather tried to. Nate's age. He shook his head. That could only mean . . .

Again the memories from their time at Hollindrake House came rushing back.

I daresay you've been eating more Turkish delight than knitting, for you've quite filled out since my arrest . . .

His hand traced in the air what he remembered of the rounded line of her belly.

No. It couldn't be. Here he'd just assumed both her children were Gossett's.

But it was that cautious turn of her voice when she'd answered Finn's question. *About Mr. Dashwell's age.*

Dash swayed in his boots. No, it couldn't be true. She would have told him. She never would have let him go, never married another if she were carrying his child. Not her. Not his Pippin. His Circe.

He sucked in a deep breath and tried to clear his brandy-mulled thoughts, struggled to put the pieces together. But all he could hear was her cautious statement.

About Mr. Dashwell's age.

How well did you ever know the lass? Hardy had once asked.

Obviously not as well as he thought.

He barged forward and shot a glance at Finn. "Don't you have work to be done?"

"But Mr. Dashwell said I was to—" The boy's round eyes looked up at him in terror and should have stayed his temper a bit, but all he saw was a child he'd never known.

His child.

Dash's fury began to boil over, and he wasn't in the mood to wait for answers. "Get to work. No one sits around on my ship," he bellowed, his voice carrying across the deck.

All the hands stopped their work and stared, and Dash didn't care who heard him, for now that the boy had scrambled out of his line of vision he had only one thought.

Getting the truth out of the woman before him. "You have a son?"

She crossed her arms over her chest. "Yes. And you needn't have bullied that child if you wanted to ask me—"

Dash marched closer to her, towering over her. "Whose son? Whose son did you have? Mine?"

She sucked in a deep breath, the sort of indignant one you'd expect from a lady of her sort. But he knew the truth. Lady Gossett was no proper matron beneath those fine silks of hers. Never had been.

He caught hold of her arms and shook her, ignoring the heavy thud of Nate's boots as he crossed the decks to come to her rescue.

But there was no saving her now. Not as far as Dash was concerned. "Did you have my child?"

She blanched, whether from his brandy-laced breath or the indecency of the question, he wasn't sure. Didn't care.

"Let me go," she said, trying to shake him off. "You're drunk, and in no condition to—"

"Lady Gossett," he sneered, "I may be drunk but I can still do math."

Nate came rushing forward. "Da, let go of her. Are you out of your mind? Accosting a passenger, yelling at the poor lad? What the hell is wrong with you?"

"Shove off," Dash told him. "This doesn't concern you."

"When you start bullying children it does. That boy is in my care—"

Dash cut him off. "Then see that he pulls his weight."

Nate shot a glance at the woman his father held in his unholy grasp, and she shook his head at him. That, however, wasn't assurance enough for the young man to butt out. "Let go of Lady Gossett. She isn't one of your crew. Let her go, Da."

"No. Not until I have some answers from her." Dash glared at her. "You might be interested in this as well, Nate. Did you know Lady Gossett has a son?"

"Of course. He's a captain—"

Dash didn't let him finish. "Did you know he's your brother?"

He might have been kinder to dump a bucket of seawater over his head. Nate stepped back and gaped at the two of them. "My wha-a-t . . . ?"

Good. Now Nate could see his precious passenger for what she truly was.

Beneath his grasp, Lady Gossett tried to wrench herself free, but he held on to her. "I'm right, aren't I? You had my son? You married another with my child in your belly."

She pressed her lips together, stubbornly refusing to answer.

So Dash continued, "There are only two ways your son can be anywhere near the same age as Nate— the child is mine, or you were sleeping with Gossett before you came for me at Marshalsea."

His words did exactly what he expected they would.

They infuriated her.

But not for the reasons he thought. And further, if he thought his son would stand behind him, he was doubly mistaken.

She shook him off with a vengeance. "I never—"

"Ha! So he is mine," Dash crowed triumphantly.

But it was Nate who got the answers. "When was your son born, madam?"

"October. October 1814."

Nate closed his eyes, and Dash just knew he was doing the math and realizing what she had done. How she had betrayed Dash, betrayed them both.

Oh, but he was so very wrong.

"You bastard. You wretched, drunken bastard," Nate said in a low, dangerous voice, before he grabbed his startled father by the collar and the throat and propelled him across the deck until he had him bent backward over the rail. "You rutting devil. My mother was barely dead, barely cold, and you were already fucking someone else. Getting another woman with child. Wasn't cursing one woman with your lust and cold heart enough?" Nate turned and pointed a finger at Pippin. "Did she know? Did she know you killed my mother?"

She gasped, her hands coming to her throat.

"Nate, it wasn't like that—" He glanced around his son at her, at Pippin, and saw how pale she'd become, her eyes wide with shock.

"When did your mother die, Mr. Dashwell?" she asked in a shaky voice. When he didn't answer right away, she came to him, flew to his side and caught hold of his arm. "Please! When did she die?"

"1813. In November. A few days after I was born."

Her hand fell from him and her shoulders sagged. "But that was only . . ." Her gaze flew up and fell on Dash, still trapped in Nate's furious grasp, and he could see her agile mind doing the math, connecting the lines that before she'd never known.

His wife had died two months before he'd been trapped in London.

But her eyes said more, spoke of a betrayal. Disbelief. *Married. A child. You never said a word of any of this.*

Dash shuddered, tried to shake himself free of Nate. Oh, bloody Christ, this was suddenly going very wrong.

A reckoning he'd avoided for twenty-some years.

"Then how was it?" Nate was saying, shaking him like a rag doll, the great, rolling waves licking at the back of Dash's head, his feet dangling.

He grappled to get ahold of the railing, anything to keep from going over.

"However was it?" Nate demanded. "Did you forget you had just buried a wife back in Baltimore? A woman who carried your child, died waiting for word of you?"

"You don't understand, it wasn't like that," Dash tried arguing. For a long, temper-filled moment, Dash thought his son was going to toss him into the deep, and he doubted there was a man aboard who would lift a finger to save him.

Nate stared down at him, the hatred in his eyes not his own, but Abigail's. A light so very much like hers. 'Twas as if she'd dropped down from the heavens to exact her revenge.

Then Nate pulled him up and tossed him down on the deck. He glanced at Lady Gossett. "You didn't know, did you?"

Wordlessly, she shook her head.

Nate stomped around him, his boots coming precariously close to Dash's head. "You drunken wretch. How was it that I was ever proud of you? Thought to save you? You used my mother to gain your ship and this lady to . . . to . . . save your worthless hide. Twice. How many others have you used so callously?"

She shook her head, backing away from the two of them. The shock on her face, the grief in her eyes rising faster than water into a cracked hull, cut through him.

He shuddered, waves of dismay rolling over him. Abigail's death hadn't been his fault, even the midwife had said so, for she'd died of a fever contracted in childbirth, but that hadn't stopped her father from blaming him. Accusing him of every crime possible, with the only one that held any merit being that she'd gone to her grave with a broken heart.

It hadn't been like that . . . he'd come to London with no intentions . . . other than to collect intelligence. He hadn't come seeking her . . . he hadn't.

And yet that wasn't quite true. He'd come to London with a thread of hope of finding Pippin, of finding the one woman who could possibly offer solace to his broken life.

The Circe who'd never stopped calling to him.

"Then you made a wise choice by marrying another," Nate was saying, taking her by the elbow and pulling her away.

Dash couldn't tear his gaze from Pippin, wished with every ounce of his black soul that she would turn around and forgive him.

Then she did. She glanced over her shoulder and looked at him.

But there was no hint of pardon. Not a bit of absolution. No sign that she wanted to hear his side of the story, to understand what he'd done, and why.

Of all the ways she'd ever looked at him, nothing burned through his heart the way she did in that moment.

Part of him wanted to be triumphant—now she knew the real poison, the worm of betrayal, but there was no celebration inside him. Only the gut-wrenching realization that she knew the truth now. She'd loved a man who'd never existed.

Chapter 12

$\mathcal{P}$ippin stood in the middle of her cabin and shook from head to toe.

She didn't know whether to cry or scream.

Dash had been married. He'd loved her, ruined her. Gotten her with child.

For all his claims that he'd loved her, he'd been lying. He had to have been.

You used my mother to gain your ship and this lady to . . . to . . . save your worthless hide. Twice. How many others have you used so callously?

Nate's ugly words rang in her ears, for they told another truth: how little she'd known of Dash back then.

When all the time he'd been married to another. Had a child.

She stuffed her hand in her mouth and clenched her eyes shut, for she wanted neither to cry nor scream in pain. Instead she sank to her knees and rocked back and forth.

Had he ever loved her? Had she risked so much for a man who would have deserted her, marooned her in some dingy port and sailed away?

What had he said before?

I never loved you. You were a soft, willing refuge on a cold winter night, but nothing more.

No, it couldn't be true, it couldn't be. For if it was, it meant she'd lived her entire life based on a lie.

Hollindrake House, 1814
Sussex, England

Dash paced back and forth in the luxurious room he was stashed away in. As the sole occupant of "Aunty Minty's" room, his only real task was to burrow down in the covers of the bed when the maids came to clean and moan and groan a bit so the duke's usually thorough staff would hurry along.

But tonight, it was different. Dash knew what he must do.

Tell Pippin the truth. Tell her about Abigail. And about the babe as well. What he didn't relish telling her was how he'd married Abigail for all the wrong reasons—that he'd let his greed and ambitions cloud what should have been a decision of his heart. Whatever would Pippin think of him?

He raked his hand through his hair and groaned. Christ sakes, how had his life come to this?

Rash, my boy, you're too rash, Mr. Hardy would say. *Diving in where you should be raising the sails and getting the hell out of there.*

Wasn't that the truth . . . it was exactly how he'd

ended up married to Abigail two years earlier. He'd come home after escaping the British, to find the *Circe* desperately in need of repairs. Eager to get back out in the fray, he'd gone to see Abigail's father, Nathaniel Jamieson, the owner of the best shipyard in Baltimore. Oh, yes, Mr. Jamieson could repair the *Circe*, but his shipyard was quite busy, what with the war and all, and it would take three months.

"Three months!" Dash had exclaimed, and in that moment of hasty sputtering and near cursing, both men took a measure of each other—Dash of the wily but gifted shipbuilder, and Mr. Jamieson of the infamous captain standing before him.

Shrewd to his very bones, Jamieson knew that Dashwell was going to make a fortune in the war, or find himself at the bottom of the sea and leave it all to waste. And after the war—if the resourceful captain lived—he'd be infamous wherever he sailed, as would the ships he sailed upon.

"Perhaps I can move your business ahead a bit, Captain Dashwell," Jamieson had said, offering to fix the *Circe* in a fortnight. "And by the way," he'd added after they shook hands on the bargain. "I'd be quite remiss, sir, if I didn't invite you to dinner tonight. My daughter will be overset to meet you."

Dash had seen right through the invitation, but he was no fool, either.

The little miss who haunted his dreams was on the other side of the Atlantic, most likely married to an earl or a baron or some other proper fellow. Not that she'd probably ever thought of him once. It was time for him to put away his ridiculous fancies about Lady Philippa Knolles.

So he'd gone to the Jamiesons' for dinner. A fortnight later he set off in the *Circe*, sparkling with new rigging, a tight hull, and fully provisioned.

And a wife waving from the docks as he sailed away. No banns, no fuss, just a hasty courtship, a starry-eyed bride, and a groom with an eye toward his future.

But the lights in Abigail's eyes had dimmed even as Dash's reputation had risen, for each time the *Circe* returned to port, shot nearly clean through, but always triumphant, she'd begged him to stay in port. They had gold enough. He needn't take such risks.

But the sea and a burning desire to wreak revenge on the British had closed his ears to her requests, her pleading. The last time he'd seen her, she'd discovered, quite by accident, that he'd also been dealing with the French, a dangerous sort of arrangement that was foolhardy at best. She'd been furious with him, threatened to tell one and all of his dealings so he could no longer take such risks, so the baby she carried would grow up to know his father.

And what had he done? Ordered her off his ship and hightailed it out of Baltimore as if his stern were on fire. Two weeks later, he'd come home with a prize, only to find her lost, and an infant in the housekeeper's arms. His son.

His father-in-law, lost in grief over his only child, had blamed him, thrown a ruckus at the funeral that became the scandal of Baltimore, and what had Dash done? Pulled up his anchor and fled.

And then done the most foolhardy thing of all—he'd decided to come into London. Sneak into the city and mine the gold of information that could be had around the docks and coffee houses and then hie his way back to the waters just off the Channel and have his pick of fat prizes.

Hardy had accused him of chasing death, and it wasn't too far from the truth. At least it hadn't been once he'd found himself marooned here in England. Stumbled into Pippin's path. Discovered love in her innocent kiss, in her passionate embrace.

Oh, why hadn't he just turned and fled his stand there on the Thames and left well enough alone?

Because he'd never loved before and right now it had him in agony.

Downstairs, whoever was playing the pianoforte had stopped, which meant hopefully the evening was drawing to a close. Whatever was taking so long? Pippin had promised she'd make her excuses right after dinner—a megrim, perhaps—and then be right back up. But that had been hours ago, and all he could hear was laughter and music—because wasn't that the point of a house party? To have the guests mix about and mingle, so courtships and unions could take root.

Well, no one had better be rooting about my Circe, he thought, striding across the room. He glanced at the bracket clock on the mantel and heaved a deep sigh. Where the devil was she?

Then again, whatever was he in a hurry for?

If only he had the charm of one of his English friends. Take Templeton, for example. That fellow would break the news with a smile and a jaunty quip.

Circe, my love, there is something I must tell you.

This marriage thing—never fear—for I am quite expert at it. Made a bit of a muddle of my first foray, but with you . . .

Dash snorted. He wasn't the sort for quips. More like pistols at the ready and "Fire when ready, lads."

"You must tell her, Dash. You must," he muttered under his breath.

"Must do what, Dash?" came a soft voice.

He whirled around and found her standing in the doorway. Everything about her caught his heart, but as he looked closer into her wary gaze he realized that somehow, some way, everything had changed in the last few hours.

What the devil had happened down there?

"I've missed you, Circe," he said, crossing the room to take her in his arms. But she sidestepped him, and, he thought, she'd even flinched when he spoke. He turned to where she'd fled across the room and faced her. "Whatever is wrong?"

"Nothing," she said in a short, clipped voice as she tugged off her gloves.

Nothing. Ah, the most forceful sentence a woman could ever use. For it meant something quite opposite. Hardly nothing. More like everything. That much he'd learned from Abigail.

"What happened tonight?"

She shrugged. "I went to dinner. Afterward, Miss Elsford played the pianoforte. Some of us danced. And then I made my excuses and came upstairs. Nothing really."

And she never once looked at him as she spoke.

Dash cocked his head and stared at her. "Are you

sure that's all, Pippin? Something is amiss. Who was at dinner?"

"All the guests. The Elsfords, Lord Cranwich, Sir Robert Foxley, Lord Grimston, Lord Boxley—" She tapped her fingers to her lips. "Oh, yes, Lord Gossett. He was most kind. He's a viscount, with a lovely holding just west of Lord John's. On the sea, I believe."

A hot flash of anger ran through him as he listened to her. Lord Gossett. "Just the sort of fellow your cousin hopes to match you with, I assume," he asked, circling her.

"Yes, quite," she said, looking up at him with a flash of challenge in her eyes.

Dash knew right then and there he should leave. Leave her to her viscount and be gone. This night. But something in the fiery light of her eyes ignited an inferno of suspicion inside him.

"So are you going to marry him?" he blurted out as he crossed the room to stand before her.

And his Circe, his beautiful Circe stood her ground. "I should," she shot back, firing a broadside meant to gut his hull. "For I doubt I would have to spend my days wondering how many other women he has dallied with. How many other 'Circes' he has stashed about the Atlantic."

Dash stilled. Her quietly spoken broadside took out his sails and cut his mainstay in half. "Wha-a-at?"

She rose up on her tiptoes. "You see, I left out one of the guests. Perhaps you recall her—she seems very well acquainted with you—"

His heart stopped.

"Miss Sarah Browne?" she finally finished. "Your

recent conquest?" When Dash still couldn't manage
to speak, Pippin continued. "She told the entire party
quite an enchanting tale of how you took her ship
at sea last December and were the most gallant man
alive. I had to stand there and listen to her tell all of
your 'kindness' to her."

"Who?" he asked, trying to make sense of what
was happening.

"Miss. Sarah. Browne," she ground out as if each
word was filled with sawdust.

"Oh, God. Not that harpy," he sputtered. "She's
here? And her mother as well?"

Pippin threw up her hands and marched around
him. "Yes, she's here. And her mother. Haven't you
been listening to me? Miss Sarah Browne is here."

Dash made a choked sound, tried to breathe. Of
all his wretched luck. Not them. "We need to leave,"
he announced. "Now."

"I'm not going anywhere with you," she shot back,
her voice growing loud enough to call attention to
them. "You lying, wretched—"

Dash caught her in his arms and did the only thing
he knew to quiet her. He kissed her. She struggled
at first, pounding her fists against his chest, but he
refused to let go, refused to stop. He let his lips caress
hers, let his tongue soothe where words would fail
him. He kissed her until she was moaning softly with
need and her body was rocking against his.

"There now, listen to me," he whispered. "That
chit is a dangerous minx. There's trouble swirling
about her skirts, and if it isn't already here, it will
be. Trouble we want nothing to do with." He leaned
back and stared into Pippin's glorious blue eyes. Eyes

filled with doubt, but a measure of hope. "She means nothing to me. Never did. I captured her ship and put her ashore as quickly as I could—"

Just as I was paid to do, he would have added, but that was an entirely different mess he didn't want to drag Pippin into.

The lies, the secrets were piling up around him, threatening to sink everything he'd held dear, had discovered could be possible between a man and a woman.

"I don't know what yarns she's been spinning downstairs," he continued, "but they're lies, Pippin. That gel is the worst sort of puss a man could ever cross paths with. Pity the devil who ends up in her sights. And I assure you, it has never been me."

God no, not with the relations that gel could claim. Relations he'd done business with, much to his misery, for they hunted him still, and Miss Browne's arrival here was like a harbinger of something far more deadly than just Pippin's fears of the Foreign Office.

Meanwhile, the wary light in Pippin's eyes studied him. "Truly?"

He nodded and was rewarded with another kiss, this one filled with promises of desire.

But instead of losing himself to the heady reward of Pippin's angelic body, Dash heard Hardy's voice nagging in his ear. *See, the truth isn't so hard to pass off, is it, lad? So go ahead, tell her the rest of it. Tell her about Abigail. Tell her about the wee lad. Your son.*

Instead he changed the subject yet again. "Now about this viscount," he teased. "Is he handsome?"

"Yes, quite," Pippin murmured as she tugged at his

shirt, her fingers splaying over his chest, though her touch didn't make her words any more palatable.

"Rich?"

"Quite."

Dash paused and looked at her. "Going to marry him?"

She stopped what she was doing and grinned up at him. "Whyever would I do that, when I have you?"

Aboard the Ellis Anne, *1837*

But she had married the viscount.

Married the wrong man. The words echoed through Dash's head as he stumbled into his cabin and slammed the door behind him. At least Dash had told himself that for years. Let that be the satisfaction in his cold heart.

She'd married the wrong man and had lived with the consequences. He paused and glanced around the littered room looking for one thing, a bottle. Yet his gaze fell not on the familiar flask of brandy, but on the mirror on the wall.

The stranger staring at him seemed to taunt his convictions. *The woman on your ship hardly looks full of remorse or anguish over her decision.*

For they both knew the truth: She'd made the right choice.

Pippin had saved Dash with her reckless, rash decision all those years ago, and herself in the bargain, though she hadn't known it at the time.

Though he had.

Just as Nate had said, he was a curse to anyone he loved, any woman who gave him her heart. For he'd killed Abigail with his indifference to her fears, and would have eventually torn Pippin apart as well, if she hadn't married Gossett.

So it was even more bitter to think she'd come to him because she loved him still, still believed him to be that man. The one everyone always expected.

Captain Thomas Dashwell. Privateer. Rapscallion. Gentleman pirate.

And no matter how hard he tried to tell people, he wasn't some demmed hero. He was just a man. And not a very good one. No one ever listened. Until today.

So now she knew. And hated him for it. As well she should.

Out of the corner of his eye, he spied a bottle. He staggered over to it and pulled the cork out with his teeth and then drank. Deeply, until he couldn't take another moment of the fiery liquor burning down his throat, carrying him to the depths of hell with it.

You never deserved her, lad. Never earned her love, Hardy's voice seemed to whisper from the walls.

"Damn you, Hardy," he called out, staggering about the room, bottle still in hand. "I loved her."

You took everything you ever wanted. You never did an honest day's work in your life. You lived by your own rules, not by hers. Not by Abigail's. You did them both wrong.

Dash shook his head like a dog, trying to rattle the damning words from his thoughts.

"I'm Captain Thomas Dashwell," he said, grinding his teeth together and trying to stand, but his legs wobbled rebelliously beneath him. "And she's mine. Always has been, always will be."

But she wasn't, and never would be, and he knew it, as did the ghost of his faithful first mate.

For Hardy wasn't done taunting him. Not yet. *You're a sad, lonely drunk and a coward to boot, and it's sorry I am to have sailed with you. Can't even set your own course. Left it all for Nate to do. Well, the lad's life ain't meant to be spent polishing up your reputation. He'll see that soon enough and leave you marooned, just like you deserve. For a drunk is all you'll ever be.*

Dash opened his mouth to argue the point, but Hardy hadn't finished. The crabbed old sailor had one more sally to lob at him. *And she'll never have you as long as you live your life at the bottom of a brandy cask . . . Never.*

"Want to see about that," he said, defiant as usual. He could march down the hallway to her room, knock on the door, and he'd charm her back into his arms in no time . . . one kiss, just one kiss and she'd be his once again.

And he almost believed it as he staggered to the door, until he caught sight of himself once again in the mirror.

There, his reflection told the truth.

Pippin wasn't his. Not any longer. Most likely, she'd toss his drunken ass overboard if he even dared.

He gaped at the man in the mirror and tried to deny that this was him. Tried every way he could to tell himself he wasn't, as Hardy had said, a sad, lonely drunk.

Yet there was the truth of his life staring back at him. And he had two choices.

Stay as he was, and live without her. Or do something about this demmed mess he was in.

There was a sharp rap on Pippin's door, and she raised her head slowly. How long she'd been sitting there on the floor crying, she had no idea, but the knock and the one that followed in quick succession dragged her back to a present she wanted nothing to do with.

"Lady Gossett?" Nate's voice held an urgency that piqued her.

"Yes?" she replied, wearily getting to her feet. Gracious heavens, her knees were killing her. She was getting older.

"You need to come up. Above deck. Now."

She glanced to the narrow window her cabin boasted and realized it was already night.

No wonder her knees ached. More the fool her for spending so much time lamenting a love that had never been.

Thomas Dashwell. *Harrumph*. She should have let him hang all those years ago.

"Please, Lady Gossett, you must hurry," Nate said, rattling the door as if he were going to barge in and cart her up to the deck against her will.

"Yes, yes, I'm coming, Mr. Dashwell. I'm coming," she said, opening the door and facing the man who looked so much like his father. She ignored the way her heart thudded, for it was only doing that because she'd always reacted that way when she'd seen Dash. "What is it?"

"You must see this," was all he said before he caught hold of her arm and pulled her along.

She followed mostly because she had no choice, but in short order she found herself on deck being led toward the stern. There at the very edge of the rail stood Dash.

Not the Dash of late, but Dash in his old clothing, the sort of pirate fashion he'd affected when he'd been a smuggler and he'd stolen a kiss from her lips on the beach in Hastings.

He wore a red bandana atop his head, along with his old tricorn hat. He had on black breeches, a white shirt, and a black leather waistcoat. He wore his gun belts crossed over his chest, and his boots, which rose past his knees, gleamed with polish, even in the dark.

But it wasn't the sight of him that took her aback, that had the entire crew gaping at him as if they'd suddenly found themselves in the King's Theatre in Covent Garden, plopped down in the middle of the second act of some ludicrous comedy, but what he was doing that left everyone aboard the *Ellis Anne* convinced that Thomas Dashwell had finally, well, to put it politely, lost his rigging.

For there he stood with a crate of bottles beside him, and a large cask, and one by one the bottles were being flung into the sea. A couple he kissed before giving them the heave-ho, but most just got raised in a mock toast before being tossed over.

Finally, there was nothing left but the cask, and as he raised this, Mr. Clemens, who stood to Nate's left, started to protest. "Oh, Captain, no! 'Tis a good vintage and worth a—"

But Nate stopped him with a curt nod of his head, and before anyone else could come to their senses and prevent Dash, the cask went over as well, and as it hit the waves, the splash was followed by a collective groan from the crew at the sight of the expensive liquor joining the bottles bobbing in the waves like a trail of unwanted orphans.

Dash stood with his back to them, as if he were all alone in the world.

Well, in many ways he was.

" 'Tis the last of his portion," one of the fellows muttered. "We're in for it now."

"Mr. Dashwell, whatever is he doing?" Pippin asked. "What does this mean?"

"I think he means to put off the bottle. Stop drinking," Nate said, an odd note to his voice. Pippin would have described it as hopeful, if it hadn't been tinged with so much disbelief.

"Just like that?" She shook her head. "Doesn't he know—"

"I doubt it," Nate said. "Da never is one to think through the consequences, but he's just cast off all his provisions, and the crew is under orders not to give him any of their ration."

"By your order?"

"No. His," he said, nodding at his father. "That's why everyone is up here. He ordered them to keep their rations locked and out of his hands and then he started tossing all his store overboard."

Now it was Pippin's time to turn and gape at the lonely man standing vigil at the rail. "He's gone quite mad."

"Yes, utterly."

"Then whyever, Mr. Dashwell, are you grinning?"

"Because he's about to pay the piper, Lady Gossett."

She glanced again at Dash. "Will it be as bad as all that?"

"Worse."

A chill ran down her spine. A premonition of what was to come. For Dash. For her. She shook her head and did her best to ignore it. "Whyever would he do such a thing?"

"Isn't it obvious?" Nate sighed and turned to the men lolling about. "Get back to work."

Pippin shook her head. Whatever would compel him to do such a thing? Her? Good God, she hoped not. For did he really think that just because he'd tossed his bottles into the sea it would undo everything?

She began to tremble. And not with pity, but rage.

And when he turned from the rail, his face triumphant at his accomplishment, his daring declaration, he grinned at her as if everything was going to be right as rain.

Except it wasn't that easy. *You can't erase the past with one gallant gesture*, she wanted to tell him. *Take away the pain and the lies by tossing your problems overboard.*

Couldn't he see that?

Apparently not.

So she did what she should have done all those years ago when she'd discovered him half frozen on the Thames. What her good sense had told her to do.

Lady Gossett raised her nose in the air, turned on one heel, and stalked from the deck with all the haughtiness of a duchess.

* * *

And she was right. Dash hadn't a clue that his grand gesture was naught but that: a gesture. But he was about to learn. Or at the very least, get a hard lesson in consequences.

Because as he watched Pippin storm off the deck with nary a word of congratulations or even a "well done," he found himself a bit stunned.

Now what the hell was he going to do?

One thing was for certain. He couldn't get a drink. For all his liquor was now floating away from the stern in a bobbing line of indifference, as if it hadn't a care that it was suddenly set free.

But he cared, grasping the railing and looking over his lost horde with horror.

Oh, dear Lord. What the hell have I done? he thought as a wave of panic ran down his spine.

And for the first time in his life, Dash was about to find out.

The hard way.

Chapter 13

$\mathcal{T}$he rap on her door brought Pippin straight out of bed. The sort of sharp, hard sound that spoke of urgency.

"Lady Gossett?" Nate's voice called from the other side.

She'd locked the door earlier, at his recommendation, and after hours of tossing atop the sheets, had finally fallen into an exhausted sleep.

Still, she stared at her door warily as another rap sounded.

"Lady Gossett, you must get up. Quickly."

Nate. Not Dash. There was some relief in that, but certainly his tone was just as imperious and commanding as his father's. No *I am so sorry to disturb you, my lady*, or *Pardon this rude interruption, my lady*.

Just a summary *Get up*.

Rebelliously she clung to her coverlet. "Why?" She didn't really need to ask, for she knew the answer.

"He's gone round the bend. Off his rocker. I fear he'll harm himself, or worse, one of the crew."

One elegant brow rose. And so Nate wanted her to step into the fray? How generous of him.

Stubbornly, she kept to her bed, her anger still too fresh to rouse the pity that would have been fully given if she hadn't learned the truth just a day or two ago.

From the other side of the door, there was a deep sigh. "My lady, please," Nate said. A soft thud on the door caught her attention more than his anxious knocking. It wasn't his fist on the panel, but his head, she had to imagine. And then there was another telling thud. "He needs you. No one else can help him."

She sputtered at this. Help Dash? She'd rather carry smallpox.

There was another resigned sigh from the other side. "Is what you said earlier true—that you had his child?"

Pippin shut her eyes, for the wistful note in Nate's voice spoke of an emptiness that had never been filled. She thought of John and Ginger, growing up together, squabbling, arguing, banding together against any and all. Through it all, they had always had each other.

And Nate had naught in his life but Dash, at least until now.

"Your son," Nate asked in a halting voice. "Is he my brother?"

Pippin tried to press her lips together, to deny it, but she couldn't. "Aye. He's your half brother."

The silence continued for a bit more. "Does he know?"

"No. He thinks himself Gossett's son. It was how it was agreed upon when I married him. The viscount, that is."

More silence followed. "You married him to save my father."

"Yes," she told him. That was how it had been. She'd been lost with grief when Lord Gossett had come to her with his impossible solution. Marry him, and he would see Dash freed.

For Gossett had been in love with her for some time, and Pippin couldn't deny the viscount was everything a woman would want in a husband.

And there was Dash, locked in the stables at Hollindrake House, having been captured by the determined Lord Larken after one of Dash's French "allies" had stopped their escape. Back then she couldn't fathom how a man could have so many enemies.

Now she was just as dumbfounded as to how Dash had survived all these years without one of them managing to finally do him in.

"Good man to have taken another's child and made him his heir," Nate added through the door, wrenching her attention back to the present.

"The finest."

And so is Dash, her heart whispered. *Despite all his faults, you'll never find a braver, more daring man alive.*

Foolish and arrogant, Pippin wanted to argue back. *And besides, the man I loved, the man I thought I loved, never existed.*

Are you so sure? that devilish voice niggled back.

"Yes, well, there is still our present issue at hand,"

Nate muttered. "I know he's not much to be proud of, and certainly no saint . . . tossing him overboard would probably be the kindest thing for him, but he's my da, and he needs help."

Dash needs you, Pippin, my girl, she could hear Aunt Minty urging her, remembering what the old girl had said the night at Hollindrake House that Dash had been captured. *The way that man looks at you. Hmmm. Never doubt he loves you, my girl, always will.*

"Oh, demmit," she muttered, resorting to the most unladylike expression she knew. But there it was. And there was naught to do but help Nate.

Yes, help Nate, she emphasized to the heavens, to the Fates who seemed to be conspiring against her. She certainly wasn't doing this for Dash. Not in the least.

Pulling on the simple gown she'd brought, she didn't even bother to discover where she'd flung her shoes when she'd come storming in the other night.

Taking a deep breath, she opened the door. Nate didn't wait but a moment, lest she change her mind, but caught her by the elbow and pulled her down the dark gangway. As they neared Dash's cabin, the door wrenched open.

"You'll not take me, you ruddy bastard," Dash shouted. "I'll not go off nicely if you think that's what is going to happen."

This was punctuated by one of the sailors flying out the door. The man hit the wall opposite and slid down until he ended up in a heap on the floor.

The poor fellow glanced up at Nate, rubbing his chin. "Yer da has a wicked facer."

Another man followed, having found the same reception by the captain.

"Send in an entire shipload of marines, you'll not board my ship," Dash raged in a murderous voice.

Pippin caught sight of him just before he closed the door on the lot of them. Her toes curled over the bare deck beneath her feet at the sight before her.

Disheveled and crazed, Dash's bright green eyes glowed with a wild, strange fury—as if the scene before him and what he was seeing were two different things.

One of the fallen mates glanced up at Nate. "He's bleedin' out of his mind. Thinks we were there to hang him. Says he'll do himself in afore he'll let us take him, take his *Circe* from him." The fellow spat out a mouthful of blood. "Knocked me tooth loose." He rubbed his jaw. "Better that, though, than a bullet, I suppose."

Nate glanced down at him in alarm. "What do you mean?"

"He's got a pistol, Mr. Dashwell. And it's loaded."

"Loaded!" Pippin rounded on Nate. "You said earlier that you'd removed all the weapons from his cabin."

"I thought I had," he shot back, raking his hand through his hair. "I never thought it would come to this—"

She let out a disgruntled *harrumph* that would have made Aunt Minty proud. *Leave it to men to make a muddle of things, my girl*, she'd said on more than one occasion.

And this was a dreadful one. Given Dash's state of

mind, there was only one thing to do, she realized, spinning around and rushing back to her cabin.

"My apologies, Lady Gossett," Nate called after her. "I shouldn't have awoken you for this. You're right to take to your cabin."

Pippin turned and faced him, hands on her hips. "I have no intention of hiding away in my cabin. I merely need to change my clothes."

"Change her clothes?" one of the sailors muttered. "Hope she's got one of them old suits of metal in there. For I don't think there is anything to stop the cap'n afore he goes over."

But he was so very wrong, for Pippin had the one thing that could stop Dash, well, quite honestly, any man in his tracks.

A singularly scandalous red dress . . .

Hollindrake House, 1814

It had all been so very simple. They were to sneak Dash out in the middle of the ball disguised as the valet of one of the guests, and then he would ride for the coast.

But it had all gone so utterly wrong.

For all Pippin's plans, she'd not reckoned on the determination of Lord Larken, the king's agent sent to capture Dash, nor that Dash had enemies far beyond England who wanted just as much as the English to see the American privateer roasting in hell.

Dash had been caught, and tossed into one of the duke's stables until he could be returned to London.

For hanging.

And now, hours later, the hue and cry having died away, the guests long gone, and the house settled into getting a modest bit of sleep, Pippin refused to give up.

Even if there wasn't a hope in hell of getting past Lord Larken. Not unless . . .

She clutched the pistol she'd stolen earlier, a mad, impossible plan forming in her mind.

Madness, she thought as she glanced down at it. Whatever was she going to do? Kill Lord Larken?

She should kill him. He'd come under secret orders not to recapture Dash, but to kill him.

But there was the rub, Larken hadn't murdered Dash when he had the chance. In truth, he'd saved his friend's life from another, more dangerous enemy.

Still, it was Larken or Dash.

If only that was the choice, for there were several other wrinkles to all this, like the fact that her cousin Tally was now head-over-heels in love with Larken, never mind that killing him would be murder and treason.

Pippin pressed her lips together and squeezed her eyes shut. Could she do it? A vision of Dash dancing at the end of a gibbet ran through her imagination. She wavered for a moment before she muttered under her breath, "Oh, they just can't hang him."

"They can and they will," a deep voice answered.

She spun around and aimed.

Thatcher, their former footman and now the Duke of Hollindrake, stepped out of the shadows. Felicity's duke. The husband of her heart.

"Pippin, put that demmed thing down," he ordered. "I didn't survive all those years fighting the French to meet my end in my own house."

But she held firm. "You can't stop me, Thatcher."

"Unfortunately, I can," he said, crossing the room, and with a single finger, pushed the muzzle toward the wall. "Because I know you won't shoot me." When he realized he'd managed to aim the pistol at his mother's favorite Ramsay painting, he pushed it a little more to the left.

Meanwhile, Pippin heaved a great big sigh, and then burst into tears. Thatcher sighed as well, and took her into his arms, patting her awkwardly.

"I could, you know. To save Dash I could," she said fiercely, her tears soaking his shirt.

He held her out at arm's length and offered a half smile. "Only by accident and then there'd be hell to pay. Felicity would have both our hides over such a nasty bit of business."

Oh, bother the man. He was too nice by half. Stepping back and embarrassed to have been caught so easily, she swiped at her tears. "What are you doing down here at this hour?"

"Obviously waiting for you."

"Me?" Pippin shook her head. "How did you—"

"I didn't. But Felicity suspected. Knew you'd come up with another featherbrained scheme and try to save that bastard. So here I am." He sighed and shook his head. "So come along. I know what you really want is to see him. See that he's well and safe." He started out the garden door she'd been about to open moments earlier.

"Can you let me see him?" she asked, turning to follow him.

"I'm the duke," he replied in an elegant tone.

"Oh, yes. I keep forgetting."

"So do I." He laughed as he closed the door after her.

Outside, the night air was cool. Pippin still wore her ball gown, the red dress she'd worn the night she'd freed Dash. The silk rustled as she crossed the lawn toward the Old Stables.

"I am so sorry to have brought this scandal down upon you, Thatcher."

He laughed a little. "Pippin, I am quite resigned to the fact that having married your cousin, my life will never be dull."

"Still, I am ever so sorry," she told him, for she was quite fond of their former footman. "I know you'll probably be compelled to cast me out now, what with all the gossip and censure this is sure to—"

He stopped and turned to her. "Cast you out? Whyever would I do that? If it hadn't been for this affair of yours, this entire house party would have been the dullest week ever."

Pippin laughed and so did Thatcher, until he paused. "But don't tell my lovely wife I said that."

"Never," she promised.

"And no more of this nonsense of being cast out," he said.

She drew up to a stop. "It is just that I heard your Aunt Geneva saying—"

His brows drew together. "Aunt Geneva? When have I ever let my aunt decide who is to live in my house?" Then he smiled and began to walk again. "Besides, if it vexes Aunt Geneva to have you in the house, I fear you are here for good no matter the scandal you bring!"

Pippin wasn't too sure he was going to be of the same mind in a few months, her hand covering her stomach where beneath her gown there were the stirrings of the life she carried. Dash's child.

She drew an unsteady breath as they came to the Old Stables, though the grand building was hardly what one would call old, a name that connoted something that should be torn down. This was just one of the many stables at Hollindrake House, built a century earlier in a large, wide open design, so one could drive a carriage inside and be able to unhook the horses without having to stand out in the weather.

The light afforded by the lamp hanging on a large metal hook revealed a large fellow, most likely a hand from the fields, standing guard on one side of the wide open doors, while there were two other fellows at the other end.

"What is this?" Larken asked, stepping out of the shadows that had kept him concealed from sight.

"Lady Philippa wants to see Dashwell," Hollindrake replied.

Larken shook his head and laughed. "What? So she can see him freed again?" He glanced at her red gown. "Rather like the stunt you pulled at Marshalsea, my lady?"

"Marshalsea? Whatever do you mean?" she bluffed, and badly at that. "I wasn't there."

"I have a report by a witness who describes a young, elegant lady, fair of hair, with bonny blue eyes, and wearing a red silk dress. Shall we go up to

London, Lady Philippa," he said, waving his hand at the silk, "and see if Mr. Dobbins recognizes you?"

She stepped back, realizing that she'd waded into deep waters. However had she forgotten she was still wearing her red silk? Oh, heavens, she'd made a terrible muddle of all this. But that didn't mean she wasn't going to stand her ground, no matter how it shook beneath her. "I prefer to stay in Sussex for the time being, my lord," she said with every bit of regal elegance her Bath education had given her.

"I thought as much," he replied. "And out of respect to Miss Thalia's feelings, I daresay I will have to forget that you possess that gown." He paused, as if he was reconsidering. "Just promise me that come morning you'll burn it so I don't have to compromise my duty to the king any further than I already have tonight."

"Burn it?" she shot back indignantly. Burn the dress she'd rescued Dash in? Why, it was her talisman . . . Dash loved it.

"My lady, it condemns you to a treason you do not want to have to answer to," he said. "Be rid of it." It wasn't a suggestion.

Her fingers curled into the red silk, clinging to it. "If I must—"

"Yes, quite," he said, flicking a glance at the duke.

"You'll let her see him?" Hollindrake repeated.

Larken gave her a curt nod, and Pippin started into the stable.

"Pippin," Hollindrake called after her. She turned to find him holding out his hand.

"Yes, Thatcher?"

"The pistol?"

"Oh, yes," she said, handing it over. "So sorry, I forgot I had it."

Larken snorted and shook his head, shooting a wary glance at the duke that said, *This folly is on your head*.

Pippin entered the stable and hurried to the stall where Dash was being held. Another man sat on a stool nearby, and with a curt nod from Larken, the man retreated to a discreet distance.

She dropped to her knees and caught hold of the bars. He lay in a crumpled lump on the far side. "Dash?" she whispered. "Dash, 'tis me. I've come to—"

To what? Save him? Help him. She glanced around the stable. Oh, demmit, she hadn't the least idea what to do now.

"I've come to be with you, my love," she said. "Please, look at me. I must know that you are unharmed."

For a long moment he didn't move, having stilled at the sound of her voice. But finally and slowly, he rolled over. One of his eyes was swollen shut, and he grimaced and clutched his ribs as he straightened. He'd been beaten when he'd been caught, and now he was suffering for it.

And so was she. For she ached down to her toes at the sight of him.

"Go away, my lady. Go away," he said, before he rolled back over.

"Dash! Whatever are you saying? Come here, I haven't much time. There is still a chance we could—"

Despite his injuries, he jerked up and turned toward her. "You will do nothing. Nothing more."

"I am so sorry," she said. "This is all my fault. I should have known—"

"How could you know I had more enemies than any man alive?" He shook his head. "Save Bonaparte."

Pippin smiled at his jest. "Dash, please come here, come closer. I cannot abide being apart from you."

"Oh, Circe, you must learn to live with it, for I fear there is nothing for us now."

The resignation in his voice shocked her. "Dash, whatever do you mean? You've been in worse spots, certainly. This is just an . . . an . . . an inconvenience," she offered, using his own description for when he'd been trapped in London by the frozen Thames.

He shook his head. "I fear this is far more than just an inconvenience. 'Tis my end. They'll hang me for certain and there will be no more chances."

"But I could—"

He struggled to his feet and crossed the narrow stall in staggered steps, before he dropped down before her, his fingers curling around hers. "You will do nothing."

"But I cannot—"

"You must," he told her fiercely. "You are safe this time. Larken has promised me. But he cannot look aside a second time. You must let me go."

Pippin shook her head, the hot sting of tears running down her cheeks. "Dash, there must be a way. I cannot let you . . . I will not . . ."

"You won't be. These are my crimes, and eventually a man must pay. 'Tis my time, little Circe." He reached through the stall and cupped her chin. "I've seen heaven in your arms, I don't fear my end. And you mustn't, either. You must promise me to get on with your life, and find a good man—"

"But I have—"

He laughed and shook his head. "No, a good man. One your cousin approves of. The sort who will keep you out of trouble."

She shook her head. "But who will teach me to be a pirate if you do not?"

He laughed again. "Ah, little Circe, you've a pirate's heart already. What more is there I could teach you? You've committed treason and been willing to commit murder for me—"

"I wouldn't—"

"Don't tell me you haven't thought of putting a bullet between Larken's eyes?"

"Well, he's rather unseemly—"

"Single-minded, but he's a good man, and you'll not harm him."

"If you insist," she managed.

"I do." He stroked her cheek, brushed the tears aside. "What more is there I could teach you?"

"But Dash, I thought—" Oh, this was awful. She'd thought . . . She looked up into his eyes and pleaded silently for him to let her . . . to let her try to find a way.

"Not this time, Circe. I know, I know. I thought we'd managed it this time as well. Thought it right up until a few hours ago." He pulled her closer and kissed her as well as he could through the bars of the stall. "Now go, lass, and don't return. If you think to save me, don't do it, for I shall not help you. I will not pull you any further into my world than I already have. I see now how wrong it was to think that we, that you could . . ." He groaned, then pulled away from her and staggered back to his corner, curling up into a ball, his back to her. "Go!" he barked.

She took a staggering step back from the stall. "No, you don't mean that, Dash. You mustn't—"

He rolled swiftly, his face a mixture of pain and fury. "Demmit, woman, go away. You've made a mess of my life—do you think I could love you? Never."

Still she couldn't move, couldn't believe what she was hearing. He didn't mean it . . .

Dash leaned over and picked up a clod of dirt and threw it at her, as if he was driving off a stray dog. It hit the bars and exploded into a cloud of dust, but it was enough to startle her out of her shock.

"Dash, I—"

He rose, his body shaking. "Leave me be, demmit. Get out of my sight. Don't you ever come back here. Ever!"

Tears blinding her eyes, she stumbled out of the stable, her world collapsing around her, one hand trembling over her rounded stomach. Whatever was she to do now?

Dash stood in the middle of the stall trembling in much the same manner as he watched her leave. It had torn his heart out to be so cruel, but it was the only way to save her.

Save her from him. He should never have sought her out, should never have kissed her, made love to her, ruined her life. He couldn't let her follow him any further, for he was more than convinced he'd come to the end of his days.

For how could he live without her?

His old friend Larken came strolling down the stable aisle.

Dash glanced away. "She thinks to save me."

"Impossible now," Larken said. "I hope she knows that."

"Aye," Dash said, ignoring the wrenching pain in his heart. "She knows."

"Then it was well done," Larken said, though not with his usual smooth arrogance.

Still, Dash couldn't look at him. "Will she be safe now?"

"Aye."

"No mention in your reports?"

"None," Larken promised. "The lady in the red gown that Mr. Dobbins saw will never be found, I fear. At least not by me."

"Thank you," Dash said. "I wouldn't have her come to any more harm on my account."

"Then, my good man, whatever were you doing with her in the first place?"

Dash shook his head and took one last glance out the stable doors, halfheartedly wishing he would find her still there. "I love her. I couldn't help but fall in love with her."

Larken nodded and turned his gaze out the stable doors, to the grand house rising in the shadows beyond. "I daresay, I understand that one."

Aboard the Ellis Anne, *1837*

Dash stalked around his cabin, a pistol clenched in his hands.

They wouldn't take the *Circe* from him. Not ever. Not his ship. Damn the British, how he hated them.

They'd stolen all his brandy, for there wasn't a

bottle left in his cabin. He knew they'd done it and that they were here now to take his ship.

He paced again, his thoughts wild and haphazard and he struggled to make sense of all of it. How had the *Circe* been surrounded? And where the hell was Mr. Hardy? Why hadn't he answered the bastards' arrival with the *Circe*'s cannons?

Dash raked his hand through his hair. If only he wasn't so demmed tired. He needed some sleep, but how could he sleep when his ship was in danger? If only he could rest, find a way to make sense of all this . . . for something wasn't quite right.

None of this was right . . . None of it, but he couldn't rest now, for there was one other problem. He glanced at the door to his cabin, now barred with his sea chest.

She was on board, and he had to save her. Save his other Circe.

He closed his eyes, the pistol clenched in his grasp. How the hell had Pippin gotten on his ship? Could it be she'd left her husband and come after him? Or was she the lure to bring him out into the open where he could be trapped for good?

The room began to spin and Dash staggered to find his footing. Images assailed him . . . his cold dark cell in Marshalsea Prison, the beach at Hastings, the sudden warmth of Pippin in his arms in the attics of the house on Brook Street. He turned and twisted, and each way he looked his past faced him, haunted him.

Sinking to his knees, his head aching, his gut heaving in need of brandy to soothe it, he knew he was going mad. He crawled to the piss pot and emptied his stomach, vomiting until he thought he was going to turn his insides out.

The room spun around him, and he would have called for help but his mouth was dry, his flesh on fire. Spent, he collapsed on the floor, his pistol cradled against his head.

They won't take me . . . not again . . . never again.

Voices in the hall drew his wary attention. He opened one eye and looked to the door, while his thumb cocked his pistol.

But instead of his enemies crashing through, all that followed was a soft scratching against the oak. Then a second scratch. "Dash? Dash, are you well?"

Both eyes open now, he struggled to get to his knees. "Circe," he croaked out, his throat raw, his tongue swollen.

"Let me in, Dash. Please, I must see you."

It was a trick. She would never be used so. Not to lure him out. No, his Circe loved him.

Enough to marry another.

He held the pistol to his head. "Never take me. Never again."

"Dash, you must let me in quickly. There isn't much time. Please Dash, help me. Save me."

He shook his head, "Go away. You're naught but a trick." He pulled himself into a sitting position opposite the door. "I could never save you. I ruined you, remember? Cursed you."

"Dash, you must let me in. I've come . . . I've come back to you."

He laughed. "You can't, Circe. Don't you know that by now?"

"I can, if only you will let me in."

He leaned forward, shaking the pistol at the door. "Sod off! You're not here, you frumpery, you whore. My lady is in London. My lady is lost." He shivered, chills replacing the fire beneath his skin. He leaned over and threw up again.

He was dying this night, he knew. One way or another, this was his last night on this earth.

"No Dash, 'tis me, Pippin. I'm here. Aboard your ship. I've come . . . I've come . . ."

"For what?" he asked, looking at the pistol and having no desire for any part of this. Any part of anything. There was nothing she could say to convince him she'd really come.

Save the words she whispered through the keyhole.

"I've come back, Dash. I've come back for pirate lessons."

Chapter 14

*W*hen Dash next awoke, it wasn't to find himself in a British cell, or even facing his Maker (or the fires of hell, which he'd always considered the more likely consequence of his ill-spent life), but rather it was the promising light of morning piercing the large window in his cabin that teased his eyes open.

Around him the chamber stood in stark contrast to its usual slovenly disorder. Neat and tidy, it smelled of lemon polish.

Egads, he must have died and gone to heaven.

"Dash?"

Pippin? He tried to get up to discover where she was, but found his arms and legs trapped. He struggled, but his limbs were held fast.

"Oh, dear," she was saying as she suddenly appeared at his bedside. "You can't move. I fear we had to tie you to your bed."

Tie him to his . . . And then memories, hazy ones at best, assailed him.

If it's not a fever . . .

Seen this afore.

How long?

Could be days. Been years since he's gone this long without a drink.

Do you think he'll . . .

No, he had heard Nate clearly say. *I doubt the devil or the angels will have him.*

Then it seems it is up to us to see him through . . .

Pippin stroked his forehead, her eyes fixed on his.

He looked up at her in wonder, but at the same felt a rakish bit of himself wrestling through the haze that still had him slightly befuddled.

"So this is what happens when you leave a woman in London Society for twenty-some years? The first opportunity she can contrive, she ties her old lover to his bed?"

Pippin glanced down at him, and moments later her eyes widened and her cheeks pinked as she realized just what he was saying. "Well, I daresay your fever is gone and you've come back to join the living, Captain Dashwell."

Then she laughed and reached for a knife, cutting off the ropes that bound him to his bed.

He reached down and rubbed his raw wrists. "Am I to understand that I didn't take kindly to my restraints?"

"You have much to apologize for. One of the mates swears he'll never have a lass again for the way you kicked him as they were trying to hold you down."

"Was it Gibbs?"

She nodded.

"Then I'll not worry so much over it. I don't think he's ever had a lass to begin with."

Her eyes widened again, and she knelt beside his bed. "Dear God, it is you," she said, her hand cupping his chin, grazing over the thick stubble. "You've come back to me."

"As apparently you've come back to me."

She nodded.

"Whatever happened?" he asked.

"You had a frightful time going without your usual rations of brandy."

Dash closed his eyes. He knew what she meant. Usual rations? Trying drinking from dawn until he passed out. "How many days have I been like this?"

"Three."

He groaned and glanced back up at her. "No wonder I feel like I've been keelhauled. Might have been kinder, Circe, to drag me under the ship a few times and be done with it."

She smiled at him, nudged him over, and sat down on his bunk beside him. Her warmth crept over him, and it was all he could do not to pull her closer.

As if she knew, she took his hand in hers.

He marveled at the warmth of her fingers, and his own capacity to feel it.

It had been a long time since he'd felt anything.

"So you saved me once again, have you?"

She shrugged.

"Why do you persist in doing so?"

At this she grinned, the smile lighting her eyes, and in the soft morning light she looked to him exactly like the lass he'd first spied on the beach at Hastings. "Someone must."

"Some would argue I am hardly worth the effort."

"Fools," she declared, "the entire lot of them."

With his free hand (for he wouldn't have let go of her for the life of him), he rubbed his aching chin, the stubble rough across his fingers. "Three days, you say?"

"Yes."

"Must look a bloody fright."

"Yes, quite," she agreed. "But not for long." Then she rose and went to the door. After a few whispered words and few more minutes, she reappeared at his side with a basin of hot water, a towel, a pair of scissors, and his razor.

Gently, she washed his face, and then went to fetch the razor.

"You don't mean to cut my throat, do you?" he asked as he eyed her coming toward him with the blade in hand.

"I could have Mr. Gibbs come down and do this, if you prefer . . ."

Dash shook his head.

"I didn't think so." She laughed, and then brought the razor up to his face, but he stopped her hand.

"Do you know what you're doing?"

She cocked a regal brow at him. "Of course." She pushed his hand aside as if he were a child and set to work.

Once he was shaved, she trimmed his hair a bit and then washed his face one more time, before bringing over a mirror for him to see.

"What do you think?" she asked.

Dash saw only what the years of drinking had wrought on his face, the lines, the haggard lack of color to his skin. "I don't like what I see."

"I do," she said, leaning over him and placing a

simple kiss on his forehead, before she turned to take the basin away.

And when she wasn't looking, his fingers went to the spot on his brow where she'd pressed her lips, and Dash glanced away so she wouldn't see the tears in his eyes.

By the time night had nearly fallen, Dash was ready to get out of bed, and he climbed out, his legs trembling beneath him, but at the same time, a strange strength filled his limbs.

And when he finally stood, he rose to his full height and stretched.

So this is what it feels like to be sober, he thought, wondering at the way his body was awakening—food tasted good again; the noises of the ship surrounded his ears, whispering all its secrets to him; he couldn't wait for morning and longed to see the sun, feel its warmth on his brow, a hint of the warmth that Pippin's kiss had brought.

Catching up his breeches and shirt, he smiled at the neatly done patches, the careful stitches showing the precision and care that had gone into their repair.

Dressed, he made his way above deck, the night breeze fresh and crisp in his lungs, bringing him fully awake. Overhead the sheets rippled and snapped in the wind, and he checked their positions.

The entire world rose before him in sharp focus, through clear eyes, and it was like finding his sight again after years of stumbling about blind. One of the crewmen walked past him, and it was only after the man was nearly past him that the fellow recognized him.

"Uh, Cap'n, didn't see you there. Fine night, sir," he said hastily, tugging at his cap in respect and moving along.

Dash nodded to the fellow, his mood slightly dampened by the sailor's ill-ease.

He made for the railing and went to check the seas. The mighty Atlantic in all her tumultuous glory lay before him. How he loved her, especially right now as she held the *Ellis Anne* atop her foamy waves, gracing his ship with a fair, easy passage, as if she were welcoming him back.

He inhaled again, realizing how much he'd missed this . . . this sense of belonging to something greater than himself.

"There you are," came a sharp voice from behind him. "I thought I told you to stay put until at least the morning!"

He turned and grinned at the lady crossing the deck. "I couldn't help myself. The sea called."

"Harrumph!" Pippin sputtered. "The sea indeed!"

He crossed his arms over his chest and leaned back against the rail. "Been my dearest mistress all these years." He paused for a moment and then grinned at her. "You wouldn't separate a man from his one true love, now would you?"

She stopped and eyed him, before she let out another *harrumph*, but this one spoke not of her disapproval. Then she came to the rail and looked out over the waves.

For a time they stood there, silent, each regarding the salty sea, and their thoughts . . . their thoughts far away from this awkward silence.

"I didn't want to be separated from you," she finally said. "'Twas the last thing I ever wanted. But there was no other way. If there had been, I would have—"

"I know," he said, cutting her off. He didn't want to know what she would have done for him.

Darkness began to surround them, and overhead the stars appeared, one by one sparkling anew with all their glory.

And then as if on cue, Orion's belt kindled its evening light, the trio of stars winking at one another as if in happy greeting.

He glanced over to see if she'd seen them as well, and the soft smile on her lips, the misty glow in her eyes told him all he needed to know. And she turned just then, and he knew it was because she'd hoped, she'd known he'd seen it as well.

Yet as close as they stood, as intimate as the moment had been, he'd never felt farther from her than he did right now.

As much as she might kiss his brow, nurse him through his private hell, stand beside him on his deck and exchange pleasantries, there was still so much wrong between them. So much between them.

Was this what time had done to them? Broken the thread that had bound them inexplicably together all those years ago? Could it really be lost?

"Pippin?"

"Yes, Dash?"

"How did we get here?"

"Aboard this ship?" she teased. "Nate ordered the sails raised and then—"

"Very funny," he said, cutting her off. "You know what I mean. Here. To this place."

"Oh, this place," she said, her face growing solemn. "I've wondered that as well, and all I can think of is that we are like our stars."

"How so?"

"You and I are the two outer stars, and the one between us is everything that keeps us apart."

He set his lips together and gazed out at the waves. "Like this ocean," he offered.

"Yes, and also all the ways we were never honest with each other."

He flinched at her words, but saw in her eyes not censure, but her own guilt as well.

She shrugged. "And I suppose we never really knew each other."

He laughed, for there wasn't an angle or line of her body that he hadn't memorized. Still remembered.

She must have seen the smoky light such memories kindled in his eyes, for she nudged him with her elbow. "Not in the way that lasts, Dash."

Again they lapsed into silence, and he glanced again at the stars overhead. If only there was a way to fill that empty space . . . Make good some promise he'd made her. Oh, but he'd broken so many.

Then the wind whispered around him, and he swore he heard her voice once again from the other night.

I've come for pirate lessons.

His gaze swung to look at her. Pirate lessons. Just as he'd promised her all those years ago. That was it.

"Pippin?"

"Aye, Dash?"

"Do you still dream of being a pirate?"

There was a pause before she choked with laughter. "No, of course not."

He turned to her and looked her up and down. "Truly?"

"No! I'm a grown woman, why, such a notion would hardly be . . . be . . ."

He cocked a brow and stared at her, and she stopped her rambling defense. "Proper?" She laughed, but he wasn't about to stop. "Are you sure about that?"

She opened her mouth to tell him the thousand ways it was all nonsense, but her lips fell shut and her shoulders dropped from their staid lines. "Oh, bother you, Dash. Maybe once in a while I still wonder." She laughed. "There you have the truth. The esteemed and respectable Lady Gossett still dreams of being a pirate." She looked over at him. "You may commence your teasing. Go ahead. I fear it not."

Instead he caught her by the hand and began towing her across the deck. "I have no intention of teasing. We've lessons to start."

She pulled him to a stop. "You can't be serious."

"I have never been so committed to a mission, my lady, in my entire life." He squeezed her hand and brought it to his lips. "I owe you my life, three times over, and now I intend to pay back a small portion of that debt by helping you discover your dreams."

Your desires . . . he wanted to add, placing one more kiss on her fingertips.

"Oh, Dash, you've gone mad," she said, pulling her hand free.

"Not at all," he said, bowing elegantly, sweeping off his hat and tipping his forehead down low in a contrite motion of supplication. "Lessons in piracy are my specialty. Swords and all." He peeked up at her and winked.

"Oh, get up," she said, tugging at his outstretched arm, and pulling him up. "I don't know if your lack of drink has made you mad, or I've caught your fever, for I daresay I am going to hold you to that promise. I want to be a pirate, sir."

"And so you shall, but first we must outfit you," he advised, grinning mischievously, for both her acceptance and the fact she still held on to him.

Was it he, or did her fingers tremble slightly in his?

As they came to the gangway, she pulled him to a stop. "Do I get a cutlass?"

Dash considered the image of Pippin in one of her fits of pique armed like Blackbeard and twice as fierce. "Have you forgiven me all my failings?"

She considered him for a moment. "Not entirely," she offered honestly.

He grinned at her. "Then the cutlass, I fear, shall have to wait."

"No, my lady," Dash said. "A thousand times no!"

Of all the pigheaded, stubborn . . . Pippin stuck her hands on her hips. "If you're afraid I'll fall, you would not be responsible—"

"It isn't that—" he began.

"And I am not afraid of heights—"

"It isn't that," he continued.

"Then why can't I climb the rigging?" Pippin stood her ground. Good heavens, she never remembered him being so . . . cautious!

He laughed and shook his head. "You've covered

this ship from stem to stern today, uncovered every nook and cranny below decks, and I will say it for the last time, the rigging is off limits."

"*Harrumph!*" she sputtered with more ire than Aunt Minty had ever managed.

Finn came up, bobbing his cap at Pippin, his eyes wide at her change of costume. Unable to tear his eyes away from her, he managed to get out his communication. "Cap'n, your supper is ready, set up in your cabin just like you asked."

"Good lad, Finn. Her Ladyship and I will be right down."

The boy's scandalized expression suggested he wasn't too sure her title still applied.

Well, she certainly wouldn't be mistaken for a proper London matron any longer. She doubted, garbed as she was, her own butler would admit her.

She'd covered her fair hair with a red bandana, put on her old muslin she'd brought, forgoing the crinolines and petticoats, affording her all the comfort and ease of movement she remembered from the fashions of her youth.

Taking a cue from the crew, she was also barefoot, for the weather was now warm, and the sun felt delicious on her toes.

To complete his offer to transform her into a "proper pirate," Dash had bestowed upon her one of his old gun belts, into which she'd tucked a knife.

She still held on to plans for a cutlass, and perhaps a pistol or two.

"Off with you now," Dash told the boy. "See to your own supper."

Finn dashed off without another word, but he did

glance back at her and wink his approval. Pippin grinned back, for she felt happy all the way down to her sunburned toes.

"Tomorrow," she prodded as Dash turned and went down the stairs to his cabin. "Tomorrow I can climb up to the nest."

"No!" he shot over his shoulder. "Over my dead body will you climb that rigging."

Pippin laughed. "Then don't give me a cutlass, for I will be sorely tempted to see you at your word."

Dash sputtered at first and then laughed heartily, the merry, rich sound sending a shiver of delight down her spine.

Pippin, don't think one day can make up for . . . she could hear her cousin Felicity chiding.

Of course one day didn't make up for everything, Pippin would have told her. But oh, what a glorious day it had been.

Since dawn they'd been like this, scrambling all over the ship like a pair of wayward children, Dash explaining every bit of how the ship worked, how the cargo was stowed, how to navigate.

For there was more, he assured her, to being a good pirate than just plundering.

But he'd also taken her below and showed her how to fire a cannon. Though, as with the rigging, he'd been adamant about not testing her knowledge and letting her fire one off, much to her chagrin.

"These guns aren't as bonny as the *Circe*'s were," he'd said, looking over the smallish guns. "She had twice the firepower. Why, one time . . ."

Pippin had paused, letting him relive the day he'd

captured a British frigate, and when he was finished, she'd asked him quietly. "You miss her, don't you?"

"Yes. Oh, this is a grand ship. One of the fleetest on the seas, but my heart, my love will always be the *Circe*." Then he'd turned and looked at her, and she knew he didn't mean just his beloved ship.

She smiled. "I would have liked to have sailed on her."

"You would have made a fine privateer," he'd said, and then the moment filled with too many memories. Of why Pippin had never made it away from England with him.

Inside Dash's cabin they found Nate at the great table, charts laid out in front of him, hastily eating his meal.

"Nate!" Dash said, with a trace of surprise. "A long time since we've dined together."

"Aye," his son said, biting off his answer with the same note of caution.

Dash nodded, and filled a plate for Pippin and then himself. They ate for a time in silence, Nate studying the charts before them. Finally Pippin couldn't take it any longer—for there was an air of tension between father and son that filled the room to the point of being unbearable.

"Mr. Dashwell, why is it you refuse to use the extra holds for smuggling?" she asked with a nonchalant air as if she'd just asked him about his plans for the evening.

Unfortunately she'd asked this at the moment Nate had taken a large gulp of tea, which he now sputtered. "Do wha-a-at?"

"Smuggle," she repeated. "French lace and ribbons are all the rage and taxed something terrible. You could make a tidy profit if only you weren't so—" She glanced at Dash. "How did you put it?"

"Starched in the shorts," he replied, his eyes sparkling mischievously.

"Yes, that's it," Pippin agreed. "Starched."

"My lady, smuggling is illegal," Nate told her, rolling up his chart and sending his father a look of censure.

"Aye, but it's profitable," she continued. "I'm certain Christopher—he's Mad Jack's oldest son, you know—wouldn't object to opening the passageway at Thistleton Park and handling all the business operations. He has his mother's genius for trade."

"I prefer to maintain a respectable business, my lady."

"*Harrumph!* You're as starched as John."

"I'm glad to hear it," he replied loftily.

Pippin glanced at Dash, and he at her, and they both started laughing.

"I don't know what we did wrong to produce such stodgy children," she said.

"I fear the entire generation is so," Dash agreed.

Nate stiffened. "I don't think of myself as starched or stodgy. I'll have you know that when I am in port—"

"Tsk, tsk, tsk," Dash said. "I doubt the lady would like to hear tales of your supposed conquests—"

"Supposed!" Nate said, taking offense until Pippin and Dash began to laugh again. Then he laughed as well. "My lady, do you tease your son, John, thusly?"

"Oh, goodness no! He is far too stuffy for such falderal."

Nate laughed. "Hardly as stuffy as you say. He is regarded as quite a daring captain. Wasn't he the one who saved all the people on the *Cadmus*?"

She nodded.

"The *Cadmus*?" Dash asked. "Wasn't that saved by a . . ."

His voice trailed off and then he glanced up at Pippin, his face pale with shock. When he spoke again, he stammered through his question. "Your son . . . my son . . . is a captain . . . an officer in the British navy?" Now it was Dash's turn to sputter over his tea.

Pippin flinched. "Yes . . . a highly regarded one," she added hastily.

"Not so funny now, is it, eh, Da?" Nate said, plucking another biscuit off the plate and munching it happily now that the tide had turned.

"The na-a-avy," Dash choked out.

"The British navy," Nate offered helpfully.

Pippin shot him a look that quelled the young man sufficiently. Good heavens, couldn't he see how hard it was for Dash? Though the United States and England had been at peace for more than twenty years, some battles never ended, at least not for the men who fought them, the ones who had lost so much in them and to them. Such bitter enmity couldn't easily be cast aside just because diplomats and governments ordered it so.

Even after so many years.

Dash pushed away from the table. "A navy officer?"

"Yes," she told him, folding her hands in her lap. And that wasn't even the whole of it, but the rest could wait.

He shuddered. " 'Tis a bitter pill, Pippin. My own son."

"Yes, but he doesn't know that he's your son, or that he isn't entirely British."

Dash's jaw worked back and forth, as if he were working a piece of tough gristle.

"He looks like you . . . and Nate," she offered. "No one could look upon the three of you together and not be able to guess the truth of the situation."

He glanced swiftly up at her. "He's a Dashwell?"

She nodded. "Through and through." And hopefully had remained blissfully unaware of his mother's situation, for Nate's announcement continued to haunt her.

I left a ransom note.

She could only pray that John had already been out to sea for his trials on the *Regina* before that wretched missive had been discovered.

Her son not only favored his father's features, but also possessed his reckless nature. Oh, John came across as the very epitome of propriety, of British stalwart spirit. But inside, Pippin knew, rode the devilish mix of Dashwell blood.

And blood always runs true when it runs in a passion.

Her brooding on what might happen was interrupted as Nate got up and reached for another chart. "I daresay I've made an error," he was saying. "For this can't be right."

Dash moved the tray aside and stood as his son unrolled the map, glancing at the chart with a quizzical expression.

"Are you sure about your reading?" Dash asked.

"Aye, I took it twice," Nate said.

Pippin got up and looked over the two men's shoulders as they consulted between Nate's notes and the chart.

Dash raked his hand through his hair. "If we continue at this speed you'll set a record for your crossing."

"Your crossing," Nate corrected. "You're the captain."

He shook his head. "I couldn't claim such a thing when I've done naught but . . . but . . . well, you know what I have and haven't done. And the log will be changed to show you as captain of record, and the record will be yours. Rightfully so." He clapped his son on the back. "Let's go up and take one more reading."

"How long until we reach Baltimore?" Pippin asked, feeling a lump in her throat over the slight smile of satisfaction on Nate's face.

He'd made Dash proud, and while he might deny he needed his father's approval, she knew well enough every son sought such.

"Ready to be rid of us?" Dash teased her.

"Quite the contrary," she said. "I merely wanted to know how many days I have left to convince you to teach me how to climb the rigging."

Dash groaned, but it was Nate's reaction that left her laughing, for he stared at her in horror. More so than when she'd come up on deck the first time in her pirate garb.

"My lady, you will do no such thing!" Nate blustered. "Passengers are not allowed in the rigging."

Dash held out his hands, as if in thanksgiving. "You see. I told you it isn't done."

"*Harrumph*. You are both a pair of stodgy old hens."

Dash looked affronted, while Nate just shook off her insult.

"Madam," he said, as stuffily as John might, "the rigging is off-limits. And I will warn you, while you think the crew finds your presence on the decks charming, they will not take it kindly if you are to ascend into their domain. You will find them quite unpleasant."

"Aye, my lady," Dash added, "listen to Nate. You'll not like the consequences if the crew catches you in their nets."

She laughed, for she was convinced they were merely trying to scare her off, and she followed them up on deck to learn how to take a reading from the stars.

And to take her own reckoning of the horizon behind them.

Two days later, while Dash was (much to her chagrin) up in the rigging, Pippin found herself standing on the decks watching him nimbly climb up the mast and then out on the spars.

He and the crew were teasing each other, and she suspected there was a fair amount of wagering being done both up in the rigging and down on the decks as to who would be faster, Nate or Dash.

Finn stood beside her, his hand shielding his eyes as he squinted up into the sunshine. "I'd never thought the cap'n could do it."

"I think he's done it a time or two before," she offered.

"Oh, not climb up there, but put off the bottle. Me mam said it's a devilish thing to get a man to wean himself off drink. Nigh on impossible."

"Well, I don't think the captain is over the worst of it yet," she said, thinking of the way his hand had shaken as he tried to cut into his dinner the night before. "But you should know that Thomas Dashwell is a man who is capable of doing the impossible, when he sets his mind to it."

"Mr. Clemens says he's doing it for you. So you'll stay with him."

Startled, she glanced down at the boy.

Oh, dear. How could she tell him that such a thing was impossible? She couldn't possibly stay with Dash. The scandal of her sailing off to Baltimore might be, as Finn had said, a devilish thing to undo, but staying?

Well, that was impossible.

Nothing is impossible if you set your mind to it . . .

Isn't that what Felicity had said when she'd moved them all to London, determined to have her duke? Or what Tally had said when she'd fallen in love with Lord Larken, with all his problems and demons?

But this was her life. And she'd made her choices long ago.

Life can change, my girl. Just look at me, Aunt Minty whispered from far away. And she would know. The disreputable pickpocket turned Society chaperone.

"I don't know if I can, Finn," she said. "Stay, that is."

"Oh, you will," he said, rocking back on his heels. "Look at them," he said, pointing toward the mast where Dash and Nate both scrambled to get above each other, a pair of good-natured monkeys laughing and insulting each other as they climbed. "That is higher than I've gone."

"You've gone up there?" she asked.

"Of course," Finn said with a shrug. "But only to the first spar."

Harrumph. "I hardly think that is fair. Your captain and Mr. Dashwell have said I cannot go up. And yet they let you go!"

"Well, of course I go up there. I'm part of the crew."

Part of the crew. She was growing tired of listening to such talk.

"I could teach you something that I doubt even the cap'n knows," Finn offered.

"And that would be?" she asked, her gaze still fixed on the space between the deck and the skies.

"I could teach you how to pick a pocket."

Instead of being shocked as she thought he expected her to be, she laughed. "I fear you are too late, lad, I already know how."

He shook his head. "You? A foyst? Now ain't that a fine one."

"I most certainly know how. I could have been quite the rum diver if I'd set my mind to it." She looked into his suspicious face and winked. "What sort are you? A knuckles, or did you work a bulk and file?"

His eyes widened at her perfect use of pickpocket cant, but he scoffed. "I didn't need no partner to work a bulk and file for I was the best nypper in Baltimore."

"You worked it alone?" she asked, for most pickpockets who used the technique worked in teams, the first one bumping into their pigeon, and the second coming along to clean out his pockets.

"Don't need a partner iffin you make it seem like some sort of accident."

"Oh, no," she disagreed. "I prefer to fork a purse without the cove knowing he's been pinched."

He looked up at her, still not quite believing her. "How is it a fine mort like you knows anything about being a rum diver?"

She settled down in the coil of rope, her arms crossed over her chest. "What does being a fine mort have to do with it? My cousin can pick a lock faster than even the best Seven Dials dubber."

Finn's eyes widened with admiration. "Can you teach me?"

She shook her head. "I don't think Mr. Dashwell would approve."

"True enough," Finn said wearily. "But picking pockets, my lady! Did your cousin teach you that as well?"

"No," Pippin continued, "I learned how from my Aunt Aramintha one winter when the weather kept us inside most of the time. She was the finest diver in all of London."

"Your aunt?" He shook his head at the notion.

"Well, she wasn't a blood relation," Pippin conceded. "But she might as well have been. When she retired from the business, shall we say, she came to live with my cousins and me in London."

"Did she help you free the cap'n from prison?"

"She stayed behind to make sure our disappearance wasn't noticed."

The boy looked disappointed, for he was more than determined to discover the identities of her co-conspirators.

"But my Aunt Minty always said it was best to lift a purse without anyone knowing you'd been there."

Nate shook his head. "Oh, they don't know when I fork 'em," he said. He waved at her to stand up and she did. Then he walked toward her, stumbled in front of her, catching hold of her and nearly toppling her in the progress. "My apologies, ma'am," he exclaimed as he righted himself and let go of her.

As Pippin found her feet again, it took her a moment to get her footing and bearings, and another moment more to realize she'd lost her belt and knife in the process.

She laughed heartily, clapping her hands together. "Well done, Finn."

He bowed. "Kept me mam and the brats fed, it did. But then Mr. Hardy caught me, and said I wasn't to steal any longer, for what would Ma and the rest of 'em do if I were hung? And he had a point, he did." He paused for a moment and then handed her back her belongings, which also included her pocket watch, which she hadn't realized he'd taken. "You won't be telling Mr. Dashwell, will you? I promised him I wouldn't steal no more if he took me aboard and taught me a trade."

She shook her head. "I promise, as long as you teach me how it was you got my pocket watch so deftly."

He grinned. "I don't know, my lady. I don't think Mr. Dashwell would—"

"Oh, hang Mr. Dashwell. If you show me how you did it, I will insist that Captain Dashwell teach you how to shoot this afternoon."

His eyes lit up like a burst of Chinese fireworks. "Truly?"

"Absolutely!" she promised.

"But I imagine if you can pick a pocket and you freed the cap'n from the prison, you can already shoot."

She put a finger to her lips. "Shhh, Finn. You are too smart by half. Of course I can shoot, but the captain thinks he is offering me a boon by teaching me to use a pistol since the rigging and the cannons are forbidden."

"I would hope so," Finn said, shuddering with something akin to Nate's proper sensibilities.

She laughed at this rapscallion's lapse into propriety. Not that she didn't want him to grow up and be a good man, but still she rather liked the little bounder, and hated to see his rakish tendencies lost. "Now how the devil did you get my pocket watch?"

Finn's dark eyes sparkled. "'Twas easy, if you know what you're doing," he offered, and then proceeded to teach her.

With Dash grinning down from the lines above, Finn reminding her of all the lessons she'd learned from Aunt Minty, the sun and sea all around her, Pippin's heart grew dizzy with joy at the profound sense of freedom she'd discovered . . . that Dash had given her with all his rekindled rakish charm.

Yet at the same time, she stopped, and another thought hit her. However would she return to her stolid life on Grosvenor Square now that she'd tasted this heady elixir, discovered her dreams could come true?

Well, nearly all of them, she thought, taking another long glance at Dash swaying in the lines high over her head, so far out of reach.

Later that evening, Pippin sat curled up on a coil of rope, out of way of the crew and happily knitting in the light of the lamp hanging over her head. The night was balmy, and it was too fine a weather to sit in her cabin. Alone.

Oh, bother, Pippin, whatever do you think is going to happen? she chided herself. *And whatever would you do if it did?*

If Dash came up to her, took her hand, invited her down to his cabin and spent the star-filled night making up for all their lost years . . .

Goodness gracious! She was waxing as foolish as she had when she'd been one-and-twenty and head-over-heels in love with Dash.

Aren't you still? that wry voice chided.

Across the deck, a few of the hands were telling Finn stories of the sea. They had the slight lad entranced by their stories, and a few of their salty tales had even Pippin smiling.

"Oh, aye, boy, you must beware the *Flying Dutchman*, I saw her meself, I did," the man said, with a sly wink to one of his mates. "Sails as red as blood and her decks glowing with a light that would put shivers down to your toes."

Finn's eyes rounded. "How close did you get?"

"Close enough to hear the crew crying out for

help, for cursed they are, as cursed as their captain," he told him.

Another mate wagged his finger, "So beware the decks at night, little lad, for I hear tell the *Dutchman* keeps a great black bird that can carry off a man, whenever an unsuspecting ship comes too close and the *Dutchman* needs to add to her devilish crew."

Finn shivered, and it was on the tip of Pippin's tongue to chide the fellows for scaring the child senseless, for she doubted the boy would sleep for the rest of the voyage at this rate.

"If only that buzzard would carry you off, Mr. Hagen," Dash said, coming up from behind them, "for if the *Dutchman* couldn't see us, I am sure your fine stench would draw her."

The idle men laughed, as did Mr. Hagen, for it had been said in jest, and even Finn managed to snicker at the captain's wry insult.

The men tugged at their caps and moved away, taking up their final tasks before their watch came to an end.

She studied Dash as he turned toward the sea and looked over the waves, his thoughts faraway. She didn't think he'd seen her over here in her little cubbyhole, and she was about to call to him when something remarkable happened.

Finn glanced nervously after the retreating sailors, and then over the rail at the dark waves beyond. "Cap'n?"

Dash turned, and if Pippin didn't know better, she thought he looked surprised to find the boy still standing by his side. "Yes, Finn?"

"Have you seen the *Flying Dutchman*?" The boy's

eyes were still wide, and he shuffled his feet a bit, his hands clenched at his sides.

Dash knelt down and looked the lad directly in the eye. "No. I've seen plenty of strange things at sea, but never a ghost ship."

That wasn't enough for Finn. Now that he had the captain's attention, he had a raft of questions he was prepared to ask. "What would you do if you did?"

Pippin covered her mouth to stifle the giggle that threatened to reveal her position.

Dash crossed his arms over his chest and made a great show of considering his course of action. Then he grinned at the lad and said, "Sail as fast as I could in the opposite direction."

His young audience didn't look overly impressed. "You'd run?"

"Wouldn't you?" Dash returned.

Finn shrugged. "I supposed I would, but you're the cap'n. Cap'n Dashwell." He made his statement with an air of awe that spoke much of Dash's reputation, his infamy as a privateer. "Wouldn't you stand your ground and fight?"

Dash laughed and rose to his feet, towering over the boy. "Lad, the reason I'm alive today is because I knew when to fight and when to run up the sheets and save my neck, save my crew, my ship."

"Hmm," Finn murmured as he considered this. The two of them stood side by side along the rail for a time, before he asked, "Is that why you didn't marry the lady in red? 'Cause you had to run?"

Every bit of Pippin froze. Oh, dear goodness, she'd never expected such a question from Finn, and certainly neither had Dash, for after he turned a shocked stare on the lad, he glanced away, looked up at the stars. At Orion's belt, she would have sworn.

She started to rise, for she feared Dash might become angry, lose his temper as he had before with Finn, but this Dash, this man who was struggling to find his footing, planted his feet solidly on the deck.

"She married someone else, Finn," he said quietly. "There was no battle to fight once she'd done that. I'd lost, and sometimes when you lose, there is nothing you can do but move on."

Finn sighed and shook his head, the arguments and problems of adults far beyond his ken, but he still he persisted, struggling to understand. "Did you?"

"Did I what?"

"Move on? After you lost her?"

Again, Dash shook his head. "Nay, I didn't. Not at all."

"'Cause you loved her?"

Dash looked away. "Aye. Without her, I lost my course and sailed about the seas rather like the *Dutchman*."

"You did rather look like a ghost when Mr. Dashwell signed me on," Finn told him, with all the straightforward innocence of youth.

"I suppose I did," Dash admitted, scratching at the stubble on his chin.

"But you've come around nicely, as me mam would say," Finn said.

Dash laughed. "I have?"

"Oh, aye, everyone is talking about it," Finn told him in a confidential tone. "They say now that you got her back, your lady that is, you'll be in a fine fettle in no time."

There was a pause in their exchange, as Dash considered how to reply. The moments held Pippin in their grasp, for she waited as anxiously as Finn to hear his reply.

"Well now, lad, I haven't gotten her back, she's only here for this voyage. Until we get to Baltimore."

Pippin pressed her lips together at the sad note to his words. Did he want her to stay?

The answer didn't sit any better with Finn. "Then you have to try harder to convince her to continue on with you," the boy chided. "Show her that you aren't sailing about witless and lost like that old *Dutchman*."

"I don't know if I can," Dash said, admitting more to the lad than he ever had to her.

The longing in his voice, the fears beneath his words, tore at her heart.

Oh, you can, Dash, you can, she wanted to cry out, but her courage failed her.

"Of course you can," Finn unwittingly said for the both of them. The boy paused and then grinned up at Dash. "If all else fails, you could get one of them black birds to go fetch her back," Finn said, teasing a bit and shifting the mood.

"Aye, that's all I need is some great nagging bird. I haven't had such a creature on board since Mr. Hardy sailed with me," Dash replied.

They both laughed, and Finn reached out and took Dash's hand. "I liked Mr. Hardy. He told me the best stories about when he sailed with you, during the war and before. I miss him, I do."

"So do I, lad," Dash said, his voice trembling. "So do I." He pulled his hand free and ruffled Finn's hair.

He took one last glance at the stars and then back down at the boy. "Did Mr. Hardy ever tell you about the time we took an English frigate off the coast of Bermuda and I nearly got shot out of the lines?" Dash turned, and started walking along the railing, away from Pippin.

"No!" Finn said, nothing but awe and curiosity in his voice as he hurried to follow. "Did you fall?"

"No, but I'll show you a trick to staying in the rigging when you think you're going over."

"Truly?"

"Oh, aye, lad," Dash teased. "You'll need to know how to hang on if ever we run across the *Dutchman*."

They laughed again, and continued along the railing, Dash regaling Finn with stories and the boy's eyes shining with pure admiration.

Pippin watched the two of them, her heart in her throat, tears glistening in her eyes. She'd seen so many sides of Dash, but this one, this kindhearted, gentle soul, was something that left her breathless. Hardly the same man she'd encountered when she first came aboard.

The *Flying Dutchman*, indeed.

He was making amends in so many ways—her pirate lessons, teasing his men with his quick wit, teaching Finn to be a good sailor. Indeed, he was becoming a new man—or rather, rediscovering the man she'd always known him to be.

And here everyone thought the change in Dash was her doing, but she knew the truth—the only person who could be credited for his transformation was him. She'd seen him fist his shaking hands at his sides to still the tremors that rocked him, as he held on through some private moment of hell. She knew he still wanted to slake his thirst, but had held fast to his resolve by the sheer force of his own strength, his will.

If he was finding a new course, shedding the ghosts of his past, she knew he was doing it all on his own. She could take no credit for it.

But that didn't stop her from wanting to discover where this new heading, this freshening breeze would take him. And whether, once he found his way, there would be room enough in his heart for her.

Chapter 15

*D*ash came up on deck looking for Pippin, even as he had to shake off the moment of trepidation that ran down his spine. Stop the trembling in his hands.

He clenched his fingers into a tight fist and closed his eyes. He didn't need a drink. He didn't.

And then he opened his eyes and looked for the vision that was drink enough.

Pippin. His Circe. He longed to see the breeze blowing her hair free of its confining pins, the long strands fluttering as enchantingly as the siren she'd always reminded him of.

It had been days since he'd awakened, cold sober in his room, and found her there waiting for him. If ever a man had to awaken from a decades-long nightmare, it should be to the vision of her.

But now what? They'd been scampering about the ship these past days, exploring it together, laughing and teasing each other as they had when they'd been young, but there was still so much between them.

So much to keep them apart.

And now they were nearly to Baltimore, and then what? He almost wished Nate wasn't such an accomplished sailor—and the journey had taken another fortnight.

It seemed even the Fates were conspiring against him, for it was as if they were filling the sails and calming the seas before them to keep the *Ellis Anne* on a straight, true course.

Each morning it was the same, Pippin would arrive on deck, bright and eager for her day's lessons, and his heart would ache at the sight of her. And then each night, his pain worsened, for there was that awkward, terrible moment when he had to bid her good night, and they'd both stand there like a pair of mooning youths (at least he was mooning), staring at each other as if they knew not what to do next.

That was the rub of it. They knew what to do. But it had been so long, would it be the same? Could they ever find that passion that had bound them together so many years ago?

Hell, he was just this side of sober, he wasn't all that sure he could even . . .

Then he imagined the sight of her, the sun illuminating her silhouette, revealing the long lines of her legs, the curve of her hips, the full rounded shape of her breasts, and he knew.

Knew he could.

If only . . .

"Cap'n!" the urgent cry ripped through his musings. "Cap'n, Mr. Dashwell needs you at the mainmast. There's trouble, Cap'n. Devilish trouble."

The mainmast? Whatever could be wrong with

the mainmast when the weather had been naught but balmy?

Then he looked up and spied what had the entire crew, as well as Nate, pacing about on the deck below like a pack of discontented alley cats with a canary just out of reach.

And it was a bird in their sights. A bird of a sort.

For up in the mainmast, high up in the rigging, holding on to a spar with a wide grin on her face, clung Lady Gossett.

The air in his lungs came rushing out in shock. Pippin! Christ sakes, she'd gone against his orders and climbed the rigging.

Nate stormed over to his side. "Is this your doing?"

"Mine?" Dash exploded. "I would ask the same of you. I told that daft woman to stay on the deck. Nay, ordered her to keep out of the rigging."

Nate cursed and paced back and forth in front of him. "No one is willing to go up and get her down. They won't risk their fool necks for her."

Dash looked up at her, and as mad as he was, nay, furious with her, he had to press his lips together to keep from smiling. She looked glorious up there, her hair streaming behind her in the breeze, the sun glinting off the long blond strands. But it was the grin on her face that caught hold of him.

He'd never seen her look so demmed happy. Ever. Not in his arms, not the night she'd freed him, not ever.

Because she's finally free . . .

Aye, he could understand that one. For he knew that while Lady Gossett had lived a conventional and proper life—for the most part—there lay inside a rather scandalous, unconventional lady longing to cut her own swath through the world.

Well, she was certainly making up for lost time.

He rounded the mast to get a better gauge of her position and then stopped stock-still—for all too suddenly he understood what had the crew goggle-eyed, and not just the sight of a lady in their rigging.

"Where the hell did she get those?" he exploded.

Nate knew exactly what he meant. "Those are Mr. Brody's breeches. He washed them yesterday and she plucked them from the line when no one was looking." He sighed. "He's demanding they be replaced, for the men are already teasing him about wearing 'lassie pants.'"

Dash choked back a chuckle, for he had to agree with Brody. No man wanted a woman wearing his pants.

Which reminded him, this was his ship and that woman had disobeyed his direct orders.

"Oh, demmit, Mr. Dashwell," one of the men shouted. "She's a going higher!"

"She's headed for the nest," another said with an air of disbelief.

Every pair of eyes rose in unison to watch as the agile lady in breeches deftly climbed higher, especially when her movements afforded each man a fine view of her rounded bottom tucked into her purloined breeches.

"Never seen your pants look so fine, Brody," Glover teased.

"Aye," Gibbs chimed in. "Cap'n, when we get to Baltimore can we get a few more of these climbing lassies? I'll donate a pair of my britches."

"I don't want to see the sort of lass who would fit into those mainsails you wear for pants, Gibbs." Mr. Clemens laughed. "But iffin you've got more britches to spare, Brody, we could find us an entire crew of ladies to send up."

"I'll go get her, Cap'n," Finn offered, his cheeks reddened with embarrassment at such discussions. "I don't want to see her . . . see her . . ."

Dash shuddered. *Fall and break her neck*, was what the lad was dancing around.

And she would if she went much higher without someone to keep her safe.

"Half my wages she falls before she reaches the next spar," one of the men called out.

"I'll take that wager," another said. "And half my wages she makes the spar but falls afore the nest."

The wagering and bets began to fly around the deck with gory details of how she'd end—on the deck or in the drink.

"Cap'n!" Finn pleaded. "I got to save her. I don't want to see her—"

"No, lad, neither do I," he told him. "But Her Ladyship is my responsibility." Heaving a sigh, Dash shrugged out of his coat and waistcoat. His boots followed, then added to the pile went the pistols he'd brought up for the shooting lessons she'd requested.

He was of half a mind to shoot her, and save himself the trouble of breaking both their necks, for it had been a long time since he dared climb that high.

Nate caught him by the arm. "Da, I'll go after her. I brought her on board."

He plucked Nate's hand off his shirtsleeve. "No, it is time I repaid the lady."

"When was the last time you climbed all the way to the nest?" Nate demanded, sounding all too much like a captain. A stodgy one. But he was also a Dashwell, and he'd started to shrug off his coat.

"I can do it," Dash told him, clenching his hands to his sides so Nate couldn't see how they trembled. Damn these shakes. He could do this. He could.

His son groaned. "You aren't steady enough to go all the way up. First bit of wayward breeze and it will shake you off like water on a wet dog."

"You are not going after her," Dash said, and when he saw that his words weren't having any effect, he added, "That's an order."

Nate ignored him, so Dash reached over and caught up one of the pistols.

Cocking it, he handed it to Finn. "Anyone tries to follow me, shoot them."

The boy gaped wide-eyed down at the gun in his hand. "But Cap'n—"

"That's an order, Finn. A single man comes along after me and I'll have you keelhauled and fed to the sharks." With that, he caught hold of the peg in the mast, hooked his toes into the ropes, and began to climb.

Nate surged forward, that was until he found a pistol shoved into his chest.

The boy gulped, but refused to move. "Sorry, Mr. Dashwell. Cap'n's orders."

"Cap'n's orders!" Nate said, taking a step back, for the boy's hand trembled so bad it didn't take a far stretch of the imagination to know that the demmed thing could just go off in such an untrained grasp.

"Fine time for him to remember he's the captain," he muttered. "Just in time for him to get himself killed."

Pippin paid scant attention as Dash climbed up after her. Once she'd gained her objective, taking up a position in the crow's nest, she plucked the spyglass she'd stolen from his room while he'd been asleep and looked with awe at the majestic sight of the ocean.

Waves and water in every direction; it was amazing, for she felt herself quite on top of the world, even though she realized she was naught but a speck atop the might of the Atlantic.

None of her titles and trappings mattered out here; it was as if she suddenly, for the first time in a long time, found her feet back beneath her and her life opened up with exhilarating clarity. Society be damned.

The rebellious thought left her grinning until she remembered two reasons that she should have a care.

Ginger and John.

"Oh, bother such things," she told the breeze. Ginger had Claremont's name to protect her. And John? Well, anyone who knew John would never doubt his sense of propriety.

This should have been a comfort to her, but instead it left her feeling slightly sad. If only John could be a little more like his father . . .

Like Dashwell, not Gossett. If only he could find someone to love him—not the viscount, not the naval hero, but the man beneath the uniform and title.

Before she could worry much more over her son's

future, Dash poked his head through the opening at the bottom of the nest. "Demmit, woman! I ought to wring your neck!"

Well, perhaps not that much like his father, she amended, even as she grinned down at Dash.

"I bloody well nearly fell halfway up," he complained. "And here you are grinning like this is some Maypole lark."

She didn't respond but let him complete his ascent, claiming the other half of the narrow perch. Red-faced and wheezing, he paused to catch his breath. "I gave you a direct order to stay out of the rigging, out of the lines, and off the mainmast," he sputtered. "You could have been killed. Demmed near killed me."

She glanced at him and tried to look contrite, but she failed utterly. She began to laugh, as merrily and brightly as the sparkled sunshine falling down upon them. Pippin clutched at the narrow basket and held on, for she couldn't help herself. "When did you become such an old hen?"

Dash's brows rose in outrage. "A wha-a-at?"

"An old hen," she said slowly, enunciating each word with precise measure. "Whenever did Captain Thomas Dashwell ever listen to someone else's orders when he sought his own course?"

His jaw worked back and forth. "It is just that this stunt of yours could have . . . could have . . ."

"Gotten me killed?"

His lips clamped shut and he nodded.

"'Tis my life to wager, Captain Dashwell. Mine to choose how I spend it. No one else's." She'd never meant something more fiercely. For in these past few

days, whatever debts, whatever grievances lay between them, Dash had washed his half of the slate
clean. He'd given her the adventure she'd longed for
all her life.

Let her live as she'd always wanted, free and without constraints. She reached out and laid her hand
on his sleeve. "Isn't that what you would wish for
me?" She left her hand there, sitting innocently on
his sleeve, but the heat between them rose with a
swift fire.

Yet Pippin didn't pull her hand back, as she knew
she should.

And Dash didn't move his arm.

"Whatever were you thinking coming up here?"
he asked, his gaze holding hers with a mesmerizing
light. "Nearly did me in when I saw you up here."

She grinned and leaned closer, feeling the pull between them. Like trying to stop a tide. "I thought
this was a better alternative to lighting off one of the
cannons."

He paused, staring at her, and then Dash laughed.
The merry, rakish sound that had lit her heart on fire
the first time she'd ever met him. The night he'd stolen
a kiss from her. Her first kiss, their first kiss. The one
that had bound them together all those years ago.

"Lady Gossett," he said softly, "you're still the
most devilish minx alive."

And Pippin thought—no, prayed—no, hoped with
all her heart that he meant to kiss her. Would take her
in his arms and plunder her lips and steal her heart
once again. Right here and now.

But the fickle winds had another thing in mind.

A roguish bit of breeze rushed past them, swaying the mast and sending Pippin flying into Dash's arms.

Her forehead crashed into his jaw, and for a precious moment she thought she was going to lose her footing and slip.

"Ooh," she cried out, her hands grasping for something to hold on to.

But it was Dash's swift movement that saved her. He caught her and held her, planting himself in the wavering nest as if it were nothing more difficult than navigating a London ballroom.

"Steady, lass," he said as she shivered, holding her, and once the worst of the swaying had passed, pulling her up along the wall of his chest until she could stand once again. "Had enough of your newfound freedom?"

"Yes, quite," she said, feeling the loss of their connection quite keenly. "But I have one last thing to do." She pulled the spyglass out and tipped it up to her eye. "I wanted to see where that ship was."

"What ship?" Dash asked.

"The one behind us," she said, searching the horizon. "Hmm. That's odd. I don't see it now. Can you find it?"

Dash took the spyglass from her outstretched hand, careful, she noted, not to touch her again. He searched the line where the sea and sky met, but shook his head. "I don't see anything, must have been a trick of the light." He snapped it shut and handed it back to her. "I remember one of my first times standing watch up in a nest, I called a general alarm on what turned out to be a pack of whales."

She laughed. "You? Never?"

"Oh, aye. Got a bit of a lashing for it 'cause they had to rouse the captain from his bed."

Chuckling, she smiled at him, then took another glance over her shoulder. "I swear I saw a ship back there."

"And back there they will remain," he told her, "for no one can catch us."

With that he began to climb down, guiding her along the way and pointing out the best places to get her footing.

Pippin hadn't realized quite how high she'd gotten herself until it was time to get down, and then she was heartily glad for Dash's advice.

Down below, the men, who had lost their apparent awe of having a real English lady on their ship, tossed up raucous comments, but by the time she'd nearly gotten herself to the deck, they were cheering her on.

Several of the men scampered up and climbed through the last bit of net to greet her.

Or at least that was what she thought they were going to do, until the pair on either side of her whipped handfuls of rope from their back pockets and swiftly and skillfully tied her hands to the netting.

"Dash! Dash!" she called after him, for he'd already hopped down to the deck and was standing there in his wide-set stance, grinning up at her. "They've tied me up. Get me down!"

He crossed his arms over his chest and shook his head. "No."

"No?" She turned to Nate. "Mr. Dashwell, order these men to untie me!"

"My apologies, my lady," he said, taking much

the same stubborn stance as his father, "but you were ordered to stay out of the lines and you willfully disobeyed that order."

"Oh, bother that nonsense! Get me down!"

Nate shook his head. "I fear I cannot."

"You cannot, or you will not?"

He glanced over at his father and grinned before he replied. "Both, I have to imagine." And then the pair started laughing.

Pippin sputtered and swore, putting the rest of the crew in the whoops until the *Ellis Anne* echoed with male laughter.

She turned helplessly to Finn. "Can you help me?"

He too shook his head. "Sorry, my lady. 'Tis the rule. Only the crew is allowed in the rigging. Passengers who don't heed the rule"—he paused and glanced around at the others, who were still laughing too hard to explain—"get caught."

"And how," she said in her most imperious voice, "do I get uncaught?"

"A boon," Dash called out. "You have to grant the crew a boon."

The men nodded and laughed. "You don't happen to have some brandy?" one of them teased. "Now that the cap'n has gone dry on all of us, we're powerful thirsty."

She shook her head, "I haven't any spirits to offer."

"That's a shame," one man said. "Dry tobacco?"

She shuddered. "Whyever would I have tobacco? Ladies do not use tobacco."

"Me mam does," the man argued. "Blows the finest smoke rings in three counties."

Pippin was growing exasperated. Smoke rings, indeed! She turned her pleading gaze on Dash. He wouldn't leave her to the mercy of his crew. Would he?

He merely grinned back at her, rocking back on his bare heels as if he had all the time in the day.

Oh, bother the man. She was heartily glad she hadn't kissed him before. Because if she got down from here she was going to brain him with the first heavy object she could find.

"Now back to work with the lot of you," Nate ordered.

To her horror, the men began to drift off, returning to their tasks. And leaving her up in the lines like so much laundry to be dried in the breeze.

Her stomach growled and her legs were growing tired, and quite frankly her infatuation with a pirate's life was being sorely tested.

"There must be some sort of boon I can offer," she called after them. "I just don't know what is appropriate."

Then from a knot of men came a small voice.

"You could kiss the cap'n."

Every soul aboard stilled and turned toward Finn.

The boy blushed furiously. "I just think Her Ladyship could kiss the cap'n and that would be boon enough."

Dash wasn't quite sure how he ended up back up in the lines; mostly it was the not-so-subtle shoving of his men that propelled him up into her company.

All too quickly he found himself facing her, with

the netting between them. The men's cheers and lewd catcalls became no more than the wind, for the moment he found himself staring into her angry, nay, furious blue gaze, he had to laugh, for suddenly the rest of the world was forgotten.

"Caught you well and good, they did, my lady," he whispered.

"This is an outrage," she shot back.

"Paying the piper, perhaps?" he offered.

"*Harrumph,*" she sputtered.

"I could send up Gibbs to collect the boon, if you prefer," he offered, making a mock attempt to climb back down. "Or Brody. Those are his pants you're wearing."

"Dash, don't you dare!" she sputtered, shaking the netting furiously.

"Is that an order?" he asked, still poised to get down.

"No," she ground out. "Get back up here."

"Ah, nothing like having to kiss a less-than-willing woman," he said as he climbed back into place. "I remember a time when my kiss wasn't so objectionable, my lady. When you even sought it out."

He thought he saw a flash in her eyes. The fire that used to burn there when he'd have her in his arms, have her beneath him.

And he suspected she was thinking the same thing, for she shifted, her legs pulling together, her hips swaying slightly.

Pleased with her response, he continued unabashedly. "I recall that you used to beg for me to—"

Her gaze blazed this time. "Oh, for the love of

God, Dash, will you just kiss me and be done with it so I can get down from here?"

"If you insist," he said, leaning closer, even as she drew in from her side of the net.

Oh, what a spectacle we must look, he thought. And then it struck him. He was about to kiss her. Kiss his Circe.

Not since the first time he'd kissed a lass had he ever felt so unsure of what to do. A chaste peck on the lips?

A wry, wicked thought whispered at him. *When will you ever have her again, bound and at your mercy? If you do this right, you could have her every night for the rest of your life . . .*

No, she'd never stay, he told himself. Never. He'd ruined it all, but that didn't mean he wouldn't take this kiss, for it might well be the last one she'd ever offer him.

For he doubted she'd go venturing into the rigging again.

And oh, how he wanted to entice her. To tease her, to rekindle in her the desires and passions that had pushed him to commit more sins than he cared to count.

"Come now, Dash," she whispered. "Kiss me."

Her words stole over him with hope, with desire.

He leaned toward her, pulling on the ropes that made up the netting. Her eyes hadn't left his, until she got close enough, that scant bit of distance before a kiss goes from being a wish to being a reality.

Her lashes fluttered shut and he closed the distance, settling his lips upon hers.

As if he should have left such heaven to his memory, for what he remembered and how he felt, touching her silken, welcoming lips, feeling her open up to him, her tongue tenderly touching him, teasing him closer.

Begging him to come plunder.

And being a pirate at heart, he did.

His arm shot through the netting and caught hold of her waist pulling her up against him, as close as he could gather her with the net between them.

Frustrated for more, starving to take in every bit of her he could discover, he deepened the kiss, sucking her lower lip into his mouth, growling . . . yes, growling with hunger.

His hand cradled her bottom, shaped and rounded as it was in those stolen breeches. No piles of crinoline or petticoats, just twill between his hand and the heaven of her skin.

She swayed in the ropes, her knee nudging at his thigh, and Dash's world crashed all around him.

For even as the cheers and jeers of his crew below started to pierce the sensual fog he'd fallen into, he heard the one sound that gave him something he hadn't had in twenty-some years . . . hope.

For when he pulled back, when he released her, she moaned.

A sensual purr that no man could misunderstand.

The lady wasn't done with him. Not by a long shot.

If it hadn't been for Dash's hold on her, Pippin knew she would have fallen from the netting when he cut her free.

Shaking from head to toe from his kiss, Pippin couldn't remember the last time she'd had her world wrenched asunder.

He'd kissed her, and suddenly she'd been seventeen again, standing on the beach, and this was the pirate of a man who stolen a kiss from her.

The moment he'd tentatively pressed his lips to hers— truly, who would have thought such a thing possible; Dash, being hedgy?—oh, yes, when he'd finally steered a true course and kissed her, everything inside her had unraveled, all her long-held desires, all her obligations.

There had been nothing to her world but this man and his kiss.

She'd leaned wantonly toward him, teased him with her tongue, nearly begged him to take her. Up here, in the rigging, in front of his entire crew. And she wouldn't have cared if he had done it in the middle of Hyde Park or in front of Parliament.

For when he'd cradled her bottom with his hand, pulled her as close to him as the netting would allow, and she'd brushed against him, she'd known he was in as much need as she was—oh, he'd sparked a tempestuous, dangerous flame with his kiss, his touch, and now she wanted him to pour kerosene atop it and let them burn anew.

Kiss me, Dash. Kiss me, again, she wanted to cry out as he helped her down from the ropes. When she dared a glance at him, she spied the truth in his glittering green gaze.

He knew. He knew what he'd done to her.

And scoundrel that he was, he knew only too well how much she wanted him to continue.

* * *

But what both Dash and Pippin forgot in their heady exchange was the one point that would have probably quenched their desires altogether.

The ship on the horizon that Pippin had spotted.

For on the deck of that mighty vessel paced its captain in high dudgeon over the proximity of his quarry and his inability to catch them.

"Damnation, Mr. Perkins," Captain Lord Gossett bellowed, "Keep us just out of sight until nightfall. Then douse the lights, pour on every inch of sail, call out every man, whatever it takes, for we must catch them before they reach American waters."

"Aye, aye, my lord," his first mate replied. "But what do you intend to do when we catch her?"

"Retrieve my mother by any means possible."

And Mr. Perkins said a silent prayer for all the souls on the American ship, for he knew that by the next dawn, they'd be at the bottom of the sea if His Lordship had his way.

Pippin spent the rest of the day dithering between catching Dash by the hand and towing him down to his cabin and, well, dithering.

And then what? she asked herself more times than she cared to count. Because she hadn't come up with an answer that would serve all the conflicting ties that bound her life together.

John and Ginger . . . she couldn't very well tell them about Dash. Her proper, all-too-English children would be scandalized. Not to mention the ruckus of gossip it would create in the salons and parlors and receiving rooms of London if such news slipped outside the family.

She whirled around and paced in the other direction. But then there was Dash. A life with Dash.

He did want her, didn't he? And not just for a night, but for always. Maybe? She pressed her fingers to her lips. She thought he did. She couldn't have been mistaken about that.

As you were about him before?

Huffing a sigh, she shook her head.

However can you just forgive the man? She could hear her practical cousin Felicity lecturing. *He deceived you utterly. Used you to save his hide as he used his first wife to gain his ship. Haven't you learned anything?*

She shook off that ugly, wayward thought.

No, certainly there had always been a footloose, wild nature to Dash that had seemed so untouchable, so free, that no woman would ever be able to tame.

And perhaps in her youth she'd never trusted him enough to tell him about the child she carried. Quite honestly, she hadn't planned on doing so until they had been married, for she hadn't quite trusted that he wouldn't bolt from her life, disappear across the seas, and be lost to her once again.

But with the perspective of years, and a life lived with restraint and caution and propriety, she now saw it a little differently.

Tame Dash? Why, she'd as likely stop the winds from blowing. And as much as her marriage to Gossett had set Dash on a sad, lonely course, it had also put her on the same isolated path. Yes, she'd loved her husband, loved her children. But gracious heavens, she'd discovered her heart, her dreams with Dash.

Now Brent was gone, her children were grown, and it was time she took over setting the course for the rest of her days with Dash.

Their days . . .

A knock on her door brought her head up.

"Lady Gossett," Dash said in all formality. "Can you come with me?"

What had brought this proper note to his request?

Wildly she glanced down at the red gown, the one she'd worn all those years ago. The one she knew would announce her intentions clearly to him, as clearly as if she'd turned up naked in his bed.

Had she been utterly mistaken about his kiss?

Shakily she crossed the room, took a deep breath, smoothed the dress into place, and opened the door.

There was Dash, cleaned and brushed and looking like a very proper captain. "Dinner is being served on deck tonight." He bowed slightly to her, and again her heart twisted with disappointment.

On deck? Not in his cabin? Not alone? This was their last night at sea, and by tomorrow . . . well, tomorrow would put them in port, and then . . .

"Thank you," she managed to say as she laid her hand on his outstretched arm and followed him toward the ladder.

"I hope you won't be disappointed," he said as he pulled her up the last few rungs until she spied the truth.

All around the deck lanterns twinkled and sparkled. For a breathless moment, she just gaped at the table set with white linen and a brace of candles. The silver-ware sparkled, and the plates were the finest china.

Then the soft strains of a flute began to play, followed by the notes of a hand accordion and then the wistful strains of a violin.

Pippin gasped. "However . . . ?"

"The men," Dash told her. "They wanted to thank you for giving them back their captain." He paused and then caught her hand, bringing her fingers to his lips. The warm brush of his lips over the back of her hand, a teasing nibble, and then she saw the truth of it all. "And I . . ."

Well, she saw the rest of his confession in his eyes.

For they glowed with a pirate's greed. And in this case, his greed was no sin.

For all he desired was she.

"Captain," Mr. Perkins whispered as the *Regina* sailed silently past the *Ellis Anne*. "It appears they are having a celebration on board." He handed his spyglass over. "Americans. Only those uncouth bastards would sail with doxies on board."

"Doxies?" Lord Gossett asked, drawing the lens to his eye.

"Yes, doxies. At least, one that I can see. Wearing a red silk gown and dancing with the crew. A shameless bawd; why, she looks old enough to be my mother."

Mother . . . red silk . . . mother . . . The words reverberated through his skull as he blinked furiously trying to focus on the ship they were stealthily moving to intercept.

"Do you see her?" Mr. Perkins said in a smug voice.

"Aye, I see her," Lord Gossett said in a tight voice. "But that woman is no doxy."

"Oh, aye, Captain, look again. The one in red silk."

Lord Gossett snapped the spyglass shut and glared at the man. "That woman is no doxy. She is my mother."

Chapter 16

$\mathcal{D}$ash watched Pippin whirl around the deck in her red silk gown, transfixed both by the alluring sight of her in that infamous dress, and by the smile that looked as if it could illuminate the darkest night.

That she wasn't too toplofty to dance with his men, that she made each and every sailor feel like a gentleman (when in truth, most of them were just one step ahead of the law) didn't surprise him.

What left him rattled right down to his boots were the looks she continued to cast in his direction when she thought no one else was paying heed.

Sultry gazes that smoldered with passion. The offer of a grown woman who wasn't encumbered by youth or inexperience or all the stays and gussets of Society.

She wanted him. Dash heaved an uneasy sigh. Didn't she?

She'd worn her red gown. The one she'd worn the

night she'd broken him out of Marshalsea Prison and at Hollindrake House for his amusement. And again a sennight ago when she'd come to him, when he'd been mad out of his wits, and she'd held his hand through the long night, endured his rantings, and steered him to these clearer shores.

Oh, yes, she'd done all that, but how could she still want him after all the lies, the deceptions?

How will you know, lad, if you don't change course a bit?

He smiled as he remembered Hardy's oft-given advice.

Pushing off the mainmast, he walked through the dancing and the hardy slaps on the back from the crew as they congratulated him.

For what? he wanted to ask. He'd done nothing.

Nothing but get so drunk he'd gone mad and thrown all his liquor overboard. And then had to live with the consequences.

Then again, if not for her, he would never have done anything so foolhardy.

Pippin. He grinned at her, reveled in the sound of her laughter as she led Finn through the steps of a country reel.

She'd always managed to get him to do the most foolhardy things.

Like the one he was about to do now.

Ask her to marry him.

Breathless and the happiest she'd been in ages, Pippin whirled to a stop and found herself steadied by Dash.

He caught her and held her by the elbows, grinning at her, his eyes aglow with a smoky passion.

If that wasn't enough to have her knees quaking, the heat of his touch sent tendrils of desire through her limbs.

She'd never realized how much a woman could crave a man's touch. For she hungered for Dash's like a woman starved. She'd found every excuse she could in the past week to be close to him. She'd turned into the clumsiest woman alive if only to have him catch hold of her, worse than the most pampered house cat going to any and all antics only to have her master's touch.

"I don't think I can dance another step," she confessed, glancing at the gangway that led down to the cabins. "Do you think the men would mind if I called it an evening?"

"Deserting us already?" he teased.

"It is past midnight," she said. "And most of the men have already sought out their beds."

Dash glanced over her shoulder. "So they have. Whatever were you waiting for, my lady?"

She shivered. Oh, curse the man. He knew she couldn't just say it . . . that she desired him. Wanted him.

"Gentlemen," Dash said, letting go of one of her arms, "Her Ladyship wishes to thank you for a perfect evening, but graciously asks to be excused."

The men laughed and cheered her, bowing as best they could as Dash led her to the gangway.

But with each step Pippin wondered what Dash was going to do. Her thoughts raced with the choices.

Escort her to her cabin and bid her a good night. Pippin shuddered. Dear heavens, what a terrible notion!

Escort her below and then wait for her to make the first move? Oh, she hoped not, for she was still new to all this pirate courage and such, and most likely would make a bungle of it.

And finally, the one she wished for, the one she hoped for: He'd sweep her off her feet, carry her to his cabin, and plunder her completely, ravishing her in ways imaginable and ways unbelievable, because of course she'd be powerless to stop him.

As if, she almost muttered, *I could be that lucky*.

Oh, bother, Pippin, she could hear her cousin Tally saying. *You've spent the last sennight learning how to be a pirate. Haven't you gained any useful bit of knowledge about seizing what you want? Pirates don't ask, they take.*

Dash caught hold of her hand just then and she glanced up, realizing they were at the bottom of the ladder.

"Pippin, I have something to say—" he began, in a voice that trembled.

Oh, good God, he was going to abandon her. Send her off to her narrow bed without so much as a kiss. Pippin couldn't let this happen. She was a pirate now, she'd take what she wanted, and what she wanted was . . .

A kiss.

Yes, that was it. A kiss. This had all begun with a kiss on a faraway beach, and Pippin wasn't going to let it slip away without another one.

She spun around and slammed into him, pushing him all the way to the wall, pinning him there. Her hands wound around his neck, and before he could sputter another word, she rose up on her toes and caught his lips with her own.

Pippin stole the kiss she'd been waiting twenty years to take.

Stole it with the impunity of a pirate.

Her hips swayed up against his, rubbing against him; no longer a house cat looking for a bit of affection, Pippin was in a fit of heat. She wanted him, wanted him inside her, wanted to feel him possess her, and she wasn't going to leave him in any doubt of her desires.

And beneath her she felt him grow hard, nearly cried out in joy as he caught hold of her backside and pulled her even closer so they slid against each other . . . searching, seeking whatever could be found in this first flame of desire.

He dipped his head down and turned the tides on their kiss, his tongue swiping along hers, hungry and fierce. With each lap, with each tangled swipe, she imagined him kissing her like that elsewhere, exploring her naked body with his mouth, his hands caressing her.

Pippin moaned, her hands curling into his hair, pulling him closer, begging him to deepen his kiss, to claim her.

To make love to her.

"Please, Dash," she gasped as his lips came away and began to tease and nuzzle at her neck, working their way down to her bodice. "Please."

And Dash, that unholy pirate of a man, knew.

He caught her around the middle and hoisted her over his shoulder. "As you wish, my lady."

Pippin laughed, her legs kicking and her hands hammering playfully against his back. For she was about to be plundered.

And it didn't hurt to protest . . . just a little bit.

Dash tossed her down atop his bed, a tangle of red silk and sudden insecurities.

Even as he turned and went to shut the door, she scrambled up, looking down at herself, pushing her wayward strands of hair out of the way.

Egads, she probably looked a tumbled wreck, one bare leg sticking out and her breasts nearly falling out of the front of her gown. And then it occurred to her.

She was going to have to take off her gown. In front of him. It was as if the deck gave way beneath her.

Oh, heavens. She wasn't twenty any longer, but a matron, a widow, a woman who'd had two children and had the lines and lumps to prove it.

But whatever insecurities she felt, they were quickly doused as Dash came back to the bed, having shrugged off his coat. He wore only a white shirt and breeches. And even having spent the last decade in a dissolute existence, his body didn't show the ravages of time she was sure hers was about to reveal.

"I love that dress," he said, reaching down and catching hold of her foot. His hand was warm against her skin, heated her thoroughly as he pulled her closer, dragging her across the bed like a captive.

And when he put his lips to her toes, she was only too willing to be in his power. He kissed her toes, sliding his tongue between them.

Her eyes closed, and she dissolved into the mattress in a shiver.

Oh, it mattered not where he put his lips, this was heaven.

His other hand roamed down her leg, the red silk falling away, into a puddle of crimson around her hips.

His touch, unlike his kiss earlier in the day, was no longer tentative, but possessive, stroking her, claiming her.

Farther and farther up her legs his explorations took him, until he was at that Y of her legs, and with a wicked grin and a saucy wink up at her, he dipped his head down and blew a hot breath over her sex. She moaned softly, shivering, anxious for him, hungry for what was to come.

His lips touched her next, his fingers slowly and tenderly opening her, but it was his kiss, the swipe of his tongue over her, at first slowly as if memorizing the trail ahead, and then insistently, going back and forth over her.

Pippin's body coiled tight, her body arching to meet him, and just when she thought she would explode, he drew back.

"Eager wench," he said, smiling lazily up at her. "Think to gain your prize so quickly?"

Panting and twisting in the sheets, she would have begged for him to push her over the edge, would have done it herself if he had not caught hold of her hands and brought them up over her head, pinning her to the mattress. His body slid over hers, seductively, teasingly, and she nearly came right there, as his erection, tight against his breeches, rubbed over her swollen sex, offering a sweet moment of promise, but not enough to turn the tide for her.

"Damn, you Dash," she cursed. "Make love to me."

"Tsk, tsk," he murmured, nuzzling her neck in the one spot he'd found all those years ago that left her dizzy with need. "We've all night."

Pippin arched toward him, "I don't care. I want you, I want you like I've never wanted a man. Demmit, Dash, make love to me."

"Circe," he whispered. "You know I never give in to British demands. Besides, plundering is an art. One enjoyed slowly . . ." He gave her a bit of what she wanted, sliding his hips to meet hers, and she moaned. ". . . deliberately," he offered, as his hands caught her by her hips and pulled her even closer to him. "And always with one eye in search of treasure." With that his fingers slid down over her, between the folds of soft skin, and again began to tease her back into that wild, blind need.

Oh, damn you. Damn you to hell, she thought as her body came crashingly close to release only to have him stop.

"This plundering," she whispered, her fingers reaching down to stroke him through the twill of his pants. "Can it be done by two?"

Dash moaned as her thumb rolled over the head of his shaft, her fingers drew lazy lines down every bit of him. "It is best done by two," he conceded, rolling her again and kissing her, his tongue sliding against hers, over and across, in and out, in a wild bit of love play that left her breathless.

"Oh, how I missed you, Circe," he said huskily as he nuzzled her neck, his fingers pulling at the neckline of her gown, until one of her breasts came free.

The cool night air of the cabin was a bit of shock, but no more a shock than when he took a nipple in his mouth and began to suck at her.

Pippin moaned, her insides unraveling.

His tongue, rough and eager, had her nipple in a tight bud, and then the greedy rake reached for the other, freeing it with the same skill from the silk, and then loving it into the same state of arousal.

"You are still the most beautiful woman alive," he told her, grinning as he slowly pulled the gown down, kissing a hot trail over each newly revealed inch of skin, including the lines over her belly, the rounded curves she'd gained as she went from being a miss to a matron.

He continued to kiss a blazing trail down her body, his hands stroking her into a flurry of desire.

"Dash," she gasped, as he tugged the dress down over her hips and plucked it free, tossing it over a nearby chair.

"While I have always loved the sight of you in that dress, the sight of you out of that dress"—he grinned—"is treasure, indeed."

The admiration in his eyes, the desire, gave her a heady power. Her insecurities over being in his bed again fluttered away with the wind. It mattered not to Dash that she was no longer twenty.

He wanted her, desired her, and she knew exactly how to respond.

She reached for his shirt and pulled it over his head. His chest, laced with scars, still left her filled with awe, for it was still muscled and toned. The only change was a bit of gray hair in the crisp triangle on his chest, and scars she didn't remember.

The scars had always frightened her, left her wondering how he could ever have survived so many battles, injuries, injustices, but now she saw them as trials that had kept him alive. Revealed the mettle of the man beneath them.

Or at the very least, his sheer tenacity to live.

He nuzzled her again. "Come, Circe," he whispered to her. "Come back to me."

She glanced up at him and realized she'd been so lost in thought, she hadn't even noticed that he had slipped out of his breeches and was now naked.

Oh, perfectly so, she thought wickedly, glancing at his erect member, her core growing wet and heated as he lay down atop her, her legs opening for him. Pippin was no longer willing to play at games, for she was hungry with need.

Her legs wound around his, her hands clinging to his back. He stretched her and filled her, and as he moved, she knew she'd found her treasure as well.

With each long, hard thrust, Pippin clung to him. This was the pirate lover she remembered, a man unafraid to love her in the rough and tumultuous way she craved. With each long stroke, he slid over her, drawing her closer and closer to her release.

"Oh, Dash! Oh, Dash!" she cried out as her peak came over her. "Oh, yes, please. Yes!"

And even as her body tumbled over the abyss into rough waters, Dash groaned as well, giving in to wild strokes and a ragged cry as his orgasm overtook him, leaving them both rocking together, dancing atop a tempestuous sea of their own making.

Pippin clung to Dash, inhaled the scent of him, let his heat encircle her, and in a daze of spent desires and awe, she drifted in his arms into a peaceful slumber that claimed them both.

Sometime just before dawn, Dash awoke and rolled over, only to find his bed empty. For a moment, he merely stretched and shifted positions, that was until he touched a warm, albeit empty spot beside him, and then he remembered.

Pippin.

After they'd nearly done each other in with their heated, frantic lovemaking, they had slept, until Dash had nudged her awake, then made love to her, tenderly so, kissing her quietly, murmuring words of love and desire in her ears, and slowly, gently, and softly bringing her back to a release that left them both spent and smiling once more.

"Pippin," he whispered, the cabin cast in darkness.

"Here, Dash," she said, near the foot of the bed.

"Come back to bed," he said, opening the covers and patting the place beside him.

She shook her head. "I would like to see the sunrise."

" 'Tis warmer in here," he offered.

She laughed. "That it is. But I want to see the sunrise."

"Were you going alone?"

"No, I was going to wake you."

"When?"

"After I'd dressed and you wouldn't be able to talk me out of this."

"Come over and we'll see if I can."

She laughed again and went to the door. "Come along and join me. I would see the sunrise in your arms, for it is something I have dreamed of for years."

And then she was gone. Slipping from the room and leaving him little choice but to follow. Happily so. If his Circe wanted to watch the sunrise, so be it.

And then he'd convince her that breakfast was best eaten in bed.

He hastened into his clothes and followed her up onto the deck. It had been a long time since he'd seen the sun rise, at least clearheaded and anxious for the new day to begin.

And what a day it would be. He'd ask her to marry him, and they would be wed in Baltimore before nightfall.

And then . . .

Dash grinned. That was the best part. He didn't know what. The future, which just weeks before had seemed a bleak coil of endless days, now unfurled before him with a maze of possibilities.

All of them with Pippin beside him.

He came alongside her and slid his arms around her just as the first bit of light began to creep over the line where the sea met the night. The stars overhead began to surrender, blinking out and hiding their magical light until nightfall when they would rule the skies again.

Soon, when the sun claimed the sky, the coastline

would appear, as would the opening into the waters that led up to Baltimore.

"Pippin?" he murmured as she shivered in his arms. He drew her closer. "Circe, my love, will you—"

"A ship!" one of the men on the watch called out. "A ship!"

Both of them turned and looked up the length of Dash's clipper, and there materializing before them, in the faint light of dawn, a mighty ship appeared, its lofty decks rising high above the *Ellis Anne*'s.

"Bloody hell! All hands! All hands!" Dash cried out, releasing her and running up the deck. "Is that friggin' bastard mad?"

The crew staggered up from below, raised by their captain's urgent shouts. He could hear Pippin zigzagging through them as she followed him, and when he came to a staggering halt she plowed into his back, her gaze set on the name embellished across the vessel.

HMS *Regina*.

Then worse yet, as if his every nightmare was about to come true, the British gun ports opened, all twenty of them, dropping in perfect unison, and the cannons they hid rolled out.

Every man on the *Ellis Anne* froze, for though most of them were too young to remember the previous war, Dash wasn't.

And he knew only too well he was about to be blown out of the water.

The captain of the HMS *Regina* made an imposing figure in his grand uniform. He was a tall, striking man, and with the great hat of his rank added to it, he towered over every other man lining the decks of the British ship.

Oh, he might have intimidated anyone else, but not Pippin.

After all, she'd changed his nappies.

Bustling up beside Dash and taking a stance that had once cowed her wayward son, Pippin shouted across the gap separating the two ships, "John Ellis Reginald Gossett, you stand down."

From beside her, Dash twisted and gaped at her. "You named my son Ellis? After the lad I lost?"

"Yes," she said. "I never forgot your story of the boy's bravery, never wanted him forgotten."

"You never cease to amaze me, Circe," he said, shaking his head. He glanced once again at the imposing and stalwart British captain. "And you want me to believe he's mine?"

"Good God, Dash! How could you not recognize your own son? He's about to incite an international incident."

Dash nodded, and bother his pirate's heart if he didn't look pleased over such outlandish behavior.

From the deck of the *Regina*, John called to her, "Madam, I am sending a longboat over and I expect you to come aboard. Otherwise, well, this pirate knows he will pay for such an egregious affront."

"Affront?" Dash bristled. "I'd saying shoving that ugly bit of sail up my arse, and in American waters I might add, is an affront, you arrogant prig."

Pippin cringed. So much for the loving family reunion she'd dreamed of last night in Dash's arms.

John turned his attention away from Dash, treating

him like an annoying child who needed to be taught a lesson. "Mother, are you unharmed?"

"Of course I am," she told him. "Whatever are you doing?"

"Rescuing you. You needn't fear this bastard ever harming you again." John flicked a glance at Dash. "He knows he has no choice but to turn you over."

Dash spat over the rail. "Oh, you and I both know that isn't going to happen. Besides, your mother finds the comforts of my ship more to her liking." With that he caught hold of her and pulled her into his arms, and kissed her thoroughly, not letting her up until every man on his ship was cheering.

Pippin swayed on her feet as he released her. Feeling giddy and disheveled—for, damn, the man could kiss a lady senseless—she knew he'd just made matters worse.

The sun finally climbed over the horizon, crossing night into day, and as it did, Captain Gossett snapped his fingers, and there was the cock of rifles all up and down the lines.

The ship's marines were all in their lofty stations, and each one had a dead eye on Dash.

"Gracious heavens, John," Pippin said, moving in front of Dash, "would you have them shoot your own mother?"

"My mother!" He stalked back and forth. "I'm starting to wonder if you are my mother. What has that devil done to you?"

"Nothing," she called back, indignantly.

"Then come aboard my ship so I can see for myself."

Did he really think her that foolish?

"I'm not leaving, John," Pippin shouted across the railing, crossing her arms over her chest.

"Captain!" came a cry from high above. "Captain, sails!"

All eyes turned toward the shore, where two ships were now heading toward them.

"The Americans," the boy called out. "A ship of the line and a frigate."

"Christ!" John swore.

"Rather gotten yourself into a tangle, haven't you?" Dash chided. "Blow me out of the water now and you'll start a war. Want that on your spotless, heroic record? A rather ugly blight on your good name if you're wrong, wouldn't it be?"

John flinched, his jaws working back and forth, because while he had the upper hand, the greater firepower, he'd caught the *Ellis Anne* too late.

Pippin watched the conflicting emotions on her son's face, saw him gauging the distance between the American ships, and weighing the worth of his own "good name."

He nodded and issued an order to his first mate. As quickly as they'd opened and appeared, the cannons slid back and the gun ports were closed. The marines came down the lines in scrambled haste, and as quickly as it appeared out of the morning mist, the *Regina* returned to all appearances as a proper ship.

A mere curiosity on this side of the ocean.

"We'll go ashore and settle this matter," he said, making a regal concession.

"There is nothing to settle," Dash told him, turning his back to the other captain and ordering the men to make way.

Pippin took one last glance at her son before the *Ellis Anne* caught the wind anew and slipped easily past the larger vessel.

John's brows sat drawn together in a stubborn line. Nothing about this boded well.

Her son was too much like his father to admit defeat so easily.

$\mathcal{D}$ash paced back and forth before the fireplace, Pippin growing dizzy at his measured fury. It was like watching a great lion who knew that any moment his cage would be opened and he'd be able to pounce.

From the table where Pippin sat, Admiral Fleeger waved a hand at the empty seat beside him. "Captain Dashwell, please sit, have some tea."

When Dash shook his head, the man nodded at Pippin as if to reassure her that he had the situation well in hand. A relic from two wars back, the man was probably nigh on eighty, maybe even drawing closer to ninety. "Coffee, then? You strike me as a coffee man. Never could stomach the stuff. Much prefer tea." He favored Pippin with a smile. "My lady?" he said, pointing at the pot and tray. "How about you? A cup of tea to settle the nerves?"

She bowed her head slightly. "That would be lovely, Admiral."

At this, the old man pompously straightened, shaking out his coat and making a great show of pouring a "proper cup" for her by knocking over the sugar pot and just about upending the cream as well.

Poor man, Pippin mused as she tried to drink the scalding concoction he managed to get into a cup. *He's rather too much like Admiral Fairham.*

A point not in his favor.

But this was the man who held her future in his hands.

The *Ellis Anne* had been met at the docks by a contingent of officers and American marines, the word of their approach and the British warship in their wake having traveled up and down the coastal waterways. With great pomp and fanfare, they'd been escorted to the Custom House, where their case was going to be heard by a hastily summoned Admiral Fleeger, who had muttered something about being roused from a good nap to sort out "more of Dashwell's antics, eh?"

This wasn't entirely a naval issue, she had to imagine, but the situation was so precarious that as the ranking officer in port, Fleeger must have seemed the most important person to muster to deal with a furious British captain making claims of kidnapping and piracy.

Piracy, indeed! Pippin mused. Why, she'd never even gotten to fire a cannon.

But then again, perhaps she should be thankful for that considering Dash's current mood. He'd been in a rare fury since he'd found himself facing a British frigate, and she wouldn't be surprised if he'd considered hauling them out and blasting a hole in the side of John's ship.

She'd tried as well to talk to him, but he'd waved her off in much the same fashion as he had Fleeger.

No, he needed to find his own heading in all this. His past meeting his present, and this time, he couldn't just settle it with a drink. Or face it down with cannon fire, pistols, and a sharp dirk into his enemy's gut.

Not when his enemy was also his son.

Standing in the corner beside her trunk, Nate also waved off the admiral's offer of tea. Instead, he continued to man his post, watching the proceedings with a wary eye.

Pippin knew this must be hard for him. All these secrets laid bare in the last few weeks had forced Nate to re-examine the hero he'd thought his father to be. That, and he'd been the one to leave the ransom note and open up this Pandora's box of trouble.

"Demmit, Fleeger," Dash said, coming to an abrupt halt. "This is ridiculous. Lady Gossett wasn't kidnapped." He turned to her. "Tell him."

She sighed. "I have, Dash. But I fear in this case protocol will have to be served. Am I not correct, Admiral?"

"Yes, quite," he said, tugging at his whiskers and shooting a glance at his aide. "Palmer, make yourself useful and go see what is taking this Captain Gossett so long."

The man looked only too relieved to go, and made haste to exit the room.

"What sort of man is this Captain Gossett, my lady?

Your son, I gather," the admiral asked. He passed a plate of biscuits toward her, and she took one.

They couldn't be any worse than the tea.

"Like his father," she said. *I fear . . .*

"A gentleman?"

She nodded, her gaze going toward Dash, and then swiftly flying to Nate, who snorted ungraciously at her assertion.

She shot a glance at him, and for half a second was about to chide him as she might John, for at times it was hard to remember that Nate wasn't John, for the two of them were . . .

Were so . . . Pippin tried to breathe, for suddenly the room got altogether too close. Oh, heavens. John was coming here.

In the same room as Dash and Nate. Oh, what a widgeon she'd been all day not to think of it. She'd been so worried about Dash doing something rash, or John for that matter—not that chasing after her with one of the queen's own ships wasn't bad enough— that she'd never considered that eventually they'd all end up here. In the same room. Face-to-face.

And it wouldn't take much more than the village idiot to have the three of them together and not see the resemblance.

Even Fleeger, as befuddled and dim as he was, couldn't fail to notice the similarities among the three men.

And most likely, given the man's bumbling nature, say something indiscreet. She closed her eyes and tried to swallow down a hurricane of panic. "Dash, I think it would be better if I—"

Unfortunately for her, Palmer turned out to be all too efficient, for he'd managed to discharge his duties in short order.

Too short.

The doors to the meeting room burst open, Palmer rushing just a few steps ahead of John, to make the introductions. "Admiral Fleeger, sir, this is Captain . . . aaah," he finished as John pushed past him.

He marched right up to Dash and caught him by the throat. "You bastard! I should kill you now!" And to make his point even clearer, he shoved his pistol into Dash's head.

From the wall, Nate only added to the fire. "Don't you think you might want to rephrase that? At least the insulting part about being a bastard. Coming from you, that's rather amusing."

John swung toward him. "Stay out of this, whoever the devil you are." But even as he said that, John's eyes narrowed.

Pippin felt the collision of her past and present as if it was ripping through her heart. It was all she could do to watch John's head shake slightly, an incredulous motion that said he didn't believe his eyes as he stared at the man opposite him, a mirror image of himself, minus the proper uniform.

Palmer was also taking in the sight before him with a look of pure shock on his face.

In fact, the moment held everyone in an expectant pause. Save the admiral, who had taken the British captain's interruption in stride, using the tense moments to wipe the biscuit crumbs from his whiskers, stand, and tug his coat over his protruding belly and then blink like an unwitting owl at the proceedings.

"There now, Captain Gossett, please unhand Captain Dashwell, stow the pistol, and then we can proceed in an orderly manner."

But no one was really listening to him.

Used to the admiral's obtuse nature, Palmer coughed slightly. "Sir, I believe this is a bit of a reunion." He nodded up at Dash and John.

"A reunion?" the admiral said, glancing around. "Thought you said there was a dispute to be heard. Kidnapping. Piracy. Dashwell up to his old tricks, I'd say," he remarked with a pleased sort of chuckle. "Demmed if the man never stops to—"

"Sir!" Palmer nudged him. "Look."

Then even the village idiot saw what everyone else did.

At the suggestion of his astute aide, the admiral called a stay in the proceedings until this matter could be sorted out.

"Family disputes," he'd said with a scandalized air, "are not my jurisdiction." Then he invited Dash to sup with him Thursday next and left.

As did everyone else, leaving Dash, Pippin, Nate, and John alone in the room.

John's first mate stood guard at the door to make sure there were no further witnesses, and even as the door clicked shut, John turned toward Pippin. "What is the meaning of this?"

She swallowed, rather gulped back the butterflies in her stomach, reminding herself she was a pirate now. Possessed a pirate's heart and courage. At least Dash had told her so. And looking at him, she knew he was as stricken by this as she was.

"This," she began, nodding toward Dash, "is Captain Thomas Dashwell."

John blew out a rude breath. "I demmed well know who he is."

"Can you say the same about yourself?" Nate asked, pushing off the wall and circling his brother, taking a measure of the man.

They eyed each other warily. "Who is this, Mother?"

"Your brother," she said.

"Half brother," Nate corrected quickly.

Shaking his head, John took a step back. "So Lady Larken was telling the truth, you and this man . . . that man . . ." he said, taking a quick glance at Dash, "were . . ."

"Yes," Pippin told him.

"And he's . . ." He looked at her, his features stricken, so much so she couldn't speak, only nod in affirmation.

"Madam," he said, his voice tight and brittle, pistol still held in his tight grip. "You want me to believe that this pompous, arrogant bastard is my father?"

But it was Nate who answered first. "At least you can be confident in the knowledge you came by those traits honestly."

Pippin shot him a black glance before she said to her son, "John, I never meant for you—" She bit off her words, for they only confirmed what he was asking.

John blanched and looked away. After a few more tense moments, he asked, "Did my father . . ." He paused and took another deep breath. "Did Lord Gossett know?"

She nodded. "Yes. He knew before we married."

"Dismal at math, aren't you, not to have figured that out before?" was Nate's comment. "At least I always knew what side of the blanket I was born on."

John turned to him, pistol raised. "Brother or not, say another word and I shall kill you."

"Nate, John, enough!" Pippin said sharply, bringing them both to attention as only a mother could. "Now is not the time."

"Would there ever be one?" Dash asked. Up until now, he'd stood in front of the fireplace, a tight, unfathomable expression on his face. "A good time, that is?" He glanced over at John. "You're a credit to your father, Lord Gossett. He was a good man. An honorable one. It matters not how you came into this world. He raised you, he guided you, and he is your father." He paused, his gaze narrowed, studying the man before him. "As for our unlikely and unwanted resemblance, I apologize." And he bowed slightly.

Pippin gazed at him, admiration swelling in her heart. She knew what that had cost him, but the honest humility in his voice touched and obviously cut through his newly met son's anger.

John took a steadying breath, his hands at his sides, his shoulders still set in their taut lines like a pair of spars jutting out. "I cannot say I am happy with the association," he began, "But I appreciate what you said about . . . about . . ."

"Your father," Dash insisted. "Don't ever think of him in any other terms. You are Gossett's issue."

John pressed his lips together, and Pippin knew

he was struggling to reconcile the staggering truth. He'd inherited a title that wasn't his, he'd been educated, raised, and promoted based on his identity as a gentleman, a nobleman, and now his world had been upended.

It was much to ask a man to whom birth, honor, and duty were everything.

Then John turned to her. "Does Ginger know?"

Pippin shook her head.

"Ginger?" Nate asked.

"My sister," John told him. When both Dash and Nate looked at him as if they didn't see the significance, he made it all too clear to them why it mattered so. "My twin sister."

A chill rushed through the room as Nate's and Dash's gazes swiveled toward Pippin.

"I have a daughter as well?" Dash managed to ask. "You mean to tell me I not only have a son I never knew, but now a daughter as well?"

John's accusing glare added to the rest. "You didn't tell him about Ginger?"

Pippin sank into a chair. "No. I hadn't had the chance."

"Not had the chance?" Dash exploded. "You've been on my ship for nigh on a month and you didn't have the opportunity to say, 'Oh, yes, my love, along with the son I never told you about, you've also got a daughter.'"

"It isn't as simple as that," Pippin shot back. "Ginger is married . . . and, oh, Dash, her husband is so . . . so—"

Even John shuddered. "Claremont would be beside himself if he knew his wife wasn't—"

"Completely English?" Nate offered. "How horrible that must be, to discover your sainted noble lines are soiled by one of us wretched Americans." He paused and crossed his arms over his chest. "You can't seriously mean that this stiff-rumped husband of hers would toss his wife out if he discovered her to be merely the by-blow of a commoner?"

"Sir, you speak of my sister!" John said, coming closer.

"I speak of my sister as well," Nate reminded him, meeting him nose to nose. "And if I don't mind the circumstances of her birth, I don't see why her husband should."

"I have a daughter," Dash was muttering. He glanced up at her, his eyes alight, his expression softened. "When we're married, I insist we go to her. Oh, we don't have to tell her, but I would like to meet—"

Pippin froze. Had he just said what she thought he had?

When we are married.

Married? To Dash?

She opened her mouth to answer him, to tell him . . .

But John beat her to it, exploding like a cannon. "Married? Are you mad? You will not, cannot marry my mother."

Dash's expression darkened instantly, and Nate, having the advantage of knowing his father all his life, wisely stepped back, leaving John to get to know the man who had sired them both. "I will marry your mother, and you have no say in the matter."

The words held all the deadly calm of the click of a pistol hammer.

John held his ground. "I beg to differ. You expect

my mother, the Viscountess Gossett, a respected lady, to marry the likes of you? Whyever would she lower herself in such a way? Youthful indiscretions aside, she is woman grown and knows that such an arrangement is preposterous." He turned to Pippin. "Isn't it?"

With both men glaring at her, Pippin's temper rose. It wasn't often that she lost her temper, having always been rather levelheaded, but when she did, that stubborn streak, the one that ran through her mother's Hawstone family line deeper than the ocean they'd just crossed, rose up and reared its very obstinate head.

"I have no intention of getting married," she told them both.

"Ha!" John said in triumph, as if he had just sunk the *Ellis Anne* with one shot.

"The hell you aren't," Dash said. "You can't tell me that you don't love me, that what happened between us last night wasn't—"

There was a sort of choked sound from John, and a discreet cough from Nate, all of which told Dash that he'd said too much. With John's cheeks flaming in outrage, and Nate's gaze tactfully pointed at the ceiling, he realized his children didn't want to know that two people who must appear as old as Methuselah to them could still . . . manage to still . . . well, make love.

Well, demmit, they had. And more than once. Furthermore, his sons had better get used to the notion, because he intended to keep Pippin in his bed until he died from happy and prolonged exhaustion.

"I love your mother, with my heart and my body, and I will not let her go." He turned to Pippin and wagged a finger at her. "And you will marry me, for I will not lose you again. Ever. You are my north and my south. My guiding star, Circe. I cannot lose you, for you hold my heart."

Pippin shivered, all her anger melting away. But still . . . "Dash, I never said I was going to leave you. I just don't want to get married again."

She might as well have told the three of them that she was considering a career as an opera dancer. For all three exploded like powder kegs with the same argument.

"Are you mad?"

An hour later Dash, John, and Nate had gone nearly blue in the face arguing with her. Finally, John asked the other two for a few private moments with his mother. Albeit with the silent understanding that he might be able to talk some sense into her.

Pippin took Dash's hand before he could refuse and said quietly, "Let me speak to him."

"This isn't over," Dash told her in a low, passionate voice.

"I don't expect it to be," she told him with a sly wink.

Dash pulled her closer and kissed her, thoroughly and soundly, and thankfully at the same moment John had gone out to say something to his first mate, who had been patiently waiting for him in the hall.

When it was just the two of them, Pippin and John, he went over to the teapot, which was now cold, and shuddered. "Barbaric country. The tea's done for. Who on earth, other than these upstart colonials, would expect anyone to drink cold tea?"

She smiled at him. For this was the John she knew. Proud of his Englishness, and always one for the proper way of things except when his Dashwell blood got the better of him. As when he'd ignored the risks and saved the *Cadmus* or come racing across the Atlantic hell-bent on revenge.

There were just some inclinations you couldn't escape, no matter how proper you tried to be, Pippin realized. Herself included.

"I am sorry for how all this has come to pass," she said. "I knew nothing about the ransom note. I only knew that Dash—"

"Captain Dashwell," he corrected.

"Dash," she told him stubbornly. "He has always been Dash to me. My Dash."

"So it would seem," he said, not sounding all that pleased over her insistence.

"He's a good man," she told him, but she might as well have been whistling to the wind.

"That depends on what uniform you wear. You should hear what the old officers say about him."

"And I believe he has some very similar accounts regarding our navy. Look at his back someday and you will see the justice he received at English hands."

John flinched. If it was from the knowledge that his mother had seen the man naked or the reference to punishments that had been meted out, she didn't know. More likely the former rather than the latter.

"There was a war on," he said, waving off her arguments.

"Ah, yes. A war. An excuse for men's greed and crimes that should put their hearts to shame." She folded her arms over her chest. "Now, tell me, John, who pays the price for those wars? I'll tell you. The women who stay home. Who find themselves without husbands, or nearly worse, the ones who have their men come home so scarred and angry that they barely recognize them. What is war to women and children? What is it? Nothing to be proud of, nothing to be excused or explained away."

His jaw worked back and forth, for this was far out of the realm he considered proper to be discussed in front of a lady, let alone his mother.

Absently, he went over to the teapot again, and as he put his hand on it, the chill roused him. "Let me see about remedying this." Crossing the room and pulling open the door, he called his first mate in.

"Mr. Perkins, have you seen to what I asked for?"

The man shot a glance at Pippin and then bobbed his head. "Aye, Captain. All is ready."

"Good."

And then without a word, John moved across the room, clapped his hand over her mouth. With more speed than she thought possible, a rag was stuffed in her mouth and a gag tied over it. Then Perkins let out a low whistle and two large fellows, men from the *Regina*, came in from the back door. With John and his first mate on either side of her, she was hauled out the back of the Custom House, her trunk following in the sturdy grasp of the sailors.

Pippin kicked and fought and twisted like a wild-cat but couldn't break free.

John groaned when she connected with his shin,

but his resolve only grew more determined. "Don't you think you've created enough scandal already? I am returning you to your rightful place. You'll thank me when you are no longer under that man's thrall and come to your senses."

If I don't kill you first, she thought as they hoisted her into a waiting carriage.

Pippin's fury only increased as she found herself being rowed out to the *Regina*.

You pompous, arrogant bastard, she wanted to cry out. *How dare you!*

But apparently he did. Only proving that while his name might be Gossett, he was entirely a Dashwell.

"You've been lied to, deceived by that fellow," John told her, as if speaking to some errant, under-age ward caught halfway to Gretna Green. "You've refused to marry him, so there is no reason not to return to London. Immediately," John said, nodding to Perkins, who, with the help of one of the sailors, placed her in a sling and had her hoisted aboard like a piece of cargo.

Up on deck, the officers appeared surprised to see their captain having returned, for the moment John's feet hit the deck, he began to shout orders to make ready to sail before the tide shifted.

One of the other officers came up, hemming and hawing over the call to haul up the anchor.

"It's just that, well, sir, my lord, it might not be so easy."

"Why the devil not?" John railed back.

The officer blanched, glancing at Pippin and then back at his captain, lowering his voice. "You see, you promised the men a bit of reward if they made the crossing quickly and they are . . . well, enjoying just that, shall we say."

"What sort of reward?" John asked, even as female laughter rose from below decks. His gaze dropped to the grating on which he stood.

"The men brought some . . . females aboard. I fear it is a bit raucous down there right now," the officer said as diplomatically as he could.

"I don't care what is going on down there. Get those . . . those . . ." He paused, glancing over at his mother. "Persons off my ship. Now."

"Aye, my lord," he said, tugging at his cap and running for the gangway, calling to the others on deck to keep the longboats in the water.

John took Pippin by the elbow and ordered one of the men to follow with her trunk.

When they got to his cabin, the first of the "ladies" were being led off the ship, disheveled and protesting about their lack of pay. None of which held much sway with the stone-faced officer leading them off the ship.

John pulled Pippin into his cabin, allowed the man to deliver her trunk, and then dismissed him. He waited until the fellow was gone and then undid the linen binding her mouth.

Pippin spat out the gag, and took a step back from her son. Before she could say a word, he stepped to the door.

"Save your breath, madam. All the raging complaints in the world will not change my mind. I'll give you a few days to regain your senses, but until then, make yourself comfortable in my cabin."

With that he shut the door, and there was the unmistakable click of the lock being turned.

Pippin flew to the door and pounded on it, because she knew that was what he expected her to do.

But she did it with a grin on her face, for her son was about to learn what other youthful indiscretions she'd failed to tell him about.

Dash had paced back and forth for nearly half an hour. "I shouldn't have left her in there with him."

Nate snorted. "Perhaps we should go see if she's done him in. Wouldn't put it past this lady of yours."

Dash grinned. "She is extraordinary, isn't she?"

"Quite," Nate agreed.

Both men approached the room, and Dash looked around. "Where is that other fellow? The first mate?"

Nate glanced around as well. "I don't know."

Dash didn't bother to knock, but went right into the meeting room, "Pippin, are you—"

But the room before them was empty.

"That duplicitous bastard! He's taken her," Nate said, pointing at the open door on the other side and the empty space where her trunk had sat. Then he looked at his father. "He is your son, isn't he?"

"Apparently so," Dash said, wheeling around and running for the docks. The tide would be turning soon, and if Gossett could catch it before it turned, the *Ellis Anne* would be trapped in port for a good eight hours, giving the British frigate a head start to anywhere in the world.

Taking Pippin out of Dash's reach forever.

* * *

Pippin marveled at how quickly she remembered the basics of picking a lock. Getting John's door open had taken a matter of a minute or so of concentration.

Really, the navy should see about putting better locks on their ships, she mused, closing the door so nothing looked amiss. Then she turned to her trunk and flung it open, digging into it and pulling out her final weapon, her infamous red dress.

Pulling off the fashionable silk she'd chosen with great care for her meeting with her son, she nearly sighed with joy as she slipped into the sinful gown.

Now all she needed was a bit of luck.

And then it came.

"Come along with the lot of you," a man was saying out in the hall. "Cap'n's orders. Off you go."

"I won't, I tell you," one of the ladies shot back. "I don't want to go back. Not yet."

"You'll all go and no complaints," he said as he led the way.

Pippin cracked the door open, and as the girl passed, she reached out and snagged her by the arm, pulling her inside John's cabin.

She looked her captive up and down and smiled as she saw a pretty girl, one whose eyes held an intelligent spark.

The girl was no fool, and that was what Pippin needed.

"Shhh!" she warned her, closing the door.

As much good as that did. The streetwise chit stuck her hands on her hips. "And who the hell are you?"

"Pippin." She thought it better to forgo the titles and rank. They probably wouldn't help her cause. But something else might. "Pippin Dashwell. And you?"

The name did exactly what she thought it might.

"Dashwell?" the girl asked. "As in the captain?"

Pippin nodded.

The girl's eyes lit up with admiration. "Molly," she said grudgingly. "My name is Molly Parker."

"You don't want to leave, am I right?"

The girl nodded. "I'm not one of them, I'll have you know. I just came along because . . . well, I needed to be away from the streets for a bit. If I go back now—"

Pippin held up her hand to stave her off. "I don't need to know. All I want to do is switch places with you. And to do that I need your hat and your shawl."

The girl tightened her grasp on her belongings, shaking her head. "Them's all I've got."

Pippin pointed at her trunk and the collection of gowns on the floor. "A trade then. All my gowns for your hat and shawl."

Molly cocked her head and stared at Pippin. "My hat and shawl for all that." She snorted. "This is some trick. I'll be hanged for stealing."

Pippin shook her head and glanced around the room. On the desk lay a pen and ink. She rushed to it and picked it up, grabbing the first bit of paper she could find. "No, I'll write a letter explaining it all." It was on the tip of her tongue to explain who John was, but she thought better of it. "I swear to you, Molly, the captain of this ship is an honorable man—"

To which the girl made an ignoble snort.

"—and you have my word he will not harm you. Can you read?"

"Aye. I can read," she said testily.

"Then you can see for yourself what I've written. All you have to do is keep to the bed, keep yourself covered for at least three days and speak to no one. And when you get to London . . ."

"London!"

"Yes, London," Pippin repeated, not even looking up as she grabbed another piece of paper and continued to write furiously. "Take this to the address there and tell the man at the door you have a letter for the duchess from her cousin. Show him this and he'll take you to her. She'll see that you are well rewarded and protected."

"A duchess? Oh, go on with you," she scoffed.

Pippin heaved a sigh. "Yes, the Duchess of Hollindrake. She is my cousin."

Molly blew out a breath. "A duchess wouldn't have nothing to do with the likes of me," she said, heading toward the door.

"Take this letter to her and she'll turn you into a fine lady." Pippin held it out and shook it under her nose. "A lady who never has to work another day in her life."

"Never?" The wary note in Molly's voice turned to something else. Something hungry.

And Pippin had just the bait. "Aye," she told her. "My cousin will turn you into a proper lady. Most likely then set to work to find you a husband. She has a talent for those things."

The girl's eyes lit up, though still wary and suspicious. "A husband?"

"Yes, an excellent one," Pippin said with all confidence.

"By excellent," Molly asked, "do you mean rich?"

"Utterly so." She thought that would be enough, but the girl had one more condition.

"He'd have to be kind."

Pippin smiled at her. "He wouldn't be anything but the man you want to marry."

"Never have to work?"

"Never," Pippin asserted.

The girl laughed. "Oh, now I know you're bamming me."

"I'm not," she told her, hearing another lot of women coming up from the hold and growing more impatient. "But even so, you'd be far from Baltimore and have all those dresses." She waved at the open trunk that held a wealth of silks and satins. The lace alone was probably worth more than this girl had ever imagined.

"Oh, but it's all madness," Molly scoffed staring down at the letters in her hands. "You've gone over to think such a plan will work."

"Oh, it will work." Pippin said, taking a chance and plucking the girl's shawl from her shoulders and hat from her head. "Just like it did the last time."

In the hall, the last of the whores were being herded off the ship, and Pippin had no time to lose. "Molly, I hope we meet again one day." Then before the girl had a chance to change her mind, Pippin slipped from the cabin, Molly's shawl around her shoulders, her wide hat pulled low over her face.

She hurried up the ladder, joining the knot of women on the deck.

A blowsy redhead in an emerald dress came to a furious halt in front of John. "I'll not leave without me money," she told him. "And who's with me?" she called out to her sisters in the trade.

And all save one of the ladies called out in agreement, standing firm on the deck and refusing to climb down into the waiting longboat.

Pippin couldn't believe her luck. She'd been so close to escaping, and now she was caught in the middle of a mutiny . . .

Dash and Nate came to a breathless halt at the docks.

"There!" Dash said, pointing across the line of ships. "He hasn't sailed yet."

One of the custom agents came ambling by, and Nate reached over and plucked the spyglass from his belt.

"Hey there, you can't just—"

Towering over the clerkish fellow, Nate glared at him, giving the man the impression that he would gut him and toss him into the harbor below.

"Well, carefully then," he squeaked, as Dash yanked it open and brought the lens to his eye.

"He's making ready," Dash said, having taken a quick measure of the anchor line and then the sails.

"What's left?" Nate asked.

"They've got longboats in the water," Dash said. "Two of them."

"What for?"

Then Dash chuckled. "Oh, this is perfect."

"What?"

"Lord Proper Pants over there has a bit of cargo to unload before he can sail."

Nate glanced at the naval ship. "Cargo?"

"Whores," Dash told him, grinning. "His men must not have expected him back so quickly and decided to have a little celebration." He laughed and handed the glass to Nate.

There was another huff from the clerk, but both men snuffed out his complaint with a pair of murderous glances.

"This buys us some time." Dash glanced around and spotted a lone rowboat tied up nearby. "There." He was off in a shot, and Nate followed.

"My glass! I demand you—"

Nate turned to the man and tossed the expensive, fancy piece at him.

The fluttery man dropped his account books and caught it. And he smiled at his own dexterity until he realized the brutish pair who'd nearly ruined his brand-new spyglass were stealing his rowboat.

Nate leapt easily down from the dock into the boat even as his father cast off the lines. They took seats beside each other and each picked up an oar, rowing in perfect accord, cutting a fast line through the crowded harbor.

"Do you have a plan?" Nate asked.

"No," Dash replied, casting a glance at the *Regina*.

"You do realize they will shoot us if they catch us."

Dash grinned. "Then I suppose the best plan is not to get caught."

"Get off my ship," John ordered, his finger pointing to the opening in the railing and looking very much inclined to start forcibly booting the ladies from his deck.

Pippin froze, raising the shawl around her shoulders a bit higher and tucking her chin down into the folds. *Oh, no. Please, no.*

The bawd next to Pippin turned to him. "We were promised good money to come aboard, and now we aren't to be paid? 'Tis wronged, we are. Wronged!"

The other "ladies" began complaining as well.

"Gold, I was promised."

"Cheap bastards."

"I think we ought to write the king and demand redress." All eyes turned to their redheaded leader. A bit older than the rest, she shrugged. "Me father was a clerk at the Continental Congress."

"You want to write a letter?" John sputtered, his hands balled at his sides.

"I can write," the bawd declared. "Got a fair hand at it, I do."

His first mate shook his head. "Educating women," he muttered. "I give this country another ten years. Twenty at the most."

"Aye," the ladies were cheering. "We'll write the king."

Pippin was about to turn and tell them the man had passed away recently, but decided against bringing any notice upon herself. Instead she continued to slide as far from her son's notice as she could.

"The king, the king!" the ladies cried.

John waved his hands at them, looking rather alarmed at this female mutiny, as did a good portion of his crew. Pippin almost pitied him, for she could see exactly the future he was envisioning: being called before their new queen and explaining to the overly sheltered, and utterly virginal Victoria why a group of Baltimore fallen doves wanted redress from Her Majesty for services rendered.

"Here now! There is no call for such a thing," he told them sharply. "Why, you were barely on the ship long enough to—"

"Oh, governor, you've some quick fellows down there," one of the girls told John.

They all laughed, and there were a few snickers from his crew.

"I hardly think a few—" a red-faced John sputtered.

"Something then for our inconvenience," the one with the education suggested. "We've lost business, we have."

"Aye, lost business," the rest agreed.

"Or it's a letter to London, it is," their de facto leader added. "What do you say, governor?"

Pippin tried not to smile at their cheek, for they had John between the crosshairs.

Turning to his first mate, John said something that had the man digging in his coat pocket and fetching out a leather purse. John did the same, and the coins were then passed around. "Will this do, ma'am?"

"Oh, fine manners now," she huffed, even as her flinty gaze glanced at the coins being dropped slowly into her outstretched hand. When the last one fell, she gave the fistful a heft, and then nodded. "Aye. This will do." She smiled at him. "For our inconvenience."

"Yes, well, now I must insist you get off my ship."

The old girl sniffed and hoisted her hemline as if she were about to step in offal, sweeping past John, and smiling at the lad who helped her down the ropes to the waiting longboat.

Pippin scrambled to follow and took a seat in the back of the boat on the far side, keeping her head down and her face hidden. As they pushed off and the lads began to row them quickly back to the docks, she looked up, her gaze caught by the sight of a rowboat beating a hasty pace toward the *Regina*.

"Dash!" she gasped. Oh, heavens, no! He was coming to her rescue, no doubt, but what could she do to stop him? She couldn't very well wave him off without calling attention to herself, yet she couldn't very well let him go blustering aboard John's ship. Because she had to imagine he had no plan other than some fuzzy sort of inclination to "get her back."

"Oh, Dash!" she muttered again.

The lady next to her mistook what she was saying and reached over to pat her hand.

"There now, dearie," the lady said. "No need to fret or curse. Look up there at that fine merchantman coming in. They'll have plump pockets to pick."

Pippin brazened a smile for her, and sure enough, the crew on the merchantman spotted them and began shouting offers to the ladies. And then she realized what she needed to do.

She bounded up to her feet, her red dress like a scandalous flag to every man in port, and waved her arms at the men, not caring a whit about the way the longboat rocked precariously beneath them or how the lads at the oars howled.

For once she'd caught the attention of half the sailors in the harbor, she turned in Dash's direction and waved gaily at him.

"Sit down there, you crazy bird!" one of the sailors shouted. "Or I'll pitch you over."

Pippin sat down and took a furtive glance at the rowboat where Dash and Nate sat gaping at her. She waved again, and this time she heard Dash's laughter drifting happily across the water.

"I think you found some business with that one," the bawd next to her said with a nod toward Dash.

"I do believe you're right," Pippin said as she watched Nate and Dash pulling hard to turn their rowboat around.

"Lovely dress, dearie," the lady added, reaching over to touch the silk. "Where did you get it?"

"London," Pippin said, smiling down at her prized red gown. "A long time ago."

Chapter 18

*C*aptain Gossett stood on the deck of his ship and frowned. For the past three days he'd been bunking in his first mate's room, and the narrow bed and cramped accommodations were hardly what he was used to.

But it was better than the alternative: entering his cabin and dealing with his mother.

He groaned in frustration.

His entire life he'd thought of his mother as, well . . . just his mother. A proper, staid daughter of an earl. Not the sort of woman who would . . . go unhinged, which was the only way to explain her association with the likes of Dashwell.

One of the younger lieutenants, the one he'd ordered to take Lady Gossett her meals and see to her comforts, came up to make his morning report.

"She's the same as yesterday, Captain."

"Still cowering in bed and refusing to speak?"

The fellow nodded. "She's eating. Got a good appetite, but I haven't seen hide nor hair of her. She just stays tucked under the covers." The fellow leaned forward and whispered. "I think she's been crying, sir."

John groaned again, this time aloud. Oh, good God! What was worse? Watching his mother suddenly turning into a fallen woman or having to face her tears over being separated from that devilish fellow?

He straightened his shoulders. Well, it was time to remind her of her duty. Not only to her noble, albeit deceased, husband and his good name, but to him and to Ginger.

John tugged his coat to make sure it was in place and went downstairs. He didn't bother knocking, just tucked the key in the lock and opened the door.

Across his cabin, in front of the windows that made up the stern of the ship, stood a woman.

And when she turned, he was struck by three things.

The brilliant blue of her eyes, and the challenge behind their bright gaze.

And the undeniable fact that she wasn't his mother.

Quickly his gaze swept the cabin but there was no sign of the viscountess, or anyone else in his cabin, only this gamine bit of female.

"Who the hell are you?" he sputtered.

Her fists went to her hips, her elbows jutting out like jibs. "Molly."

He cocked a brow at her defiant tone and stance. No *sir* or *captain*, or *if you please*. Just *Molly*.

"Where is my mother?"

Her eyes narrowed. "Your who?"

"My mother. The woman who is supposed to be in this cabin?"

She sucked in a deep breath. "That was your mother? And here I thought she was . . . Well, never mind what I thought."

"I hardly care what notions you harbor," he said, slamming the door behind him lest anyone see this Molly. "Where is she?"

The girl took a wary step back. "You aren't going to throw me overboard, are you?"

This stopped John. "No. Of course not." Not that the thought didn't cross his mind for one mad moment. "Now where is she?"

"You mean to tell me that mort in the red dress really was your mother?"

For a moment John found himself transported back to the scene a few days earlier when he'd been trying to remove the whores from his ship.

Oh, good God! There had been one in a red dress. John shook his head. But that hardly explained how she'd gotten out of his cabin, or how she'd convinced this Molly to take her place.

It all was too much to believe. He'd been outwitted by his mother. Thoroughly and completely.

And instead of being furious, all he could do was marvel at her bottom, at her remarkable ingenuity. Then he remembered. She was the lady in red. The one who'd gotten Dashwell out of Marshalsea Prison. He'd been a fool to forget that.

Something he doubted Dashwell ever would.

"She said you wouldn't throw me over," Molly was saying, coming closer. "Left this for you."

The girl reached inside a pocket in her dress and pulled out a letter. "She said you'd understand once you read this. Said you were an honorable sort."

John took the letter from her, looked down at the familiar, if not hasty hand, and tugged it open.

John,

I've lived twenty years to see you and Ginger have the best of futures, so now please, I beg of you, let me live the life I have longed for. Give me the freedom you take so for granted. I love him. I have always loved him, and he is my life. You can no more separate my affection for him than you can disavow that his blood is yours.

One day, I pray you will fall in love and understand. Completely and utterly. And not with some admiral's daughter, but a woman who will illuminate your heart. Settle for nothing less. It is the only thing that matters.

And please, be kind to Molly. She is innocent of all this and seems a good sort.

Complete and utter ruin was what this all was, John would have added. Illuminate his heart, indeed! What romantic rubbish!

But there was nothing he could do now. Even if he sailed back to Baltimore, Dashwell could have gone anywhere, by land or sea, and who was going to help a British captain track down their beloved hero and his long-lost love?

He crumpled up the letter and tossed it to the floor.

"Well?" Molly asked, hands on her hips. "Are you?"

"Am I what?" he asked, feeling a bit disconcerted by her impudent nature.

"Going to be honorable?"

And then John looked again at his unwanted passenger, and realized for the first time in his life, he was in over his head.

For she was just the sort of troublesome, pretty bit of muslin that could upend even the most stalwart of men.

And he answered her quite honestly. "I don't know. That quite depends on you, Molly."

Aboard the Ellis Anne, *three months later*

"Demmit, Mrs. Dashwell, why do you insist on starting every day up here in the sheets?" Dash asked, as he climbed the last few feet into the crow's nest.

She laughed. "Because I find it exhilarating."

Dash snorted. "I have some sheets down below that you'll find just as exhilarating, if not more so, Mrs. Dashwell."

Pippin blushed and then turned to take in the brilliant blue sky overhead and the vast expanse of waves before them. "I will remind you not to call me that."

"Call you what, Mrs. Dashwell?" he asked innocently.

"That!" she said, wagging a finger at him. "I am not Mrs. Dashwell. I've told you a thousand times I have no intention of marrying again."

"Oh, Pippin, you are being stubborn, of course

we must marry," he said, crossing his arms over his chest. "It wouldn't be proper otherwise."

She made a very improper *harrumph* and reached over to steal his spyglass. "I don't care. I rather like my freedom."

"And how will you not be free if you marry me?"

She shrugged. "I rather like being fallen. It lends such a scandalous air to our situation."

"Our situation," he huffed. "Is that all this is?"

Pippin turned to him, closing the narrow gap between them and kissing him, her lips parting eagerly, her tongue tangling with his and her body coming alive as he responded with the same hunger.

"Dash," she whispered. "I'm not going to be anywhere but by your side and in your bed for the rest of my life. You are my heart, my guiding star."

"Then marry me," he persisted. She leaned forward to kiss him anew, but he stopped her. "I'm not joking, Pippin. I'll cast you adrift if you refuse."

Swatting his shoulder playfully, she laughed. "You would not. Would be a waste of a perfectly good longboat."

"True," he agreed. "I could keelhaul you."

"Rather messy business, isn't it?" she asked with a shiver.

"Terribly so," he admitted. Then a mischievous light illuminated his eyes. "I'll put you ashore. Right back in London."

Pippin's eyes widened with horror. "You would not!"

"I would. Feed you to those satin-clad sharks in Mayfair," he declared, crossing his arms over his chest, feet planted and looking very much like the ruthless, determined pirate she adored. "Lady Gossett, you had best marry me or suffer the consequences."

"*Harrumph,*" she sputtered. "'Tis hardly a fair bargain."

"Well, you do get me," he offered.

She shrugged. "That is a measure in your favor."

"I'll take you to China for our honeymoon." He waggled his brows at her.

Pippin's gaze swung up. "Truly?"

"Aye, Circe. Anywhere your heart desires."

"Will we go around the Horn?" she asked, her eyes alight and starry again.

"Only if you agree to stay out of the sheets while we make the turn."

"When did you get to be so starched?"

"Starched? I think not." He looked overly affronted until he drew her closer still and whispered with a warm breath, "Did I mention that I have other sheets, much finer sheets that you'll find just as entertaining?"

"Yes, I believe you did," she murmured, sliding against him.

"Would you like to go explore them right now?"

"I thought you would never ask," she said, casting one last glance at the horizon and then bounding down the lines toward the deck like a hand half her age.

"And the wedding?" he said as he led her to his cabin.

"We'll discuss that when we get to China," Pippin told him.

"I should never have ruined you all those years ago," he chided. "For I've made you into a scandalous romp."

"And I have every intention of thanking you for that," she said, tugging him into his cabin, and kicking the door shut behind them with her foot, "for the rest of my life, Captain Dashwell."

"Glad to hear it, Mrs. Dashwell. Very glad to hear it."

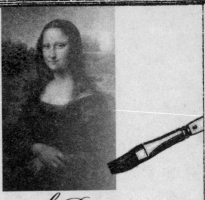

History of Passion ...

Dearest Reader,

Don't be deceived. Behind her demure smile and guarded gaze even the most proper lady has a secret. But what happens when the sting of betrayal, ache of sacrifice, or ghosts of lovers past return, threatening to shake that Mona Lisa smile?

This summer, Avon Books presents four delicious romances about four women who are more than what they seem, and the dangerously handsome heroes who are captivated by them. From bestselling authors Elizabeth Boyle, Loretta Chase, Jeaniene Frost, and a beautifully repackaged edition by Susan Wiggs.

Coming May 2009

Memoirs of a Scandalous Red Dress

by *New York Times* bestselling author

Elizabeth Boyle

Twenty years ago, Pippin betrayed her heart and married another in order to save Captain Thomas Dashwell's life. Now their paths cross again and Pippin is determined not to let a second chance at love slip away. Dash's world stops when he sees her standing aboard his ship but promises himself he'll never again fall for the breathtaking beauty.

Dashwell's nostrils were filled with the scent of newly minted guineas. Enough Yellow Georges to make even the dour Mr. Hardy happy. Nodding in satisfaction, he whistled low and soft like a seabird to the men in the longboat.

They pulled up one man, then another, and cut the bindings that had their arms tied around their backs and tossed the two over the side and into the surf.

That ought to cool their heels a bit, Dashwell mused, as he watched the Englishmen splash their way to shore. His passengers had been none too pleased with him last night when he'd abandoned their delivery in favor of saving his neck and the lives of his crew.

Untying the mule, he led the beast down the shore toward the longboat. It came along well enough until it got down to the waterline, where the waves were coming in and the longboat tossed and crunched against the rocks. Then the animal showed its true nature and began to balk.

The miss who'd caught his eye earlier came over and took hold of the reins, her other hand stroking the beast's muzzle and talking softly to it until it settled down.

"You have a way about you," he said over his shoulder, as he walked back and forth, working alongside his men, who were as anxious as he was to gain their gold and be gone from this precarious rendezvous.

"Do you have a name?" he asked, when he returned for the last sack. This close he could see all too well the modest cut of her gown, her shy glances, and the way she bit her lip as if she didn't know whether to speak to him.

Suddenly it occurred to him who, or rather what she was, and he had only one thought.

What the devil was Josephine doing bringing a lady, one barely out of the schoolroom, into this shady business?

"What? No name?" he pressed, coming closer still, for he'd never met a proper lady—he certainly didn't count Josephine as one, not by the way she swore and gambled and schemed.

As he took another step closer he caught the veriest hint of roses on her. Soft and subtle, but to a man like him it sent a shock of desire through him as he'd never known.

Careful there, Dashwell, he cautioned himself. If the militia didn't shoot him, he had to imagine Josephine would. "Come sweetling, what is your name?"

There was no harm in just asking, now was there?

The wee bit of muslin pursed her lips shut, then glanced over at her companions, as if seeking their help. And when she looked back at him, he smiled at her. The grin that usually got him into trouble.

"Pippin," she whispered, again glancing back over toward where Josephine was haranguing Temple and Clifton for news from the Continent.

"Pippin, eh?" he replied softly, not wanting to frighten her, even as he found himself mesmerized by the soft, uncertain light in her eyes. "I would call you something else. Something befitting such a pretty lady." He tapped his fingers to his lips. "Circe. Yes, that's it. From now on I'll call you my Circe. For you're truly a siren to lure me ashore."

Even in the dark he could see her cheeks brighten with a blush, hear the nervous rattle to her words. "I don't think that is proper."

Proper? He'd fallen into truly deep waters now, for something devilish inside him wanted to make sure this miss never worried about such a ridiculous notion again.

But something else, something entirely foreign to him, urged him to see that she never knew anything else but a safe and proper existence.

A thought he extinguished as quickly as he could. For it was rank with strings and chains and noble notions that had no place in his world.

"Not proper?" He laughed, more to himself than

at her. "Not proper is the fact that this bag feels a bit lighter than the rest." He hoisted it up and jangled it as he turned toward the rest of the party on the beach. "My lady, don't tell me you've cheated me yet again."

For indeed, the bag did feel light.

Lady Josephine winced, but then had the nerve to deny her transgression. "Dash, I'll not pay another guinea into your dishonest hands."

No wonder she'd brought her pair of lovely doves down to the beach. A bit of distraction so he'd not realize he wasn't getting his full price.

"Then I shall take my payment otherwise," he said, and before anyone could imagine what he was about, he caught hold of this tempting little Pippin and pulled her into his arms.

She gasped as he caught hold of her, and for a moment he felt a twinge of conscience.

Thankfully he wasn't a man to stand on such notions for long.

"I've always wanted to kiss a lady," he told her, just before his lips met hers.

At first he'd been about to kiss her as he would any other girl, but there was a moment, just as he looked down at her, with only one thought—to plunder those lips—that he found himself lost.

Her eyes were blue, as azure as the sea off the West Indies, and they caught him with their wide innocence, their trust.

Trust? In him?

Foolish girl, he thought as he drew closer and then kissed her, letting his lips brush over hers. Yet instead of his usual blustering ways, he found himself reining back his desire. This was the girl's first kiss, he knew that with the same surety that he knew how many casks of brandy were in his hold, and ever-so-gently, he ventured past her lips, slowly letting his tongue sweep over hers.

She gasped again, but this time from the very intimacy of it, and Dash suddenly found himself inside a maelstrom.

He tried to stop himself from falling, for that would mean setting her aside. But he couldn't let her go.

This Pippin, this innocent lass, this very proper lady, brought him alive as no other woman ever had.

Mine, he thought, with possessiveness, with passion, with the knowledge that she was his, and always would be.

He wanted to know everything about her, her real name, her secrets, her desires . . . His hands traced her lines, the slight curve of her hips, the soft swell of her breasts.

She shivered beneath his touch, but she didn't stop him, didn't try to shy away. Instead, she kissed him back, innocently, tentatively at first, then eagerly.

Good God, he was holding an angel!

And as if the heavens themselves rang out in protest over his violation of one of their own, a rocket screeched across the sky, and when it exploded, wrenching the night into day with a shower of sparks, Dashwell pulled back from her and looked up.

As another rocket shot upward, he realized two things.

Yes, by God, her eyes were as blue as the sea.

And secondly, the militia wasn't at the local pub bragging about their recent exploits.

*L*aura seated herself, and Sandro took the opposite
chair. The fire crackled cheerily in the marble framed
grate. "Have you run afoul of the law, madonna?"

"Of course not." She folded her hands demurely in her
lap. "My lord, I have information about Daniele Moro."

Her words pounded in Sandro's head. Disbelief made
him fierce. "How do you know of Moro?"

"Well." She ran her tongue over her lips. Sandro knew
women who spent fortunes to achieve that beautiful

shade of crimson, but he saw no trace of rouge on Laura. "I have a confession to make, my lord."

A denial leapt in his throat. No. She could not be involved in the butchery of Moro. Not her. Anyone but her. "Go on," he said thickly.

"I heard you speaking of Moro to Maestro Titian." She leaned forward and hurried on. "Please forgive me, but I was so curious, I couldn't help myself. Besides, this might be for the best. I can help you solve this case, my lord."

He didn't want her help. He didn't want to think of this innocent lamb sneaking in the dark, listening at doorways, hearing of the atrocity that left even him feeling sick and soiled.

Without thinking, he jumped up, grasped her by the shoulders, and drew her to her feet. Although he sensed the silent censure of Jamal, he ignored it and sank his fingers into the soft flesh of her upper arms. He smelled her scent of sea air and jasmine, saw the firelight sparkling in her beautiful, opalescent eyes.

"Damn you for your meddlesome ways," he hissed through his teeth. "You have no business poking your nose into the affairs of the *signori di notte*."

She seemed unperturbed by his temper, unscathed by his rough embrace. She lifted her chin. "I'm well aware of that, my lord, but remember, I did warn you of my inquisitive nature."

"Then I should have warned you that I have no use for women—inquisitive or otherwise."

She lifted her hands to his chest and pressed gently. "Your fingers are bruising me, my lord."

He released her as abruptly as he had snatched her up. "My apologies."

"I wouldn't worry about it, but Maestro Titian will

question me about any bruises when I model for him."

Sandro despised the image of Laura laid out like a feast upon the artist's red couch, lissome and sensual as a goddess, while Titian rendered her beauty on canvas.

"Do you truly have no use for women, my lord?" she asked. "That's unusual, especially in so handsome a man as you."

Sandro ignored her insincere compliment and paused to consider his four mistresses. Barbara, Arnetta, Gioia, and Alicia were as different and yet as alike as the four seasons. For years they had fulfilled his needs with the discretion and decorum he required. In exchange, he housed each in her own luxurious residence.

"It's my choice," he said stuffily, settling back in his chair. He did not need to look at Jamal to know that he was grinning with glee.

"Well, I believe my information could be useful to you." She sent him a sidelong glance. Not even the demure brown dress could conceal her lush curves. "That is, if you're interested, my lord."

As she sank gracefully back into the chair, he stared at the shape of her breasts, ripe beneath their soft cloak of linen. "I'm interested."

She smiled, the open, charming expression that was fast becoming familiar to him. "I happened to mention the murder of Daniele Moro to my friend Yasmin—"

"By God," he snapped, "don't you understand? This is a sensitive matter." He gripped the chair arms to keep himself anchored to his seat. "You can't go airing police business all over the city."

"I didn't." She seemed truly bewildered. "I told only one person."

"You could endanger yourself, madonna. The killer is still at large."

"Oh. I'm not used to having someone worry about my welfare."

"It is my vocation to worry about the welfare of every citizen of the republic."

She shifted impatiently. "Never mind all that. I found someone who saw Daniele Moro on the night he was killed."

Once again, Sandro came out of his chair. *"What?"*

"I'll take you to meet this person, my lord."

"Do that, and I'll think about forgiving you."

Coming July 2009

Don't Tempt Me

by *New York Times* bestselling author

Loretta Chase

Imprisoned in a harem for twelve years, Zoe Lexham knows things no well-bred lady should . . . ruining her for society. Can the wickedly handsome Duke Lucien de Grey use his influence to save her from idle tongues? A simple enough task, if only he can stifle desire long enough to see his seductive charge safely into respectability . . .

Zoe went cold, then hot. She felt dizzy. But it was a wonderful dizziness, the joy of release.

Now at last she stood in the open.

Here I am, she thought. *Home at last, at last. Yes, look at me. Look your fill. I'm not invisible anymore.*

She felt his big, warm hand clasp hers. The warmth rushed into her heart and made it hurry. She was aware of her pulse jumping against her throat and against her wrist, so close to his. The heat spread into her belly and down, to melt her knees.

I'm going to faint, she thought. But she couldn't let

herself swoon merely because a man had touched her. Not now, at any rate. Not here. She made herself look up at him.

Lucien wore the faintest smile—of mockery or amusement she couldn't tell. Behind his shuttered eyes she sensed rather than saw a shadow. She remembered the brief glimpse of pain he'd had when she'd mentioned his brother. It vanished in an instant, but she'd seen it in his first, surprised reaction: the darkness there, bleak and empty and unforgettable.

She gazed longer than she should have into his eyes, those sleepy green eyes that watched her so intently yet shut her out. And at last he let out a short laugh and raised her hand to his mouth, brushing her knuckles against his lips.

Had they been in the harem, she would have sunk onto the pillows and thrown her head back, inviting him. But they were not and he'd declined to make her his wife.

And she was not a man, to let her lust rule her brain. This man was not a good candidate for a spouse. There had been a bond between them once. Not a friendship, really. In childhood, the few years between them was a chasm, as was the difference in their genders. Still, he'd been fond of her once, she thought, in his own fashion. But that was before.

Now he was everything every woman could want, and he knew it.

She desired him the way every other woman desired him. Still, at least she finally felt desire, she told herself. If she could feel it with him, she'd feel it with someone else, someone who wanted her, who'd give his heart to her. For now, she was grateful to be free. She was grateful to stand on this balcony and look out upon the hundreds of people below.

She squeezed his hand in thanks and let her mouth form a slow, genuine smile of gratitude and happiness, though she couldn't help glancing up at him once from under her lashes to seek his reaction.

She glimpsed the heat flickering in the guarded green gaze.

Ah, yes. He felt it, too: the powerful physical awareness crackling between them.

He released her hand. "We've entertained the mob for long enough," he said. "Go inside."

She turned away. The crowd began to stir and people were talking again but more quietly. They'd become a murmuring sea rather than a roaring one.

"You've seen her," he said, and his deep voice easily carried over the sea. "You shall see her again from time to time. Now go away."

After a moment, they began to turn away, and by degrees they drifted out of the square.

Coming August 2009

Destined for an Early Grave

by *New York Times* bestselling author

Jeaniene Frost

Just when Cat is ready for a little rest and relaxation with her sexy vampire boyfriend Bones, she's haunted by dreams from her past—a past she doesn't remember. To unlock these secrets, Cat may have to venture all the way into the grave. But the truth could rock what she knows about herself—and her relationship with Bones.

If he catches me, I'm dead.

I ran as fast as I could, darting around trees, tangled roots, and rocks in the forest. The monster snarled as it chased me, the sound closer than before. I wasn't able to outrun it. The monster was picking up speed while I was getting tired.

The forest thinned ahead of me to reveal a blond vampire on a hill in the distance. I recognized him at once and hope surged through me. If I could reach him, I'd be okay. He loved me; he'd protect me from the monster. Yet I was still so far away.

Fog crept up the hill to surround the vampire, making him appear almost ghost-like. I screamed his name as the monster's footsteps got even closer. Panicked, I lunged forward, narrowly avoiding the grasp of bony hands that would pull me down to the grave. With renewed effort, I sprinted toward the vampire. He urged me on, snarling warnings at the monster that wouldn't stop chasing me.

"Leave me alone," I screamed as a merciless grip seized me from behind. "No!"

"Kitten!"

The shout didn't come from the vampire ahead of me; it came from the monster wrestling me to the ground. I jerked my head toward the vampire in the distance, but his features blurred into nothingness and the fog covered him. Right before he disappeared, I heard his voice.

"He is not your husband, Catherine."

A hard shake evaporated the last of the dream and I woke to find Bones, my vampire lover, hovered over me.

"What is it? Are you hurt?"

An odd question, you would think, since it had only been a nightmare. But with the right power and magic, sometimes nightmares could be turned into weapons. A while back, I'd almost been killed by one. This was different, however. No matter how vivid it felt, it had just been a dream.

"I'll be fine if you quit shaking me."

Bones dropped his hands and let out a noise of relief. "You didn't wake up and you were thrashing on the bed. Brought back rotten memories."

"I'm okay. It was a . . . weird dream."

There was something about the vampire in it that nagged me. Like I should know who he was. That made no sense, however, since he was just a figment of my imagination.

"Odd that I couldn't catch any of your dream," Bones went on. "Normally your dreams are like background music to me."

Bones was a Master vampire, more powerful than most vampires I'd ever met. One of his gifts was the ability to read human minds. Even though I was half-human, half-vampire, there was enough humanity in me that Bones could hear my thoughts, unless I worked to block him. Still, this was news to me.

"You can hear my *dreams*? God, you must never get any quiet. I'd be shooting myself in the head if I were you."

Which wouldn't do much to him, actually. Only silver through the heart or decapitation was lethal to a vampire. Getting shot in the head might take care of *my* ills the permanent way, but it would just give Bones a nasty headache.

He settled himself back onto the pillows. "Don't fret, luv. I said it's like background music, so it's rather soothing. As for quiet, out here on this water, it's as quiet as I've experienced without being half-shriveled in the process."

I lay back down, a shiver going through me at the mention of his near-miss with death. Bones's hair had turned white from how close he'd come to dying, but now it was back to its usual rich brown color.

"Is that why we're drifting on a boat out in the Atlantic? So you could have some peace and quiet?"

"I wanted some time alone with you, Kitten. We've had so little of that lately."

An understatement. Even though I'd quit my job leading the secret branch of Homeland Security that hunted rogue vampires and ghouls, life hadn't been dull. First we'd had to deal with our losses from the war with another Master vampire last year. Several of Bones's friends—and my best friend Denise's husband, Randy—had been murdered. Then there had been months of hunting down the remaining perpetrators of that war so they couldn't live to plot against us another day. Then training my replacement so that my uncle Don had someone else to play bait when his operatives went after the misbehaving members of undead society. Most vampires and ghouls didn't kill when they fed, but there were those who killed for fun. Or stupidity. My uncle made sure those vampires and ghouls were taken care of—and that ordinary citizens weren't aware they existed.

So when Bones told me we were taking a boat trip, I'd assumed there must be some search-and-destroy reason behind it. Going somewhere just for relaxation hadn't happened, well, *ever*, in our relationship.

"This is a weekend getaway?" I couldn't keep the disbelief out of my voice.

He traced his finger on my lower lip. "This is our vacation, Kitten. We can go anywhere in the world and take our time getting there. So tell me, where shall we go?"

"Paris."

I surprised myself saying it. I'd never had a burning desire to visit there before, but for some reason, I did now. Maybe it was because Paris was supposed to be the city of lovers, although just looking at Bones was usually enough to get me in a romantic mood.

He must have caught my thought, because he smiled, making his face more breathtaking, in my opinion. Lying against the navy sheets, his skin almost glowed with a silky alabaster paleness that was too perfect to be human. The sheets were tangled past his stomach, giving me an uninterrupted view of his lean, taut abdomen and hard, muscled chest. Dark brown eyes began to tinge with emerald and fangs peeked under the curve of his mouth, letting me know I wasn't the only one feeling warmer all of a sudden.

"Paris it is, then," he whispered, and flung the sheets off.

At Avon Books, we know your passion for romance—once you finish one of our novels, you find yourself wanting more.

May we tempt you with . . .

- **Excerpts** from our upcoming releases.

- Entertaining **extras**, including authors' personal photo albums and book lists.

- Behind-the-scenes **scoop** on your favorite characters and series.

- **Sweepstakes** for the chance to win free books, romantic getaways, and other fun prizes.

- Writing **tips** from our authors and editors.

- **Blog** with our authors and find out why they love to write romance.

- **Exclusive content** that's not contained within the pages of our novels.

Join us at
www.avonbooks.com